AN ENDLESS EXILE

AN ENDLESS EXILE

by

Mary Lancaster

Published by
Bladud Books

FOR MY MOTHER AND MY FATHER

Present: March 1076

CHAPTER 1

"Hereward is dead."

Whatever I had expected of my husband's nephew, rousing my household in the middle of the night to throw his dripping person and its accompanying blast of cold air at my feet, it was not that. Even though there can have been few men more likely to die.

Just for a moment, I could only stare at the bent, agitated head, watching the rivulets of water run down his hair to join the thousand others on his sodden cloak. By the trembling, almost sinister flame of my porter's lamp, I could even see the little pool of water forming between us. Just for a moment, that fascinated me too.

Hereward is dead. Was this news, then, already galloping and spreading under the night-stars? Northwards, perhaps, to York and beyond, to his sister and to his erstwhile Danish friends of Northumbria. West too, to the old rebels of the Welsh marches – would Edric the Wild weep for the ally he had never met? South, probably, to the King in London or Winchester or wherever he was, and whatever pity was in his heart today. And eastward – was it eastward? – among the fens which had always been his. Were his people, the lost and despairing, loud in lament for their last great hero? Wildly – or silently – inconsolable? Or did they close their eyes in peace, breathe a mighty sigh of collective relief and say, "Thank God it is over at last: Hereward is dead."

Perhaps, in the end, it would even be the Normans who mourned most for their new and prestigious friend. Or were the present masters of this land too full of such an unexpected triumph over their one-time enemy? An enemy who could never, after all, have become one of them; only a dangerous rival. Perhaps they would be unable to believe their luck, passing on the news in superstitious whispers through the great estates and courts of England and Normandy, that Hereward the Exile, the Outlaw, was dead.

There is a dreadful finality about that word. Even through the detached

1

ramblings of my mind, I was aware of it. Gradually too, I became aware of the pain in my hand where Siward, my husband's nephew, was pressing it into his face. He was kneeling still at my bare, icy feet as though begging forgiveness for the news he bore, and in his own torment of grief – or his completely misplaced fear for mine – gentleness was forgotten.

Still distractedly, I began to draw my fingers free. They were wet. Releasing me, Siward dashed his hands across his eyes, and rose slowly to his feet, sword clanking dully at his belt and brushing against the fur cloak I had dragged around my chemise to receive him. In the dimly flickering light of the lamp that my porter held unsteadily above us, the skin of his still young face looked taut and sickly, the hollows around his exhausted eyes black. The tangled mass of fair hair, palely imitating his uncle's, fell damply forward over one cheek; then, impatiently, he pushed it back, the better to peer at me, I think, for signs of emotional disintegration. Baffled, I gazed silently back at him until in pity he lifted both arms for me.

Instinctively, I stepped backwards out of his reach, and as his arms fell again, a frown of puzzlement creased his low brow.

"Torfrida, he is dead," he repeated deliberately, as if to a child, or to an imbecile who could not understand simple words. "Hereward, your husband, is dead."

And at last the breath seemed to seep back into my body.

"Good," I said with satisfaction. "Then I can go home to Bourne."

In the first light of a grey, wintry morning, I prepared with some care for my ride from Lincoln to Bourne. I dressed in a warm woollen gown of bright, sky blue, over a fine yellow under-dress. Beneath my veil, which was circled with a braided ribbon of the same blue and yellow, my hair was as neatly and becomingly pinned as I could make it. I had no intention of being surprised by anyone at any time.

That done, I drew the sable travelling cloak about me and regarded my reflection in the sheet of polished bronze which was the one extravagance of my solitary, sterile bed-chamber. My face was too thin now, marked by life like the grey streaks in my once jet-black hair. I looked, in fact, disconcertingly frail. My eyes, too large and bright for that face, stared back at me, half-frightened, half-excited; and in my breast my heart beat and beat and beat.

"Stop it, Torfrida," I whispered. "Stop it . . ."

Then, taking a deep breath, I rose and went to collect my children. I was thirty-two years old, and felt as if I were waking up after a long, expectant sleep.

The journey was accomplished mostly in uncomfortable silence, at least after we had drawn away from the children. Siward the White, torn be-

2

tween his own grief and an increasingly desperate, if covert, search for signs of mine, began to withdraw even further into his own private misery. I could not help that. It was not the time to try. For my own part, I think I sang a little, snatches of a merry French song that brought Siward's eyes round to me with an astonishment that was far from admiring.

I smiled at him, beatifically, and twisted back in the saddle to give one last wave to the children. They were riding two ponies – Frida on one, the two little boys together on the other – in company with their nurse and most of the men-at-arms. We had agreed that they would go directly to Folkingham, to Gilbert of Ghent, their father's godfather, while I insisted on riding ahead with Siward the White, to visit Bourne on the way. Siward said it was not fit for me. It was where Hereward had been killed.

"Do they know?" Siward asked abruptly.

"Know what?" I asked vaguely, straightening in my saddle, and adjusting the warm, soft cloak at my throat.

Siward said sharply, "That their father is dead, of course!"

"Oh no. I see no point in spoiling their treat. They are going to see their grandmother and Aunt Lucy, and stay at Uncle Gilbert's hall; and Aunt Matilda will spoil them mercilessly. Now, Siward, add to *my* personal well-being: *who* had the ultimate honour of killing Hereward?"

This time he did not even try to keep the accusation out of his face or voice.

"The *honour* of killing your husband? Some treacherous Norman knights, purporting to be his friends! They were dining with him – it was the lady Aediva's birthday feast – when their servants, who had hidden weapons under their clothes, fell on his men and . . ."

"Yes, so you told me last night," I interrupted, waving that aside. "But who were they?"

"I don't know," Siward said bitterly. "I was not there. The assassins had fled by the time we came to his rescue. But it was Deda who escorted Aediva and Lucy to safety at Folkingham."

My lip twitched as I regarded his averted face. "Deda," I said with blatant mockery. "*Deda* killed Hereward?"

"Hardly!" said Siward sharply, displeased all over again by the flippancy of my tone. Well, what did he expect? "From all I can gather, Deda did everything possible to try and stop the fight. But I doubt the same could be said for that swaggering fool, Asselin!"

I had no quarrel with that description, but glancing up at him from under my lashes, I pointed out, "You told me they fled before you got to them."

Siward's pale skin flushed, but his eyes met mine squarely. "I heard from those who survived."

"Yes," I agreed evenly. "I expect you did."

3

"Torfrida!"

I lifted my brows at him, watched him take a deep breath. Then: "Torfrida, I know this is hard to take in; after all he has done, God knows I never thought he would die like that, foully, in his own home . . ."

"That's just it, Siward," I murmured. "It wasn't his home."

Siward blinked his pale eyes once. "Wasn't his . . .?"

"No. He gave Bourne to me, in trust for Frida."

Siward was staring at me. In truth, the contempt in his eyes hurt me far more than it should. What in the world did he imagine I still owed to a troublesome and adulterous husband I had cast off four years ago? Bourne was all I had had of him, and that I had looked after mainly for his mother and widowed sister who still lived there! My own efforts, my own reviving of my father's trading ventures, had fed and clothed my children and me . . .

But Siward was angry now. I tried to make allowances for his grief.

"Are you really counting property while he lies cut to pieces not twenty-four hours since?" he said harshly. "He may have behaved ill to you once, Torfrida, but before God, he was still your husband!"

There was a short pause. Then: "Was he?" I actually sounded amused. Mind you, I had not been, although I had tried quite hard, when I first heard the song linking Hereward's name to Aelfryth's, and calling her his wife. It had been yelled out joyously by a couple of drunks in imperfect harmony one market day in Lincoln. Well, being young and fair and Saxon, she made a better heroine for the story than I – well past my first flush of youth, Flemish, and endowed with rather dubious knowledge for a Christian.

"There seems," I remarked judiciously, "to be some doubt."

Hereward is dead. What would she do when the news got to her? Was someone else – one of the twins perhaps, or Leofric the Deacon – even now riding across the country to tell her what Siward had already told me? Would she come crashing into Bourne, claiming to be his widow? Well, Bourne was one place she would have no such rights. Bourne, as I had just reminded Siward, was mine. Mine and Frida's.

Avoiding the village and the monastery, and the wide, stricken eyes of the few frightened people we encountered on the road, I came home to Bourne. His presence there, unexpected and uninvited, had prevented me returning at all for the last month, even for Aediva's birthday, and I had missed it. I acknowledged that as my tired horse picked its way daintily across the stream which flowed from St. Peter's Pool, the natural fountain close by. Above the stream rose the earth mound and stockade that protected my hall.

Whatever occurred here yesterday, Hereward's people had not deserted his ancestral home. The gates were closed and guarded by a man I knew well: he had a sword-scar on his left buttock. I tried to bear that in mind as he greeted me, disconcertingly with tears rolling unchecked down his rough, pitted cheeks.

While I stared carefully between my horse's ears and urged it through the gates, I heard Siward quickly questioning the man.

"Where is he?"

"In the hall . . ."

"Is he fit . . .?"

"As he can be."

I rode carefully on, and my heart beat and beat and beat.

There had certainly been a battle here. The whole yard and the burned and damaged buildings around it bore unmistakable witness to that. For the first time, foolishly, I wanted to weep, because in all the years of war, for all the halls and towns and castles I had seen destroyed by one side or another, Bourne had never before been one of them.

But *they* were there, Hereward's 'gang'. Just as in the old days, they would have had word this last half hour and more of my approach. And as my horse picked its way slowly into the devastated yard, they emerged from the hall and the outbuildings, pausing in their tasks of clearing and burying and putting to rights, to stand and move silently towards me, united as one in their enormous loss, in their pity, and in the great grief they assumed, despite everything, that I would share.

"Fools!" I thought, with a sudden fury that could never be free of affection. "Fools, fools!"

Forcing myself, I picked out with my eyes those of them I had known and loved best, marked with my mind those who were notably absent.

"In the hall," the soldier had said. And since I had no words to offer the men I had laughed with and suffered with for so long, I half-turned, till I could see the hall door. It lay open, half ripped off its hinges, and the twins, Hereward's cousins Outi and Duti, stood on either side of it, shoulders sagging with fatigue, mouths drooping with misery. And yet they tried to smile at me.

I did not know what was going on.

My limbs were trembling slightly, and not just with the cold. Lifting my head, I drew the sable close around my throat and moved forward to the hall. Men moved respectfully to let me pass. Behind me, I was aware of Siward saying urgently, "Torfrida, wait a little. At least let me ensure . . ." But I heard no more. At the door, Outi embraced me, briefly, and because I could not stop it, I let him. And then I was past them, in the hall itself.

The battle had been in here too. They had made some effort to clear it up, but broken benches and tables lay piled on both sides and hangings

5

had been torn down or shredded. The walls were scarred and pierced by weapons, stained by many liquids, some of which, at least, must have been blood. There was always blood. And at the far end, even the high table had been damaged: one of its legs was propped up now on a broken chair. I could see that, although I could not see what was laid upon it. In front of it stood Leofric the Deacon, a stained, ragged bandage askew about his head, and Siward the Red, friend and cousin of the White Siward who had followed me inside. From the footsteps I heard, so had the twins.

For a moment, we stared at each other. Then my eyes flitted beyond them, and around the hall, and back to Leofric. It was he, inevitably, who moved first, stepping down from the dais, and coming straight towards me, a thousand expressions flitting across his open, gentle face.

I decided to strangle the pity at birth.

"Very well," I said sardonically. "Where is the body?"

Shock brought him to a standstill. Beside him, I saw Siward the Red's eyes fly to his cousin's. I even felt the movement of Siward the White's tired shrug.

Leofric said, "It is here; but I have to warn you, lady . . ."

"I have seen dead bodies before," I interrupted drily. "You must remember *that*, Leofric – you were generally there." And I moved forward, brushing past him. At the last moment, he reached out and caught my arm. He was strong enough to force me, but I did not struggle. Instead, slowly, I looked back at him over my shoulder. His dark eyes gazed at me, serious, intense, *pleading*.

"Torfrida, don't . . ."

I laughed. "Don't what? Don't look? Why do you think I came?"

I think it was the laughter that shook him off. At any rate I was free, with no inclination, or time, to think about what was in his face. There was only one obstacle left, on the dais: Siward the Red, planted firmly in front of me. On his left, on the table, I could see someone's up-turned boots.

"Stand aside, Siward," I said quietly, and reluctantly, slowly, he did.

I took my time. There were the boots, and leggings, and a short tunic worn without armour, save for the red painted shield still slung around his body like his sword-belt. There was a black dragon on the shield, with fierce, jewelled, emerald green eyes. My lips parted.

For the first time, I acknowledged the stale smell of burning that came off the body. His hair and head had been badly burned, beyond recognition. That should not have surprised me. I think it was the isolated clumps of thick, golden hair clinging still to his shoulders and chest that threw me off balance. Siward was right: he had been hacked to pieces. Bits of limbs were missing, there were massive, gory wounds in his legs and body, and his face, dear God, was enough to make seasoned warriors cringe.

I had seen enough. Sickened, I was already beginning to turn away when something on the body caught my eye: something frail and small and stained, but once, unmistakably, yellow. It shone through the singed, filthy, bloody rags of his clothing, somewhere between his chest and his left shoulder. Involuntarily, my hand reached out and touched it.

A braided ribbon, sewn with tiny gems.

My mouth opened, soundless at first, then gasping, and gasping again. Another storm filled my ears, rushing, swelling, endless. "Jesus Christ," I whispered, twisting with the awful, unbearable thing I had found. "Jesus Christ . . ."

Leofric said urgently, "What . . .?"

And Siward the White interrupted him savagely, "She did not know! She would not believe me!" Blindly, I looked at him while he strode up to the dais and seized me by both arms. "You didn't, did you? That is why you behaved so – said all those things! For God's sake, Torfrida, what do you take me for?"

A queer, animal noise burst from my throat.

Leofric said sharply, "Leave her!" And as soon as the fingers slackened on my arm, I was away, bolting for the door, away from the tragedy I had not foreseen and would never be able to run from. The dreadful finality of death was upon me at last, and now, *now*, I was lost.

Hereward is dead.

CHAPTER 2

They let me run, as if they knew it was the only thing I could do, as if they knew I had done much the same thing before, over another, less terminal parting. And I suppose they knew I would come back.

And I did. Not so very much later. And I was calm, with the calm that can only be induced in me by fixed purpose. Yet, mostly, I felt detached from my surroundings, as if I were somebody else entirely.

Walking sedately back across the yard, I was aware of the men watching me with varying degrees of subtlety. Only Wulric the Heron, slumped in the open doorway of what used to be the men's house, had no such pretensions. His white, ugly face looked wrung dry, his muddy eyes huge as they stared at me unblinkingly. His arm was roughly bandaged, and there was blood all over his coat.

Abruptly, I changed direction and walked over to him. Some habits are hard to break, whatever the circumstances.

"You are hurt, Wulric," I observed, much as I had on many occasions past.

"I am alive," he corrected me, without noticeable pleasure.

"I would like you to stay that way. May I see your wounds?"

"If you like. It's nought to me."

Taking his less bloody arm, I led him into the house. I said carefully, "You are grieving for him."

"For him," Wulric agreed. "Who is not? And for the lesser men."

The lesser men. I remembered one, notably absent from the crowd in the yard. Why was it, I wondered with detachment, that one all-consuming pain could not dull the many lesser griefs? Instead, it seemed to sharpen them, so that I could not speak again until I had sat him down upon the nearest bed and unwrapped most of his filthy bandages.

"Have I taught you no better than this?" I asked severely, dropping the rags with exaggerated distaste.

"I did not care," he said without emphasis.

"Wulric the Black is also dead?" I asked calmly, and the dead man's friend nodded once, dumbly. His Adam's apple wobbled precariously, making him look so ugly that I wanted to put my arms around him. However, since I didn't think either of us could bear that, I stood up and went to fetch the water bowl lying on the table under the window. It looked clean.

Wulric the Heron watched me return to him, and when I had begun to wash, he said without flinching, "I'm sorry. I didn't mean to add to – to . . ."

"They will all be added, Wulric." My voice sounded perfectly calm, a little tight perhaps, but calm. Somewhere, I could still wonder at that, that I could still act and think as before.

Wulric's eyes had lifted to mine, widening. A faint light even gleamed there, briefly. "God must have spared me to be revenged . . ."

Ignoring this slightly unlikely interpretation of God's will, I said only, "What happened here, Wulric?"

"*They* were here," he said. "Visiting the lady Aediva, or her daughter, I don't know. But Hereward asked them to sit down for dinner. Again."

"Who?" I asked. "Who did he ask?"

Wulric frowned. "That parcel of Normans. Asselin, Ralf of Dol, Hugh of Evermouth, Ivo de Taillebois . . ."

I glanced down at his face. "Ivo was there?" I asked quickly.

"Yes, and Deda. They all had their retinues of servants and soldiers, and they were all given hospitality."

"Siward told me the servants carried weapons hidden in their clothes."

Wulric stared unseeingly at the gory arrow-hole in his shoulder. "They drank with us. I think there was something in the ale. Or in some of it. I think they brought more to Wulric when he was on watch outside the hall, for he fell asleep. Wulric never sleeps on watch. They could have stepped over him to do their work, but they didn't. They killed him anyway, when he could not fight back."

I frowned at him. "You know this?"

"No, I'm guessing that part. I was inside the hall, with *him*. The first I – the first any of us knew, was when the door burst open and the Normans' servants and soldiers rushed in. As if it was a signal, the others rose to their feet, swords were out, and the fight began. If you can call it a fight. With Hereward there was only Wynter and Martin and Leofric and me – and the two servitors who could not fight off their own grandmothers . . . Hereward saw at once we were lost and ordered me to bring the others – they were hidden in the old forest camp – but someone saw me opening the door and shot this arrow that pinned me there some time before I could get it out . . . And when I did, and I got out of the door, I tripped over something. They told me later it was Wulric the Black . . . I ran till I thought I would burst, giving the whistles as I went – they met me half way, but even so, we were too late . . ."

I wanted to close my eyes, as if that would shut it all out, make it unreal. I said prosaically, "That will be more comfortable. I'll bind it for you now. Tomorrow I'll put some ointment on it that will keep infection away and help it to heal faster." Binding it with torn linen from the other bed, I said determinedly, "So the Normans' servants conveniently began it. Did Hereward turn on their masters? Did any of you?"

"Hereward drew his sword," Wulric said, after a moment's frowning thought. "It was instinctive, and you know how quick he is . . . Was. He leapt over the table, to meet those charging into the hall, and they were upon him in a trice."

"Who were?" I asked patiently.

"The boy who came to Ely once – Ralf. Hugh of Evermouth. Asselin. Chiefly."

"Not Deda?" I asked, because I had to.

And even like this, Wulric could spare a faint upward tug of his torn lips for Deda. "No, not Deda. He was shouting furiously at the others, trying to push up their swords, but no one paid him any attention. All he could do was hustle the ladies away before they got hurt. Unless he'd been prepared to join *us* – a gang of Saxons fighting his own people!"

"And Ivo de Taillebois?"

Ivo, who would marry Hereward's sister, if he could, yet who could not keep his black, sparkling eyes away from me . . .

Wulric frowned. "He's a cool bastard. He fought if anyone came near him. Otherwise, he stood, or even sat, and watched. Sometimes, often

9

when Hereward confounded the others, he laughed. I had an idea he disapproved of his countrymen, but he did nothing to interfere. I suppose he wouldn't. Anyway, all that was at the beginning, before I got away . . . I wish I had never left him."

"You could have changed nothing," I said dully. "And you would be dead as well."

He looked at me bleakly. "I know."

Leaving Wulric, I resumed my journey to the hall. My feet felt heavy and reluctant. I did not want to go in there. Not because I was afraid of the awful thing on the high table that had once contained the huge life of Hereward, but because I was afraid of his friends, of their effect on me, of their need of me. But I had to go to Folkingham. My children were there.

The door still hung crazily open, so they did not hear me come in. For a moment, I stood in the shadows, more from an inability to act than any desire to hear what they said.

And they were talking about me.

". . . don't care!" Siward the Red was exclaiming, violently punching his own leg as he half-sat on one of the trestle tables. "Why should you lie to her?"

"She didn't think I had," said Siward the White tiredly. "She thought I was – mistaken."

"Why, in God's holy name?"

"I don't know. I think – probably – because she did not see it in the stars." There was silence.

Then: "But she cannot have imagined he was playing some trick!"

"I think that is exactly what she did imagine."

"Dear God . . ." Duti said, sagging into an empty bench. "With what possible purpose?"

"Well think about it!" Siward the White said impatiently. "He arrived here over a month ago, giving no reason and making no attempt either to go to her in Lincoln or to bring her back to Bourne. She must have thought, like the rest of us, that he was seeking reconciliation at last. She must have thought he wanted her back, that he was too proud to beg or to chase, so she played along with his game, as she thought, to get her home. It probably suited her pride as well. White Christ! I don't know what goes on in the minds of those two . . ."

This was unbearable. I found my eyes were closed, tightly, till some movement in the hall made me open them again in alarm.

"Well what convinced her you *weren't* mistaken?" Outi was demanding, coming down from the dais with his quick, nervous tread. "That none of us were?"

The Siwards exchanged glances. This time, I would have intervened, but my tongue had got stuck, cleaving to the dry roof of my mouth.

"The ribbon," said Siward the White at last, reluctantly, finally revealing the secret that he and his cousin had kept so long. "The ribbon that's tied around his shoulder. He always wore it in battle, under his shirt – ever since Flanders. It was the first token she ever gave him."

I moved forward then, suddenly, because my body could not bear to be still. Almost as one, they swung round to face me, and I saw without surprise that Deda was there too, now, seated at the table and half-hidden still by Siward the Red. He rose, abruptly, coming towards me and then, helplessly, pausing, as if he did not know how he – one of the party of Frenchmen who had killed Hereward – would be received.

"She doesn't blame you," Siward the White said quickly.

"Of course I don't," I said, just as hastily. "Later, later I will thank you for your care of my mother- and sister-in law. I am ready to go to Folkingham now."

"Of course," said the Siwards at once, and the twins too prepared to accompany me.

But I had seen Deda's face, and when my enquiring gaze did not leave it, he said slowly, "Ivo de Taillebois is at Folkingham."

A snarl that was only half pain writhed across the twins' identical faces.

I said calmly, "Then Gilbert had better keep him away from my cousins. Shall we go?"

I had done this before, ridden this path up to Folkingham Hall, just before dusk, with fear of the future in my heart. We had come into this very yard, and someone had helped me to dismount. Just as then, I did not look at the man who was setting me on my feet, for I was busy trying not to remember.

The yard was full of men, soldiers, gathering and drilling in expectation of the trouble Hereward's murder was bound to inspire. Somewhere inside, in the hall probably, were my children, waiting to be told that their father was dead.

And coming out of the hall door, Gilbert of Ghent, Hereward's godfather, wearing a breastplate over his rich tunic, and a sword at his belt. Gilbert in martial mood, though with what purpose I had yet to find out. At his heels came his son and heir, a worried frown creasing his serious brow, and beside them, the lady Matilda, who had been weeping.

Weep, Matilda, weep . . .

I think I would have coped if she had not smiled. But though the tears still glistened wetly on her puffy face, she tried to pull herself together when she saw me. Her hand lifted in sorrowful welcome, and yet she tried to smile, a quite inappropriate, almost grotesque effort in all its false brightness. Just so, flanked by her husband and a son, had she smiled at

11

me when I had first come here twenty years ago, a furious but determined child of twelve, sent from Flanders by my own parents with the incomprehensible purpose of marrying me to Matilda's eldest son.

Inevitably, the memories burst on me, overwhelming me until my breath rasped in my throat, and I gave up the fight, and let them come.

Past: Into Exile:
April 1056 - January 1057

CHAPTER 3

My betrothed was not a handsome man. Gangly to the point of gawkiness, his mousy hair already thinning, although I knew for a fact he was only nineteen years old, he stood hunched between his fixedly smiling parents. The unpleasing contours of his face were only emphasized by the general mottled redness of his complexion – to say nothing of the even less becoming hue of his puce, bulbous nose, above which rather weak, sullen eyes regarded me with a depressing mixture of desperation, dejection and straightforward dislike.

I didn't blame him for that. I was not much of a bargain myself from a physical point of view. Besides being only twelve years old, plain and short, with the odd sort of pre-adolescent body that humorously manages to combine skinniness and lumpiness, I showed little promise of improvement.

On top of which, I had a cold.

"This," beamed Gilbert de Ghent, the sleeves of his long, heavily embroidered tunic rustling expensively as he cast one arm around my intended, "is my son, Robert. Robert, make your bow to the fair lady Torfrida who has come to us all the way from my good friends in Flanders."

Robert obediently bowed, a jerky, graceless motion that held neither courtesy nor respect. Even his dress, muddied and plain and short, and quite unadorned save for a rather grotesque, wrought silver buckle at his belt, spoke of neglect that amounted to insult. Obviously he had been among English Saxons too long.

He still was, for the yard in which I was met by this daunting threesome seemed to be teeming with young men engaged in wrestling or contests of arms or other manly sports, while several ladies watched from the edges, or from the great doorway of the low, sprawling house facing me.

The fair lady Torfrida, seeing nothing worthy of comment, sniffed with watery disdain.

Robert, surreptitiously pinched by his still smiling mother, forced himself to speak, muttering ungraciously, "I trust I find you well?"

Inevitably, I sneezed. I made it loud and enthusiastic, although I glared balefully at him over the top of my handkerchief.

"Do I look well?" I demanded.

There was a short silence while they all stared at me in blank dismay. Even without the cold, it must have been apparent that I didn't look too well.

I sniffed again. Some of the young men, grubby and panting still with their exertions, and most of the observing women, were gazing in our direction. I expect it was the sneeze. I am good at sneezes.

The lady Matilda said smoothly, "You will be exhausted after your long journey."

I did not answer at first, for a wink of startling golden hair, gleaming among the many paler heads around it, had caught my attention – probably because it was the brightest thing I had yet seen in this grey, dreary place. It belonged to a fair youth in a rough, sleeveless leather tunic with a sword belt slung over his broad shoulder. Wild, beardless and dirty-looking, with the barbarically long, tangled hair favoured by Saxons of a certain type, he was strolling among the combatants in the yard as if they were so many flowers in a field; and though it was hard to tell – for his eyes seemed to dart constantly and his whole body was somehow *unstill* – I thought he was looking mainly at us.

Then, abruptly, he dropped out of my view – felled, I perceived, by several other young men at once. The one at the top looked as dark as the victim was fair, but indescribably neater and cleaner. It crossed my mind that the golden youth was probably the sort who invited such unequal attacks. Or perhaps it was all part of their silly games. I didn't care. I already disliked the entire country.

Looking away, I realized that the lady Matilda, still determinedly smiling, was holding out her arm, dripping at the wrists with fine, English lace, in the direction of the house. The invitation was obvious, but I made her say it.

"May I give you some refreshment in the hall? Or would you prefer to retire and rest before supper? Come, I shall take you myself."

I glanced coldly at the men of the family. Robert, my betrothed, bowed again, jerkily. I ignored him. His father, a powerful, handsome man not yet forty, idly fingered the fine gold filigree brooch at his shoulder, and smiled. It was a distracted smile, as if he were thinking about something – or someone – else entirely. Why then was I so sure he disliked me? Apart, of course, from the fact that I had done nothing so far to be liked.

"I hope you don't mind this rabble, by the way," the lady said brightly, guiding me safely round a pair of worryingly inept young archers. "My husband encourages all the young men of the neighbourhood to practice sports and arms here – a sort of informal tourney. We do it several times a year, but I assure you it is not constant!"

"I have just been fortunate," I said sardonically, stepping over a fallen wrestler in my path. "Again."

She did not take me into the hall – the main house, long, large, single-storied, flimsily wooden – but as we skirted it, a sudden commotion above my head startled me into glancing up at the roof with extreme apprehension. Somebody was pulling himself up the thatch from the other side, throwing one bare, brown leg over the ridge of the roof, and perching there like a weather vane.

It was the same golden-haired youth I had last noticed vanishing under an apparently irresistible onslaught of fellow brutes.

The lady Matilda stopped. So did I. The boy on the roof, a little battered about the face, drew one deep, reviving breath, and grinned. It was an insolent, provoking sort of a grin, though there seemed to be genuine laughter there too, and it was aimed at someone below him on the far side of the hall.

"Oh no," the lady uttered – involuntarily, I thought.

Then the youth said something I didn't catch. It sounded deep and sharp, like a command, and immediately two dark boys near us – whom I hadn't even noticed before – started throwing things at the roof. Or no, not *at* the roof, but *to* the youth astride it. Sticks, stones, tree-branches, hats, buckets, old bits of broken armour – it seemed they were not choosy – and all tossed up with blood-curdling, martial yells.

And the golden youth, catching most of them, at once began hurling them at some unseen foe, or foes, on the other side of the building. Sometimes he called out a name before he threw, as if giving an impudent warning. Once I heard him laugh, quick and clear and incongruously joyous.

All around us now, like some noisy nightmare, I could hear people cheering and laughing and shouting out advice. One or two others moved disgustedly away, some calling warnings to friends or to the agitated women on the fringes, but in the main, all over the yard, men were dropping their weapons and their opponents and running over to watch the fun. Or to join in.

And they said this was a civilized country. I didn't understand how the lady Matilda could tolerate such behaviour.

Apparently she couldn't. When I looked at her, her face was still turned upwards; but her eyes were closed, as though praying for strength. It made her human for the first time.

Ineffectual, but human.

"Where," uttered the lady, opening her eyes at last, "is Gilbert?"

Looking about me, I saw no sign of him. Instead, I found two young women beside us, the smaller open-mouthed and scared looking, though her eyes still sparkled with some sort of delighted anticipation. Stupid, I judged. It was to the other maiden, tall, spotlessly clean, that Matilda spoke.

"Emma," she said, and I remembered that Emma was the name of her eldest daughter. "Emma, fetch your father or we'll have blood before supper . . ."

"You'll have it any way now," the tall girl returned, managing to convey both resignation and annoyance. "If you *will* invite him, you must expect trouble."

"Well I could do without it today!" Matilda snapped. She wasn't smiling any more. She hadn't been for some time. "*Will* you fetch your father when I tell you? You shall meet Torfrida at supper. Come, my dear . . ."

I cast another glance at the roof. The opposition appeared to be fighting back to some purpose, for the golden youth now sat among a positive hail of missiles hurled from the far side of the hall, many of which struck their target. On the other hand, more men were climbing up to join him from our side, while others again ran in with fresh ammunition. Even as I watched, I saw the boy's far leg jerk violently. The thud and the scream from the other side of the building, told me the rest – that he had just kicked some would-be interloper off the roof.

"Two in one blow!" he yelled triumphantly, confirming my prognosis. "One slitherer, one flyer!"

A rousing cheer went up from his own side. Behind me, I heard the smaller, sillier girl gurgling with laughter. "Isn't he splendid?" she demanded, followed by a decided slap and an aggrieved, "Ouch!"

By quick thinking, I managed to turn my hysterical laughter into a sneeze. Hastily following the lady, I observed, "You appear to be hosting a battle."

"Oh no, my dear, nothing less than a war," Matilda said with suppressed savagery as a rock fell alarmingly close to us. I stepped over it, and paused.

"Do you want him down?" I offered. "This stone, scientifically aimed . . ."

"By whom?" she interrupted bitterly. "My husband or my son?"

I stared at her. "By me, of course."

Matilda closed her mouth. Swiftly, before she could recover, I bent and took hold of the rock in both hands, lifting it and walking away almost in the same breath. It wasn't easy, for the stone was heavy, and now that I had it, I was no longer quite so sure of my ability to bring the golden barbarian down. However, since that was of purely secondary importance to me, I kept going, ignoring her alarmed, "Torfrida! In God's name, come out of there!"

By the time I was in among those who were trying to dislodge the boys on the roof – there were three of them up there now – I had planned my angles and my distance. Stolidly, I was ignoring the blunt objects that whizzed past my ears and flew over my head. Once in place, slightly aggrieved that no one but the lady Matilda seemed to be paying me any attention, I hefted the stone to my shoulder, and took aim.

Only then did the golden youth perceive me. Laughing aloud, he said something to the boys behind him, while still hurling sticks and a particularly nasty looking stone – fortunately not in my direction. At the same time, he appeared to be impudently offering me his yellow head as a target. Accepting with alacrity, I altered my aim slightly, and let my hand fall back to throw, but then, before I could, I was suddenly pulled unceremoniously aside and only just managed to avoid dropping the stone on my own foot.

There was an ante-chamber with sweet-smelling rushes on the floor; small but furnished with several stools and a chest in the French style. Beyond it was a large chamber, full of beds. My step faltered. Was I to have no privacy, even at night? I didn't know whether to scream or weep or wrestle my mother-in-law to the ground in what seemed to be the fashion of her adopted country.

In the end, I did none of these things, which was just as well, for my fate was really not quite so bad. She had given me a corner of my own, curtained off from the others by bright, heavy hangings. I even had a window.

"You will not mind the others," the lady told me in a way that made me want to mind them very much. It was the first thing she had managed to bring herself to say to me since dragging me away from the battlefield. She was smiling again. "They are all young, like yourself, and well-born. Now I shall leave you – but I'll send someone with a posset to make you feel better."

"Please don't trouble," I said coldly, but she was already half way across the main chamber. I don't think she even heard me.

I stood still, counting silently to twenty. Then, in the heavy silence – someone must have stopped the battle in the yard – I let my shoulders slump. Slowly, I unfastened my sable-lined cloak and dropped it on the bed. I hoped no one had seen me shaking. Now, remembering vividly the recent tedious hours at sea, spent mainly with my stuffed and runny nose pressed into my knees, and a few brief glimpses thereafter of endless grey skies and vast, dreary marshes beyond the river's shores – to say nothing of the bumpy, lonely ride here after my people had abandoned me to the servants of my betrothed – I just felt cold.

I sat down on top of the cloak, and tried to think.

I hadn't got very far when the hanging moved and a bright voice in the gap said, "Hallo! You must be Torfrida."

I looked round to see a pretty girl just a year or so older than myself; she was smiling at me. Her hair was long, loose and gleamingly fair, confined only by a braided circlet of blue and red ribbon around her forehead. She wore a simple gown of fine, sky-blue wool – woven in Flanders, I rather thought, by the new processes which were making my father so wealthy – fastened with small, old-fashioned snake-shaped brooches at either shoulder. Between, she wore a string of pretty but inexpensive glass beads.

In her hands she held an ornate, silver cup. Without enthusiasm, I looked from it up to the girl's open, merry face.

"So I must," I agreed. "Who are you?"

"Lucy," she said amiably. "Lucy of Bourne. One of the lady's ladies – if you see what I mean!"

"I expect I can work it out. Given time and a sharp pen." I sneezed again, accusingly. "Lucy is hardly an English name."

"I was named after my lord's – that is, the Earl of Mercia's – granddaughter, but the lady Matilda always calls me by the French form. I don't mind – it distinguishes us! And anyway, my sister in Northumbria is English enough for both of us – Aethelthryth, after the saint of Ely. And her son is Siward, to please the Norsemen, I suppose, though I can't see that any of that stuff matters. And I must say," she added, coming further into my corner, "I am very glad that *you* speak Saxon, for my French is atrocious and I don't have a word of Flemish. This is for you," said the girl, as if she had suddenly remembered the cup in her hands. "To help your poor cold."

"Thank you," I said distantly, turning back towards the window. "Please leave it on the side."

She did as I bade her, but the unspoken command – namely to take herself off and leave me alone – was obviously too subtle for her. Dropping familiarly on to the bed beside me, she said cosily, "So! How do you like your betrothed?"

"At a distance," I said shortly. With luck it would get back to him, suitably embellished. However, instead of looking shocked, the girl only smiled.

"You must not mind Robert. He will have been nervous of meeting you. Really, he is very amiable and very gentle. You are lucky."

17

I stared at her. "Then you marry him."

She only grinned again, impishly, but in a way that disturbed her angelic beauty not at all. She reminded me of someone.

"I could do worse," she acknowledged regretfully. "But I have other plans. So do my parents, more to the point! The lady said, by the way, that I should let you rest before supper – old people are always saying things like that. Do you *want* to rest?"

"Would you go away if I said I did?"

Rudeness, like subtlety, seemed to float right over her head. She said distractedly, "Of course, if you asked me to," quickly followed by, "Are you missing your home? Or perhaps, like me, you're just glad to escape parental restrictions!"

I turned away from her again, quickly, saying coldly, "I was never much restricted." Until now . . .

"Lucky you! *I* was, quite horribly, I assure you! Life is much better now – although at times my parents are still too close for comfort. When we are here at Folkingham, the lady can complain of me too easily! Bourne, my father's favourite hall, is only eight miles from here."

Eight miles. What would I give for a mere eight miles? And eight years . . .

"Still, at least I need seldom be home-sick," the strange girl comforted herself, belying her previous joy in her escape. "Nor, more importantly, need I listen to the perpetual quarrels of my father and brother!"

At that I did regard her with only slightly distracted fascination. "Your family *can* quarrel?" I had more or less given up trying to provoke one with her.

"Oh yes," she said blithely. "Hereward, you see, is my brother."

Lost but not yet despairing, I enquired, "Is that a matter for congratulation?"

And she laughed. "I hardly know! Certainly, it gets one noticed, but as for congratulation – well, you will have your own opinion by now. You must have seen him on your way across the yard."

I looked at her. "One of the wrestling young men?" I hazarded, without much hope; there was a certain inevitability about all this.

"No," she said apologetically. "The one on the roof. The first one on the roof."

CHAPTER 4

The main hall at Folkingham, as befitted the home of so close a kinsman of the Count of Flanders, was a large, well-proportioned chamber, hung with rich, Flemish tapestries. The wood panels and beams, high tables and chairs and benches, were all decorated with wonderfully detailed, yet fantastically ugly animal carvings, and the high-backed chairs on the dais seemed to be studded with gold. Already, the high table had been set with fine plate and coloured glass beakers lying at every place. To me, it was a very alien mixture of luxury and grotesque barbarity; but I took a perverse pleasure in the knowledge that my mother would not approve of it. I would describe it vividly in my first letter. Tomorrow.

Now, for supper, the hall was laid out with lots of trestle tables and benches, and it seemed the entire floor was covered with people waiting to take their seats. I could no longer, with justice, accuse the company of dullness. My eyes were quite dazzled by the sea of brilliantly coloured silks and wools adorning the ladies. Much gold and silver winked in the fading sunlight that still peeped in the many windows.

I would not have been surprised to see the men sitting down to supper with swords and scramasaxes at their belts, shields and bows slung at their backs and spears propped against the tables. I hardly knew whether or not to be disappointed by their restraint. Some of the assembled noblemen certainly wore swords, but almost as decoration, and the hilts on display were all of fine wrought metal; some were even jewelled. Otherwise, the only weapons in evidence were the painted and bossed shields on the walls, much as you would expect.

No one could say our entrance upon this surprisingly glittering scene was not effective. I chose to stand for some time just inside the door, in the full glory of my violent red gown, ridiculously festooned with every item of clashing jewellery I could find; and Lucy, perforce, had to wait nervously with me, while heads turned in our direction, one after the other, more and more of them in rapid succession – including the lady Matilda's, gratifyingly appalled before the smile managed to resurface. The babble of voices and cheerful laughter sank, paused in near silence for what seemed to be several seconds, and then rose again with renewed vigour.

The first voice I heard clearly came from a woman standing near me at the door. With a tinkling, very feminine little laugh it said to her companion, "Oh my dear, is that the bride? Well, what can one expect from the biggest swamp in Europe? Poor Robert! But what a charming couple they will make!"

19

I did not mind the opinion; it was the one I was seeking after all. It was the calculated malice behind it that threw me, so that although I turned my head boldly to look directly at her, I could think of no words. She was young, tall and graceful, slender and plump in all the right places, with bright, sparkling blue eyes that were used, I thought, to laughing, even if only at other people, and a charmingly full-lipped mouth. She wore amber silk, finely embroidered with green and gold leaves, and fastened with rather beautiful gold inlaid brooches. Necklaces of gold and pearls hung between her breasts. And though the veil of the matron was apparent, it hung loosely on her head to reveal the luxuriant chestnut locks beneath.

And at her side, surely, the husband: tall, dark, short-haired, good-looking. He had the grace to blush for his wife, whose smirk had become slightly fixed under my continuous stare.

Lucy whispered breathlessly, "The lady Edith. Ignore her. Her husband, Godric of Lincoln, is an important man, so the lady tolerates her. No more."

Here she pulled me physically forward to greet with enthusiastic affection two people whom I took to be her parents – a still pretty but tired looking lady with a permanent frown, called Aediva; and Leofric, a tall, fierce man in the Saxon-Danish style, whom I thought not incapable of causing and maintaining that frown of his wife's.

From old habit, I accepted Lucy's introduction courteously enough. Then Aediva's polite, "Let me present my son . . ." made me glance hastily at the figure beside her.

Not the golden youth from the roof, but a much younger lad, barely my own age, with hair as fair as Lucy's – and his tongue protruding charmingly in the direction of his sister. Under my gaze, it vanished sharply, and the lips around it grinned.

"Alfred," said Lucy with resignation, as if she had long ago accepted that she was not to be fortunate in brothers.

"Is Hereward here?" Alfred demanded by way of greeting. "Is it true he started a battle from the hall roof and split open Roger FitzGeoffrey's head?"

Lucy cast a quick, nervous glance at her father, who muttered something under his breath and glared ferociously back at the heads that had turned sharply at the sound of his delinquent son's name. Or perhaps at the injured man's.

Alfred said impatiently, "Well? *Did* he roll Roger off the roof?"

Lucy hissed, "Alfred, be silent!"

I said helpfully, "I understand he flew off. Or perhaps he was the slitherer?" And Alfred let out a crack of delighted laughter. Aediva closed her eyes. Leofric muttered something enraged that sounded like, "White Christ!"

I was seated beside my betrothed at the high table. More surprisingly, on our hosts' other side sat Lucy's parents, clearly special and honoured friends. I was still digesting this when Robert sat down clumsily at my side.

"Did you win all the contests?" I enquired amiably. "Or just the archery?" In the pregnant silence, I at last spared him a glance. His weak eyes had narrowed, and there was a spark of irritation there that convinced me that this time his reply would be blistering. My breath caught.

And then, infuriatingly, the outer door burst open and someone erupted into the hall, and at once, by his very presence, caused a violent stir: the golden youth, Lucy's brother, Hereward.

I had the feeling that this wretched boy would always draw attention to himself, even without such nefarious exploits as this afternoon's. It was something in the powerful urgency of his step – like some unpredictable beast whose ferocity is only temporarily contained – combined with the careless pride of his tilted head. And the weird, irregular beauty, for that was there too. I had noticed no such thing this afternoon, but it was certainly glaring at me now, beneath the bruises and the half-scrubbed grime.

He had not even bothered to change his dress for the occasion. Only his slightly discoloured face and grazed, powerfully muscled bare arms appeared to have been anywhere near water, and he still wore the battered leather tunic, spattered with mud and blood and God knew what else.

Everyone looked, and everyone saw. And heard, for after a sudden upsurge in noise as he strode in, the chatter all dropped away to an expectant silence, into which we could hear his shoes thud across the floor, scattering rushes, and his sword and barbaric knives clank at his hip as he brushed past the tables. He could only have been sixteen years old.

Suddenly, Robert's chair scraped back. I thought he rose involuntarily, appalled by the late and unwanted guest. But Hereward saw him immediately, and swung round in our direction.

It was only as I watched it vanish from his face that I realized he had been angry. Then he grinned, the same radiant, impudent grin I remembered from the roof.

In his own language, he called out, "Where is she then, Rob? Is she hideous? Does she squint like a bag of nails? Does she screech like a shrew with toothache?"

This time, the silence was definitely appalled – not least, I suspected, because there was more than a grain of truth in Hereward's unflattering description. Only I was unperturbed, for the spite was not inspired by me but by whatever hidden anger was churning him up; I understood that perfectly.

Somewhere, somebody giggled. The lady Edith again? Robert's hand lifted and floundered helplessly. The youth Hereward, coming to a halt before us, continued to gaze up at him innocently, the laughter slowly dying in

21

his stormy eyes – strange, mismatched eyes, I could see now that he was close enough. One was a sharp, wintry blue, the other a definite, boiling grey; like two shades of the same violent sea.

An embarrassing scene beckoned. Deliberately, I stood up.

I said, "I believe I don't squint. I do, however, have a facility for languages."

The strange, intense eyes shifted quickly to me, and rested without blinking – or apology.

He said mildly, "Do you, by God?"

He had, I saw, very long, almost womanly lashes, darker than his hair and slightly incongruous in that hard, curiously asymmetrical young face. I had no way of telling if he recognized me from the afternoon.

Robert made an odd, strangled sound in his throat. On his other side, I could hear the lady Matilda furiously whispering.

Hereward, still examining me, said consideringly, "You're very small."

I blinked. "Yes? But then I am twelve years old. What is your excuse?"

His height, in fact, was neither tall nor short. I only picked it as a point of insult because he brought the subject up and I aimed to shock. I succeeded too, though not, it turned out, for quite the reasons I was imagining.

At my words, startlement leapt out of his brilliant face. His eyes sprang involuntarily to Robert's, and he uttered, "*Twelve?*" in accents that left me in no doubt of his amazement, or of the fact that he expected Robert to share it.

And abruptly, all the tiny things fell into place. The shock of my arrival, which could hardly, after all, have been entirely unexpected; the fixed smiles of the lady Matilda; the elusive anger of her genial husband. They had been misled by my own desperate parents. They did not want me. They wanted someone who could be married *now*, to allow Robert, and therefore Gilbert, some real control in my father's affairs *now*. The knowledge should have brought me hope; so why was it I just felt smaller and more isolated than ever?

The entire hall seemed oppressive, unnaturally dark with the sinking of the sun; and the grotesquely ugly wolves, or dragons, or whatever they were, carved into the beams above my head, and the walls on either side of me, seemed to take on expressions of extreme malevolence, as though closing in upon me for the kill. I could not imagine ever wanting anything as much as I wanted to be out of there . . .

I started violently as cool fingers touched my hand. They were Hereward's, quickly and efficiently prising mine off the table. Only then did I realize I was gripping it so hard that my knuckles shone white.

And Hereward himself, vitality still blazing out of his wild eyes, was grinning at me with more amusement than anything else. I found, pathetically, that I was grateful to him.

"Lady," he said, as he raised my hand and soundly kissed it. "*Young lady – I salute you.*"

Falling back into my seat, I took time to gather my breath and my wits, and what was left of my poor pride. And when I could take an interest again, I realized that Matilda was talking, lightly and easily; yet with morbid sensitivity, I sensed the nervousness behind it.

She was saying, "I have a most fitting punishment for you! I send you from my table, Hereward! You lose your place of honour as champion, and are banished forthwith to sit with – your brother! And that only on condition you greet your parents with proper respect and affection."

Beside me, Robert muttered something under his breath.

Hereward's eyes turned slowly, as though reluctantly, upon his mother, then quickly on to his father.

I leaned back in my chair in order to see better, but there was no visible emotion in the boy's face, or in his voice as he said, "If my parents wish to receive it, then they have it."

Perhaps if there had been the remotest trace of contrition or appeal, he might have got away with it, for the words themselves were not ungracious; but as it was, their coldly spoken tone acted as tinder on his father, who suddenly exploded.

"I am *sick* of receiving it, for it is worthless!"

"Leofric . . ." The word formed soundlessly on Aediva's faded lips; but Hereward didn't even flinch. He just shrugged.

"Then don't," he said carelessly, and turned away from them.

"You see?" said Leofric with contempt. "What is the point in continually forgiving him? He crowns every sin with another until this of yesterday!" His voice rose, like that of a priest pronouncing damnation. "Well, *this* time, I swear before you all, before God Himself, that I will accept him back now only on *my* conditions. Namely, his *abject* apology, the return of all he stole from me, *and* the surrender of his sword."

There was a universal ripple, almost a gasp – of shock, or dismay, or just insatiable curiosity.

"What do you want with my sword?" Hereward said insolently into the still rising buzz of comment. "You already have everything else I own."

"You own nothing!" Leofric flashed. "Nothing that is not given by me!"

"I do now," said Hereward provokingly – referring no doubt to whatever it was he had stolen. I thought his father would burst. So did Gilbert, apparently, for our host said hastily, "Get to your place, Hereward. We are all hungry."

Hereward shrugged and sauntered with deliberate impudence on his way.

"What," I said curiously to Robert, "has he done?"

"Ask him," said Robert shortly.

I stood up purposefully, and at once several eyes turned on me in surprise. The servants with the washing bowls paused, eyes flying to their mistress for guidance.

Robert's hand jerked me back into my seat. "Be still, in God's name," he breathed.

"Then tell me."

"I would need *days* to tell you all he has done!"

"I only want to know why his father won't forgive him. He said he stole from him."

Robert said reluctantly, "I suppose he did." Quickly looking about him, he added low, "They have been quarrelling for years over Hereward's behaviour. They say he provokes discontent among the lesser people, taking their sides against their lords, defending their every minuscule right. Which inevitably leads his parents into all sorts of fights with their noble neighbours. Periodically, Leofric gets fed up and throws him out."

"Ah," I said, pleased to have the mystery of the unchanged clothes solved at least.

"This time, " Robert continued, getting impatiently to the point before the washing bowl came to him, "he threw out all Hereward's friends and companions with him. Hereward had nothing with which to support them, so yesterday . . ." He paused and drew breath, then lowered his voice still further, so that I had to bow my head to hear him at all. "Yesterday he went and collected some of the tributes due to his father and distributed them among his own men."

I felt my eyes widen. "An ingenious and amoral youth," I observed.

"You know nothing," said Robert contemptuously, submitting to the hand-washing ritual. Interestingly, Hereward's confrontations seemed to have abolished Robert's tolerance of me. I supposed hopefully that it was progress. Until we sat down I hadn't even managed to elicit a mild retort from him. And supper was not over yet.

Poor Robert.

CHAPTER 5

It was a bright, pleasant spring morning to be riding. Maddeningly enough. I would have preferred rain and fog, so that I could, with some justification, wallow in my hatred of the place. With my melancholy betrothed as escort, I was being taken on an expedition to Crowland Abbey, a remote monastery in the midst of the fens, founded, so the lady Emma had informed me, by St. Guthlac.

"Who was he? Some masochistic hermit?" I had demanded rudely.

"Actually," said Emma coldly, "he was a prince of the Mercian royal house."

I did not like their fen. It resembled too closely the marshes of home, only it was poorly drained, largely unreclaimed, and stretched as far as the eye could see. It's sheer size alone made me feel small, which hardly improved my temper.

When our horses had left the old Roman road and began to pick their way through damp marsh paths, skirting hamlets of tiny, sunken huts, I determinedly paid no attention to the big over-hanging willows or to the really quite attractively glinting pools which could be made out in the distance. From the corner of my eye, I did catch some odd, isolated sights, including a man striding over the marshy land on stilts, and another who vaulted over obstacles in his path by means of a long, wooden pole, but those I refused to acknowledge. Instead, I noted with interest that Robert was riding very close to Lucy.

And then, quite abruptly, a group of men seemed to rise threateningly out of the reeds ahead of us.

I heard Lucy gasp.

Then I realized that two of the men, who must have been bending down for some time to have remained hidden from us until now, had reached back to pull a third up to join them, as if from some way down. And almost immediately, this third was enthusiastically clapped on the back by the rest of the group, not withstanding his almost total covering in mud.

It became clear to me then that none of them even saw us, let alone threatened us.

The third man shook his head like a dog, causing mud to fly in all directions, and through it, I saw the shining gold of his hair – some small patch freakishly saved from the filth – caught in the shaft of sunlight which wriggled through the trees on our left.

I laughed.

Matilda turned sharply in the direction of my gaze. So did the others. Emma muttered something under her breath. At the same time, the fenmen became aware of us. One of them laconically pushed Hereward's shoulder, and the youth, breaking off from some explanation that involved much gesticulating, looked round and saw us.

Interestingly, I thought he swore. Certainly there was no response to Lucy's joyful cry of his name. Relief seemed to be flooding out of her very pores now, as if she had been imagining him shivering himself into an ague in the night.

I couldn't imagine any such thing. The last I had seen of him, he had looked massively healthy and almost outrageously comfortable, lounging back on his bench, feet up on the table and tipping wine haphazardly into a drinking horn with his toes, while he called out irreverent and frequently ribald remarks to the Saxon poet who had entertained us during supper with stirring and melancholy verse. His antics had appeared to inspire annoyance in some quarters, amusement in others. Even the poet himself hadn't seemed clear as to whether or not to be offended.

Now, Lucy began the surge towards him, Robert at her side; but rather than meet it, he actually turned his back, quite deliberately.

"What are you doing out here so filthily?" Robert demanded amiably, apparently undeterred by the other's blatant rudeness. I suppose it explained his imperviousness to mine.

"Sewering," said Hereward shortly over his shoulder. With extreme reluctance he half-turned back towards us, though his eyes were wintry, unwelcoming. Some northern, icy sea.

Closer now, I could make out that the fenmen stood beside a channel dug through the watery land around them, and stretching in both directions as far as I could see.

"It doesn't work," I observed flatly, and the hard, disconcertingly different eyes flickered over me without interest.

"It will now," he said briefly. "We unblocked it."

"With your head?" Robert asked humorously, and the youth smiled in a cold, perfunctory sort of a way that didn't get near his eyes. He was irritated by our presence here. Whether because of his company, or his dirt, or his behaviour yesterday, or some other cause, I didn't know. Or care.

"The lady Matilda of Ghent," he observed offhandedly to his companions. "Better make your bows to her before she goes."

And he jumped deliberately back into the ditch, reaching into the murky water to fish out some long, spiky tool on a wooden pole. This time he leapt up again unaided, with the same peculiarly wild grace he seemed to bring to everything physical. Over-developed muscles in his arms rippled through their coating of mud. His legs, bare and brown and wet, were like tree trunks.

"And to the child-bride," he added, causing my eyes to fly resentfully to his. They were smiling now, maliciously. Following Matilda's example, I sniffed, though much more productively than she. In fact, I didn't mind in the least being the scapegoat for his ill-nature. It made my own simpler.

"What about Emma and me?" Lucy was demanding indignantly. Her brother lifted one arched eyebrow at her.

"Why should they bow to you? You don't frighten me in the least."

"I wish someone did," Matilda retorted. It seemed she was ready for the fight now. "Before you turn the whole of Mercia against your parents!"

"Oh oh," Hereward mocked insolently. "You are going to beat me – verbally but mercilessly – over yesterday afternoon."

"Don't you think someone should? You know perfectly well your behaviour was *abominable*! What have you got to say for yourself?"

Hereward appeared to think. "It wasn't my fault?" he suggested, with no pretence whatever of truth. "Or – it was in self-defence?"

"Rubbish!" Matilda said angrily.

"Actually," I said delicately, for I had spied a new means of annoying her, "it probably was. Self defence."

Inevitably, all eyes swung on me, with varying degrees of surprise. Gratified, I deigned to explain. "Just before the – er – war, I saw some five or six men fall on him from behind."

Though I wasn't looking at him, oddly enough it was of Hereward's unblinking regard that I was most aware. Robert was frowning. Emma's mouth had fallen open. Matilda turned sharply towards me.

"I expect," I said kindly, turning my gaze at last upon the delinquent himself, "I expect they eventually cornered you against the back wall of the hall, forcing you on to the roof for your own safety."

There was a pause, during which I tried and failed to read the expression in his strange, intensely mismatched eyes. Then he said obligingly, "I expect they did."

I heard Matilda breathe in deeply. "Is this true?" she demanded.

"I couldn't dispute the word of the child-bride," Hereward said apologetically. Having caught my eyes, he seemed reluctant to release them, and I wasn't going to back down.

Matilda repeated, "Is it true?"

And at that, he let me go to turn to her; but even then, instead of answering her question, he posed another, quite abruptly. "Will you tell Gilbert?"

She stared back at him. "Why didn't you?"

The ridiculously long lashes swept down over his smooth cheek, then flickered up once more. "A previous quarrel got in the way."

Matilda's brief softening was over. "And that's another thing," she fumed. "What are you going to do about your father?"

Hereward smiled dazzlingly through his mud. "Send in the child-bride to make my excuses?"

"If," I said pleasantly, into the sniggers of the fenmen and the servants and the men-at-arms, and the slightly shocked giggles of my companions, "*If* you call me that once more, I shall cut out your tongue. Through your ears."

"Torfrida!" cried Matilda, properly shocked this time, but she was drowned out by Hereward's shout of laughter.

Hereward refused to come to Crowland with us – on the presumably reasonable grounds that the Abbot was liable to clap him in chains –

though he did come with us part of the way, striding along in the midst of the horses, exerting himself to entertain. In fact, he turned out to be rather funny.

He made no effort to speak to me, though, and I made no effort at all, except to be nasty whenever opportunity offered. Only once, as he swung along beside Robert, did I hear my betrothed exclaim, "*Spirit*? *You* try sitting beside her for two hours! The girl is *relentless*!"

I managed to look away before Hereward's gaze found me, but I don't think I had wiped the smile off my face.

Emerging from a thick clump of trees onto much more marshy paths, we finally saw the abbey. It stood on an island – little more than a green hillock, I thought disparagingly – rising out of a murky lake. Some people might have found it picturesque, for there was a sort of still, lonely distinction to the scene; I wasn't in the mood to appreciate holiness.

"Bourne is that way," Lucy informed me, pointing vaguely away from the river. "Just on the edge of the fen." She looked at me expectantly. "So, what do you think?"

I curled my lip.

"I think there will be flies," I said shortly.

"Optimism," said Hereward, appearing suddenly between our horses, "is such a blessing in the young."

Without invitation or instruction, his hands were on my waist, lifting me out of the saddle. He was little more than a boy, yet the strength rippling through those brawny arms made me feel like a piece of straw plucked helplessly out of the air by a mischievous wind. It did not improve my temper.

As my feet landed, I glared at him with quite genuine irritation, and he paused, holding me still while he regarded me, his fair head slightly on one side. I suspected that, young as he was, other people found it hard to withstand that peculiarly forceful gaze. I was glad to be made of sterner stuff.

Unexpectedly, he lifted his hand from my waist and touched my one eyebrow with a large, unclean thumb, unhurriedly tracing its long, thick line from one side to the other, and then returning to its middle across the bridge of my nose, where the thumb stopped, and lightly pressed.

"What is it," he wondered, "that pulls down this frown of yours so constantly? The weight of the splendid eyebrow?"

My mother had tried to pluck it before I left. I had only got away by swearing I would do it myself on the journey. I think that was what brought the blood seeping up to my cheeks. That, or the fact I did not care to be laughed at.

Hereward's finger fell away, but his other hand did not release me.

He said lazily, "There is no need to be so frightened, you know. You might even find that your parents have not made such a bad bargain for you."

Stricken. So much armour, so much effort, and all it took was the careless, mismatched eyes of a delinquent boy.

I closed my mouth, still bereft of words, still bombarded by a mass of confused emotions, the chief of which seemed to be that he had no right to say I was frightened, no right at all.

Still he was not finished with me. Leaning forward so that his breath actually tickled my cheek, he whispered, "Besides, they won't send you home, however ill you behave. They are too honourable. I should know."

"Torfrida?" It was Lucy, pushing my pony out of the way to get to us. "Hereward, leave her alone; she's not used to you."

"Oh, I think she is," Hereward said, stepping back. A smile danced across his face. He closed one eye – the blue one – so quickly that if I had blinked myself, I would have missed it, and then he had turned away, saying regretfully, "On the other hand, I think it's time I stopped teasing all of you. I'm off, back to my lair. See you next week, Rob? In Lincoln . . ."

"Lair?" said Lucy revolted, while I let out my breath and wondered in panic what had just happened to me. "Wait, Hereward!" she shouted after his grimy, retreating back. "Hereward? You're not – you're not going to *rob* someone?"

He didn't even turn, though his laughter came back to us clearly enough. So did his carelessly called reply: "Not unless I come upon a fat abbot, or a sleek Norman. Or, even better, a fat, sleek Norman abbot!" And then he was striding back the way we had come, leaving me to wonder distractedly what peculiar grudge he could possibly hold against fat abbots.

But I was glad at his going. I felt quite strongly that I never wanted to set eyes – or ears – on him again.

Bourne, the hall from which Lucy's family held together innumerable scattered properties, was a pleasant place, comparable in size if not in comfort with Folkingham. But here were no Flemish tapestries. All the decoration was quite fiercely English – crude hangings, animal-like carvings and rough wall-paintings of brilliant reds and blues and yellows. But at least the feast to which we were bidden was unstinting in both quantity and quality. And to my relief, there was no sign of the errant elder son, invited or otherwise, so I felt able to relax, just a little.

In the interests of a peaceful meal, no doubt, the lady Aediva had separated me from my betrothed, placing me between the youthful Alfred and a plump clergyman of uncertain years who was introduced with casual disrespect simply as Brand. I wondered if I were being punished. The clergyman, however, persisted through all my monosyllables and silences and curt replies of undisguised boredom, until, pushing my bread away, I turned my head to look at him.

He smiled peacefully, and a small piece of fish tumbled off his lip to join a considerable proportion of the previous courses on his chest. He had a round, smooth moon-face beneath a shiny tonsure, and large, amiable eyes, blinking sleepily at me. I may be slow, but I am not stupid.

"You are not, I think, the family chaplain," I observed. His disordered eyebrows heaved themselves up in surprise, then collapsed again with the effort.

"Oh no."

I waited, but the old buffoon was determined to make me ask. Nothing loathe, I said bluntly, "Who are you then?"

Brand wiped his fingers on his habit. Some breadcrumbs leapt up in alarm and resettled themselves more comfortably about his person, or on the table or the floor nearby.

"Brand," he said, holding out his hand to me. We had done this already. I wasn't sure whether or not he was joking, but I chose to take the hand – gingerly, for I had no idea what lurked there.

"Torfrida," I said gravely. For a moment I thought I would have to ask again, but he had obviously tired of the game.

Dropping my fingers, he said, "I have the honour to be Aediva's brother. Aediva," he added kindly, "is your hostess."

"Thank you," I said politely. "It is more comfortable to know."

"Exactly. I have also," he continued ponderously, "the *almost* as grave responsibility of being Provost of Peterborough Abbey. Which is why I am here today, visiting our cell by the village."

I blinked. I said curiously, "Do you get on with your elder nephew?"

Again the eyebrows lumbered up and fell with a silent crash.

"Don't be ridiculous," said the Provost of Peterborough mildly. "No one gets on with Hereward. Why do you ask?"

"Fat abbots," said Alfred, unexpectedly and succinctly on my other side.

"I am getting on in years," Brand said peaceably. "I am allowed to be fat. I may even be allowed to be an abbot one day. But still, in my current, lowly position, I am allowed – nay, positively *encouraged* – to beat boys for impudence."

Alfred cast me a careless, Lucy-like grin, though I noticed he ducked rather swiftly back to Emma.

"Ah," said Brand with satisfaction. "Roast duck. Excellent. Now then, young lady – tell me the gossip from Flanders. What is the opinion there about the English succession?"

"Indifference, I should think," I said dryly, and watched his eyebrows struggle briefly. Apparently deciding it was not worth the effort this time, he only twitched them.

"Really?" he marvelled. "Yet surely there would be untold advantages for your people if William of Normandy became king here?"

"Maybe," I allowed. "But I doubt it keeps them awake at night worrying. King Edward is hardly on his last legs, is he? The next ruler . . ."

"*Next?*" Alfred interrupted again. "King Edward doesn't rule now! He prays and builds abbeys. Harold of Wessex rules."

"Hold your tongue, ignorant boy. The King," Brand added to me, "is advised by his chief nobles . . ."

"Harold of Wessex!" Alfred repeated triumphantly.

"And our own Earl," Brand said mildly. "Only a silly boy would write off Leofric of Mercia."

"Leofric is old," Alfred said stubbornly.

"He has Aelfgar to succeed him."

"Aye, with boat loads of Irish or Welsh at his back! Or even, God forgive him, Norwegians!"

Half-heartedly, Brand swiped some unsuspecting crumbs off his chest and reached for his duck. "You have been listening to Hereward," he observed.

"No I haven't!" Alfred protested, and when his uncle looked at him speakingly over a duck leg, he added defensively, "It is my father's opinion that Mercia is no longer capable of balancing the ambitions of Wessex. It is my opinion too!"

"Oh well, if it's *yours*," Brand said sarcastically. "But we were not discussing over-powerful subjects. We were discussing kings."

I said quickly, "What is there to discuss? If King Edward has no children . . ."

"He won't," said Alfred irrepressibly. "It would involve lying with his wife."

"Well," Brand confessed, distracted, "I'd as soon lie with a snake myself as with one of Godwin's brood."

I looked at him. "But then you," I reminded him, "are a monk."

A smile flickered through his round face. "So I am."

"And Edward might as well be," said Alfred. "So – no children."

I said, "Then there *is* only William to succeed, his nearest full-grown relation of any standing. And he is promised it, is he not?"

"So, they say, was Eustace of Boulogne," Brand said apologetically. "And I don't see the King of Norway sitting still when the throne of Canute's kingdom is vacant again. And then there is the Aethling . . ."

"Who won't leave his comfortable home in Hungary," I said wryly. "Forget your Aethling. Actually, you would be wise to. William the Bastard is an ill man to cross. But what is the point of guessing? Who knows what will happen in ten or twenty years or whenever King Edward dies?"

"God and the astrologers," said Brand flippantly. He slapped his lips over a minutely clean bone and dropped it on the table. "I can't speak for the All Mighty, of course, but the astrologers seem to be in favour of William the Bastard."

I looked at him sideways. "How many astrologers do you know?"

"Oh, two or three," he said vaguely.

I laid down my duck wing carefully, gazing at it as if I expected it to fly off at any moment. I said, "Can they really predict the future that way?"

"Some of it. If they ask the right questions."

I looked up at him thoughtfully through my lashes. It was an idea I had had before. Something told me it could not be mere chance that brought it to my attention again here. At any rate, I saw no harm in testing it.

I said shrewdly, "Do *you* ask the right questions?"

He smiled faintly. "My studies involve the prediction of nothing more or less momentous than Easter or the matins bell."

He was not, of course, being strictly honest. Even then I knew that no one of intelligence could cut such studies off there. Smiling back, I pursued him.

CHAPTER 6

I was so used to being clever. I had thought I could study astronomy for a week or so, and then work it all out for myself. After my first visit to Peterborough, I felt very childish and foolish. But more determined than ever.

Of course, I could not keep visiting the Abbey in isolation if I did not wish to excite too much curiosity. Even though the adults were increasingly distracted by tidings that the Bishop of Hereford was marching against the turbulent Prince Gruffydd of Wales – apparently an ally of the Earl of Mercia's son Aelfgar – I still felt obliged to cover my tracks with other expeditions and visits, and yet still deny any pleasure or interest in the country. Which was how we came to be in the city of Lincoln on a market day.

I liked Lincoln. Big and bustling with noisy prosperity, it reminded me a little of Bruges: stone churches and large wooden halls with gardens, neatly laid out with more haphazard arrangements of lesser houses and sunken huts in between; noisy streets alive with animals and people, and clusters of booths selling everything from meat and bread to cloth and jewellery. In the market square, gaudy tumblers and jugglers throwing brightly coloured balls and plates walked among ceorls and fishwives and well-to-do burghers. Drab serving men and women, buying for their masters, rubbed against brilliantly-gowned ladies in search of silks and lace and new trinkets. Rich scents of spice and fish and fruit filled the air.

It all made me so wretchedly homesick that I had no difficulty at all in appearing bad-tempered and sullen for all of the first hour. But it was a warm, May morning, bidding fair to be positively hot by the afternoon, and I found I did not mind the press of people, the raucous calls of the street pedlars or the close stench of over abundant humanity. It made me feel comfortingly anonymous – so much so that I had bought some lace for no better reason than that it was pretty, before I realized I could never wear it here. Not if I was to keep up my dismal role.

"It's for my mother," I told Lucy shortly when she pounced admiringly upon it. After which I made a point of haranguing Robert into buying me a particularly large and vulgar garnet brooch set in gold with which to fasten my cloak. I wore it immediately, with pride.

Robert, having obvious difficulty in dragging his eyes from this new piece of gaudery, was conducting us away from the seductive smell of a pie-seller's booth towards some more respectable alehouse for dinner, when I saw Hereward again.

He was in a smaller square formed between the church and the inn, with a crowd of other young men, and he was crouched on the ground playing dice, his head bent in concentration so that his face was invisible to me. But still I knew him as soon as I saw the shock of bright gold. It didn't need the shout of laughter or the quick, upward toss of his fair head as he grinned across at his companions.

I looked away at once. I didn't want to meet him again. I didn't like him. I didn't like the way he *bothered* people. And if I was honest, which I generally was, I didn't like the way he bothered *me*.

Besides, I had learned rather more of him now: normal, decent people did not just disapprove of him, they feared him, because his behaviour was not simply wildness, it was *rebellion*, a rebellion that struck at the heart of all civilized societies. He obeyed nobody, appeared to consider that neither he nor anybody else owed loyalty to any lord, and his only purpose in life seemed to be anarchy. All of which would have been bad enough, but he swept others along in his wake: the youths who had joined him on the hall roof, by name Wynter and Leofric the Black, were apparently just two of the boys of good family who were in his thrall.

So it was with dismay that I belatedly recalled his casual arrangement to meet Robert here, and I could only hope that it would be forgotten.

However, Robert and Lucy had both heard the distinctive, wild laugh, and inevitably Robert was already starting across the square towards him, Lucy trotting delightedly at his heels. Short of stamping into the alehouse on my own – which I considered quite carefully – there was nothing I could do but trail after them.

Of course, he showed no surprise at seeing us. An engaging smile broke out, but otherwise he might have been meeting us for the third or fourth time that day. At first he did not even rise to greet us, merely stretching up one lazy, brawny arm to shake Robert's hand. He said something to Lucy, but I didn't catch what it was, for his attention had already returned to the dice, and with it went everyone else's.

Hereward, dressed for summer, apparently, in a short, belted tunic of some light, frayed material carelessly open at the throat and chest, and his brown legs still bare, was flanked by two youths of about his own age: one sinewy, wispy, impassive and rough; the other not much taller, but considerably stronger looking, with a massive tangle of black hair and fluffy young beard, and a continually fierce glower. His eyes were a sharp, unexpected blue. After a moment, I recognized this latter as Wynter, one of the boys from the hall roof. And a little way off, sitting on a barrel and idly swinging his long legs, was the other rooftop culprit, the dark, gangly and slightly distracted Leofric the Black.

All four of them were hung about with an impressive array of weapons, some of which I still lacked names for, but the only ornament between them was the intricately carved dragon buckle on Hereward's belt.

The others of the group, some five or six of them, appeared from their dress to be wealthy burghers and noblemen, also young, though rather older than Hereward himself; some even wore long tunics and short hair. Civilized men, I thought with some surprise – apart, of course from their youthful folly in playing dice in the street with a delinquent of Hereward's reputation. Having hastily greeted Robert and Lucy – I was still dragging my heels on the outskirts of the group – these worthies all directed their eyes expectantly at Hereward's hand, which was almost idly shaking the dice.

Perhaps it was that – the game, for stakes that no doubt none of them could really afford – which explained the tension in the square. But it seemed to me that no one, except he who held the dice, was free of it.

Hereward threw. All eyes followed the dice. Hereward smiled. One of the men groaned. Another muttered. Hereward scooped up the dice and rose in one clean, easy movement.

He said provokingly, "See?" his voice maddeningly self-satisfied, even smug.

"Too well!" exclaimed one of the men in inevitable retaliation. Hereward paused in the act of turning towards us. Instead, he glanced up at the speaker through his long, golden lashes.

"Meaning?" he asked gently.

And the other, looking slightly taken aback to be taken up so quickly, took a deep breath before he replied boldly, "Meaning you have all the luck. *All* the luck."

It was alarmingly plain, even to me.

Robert said hastily, "What are you playing for, anyhow? Surely not money!"

"Oh no," said Hereward. "We're playing for honour. Godric has just lost his."

Someone laughed. Others smiled, as though too nervous not to make a joke out of the words; and it was only then I realized that Godric was not the man who had accused him, but the man he had just beaten, the most respectable of the whole group, by his appearance. I had only met him once before, through a haze of anger against his wife and the rest of the world, but after a moment, I did recognize him. Godric of Lincoln.

Flushing under Hereward's limpid gaze, Godric's eyes narrowed, and I knew instinctively that this was a far more dangerous man to provoke than the first. And that this was the fight Hereward really wanted.

Now why, I wondered, was that?

Godric's mouth snapped open to retort, "It is not *my* honour which concerns us!" But again, before he had even finished speaking, Robert intervened.

"We're dining across the road, if you care to join us," he said quickly. I didn't know whether to feel relieved at escaping this suddenly fraught situation, or simply appalled at the prospect of Hereward's further company, though in the end it didn't matter.

Hereward said, "Thanks," but neither his eyes nor his smile ever left Godric. His hand lifted, carelessly, indicating the barrel under Leofric's lanky person. "I have my dinner here."

Then, quite without warning, he moved, taking me by surprise. "Is that Torfrida? Can you dice?"

And I, finding his erratic yet intense attention suddenly upon me, could think of nothing to say except, "I can try."

"Good girl." Without hesitation, he held out the dice to me, but abruptly Lucy slapped his hand away.

"Don't be ridiculous! What will people say if she's seen dicing in the street?"

"They'll say I'm a child," I said prosaically, "who knows no better. What's the matter?" I asked Hereward, boldly stretching out my hand. "Don't you have another set?"

Hereward's eyes smiled disarmingly, dropping the dice into my palm. "I'd hate to split them for nothing."

Withstanding the intense gaze, I realized the storms were back. If he was not angry, he was certainly restless, profoundly reckless. And with a jolt, I caught that mood from him, feeling it rise up like a torrent.

I said breathlessly, "What if I win too?"

"I fully expect you to. God is on the side of angels and child-brides."

"You're drunk," said Lucy contemptuously.

"Give them back, Torfrida," Robert said commandingly. And then to Hereward, more enraged than I had ever seen him, "She's not a toy in your games, Hereward, and I won't have her . . .!"

"I believe the young lady has already spoken," Hereward interrupted, mildly enough. "Do you know our opponent, Torfrida? Godric, noble coiner of this town."

I glanced impatiently at the respectable young man, who really looked old enough to know better than this. He also looked decidedly uncomfortable suddenly, as if he wished he had never started this; which, of course, he hadn't – his friend had. Only Hereward, for reasons of his own, had crudely turned the confrontation against him . . .

"We have met," Godric said with difficulty. "At Folkingham."

"My betrothal supper," I agreed cordially. "You are husband to the beautiful Edith."

He smiled. "As a reason for fame, I could do worse."

I doubted it. However, keeping that to myself I crouched down as I had seen the others do, and somewhat inexpertly rolled the dice.

"Torfrida!" Lucy wailed. Some people had come out of the inn and were staring across at us. I smiled and waved to them. A breath of surprised laughter broke from Hereward, feeding my pleasure in rebellion.

I hoped very much that this would get back to Gilbert and Matilda. In fact, Robert should tell them, in his best tones of very genuine outrage.

Hereward, who had been standing above me, leaning one elbow negligently on the ale barrel beside Leofric's thigh, swooped down upon the dice and dropped them into the purse at his belt.

"There now," he said amiably. "Is your peculiar honour satisfied?"

"Of course not," Godric snapped. "How could it be?"

"Did I win?" I asked with interest.

"Of course you did," said Hereward, reaching down unexpectedly to draw me to my feet. "Even though Wulfstan here moved it with his toe."

For no reason, I laughed. Robert groaned. Wulfstan, a rather shifty looking individual, did his best to appear affronted.

Godric said angrily, "You are impossible!"

"I am victorious," said Hereward flippantly. "And you have still to apologise. So has Edwin, who first voiced your rude suspicions."

"Leave it, Hereward," said Robert sternly. "You are drunk, and Lucy and Torfrida . . ."

"Take them away then. Godric wants a fight."

"I do not," Godric said at once; and then, because there was no other option for a man of standing, he added, "But I am prepared for one, since your pointless little play has proved nothing – except that anyone may win with your dice!"

"Trial by combat," said Hereward happily, and abruptly my rebellion was over. "Martin, fill the horns first. Have a drink, Rob, or go away."

Lucy had me by the arm. "Come," she said nervously. "There's no doing anything with him in this mood. Just pray he doesn't kill anyone . . ."

I would have gone with her tamely enough now, my silly recklessness
vanishing into so much dust at the prospect of real violence, but Robert,
oddly, would not leave it, even though he was still rigid with anger.

"You want to be taken up by the Sheriff's men?" he demanded. "For
fighting in the street? You especially cannot afford such an outcome,
Hereward! Can't you solve your childish quarrel by less lethal means?"

I regarded my betrothed with new respect. So, I think, did everyone
else.

"Such as?" Hereward said thoughtfully.

"Ah . . .er . . . a . . . a race!" Robert said, floundering at the last, and
Hereward let out a crack of laughter.

"Oh, tame stuff, Rob," he mocked.

"All right then, a race on *stilts*, if you will!" Robert retorted. And a light
of pure mischief began to blaze in Hereward's strange eyes, blocking out
whatever ugliness lay underneath. Leofric's gaze came back into focus;
he had begun to grin.

"On stilts," Hereward repeated thoughtfully, as though the suggestion
showed promise. "On stilts! A *three-legged* race on stilts, the stilts to be
made by each team. If I win, Godric apologises. If Godric wins, I'm a rotten, stinking cheat and he can have my loaded dice. Fair?"

"Ridiculous!" said Godric indignantly. "And I have better things to do!"

"Don't be feeble. Just because you're an old married man these days,
and scared of your wife, doesn't mean you have to be boring too. What do
you say? Two couples in each team?"

I'm sure Godric would have backed out. Certainly he wanted to, but his
own supporters would not let him. In no time, Martin – the roughest and
wiriest of Hereward's three present henchmen, who seemed to stand somewhere unclear between friend and servant – was filling drinking horns,
and the men were all sitting or lounging about the barrel, drinking and
arguing over the rules of the contest till even Robert had recovered his
temper.

They decided in the end to start from the front door of the alehouse, to
race across the road to the church, then once around the square and back
again. If everyone fell before the end, the couple that got farthest would
win. And Leofric the Black, for some reason, was appointed the race
judge. Somebody had suggested Robert first for this task, but Hereward
claimed indignantly that Rob was his partner, at which Robert looked distinctly alarmed, although as the ale went down he appeared more
reconciled to it.

By the time all this was established, Martin and a couple of the towns-

37

men, who had disappeared round the back of the alehouse, returned with armfuls of long logs – once clearly intended as fire wood – and a couple of axes. So we split into two camps. Leaving Godric and his cronies in triumphant possession of the square, happily chopping logs into usable sizes and shapes, Robert and Lucy and I accompanied Hereward and his henchmen back across the road to the alehouse – where Hereward led us straight through to the yard, ignoring the protestations of the keeper, who flapped his arms helplessly at us as we passed through his house.

"Tactics of surprise," Hereward explained. "We have to make our stilts bigger."

Robert transferred his doubtful gaze from our logs, which Martin had just dropped with some relief into the yard, up to Hereward.

"Why?" he asked succinctly.

"Bigger strides, of course," Hereward said, crouching down to pick up a log and measure its length. "What's the matter with you? We used to be good at this as children, in the fens – don't you remember?"

"I remember *you* being good at it. I remember *me* falling off."

"We'll make them stout so no one falls off. What do you think, Martin? Could we keep our balance if we made all the stilts the full length of this log?"

Martin shrugged.

"You and I could," he said ambiguously, and Lucy laughed. I swallowed my own sudden mirth back down, for it felt too wild. The recklessness was back.

"Excellent," said Hereward, reaching to his belt for a knife. "Set to then. We'll need to match the stirrups quite carefully."

I brushed past him, thoughtfully picking up one log and then placing another rather precariously on top. The result was several inches taller than me.

"What are you doing?" Robert asked uneasily.

I looked at Hereward. "What," I said, "if you used two, end to end? No one – but no one – would then have bigger strides."

CHAPTER 7

Hereward's lips twitched. Regarding me, head slightly on one side, he said, "We could splice them together. They might be strong enough if we left them this broad. But it would be quite a weight."

"Who cares? With legs this long, you'll have won in about four steps."

I heard another breath of his laughter – reward enough for my creativity – but he was already setting to work with quick, deft fingers. Robert looked at me without affection.

Lucy said severely, "You're as bad as he is. In fact, you make him worse!" Yet I had the impression her mischievous soul was actually delighted, now that the prospect of lethal violence between her brother and Godric had been commuted to mere horseplay.

Not that Hereward wasn't taking his game seriously. While he worked, issuing practical advice with increasingly outrageous humour, till even Wynter was grinning, Robert was sent to spy on the others, to make sure no one else had the same idea. Leofric the Black, excused work on the grounds of his supposed impartiality, had little to do but watch and smile his faint, slightly dreamy smile, contributing little to the repartee beyond an occasional blasphemous, "Bless you, my son," whenever Hereward requested it.

"Why is it your task to bless?" I asked curiously. "Are you destined for the Church, or something?"

"Terrifying, isn't it?" said Hereward. "Your soul in his hands."

Leofric smiled amiably. "It is my ambition to join the Church," he said peaceably. "Not as a monk, but as a priest of the world."

"It would have to be the world," said Hereward irrepressibly.

"Why do you mock him?" I demanded. "I thought it would be an untold advantage for you to have a tame priest to grant you absolution!"

Hereward shot me an upward grin from behind his hair, and carried on working. Once, I remember, he laid down his knife to concentrate more on his ale and on some hilarious argument with Leofric and Robert which, I thought, went over Wynter's head as well as Martin's. Yet I noticed Wynter's blue gaze rose frequently from his well-fashioned stilt to his friend.

Thinking aloud, I said abruptly, "Is he really as carefree as he seems?"

Wynter had no difficulty working out who *he* was. To his men, even then, there was only one *he*. But he appeared unoffended. With a quick shrug, he said, "Needs to go home, I suppose. Needs something to do."

"Perhaps you all do."

"The fun wears thin after a bit," Wynter confessed. "But Hereward's as stubborn as his father."

"Would not the lord of Bourne take you back now, if you came home without him?"

Wynter stared. "I would not go without him. None of us would."

I looked at him curiously. "You would do anything for him, I think."

"I would die for him," Wynter said simply. Then, under my clear gaze, he flushed with rough embarrassment and looked away. "It's the way things are," he muttered.

And then Hereward rose to his feet, holding up the new stilts to their full, impressive height. Robert broke off in mid sentence; his mouth remained open, his eyes fixed in horror on the completed stilts. Slowly he swallowed, lifting his gaze to Hereward's.

"No," he said with finality.

"Don't be a baby. It's not so high."

"Supposing I could get on, I'd only fall off! Aye and that's another thing! How *do* you mean to get on? Exactly?"

Hereward looked at me.

I said promptly, "From the roof. You like roofs."

Hereward's eyes danced. "There you are then."

Only Hereward and Robert had the long stilts. Martin and Wynter made do with more moderate models. "In case we fall off," Hereward had explained. "You'll still have a sensible chance to save my honour – and my dice, more to the point."

The shorter stilts were mastered encouragingly quickly; practice on the others, however, did not go so well. Amid increasing hilarity – fostered among the men, I have to say, by further draughts of ale – Hereward and Robert got up on the low inn roof, and sat with their legs dangling down the wall, while Lucy and I held the stilts for them, and I tied their legs together at the ankle.

"Ready?" said Hereward. "Now!"

Lucy and I let go. They both heaved their outside feet forward – and fell off. The third time they got two steps before they fell in a mirthful heap, and by then it was clear that it was Robert's balance which was the problem. Still laughing, Robert offered to swap places with Martin or Wynter, but Hereward, apparently determined to make him suffer, wouldn't hear of it. Which is why they tried a fourth time, got three steps and fell again, this time spraining Robert's ankle in the process. Fortunately, he found the whole thing so funny that he was able to grin through what must have been considerable pain, and when Lucy bound the ankle for him, he was so far enchanted as to be quite reconciled to his injury.

Not so Hereward. When Wynter said, "Do you want my place?" he answered, "I do not!" quite roundly.

"Martin should go with you," Robert suggested. "He has much better balance than me anyhow."

"Yes, but he and Wynter are used to each other now . . ."

Speculatively, his eyes flitted from them to Leofric, then regretfully on to Lucy, to the alehouse keeper, trotting off with further orders, and finally to me.

He smiled.

"Torfrida. How is *your* balance?"

"No!" said Robert and Lucy together. But I knew only a wild desperation for the fun I had been deprived of for so long; the reckless laughter was back in me now with a vengeance, gurgling up and spilling over. And Hereward's wicked eyes were answering me, urging me on.

"It's all right," Hereward assured the others, although I didn't think he was even listening to them. "I can carry her weight so easily that even if she falls, I'll make sure it's on top of me."

"I won't fall," I assured him breathlessly, anxious now only to begin.

Scrambling on to the low roof was easy. The hardest part, surprisingly, was the embarrassment of Hereward's arm around my waist, and his warm, muscled leg moving against mine. I was not used to being this close to any man, let alone one so physically *intense*, and if I was not yet a woman – well, I was not a child either, and for several moments I lost my concentration in trying to cover my confusion. However, the threat of toppling from such a height does focus the mind wonderfully, and since Hereward's manner to me did not change in the slightest – except, perhaps, in increasingly rollicking humour – I quickly lost my unease and re-entered the spirit of the game.

The stilts were heavy. On the first step, Hereward was obliged to heave me forward, which upset our balance so far that I still don't know how we kept upright. However, arms stretched outwards on either side, like some monstrous, two-headed bird, we found we could *swing* our steps, which had the added advantage of speed.

"A lady of experience, I perceive," Hereward observed. He seemed to be laughing inside, constantly, which was just as I felt, now that my childish embarrassment was over.

"I was only nine," I said breathlessly, remembering a wild summer with my cousins. "And I confess I was not this high. Nowhere near! Do you think they can see us over the roof?"

"Who cares? Can you turn? We'll have to go round the side of the house."

"Are they ready to start the race?"

"They'd better be: I haven't worked out how to stop yet."

Martin and Wynter led the way. Lucy, taking over my role, had tied all the necessary legs, and Robert, hirpling through the inn to the front door, with Leofric's aid, prepared to supervise all.

Through my concentration, I heard the catcalls and laughter as the two teams reviled each other's stilts and prepared for the race.

"Where are the others?" one of the townsmen demanded. "If Robert is here, *where* is Hereward?"

"Here," said Hereward, as we swung to the front of the house in perfect harmony. I heard the dazzling smile in his voice before the deafening silence, save for our own breathing and the deliberate thud of our stilts. Someone swore, long and admiringly, and then the laughter came.

A group of people in the square were pointing at us, open-mouthed.

"Now, Leofric," Hereward said significantly, although we were not yet abreast of the others. And Leofric, doubled-up with Robert in the throws of helpless laughter, waved one desperate hand.

"Go," he managed, obligingly, and the race began.

The first stride brought us close behind the others, although Godric and his partner were still well ahead. On very short stilts, they seemed to have an excellent and speedy system that made them look like bouncing rabbits. The effect was so ridiculous I wanted to howl with glee, but even I had to confess it worked rather more efficiently than our spectacular lumbering.

Our second stride took us almost to the road, where Godric's second team fell, much to the vocal joy of the watchers. We swung past them amidst great cheers. However, the force of the movement was now propelling us so fast that I thought my legs would break with the effort of controlling them; and yet Hereward's hilarious commentary on the proceedings – some to the world, some for my ears alone – ensured that I could barely see for the tears of laughter clogging in my eyes.

Now only Godric was in front of us. Behind us, Lucy's wail – she was nothing if not partisan – told us that Martin and Wynter had fallen. A bad time, for we were negotiating the turn of the square and the open-mouthed, frequently ribald spectators were too close for comfort.

"If you're going to fall," said Hereward, "aim for the fat old bore in red."

I said breathlessly, "I was thinking more of his wife."

"Less padding," he said judiciously. "But I suppose such po-faced disapproval does deserve to be squashed. Will you hate me for this?"

"I hate you already. My legs are breaking. Look! Godric's over!"

"What are you laughing at? He's right in our path, the bastard, and we have to get past to win . . ."

"Can't we veer round them . . .? But that's not fair! He's deliberately getting in our way!"

"Can you stop?" Hereward asked with interest.

"Not unless I fall off."

"Then it's over the top. Ouch," he added as my fingers involuntarily pinched his waist in fear.

"Can we?" I breathed.

"We'll soon find out."

I had a glimpse, through my mirth and terror, of Godric's suddenly horrified face, of Edwin's open-mouthed resignation; and then they seemed to pass underneath us, between Hereward's swinging legs. And Hereward's laughter was no longer just inward. His whole body was shaking with it, and so was mine. We never stood a chance after that.

It was his own fault in the end. I think he was trying to knock Godric back over as he passed, and the unnecessary force upset his balance even more. We veered drunkenly, out of control.

"We've won," Hereward gasped, with another lurching step. "It's all right."

"From whose point of view, precisely?" I demanded, and was suddenly yanked aside.

I was falling from a great height, on Hereward, and nothing in the world had ever been quite so funny before. I heard the warning cries of the crowd. I heard Hereward make a sound like "Ouf!" as the air was shot out of him by a combination of the road below and me above. And then we were a tangled heap of arms and ridiculously long legs, weighed down by impossible weights. I was laughing so hard that the tears streamed down my cheeks, into my mouth and my hair, as I raised my face to Lucy's frightened concern and Robert's white-skinned guilt.

"Here's to Godric, beaten by a girl!" Hereward said ecstatically, when he could breathe. I turned my wet head in the rubble to find his wild eyes blazing at me with a joy like lightning. "Torfrida, I love you!"

CHAPTER 8

The Earl of Mercia was old – so old that the son at his side was already middle-aged. Yet Aelfgar seemed to be one of the eternally youthful – all restless eyes and charming smiles. And only half the man his father was. Of course, even his mother, the lady Godiva, was the stuff of legends, her beauty being famed as far afield as Flanders. But she was not here.

She was the only one, I thought, amazed, as I slipped into the hall with Lucy behind some eminent lord and his wife. Half of Mercia seemed to be present at Folkingham, to discuss Prince Gruffydd and Earl Harold and the militia of all England. For Gruffydd of Wales had soundly defeated – and killed – the over-confident Bishop of Hereford, resulting in the calling out of the militia of all England against him – with Mercia's bug-bear, Harold of Wessex, at its head. Which was why most of them were here. Lucy, on the other hand, was more concerned about her brother.

"Is he here?" she hissed at my back.

"He could be," I said noncommittally. "My own mother could be here and I wouldn't see her in this throng . . . Here's your father, though, and Alfred." And behind them, the lady Aediva. Nothing, I supposed, would keep her from seeing her son, from the reconciliation I prayed was about to be effected. I was sure, you see, that this reconciliation was Hereward's only chance of salvation, whether or not he saw it that way. Without it, he would just grow worse and worse until everything good, even his loyalty, his care for his own people and for the unfortunate, was lost.

"You are not meant to be here," Leofric of Bourne growled at his daughter. Penitently, she stood aside for him and her mother to pass, but she looked up in time to exchange grins with Alfred, and to be ushered exaggeratedly in front of him. For once, they were in alliance to meet their brother and reunite the family. And I did not intend to miss it. Fortunately, Alfred seemed to be in favour of that, for I was allowed to go before him too.

By jumping and peering over heads, I could make out the Earl with Gilbert and Matilda, and some of the greatest men, over beside the high table.

"I suppose," said Lucy disappointedly, "that if we stood on each other's shoulders, they'd send us both home."

That jolted me. For the first time, going home had not been my first motive. Of course, by then my astrological studies with Provost Brand were encouraging me to believe in my father's eventual recovery; and although, in order to postpone the marriage, I had resorted to the untruth that I had not yet reached womanhood, Robert and I had achieved a much better understanding since Lincoln. We were now allies in the cause of our 'detrothal'.

Assuming us to be one of Leofric's party, the crowds were still parting to let us through in his wake. And I peered around them to the best of my ability. And then Leofric stopped. I know because I bumped into him; and Alfred promptly walked up my heels.

"Ouch!" I said loudly, and Alfred and Lucy both giggled. Only then did I register the sudden silence in the hall.

Into it, before I could even be alarmed, a familiar voice said blandly, "I hear you brought the children. How nice."

"Hereward!" roared Alfred. Unceremoniously, I was pushed aside as the boy raced past, round his still father and Gilbert, who had materialized in our midst, and into the arms of his brother. Lucy seized my hand and squeezed.

Craning my neck, I saw Alfred bury his face in the other's tunic – an almost respectable one of good burgundy wool – his fingers gripping fiercely. For the briefest moment, Hereward's hand touched his head; I saw his lips move as he said something into his hair, and then Alfred laughed and hiccoughed together, allowing himself to be pushed away. Over the boy's head, Hereward's eyes met his father's.

I watched with the anxiety of a mother hen. I found myself praying afresh that he would not say anything insolent or flippant and lose this chance . . . If he wanted it. I realized I wasn't even sure of that.

44

The pause was long and pregnant. Hereward's lips stretched into a faint smile, parted so that I knew he was going to speak – *Please, God, let it be conciliatory!* – and then the Earl himself stood between them.

"I see," he said with dignity, "that you have found each other. Shall we step into the lord Gilbert's private chamber, and deal with this matter first?"

Someone, I could not see who, said, "Why in private? The world knows his sentence though no court decreed it! Let the justification or withdrawal at least be done in public."

There was a rush of agreement around the hall. But Hereward himself frowned, irritated for once by this vocal support.

Leofric of Mercia regarded his namesake of Bourne, one white eyebrow raised in interrogation. Hereward's father squared his shoulders. "We have nothing to hide, and nothing, I hope, to be ashamed of. Let it be in public then."

The Earl inclined his head, the picture of ancient, yet still powerful grace.

"Very well. Hereward." The Earl turned to the youth, who met his gaze directly, fearlessly. But his face was serious now to the point of sternness. "This long-running dispute between you and your father is so damaging that it affects not only your family but the whole earldom, and as such, I have seen fit, as your lord, to intervene."

Hereward nodded. It was accepting, but also curiously impatient: he wanted the Earl to get to the point, while the rest of us – I was not the only insatiably curious observer – simply drank in his every word.

"You know," the Earl went on in his stately way, "that I have cause to value your father, as I hope in the future to value his son."

There was another pause. This time, Hereward spoke into it, without flattery or affectation.

He said, "I have every desire to be of service to you."

Leofric of Mercia took it as his due, merely nodding. "Yet the crimes you have committed against your father and his neighbours – no, you need not dispute them, they are common knowledge and irrefutable – are so serious . . ."

"I do not dispute I did them," Hereward said impetuously. "I dispute only that they were crimes."

"Do not interrupt me!" Leofric uttered, his face changing suddenly, reminding the world of his power in it and how it was he had hung onto it for so long. "I have brought you here to answer for your crimes, not to a court that would undoubtedly find you guilty, but to your father, who is prepared to forgive you."

I let out my breath with relief. That was the first hurdle. Leofric's forgiveness.

45

Hereward's eyes left the Earl's for the first time since the conversation began, moving directly to his father. A faint, half-mocking, half-rueful smile lurked about his mouth.

Echoing his father's words of months ago, he said, "For my submission, and what I took from you, and my sword?"

"For your submission," the Earl said. Leofric of Bourne said nothing at all. I shifted my position to try and see his face, but it was impossible. "And my own adjuration that you reach a better understanding together."

The conditions had been lowered. I recognized that at once. To all intents and purposes, Leofric of Bourne had given in to his turbulent son. And the son knew it. Yet I saw no triumph in Hereward's eyes, only a swift confusion of regret and guilt and gratitude, and something else quickly veiled by the ridiculously long lashes. The rebellion was over, and reparation about to be made.

Hereward's fingers gripped his sword-hilt, began to draw the weapon loose; and I understood the gesture he was clearly about to make. To deliver up the sword to his father who no longer demanded it.

I swallowed a sudden lump in my throat. I felt curiously proud of him, for in this one act of generosity, he was doing all I had hoped of him, and more.

Later, I thought angrily that there was no excuse, that both Leofrics, who knew him so much better than I, should have known to leave it there. But they had given in and had to justify it, with or without Hereward's humility.

As if he had not even seen the youth's move, the Earl, suddenly grim, said, "If you choose not to submit, you leave me no alternative but to send you away from my lands, to withdraw my protection from you, to make you an exile without a lord. Is it clear?"

I saw at once what they had done. Why didn't they? A gasp rippled around the hall, of approval in some quarters, and outrage in others. Hereward himself stood unmoving, his hand still on his sword hilt, his eyes still locked to his father's. Waiting, I realized. Waiting for him to argue, to show his denial of the Earl's ultimatum. But he couldn't deny it. They had cooked it up together, and if Leofric of Bourne regretted it, he hid the fact in the determination of his glare. Only his hand, convulsively gripping the skirt of his tunic, gave him away.

Slowly, Hereward's fingers slackened their hold on the sword, let it slip back with a tiny shriek into its scabbard.

He said, "You would do that?"

His voice sounded merely conversational, but there was a desperate struggle going on to keep the hurt out of his eyes as well. To Hereward, *this* was betrayal. Aching for him, I wondered how far he had thought his father would let him go. I wondered why they could not understand each other's own foolish pride.

Low-voiced, more so than he had meant, I think, Leofric of Bourne said, "What do you expect? I have forgiven you so often, Hereward, and each time you have reoffended, worse than before. I *will* have your obedience!"

"Will you?" said Hereward, deliberately. Beside him, Alfred was gazing open-mouthed from his brother to his father and back, as if he didn't understand what was going on. I wondered who did.

Lucy. She was silently weeping on my hand.

Just for an instant, I thought that even Hereward was unsure what to do, what to say. Like a sail suddenly deprived of wind. His restless eyes fluttered over his anguished mother, silently suffering throughout; then they wrenched away, quickly, back to the Earl.

"I thought you had summoned me to serve in your army," he said brittlely. A boy, just a boy thwarted in his quest for honour. No wonder they had been so sure he would come. Betrayed again. I wanted to cry, and it had been so long since I had cried for anyone.

The Earl said brutally, "What use to me is the sword of an unreliable man?"

It was harsh, unnecessarily harsh. They were trying to shake him up, bring him back to a sense – *their* sense – of right. But they had chosen the wrong way, and the wrong man.

Hereward laughed, and if there was a catch in it, very few could have heard. "Don't ask me. I have no unreliable men. Mine all give – and receive – complete loyalty. Well, my lords, if my sword is not required here, I shall take it elsewhere."

"Where?" demanded his father, disgusted yet desperate. "Who would accept it?"

"Alba?" Hereward said, as though suggesting it to himself. "I believe there is a spot of trouble up there still . . . Oh, don't worry, my lord," he added to the Earl. "I mean to go to King Macbeth himself, not to the protégé of any enemy of yours." Not to Malcolm, he meant, not to the foster-son of old Earl Siward of Northumbria, not to the friend of Tostig, Harold's brother. "I told you, I take my loyalty seriously."

He laughed again, bowing to the Earl with almost inhuman, unhurried grace, before he deliberately walked past his father. He didn't even see me, for Aediva was catching at his sleeve, as if she could not help herself. But Hereward shook her off – not, I saw, to be cruel this time, but because he could not bear any more.

"Hereward!"

Alfred was running after him, but his father caught him fiercely, growling something under his breath that kept the boy anguishedly still. And the crowd parted to let the outlaw through. He swaggered past till I could not even see his unconcern belied, as I knew it was, in his pain-filled eyes. He was an oddly dignified figure, alone, defying rejection with calm unconcern, although his every loose-limbed movement, like some half-tamed young wolf, reminded me that the violence in him was barely controlled.

When the door banged shut behind him, we even heard him whistling before the noise broke out in the hall. Through it, I saw Gilbert, slipping among the eagerly arguing Englishmen to the door.

At least, I thought, angrily dashing my hand across my eyes, his godfather would bid him farewell. I was conscious of gratitude to Gilbert for that. For the rest, I was aware chiefly of fury, because they had sent away my friend before he had even had the chance to become so.

CHAPTER 9

"What do you think, Torfrida? Am I too mature to wear this veil loose?"

I looked at Matilda critically. Dressed in a new gown of fine, bright yellow wool, she seemed to radiate excitement, like a child about to receive a present. I supposed she was, since this was her first dinner in the hall since we had arrived in Northumbria two months ago. For with Gruffydd duly dealt with – largely by giving him vast swathes of land – Gilbert had decided it was time to hurry up to the northern estates. Considering how much I disliked Folkingham, leaving it proved to be surprisingly difficult – not just because of the fascinating knowledge I was gleaning from Brand – about Boethius and Geber and their astronomical teachings – but because of the moth-eaten old monk himself.

Now, to the lady's sartorial problem, I said unhelpfully, "Just be comfortable. Abandon it altogether, if you like."

"Oh no," Lucy objected. "It matches the gown so exactly, it would be a crime not to wear it! Let me drape it like this and tie it loosely so that we can still see your hair? Which is very pretty," she added generously, while Matilda surveyed her reflection in the bronze mirror that had come all the way from Folkingham with us.

I had never seen her like this before. She was behaving more like Lucy.

I said prosaically, "I hope you do not mean to walk." For the lady had been badly injured on our journey, breaking her leg in two places. "Shall I call someone to carry you?"

"Oh no," she replied brightly. "Hereward will carry me. At least as far as the hall door."

That had been our other Northumbrian surprise, the reason for the unseemly speed of Gilbert's departure: Hereward was not in Alba, but in Gilbert's northern hall. In fact it was he who had rescued the lady, hauling the heavy carriage off her poor, crushed legs and carrying her safely out of the ravine and home. I had trailed after them, as dazed by his sudden appearance as by the pain of my own broken arm.

"He isn't here," I pointed out now.

But inevitably, "Yes I am," came his voice from behind the hanging. "May I come in?"

The lady's face broke at once into smiles. These days, he was a welcome visitor. "Of course!" she cried. "Lucy, bring him in!"

He had made an effort for her important day. I allowed that. His hair was brushed and gleaming, his burgundy tunic new and unexpectedly splendid, heavily embroidered and with sleeves to cover the uncivilized bulging of his muscles. In fact, he looked almost courtly.

The lady was enchanted.

"How smart you look!" she said warmly.

"A pig in a coat," said Lucy darkly, "is still a pig."

Matilda did not hear her. Hereward amiably pulled his sister's hair, while simultaneously complimenting the lady on her looks, choice of dress and general health. Rather to my surprise, she blushed. The lady was indeed in sad need of company.

"Oh you are being kind to an old woman," she protested, though I thought critically that her eyes pleaded a little too hard for argument.

He obliged. "I don't know any old women. None without beards at any rate. Are you ready to go?"

"I can't make up my mind about the veil. Lucy tied it like this – what do you think?"

"I think it's charming," he said patiently – so why did I think he was anything but? "Even if Lucy did do it."

That was when I began to worry, though I could not, at the time, put any reason to it. He was not paying attention to me – very often he didn't – so I was able to observe him closely without being noticed. His eyes were on the lady with the very real respect which he nearly always accorded her; his usual humour leavened his civil words. And yet it struck me that those words were . . . mechanical, as if they were nothing to do with the thoughts in his head.

And surely there was an odd tension in his stillness? As though he was forcing his body into unnatural inactivity. As though he had been good for too long.

I heard him ask now for permission, and his patience still sounded too deliberate, too stiff to my over-sensitive ears. I watched him bend and lift the lady from her stool, one arm at her back, the other behind her knees, just as he had carried her away from the broken carriage and out of the ravine. And as then, she lay back trustfully in his arms.

Yet surely there was a difference now. To her he was no longer simply the wild, troublesome boy she could never quite dislike. He had become a man in her eyes, a man with the strength and the courage to save her life. And, of course, despite the strange irregularity of his features, he was beautiful. I forgot that sometimes . . .

". . . if it's not too much trouble."

With a start, I realized Hereward was addressing me, heavy irony in his face and voice. I blinked at him.

"I could use my teeth," he offered, "or sling the lady over one shoulder. Alternatively, I could use her as a battering ram. But I feel we would all prefer it if you just lifted the hanging and opened the door."

I was nearest; and I was blocking their way. On the other hand, I had never been spiritless.

"A little courtesy," I said disdainfully, as I moved to obey him, "would not go amiss."

"True," he said at once. "Keep trying."

Sometimes, I didn't like him at all.

She made quite an entrance, the lady on Hereward's arm. He had set her down at the doorway, so she entered the hall in the full dignity of her own elegant bearing, the centre of all eyes and the cause of the expectant hush all around us.

And then the household cheered her, rising and applauding, bowing as she passed them with her most gracious smile.

Gilbert came to meet her, of course, receiving her rather proudly from his godson. She spared a last, radiant smile for the younger man, cast quickly over her shoulder so that I felt blinded by the strength of it.

But my mind was focused on Hereward. I wanted to know what was going on in his head, to try and calm the storm before it broke and damaged everyone in its path. I had even taken a hasty step forward, reaching out for his arm, now that it was free of its burden, but his whole body suddenly moved, swinging aside with a kind of massive relaxation as he strode off to join his friends, dodging under arms still raised in applause, good-naturedly heaving others out of the way and then springing out of their reach as they sought mock-retribution.

My relief was intense. There may have been a little extra wildness in his clowning, but at least that peculiar, uncharacteristic *stillness* had vanished, just as though it had never been.

It was the lady herself who had been the cause of it, I realized as I took my place beside Robert. He was uncomfortable with her new attitude to him. And yet that in itself was odd, because he was used to the admiration of women. I had discovered that since coming here.

Shrugging off such troublesome concerns, I turned to my betrothed and studied him, for although the doctors could find nothing wrong with him, he seemed to be taking a long time to recover from his journey.

"You look better today," I approved at last.

"I feel better," he said gratefully. "So, I should guess, does my mother."

"The company cheers her, I think. And she must be glad you managed to come to the hall today . . ."

"I doubt she knows I have been absent."

Sometimes these days, he eluded me. Such as when, hearing from home of my father's partial recovery, I had offered to jilt him immediately, and he had generously – and frustratingly – offered to do it instead. Several months too late! In the end, neither of us had, for I suspected neither he nor my father was yet well enough for the ensuing furore.

I said abruptly, "I think you should see another physician," and he laughed.

"I'm better," he reminded me.

Everything went well until the poet stood up in the middle of the hall to recite. By then I was lulled by the good will of the household and the stunning realization that somehow I had become part of it. Or perhaps the heavy mead had gone to my head, for I seemed to be watching the poet, Wulfstan, through a mist, as he rose and walked to his accustomed place. The hall grew hushed in expectation.

Gilbert, neither Saxon nor Dane, nevertheless kept a Saxon poet as much for the entertainment of his English friends as for his own standing. And Wulfstan was really very good. He had a fine, resonant voice with depths that could tug at your heartstrings, drive you to anger or even surprise you into laughter.

As if to warm us up, he began with the poetic riddles of the type I had heard before. After a rather witty introduction, he began sadly, "Sometimes my lord confines me fast . . ."

"Good thing too," said someone promptly, and was shushed down by his neighbours. It was Hereward, of course. I could see him lounging back on his bench, resting against the youth called Hrofgar, who didn't appear to mind; he had one foot up on the table and a wine cup in his hand. The food in front of him looked barely touched to my suddenly sharp eyes. Abruptly, the misty ease of my existence vanished.

I had been right in Matilda's chamber; he was ripe for trouble. I felt slightly sick with the knowledge.

Wulfstan began again, staring quellingly at Hereward as he vividly described some mysterious, all-powerful yet half-bridled force. Hereward met the poet's challenging gaze with enough interest to convince the poet that he was listening. Then, when I had begun to suspect the riddle's solution – "*Sometimes, I have to whip up the waves . . .*" – Hereward observed distinctly, "I always said you were windy."

Wulfstan glared at him. Someone laughed. Someone else shouted, "The wind! Of course it is!" And everyone clamoured for more.

Wulfstan hunched one shoulder at Hereward and began another: "My father and mother abandoned me . . ."

"Cuckoo," said Hereward mildly.

"Spoil-sport!" retorted one of his friends – I couldn't see which. "Another, Wulfstan!"

The poet's breath had quickened. I watched him quell it with considerable effort, for he was not a patient man. Then, determinedly, grimly, he said, "I am one on my own, wounded by weapon of iron, scarred . . ."

"Shield," said Hereward, clearly bored. He put his other foot up on the table and took a long draught of wine. Wulfstan swung on him. I thought he was actually gritting his teeth.

"I see we are in humorous mood," he said brittlely. "So I shall follow you. Solve this, my lord Hereward: I am a wondrous creature: to women a thing of joyful expectance. My stem is erect and tall . . ."

"Oh my," said Matilda faintly among the shocked screeches of her women and the ribald snorts of the men.

"I stand up in bed," Wulfstan continued, clearly heartened by his effect, "am whiskery down . . ."

"You," said Hereward, "are a great big onion."

There were shouts of laugher and disappointment, through which Wulfstan again glowered at Hereward. I didn't blame him. He had run out of ways of dealing civilly with these interruptions, and I could see it was all going to come to a violent head unless someone did something.

Hereward was looking mildly surprised at the poet's reaction.

"Sorry," he said carelessly. "I've heard them all before."

"Well the rest of us haven't!" Tostig of Rothwell said indignantly. "So hold your jabbering tongue!" Tostig was kinsman – some said natural son – of Northumbria's Earl Tostig, brother of Harold of Wessex. One of the more brilliant of the young men training for knighthood in Gilbert's household – reciprocally, Gilbert's second son, Walter, was placed in the Earl's. Tostig was Hereward's friend and rival in many things, not just in the matter of the bear . . .

Robert called out, "Better still, Wulfstan, don't give him the opportunity. Let us have a poem instead."

Robert the peacemaker. I nodded at him gratefully. A straightforward poem provided less excuse for interruptions, although if Hereward was intent upon causing trouble, I didn't really see how any of us could stop him, short of physically ejecting him from the hall. I would have suggested it too, if it hadn't been for the lady. Already Hereward was well on the way to ruining her evening.

Temporarily, I had forgotten that I had once considered this to be my own special duty.

After a few moments of silence, while the poet stood still, with his eyes closed, gathering his muse and his atmosphere and the attention of the audience, he began to speak again.

This was the kind of poem the Saxons loved best, full of heroism and nostalgia and unswerving loyalty. His audience, both Dane and Saxon, listened, rapt, to the story of a wandering knight, cast out from his home and his lord, confronting terrible odds in his adventures while he searched for the simple joy to be found only in the fellowship of a master's hall.

Men and women hung on his every word – and not because the poem was new to them – most of them had probably heard it before, several times. But men's heads came up, brows furrowed and cleared and smiled in sympathy with the hero's changing emotions. Once, this unity they found in such poems had served only to add to my sense of alienation. Yet somehow, very gradually, it seemed they had got to me too . . .

"A- a-ou- ur-pp!"

The disgusting noise came, inevitably, from the young men's table. It was Hereward, of course, lounging at his ease, making silver pennies jump over each other, by pressing on their edges with the base of his cup; the only man in the room paying no attention whatever to Wulfstan, until Wulfstan, as distracted and thunderstruck as the rest of us by the abrupt rudeness, fell silent, and all eyes in the hall glared at the perpetrator.

As if just becoming aware of it, Hereward glanced up and around the hostile faces of his neighbours. A coin span noisily on the table and was still.

"Pardon," he said mildly, and ground his cup into another coin. Wine sloshed onto the table, the penny jumped, landing flush on top of the next. Hereward seemed pleased.

"What is the *matter* with you?" That was Tostig, leaping up from the bench, exploding with a passion that had gone well beyond mere irritation.

"With me?" Hereward responded, apparently surprised. "Nothing at all."

"I think," said Wulfstan, taking an aggressive step towards him, "that you do not care for my poetry?"

"You're right there," Hereward agreed. "It's horrible stuff."

Shockingly, part of me wanted to laugh. Yet there was nothing funny about the situation. Wulfstan was mortally offended. Tostig and many of the others had clearly had enough of the interruptions and were now outraged by this last carelessly uttered insult. Hereward, once again, had gone too far.

Yet he seemed unaware of it. Seemed. Yet suddenly I knew – I *knew* –

he had heard every word of Wulfstan's poem, had judged the timing of his insulting belch to a nicety, and was now deliberately, destructively intent on provoking anyone and everyone who could possibly oppose him.

Robert's eyes were closed, as though suddenly too tired again to deal with this. Beyond him, Matilda looked oddly desperate, while her husband, merely watchful, continued to eat his soup, as though he imagined his own calmness would somehow influence the confrontation further down the hall. Or perhaps he had learned over the years when it was best to let Hereward have his head; if so, I thought his instincts had let him down tonight.

The whole evening had turned suddenly ugly. Hereward had deliberately made it so, and only blood would sweeten it now for the men.

And for Matilda? And Lucy? And me?

Suddenly Tostig leaned across the table, sweeping the coins off with one aggressive arm.

"Damn you!" he roared, while Hereward's cup tumbled over; the rest of the wine spilled out, splashing on to the floor.

Hereward stayed where he was, gazing up at the other man.

"You want a game?" he hazarded.

I thought, almost resignedly, that Tostig would burst. But before he could, the poet too had closed in, made all the braver by the evident hostility surrounding his tormentor.

"You were about to tell me what parts of my poetry you disliked," he sneered. "And why."

"I hate all of it," said Hereward largely. "I hate the maudlin nonsense about exile, and the daft heroics against mythical monsters, and your hero's spineless whining for some master to give him expensive trinkets and tell him what to do."

Hereward had not finished. He merely paused to draw breath, but Wulfstan pounced at once. "You don't believe in loyalty! In a word!"

"In a *word*? No."

"Or the generosity of your lord?" Tostig flung in, ignoring if he heard it the ambiguity of Hereward's reply. "I wonder what the lord Gilbert thinks of that!"

"It has nothing to do with him." Calmly, Hereward was pouring himself more wine. "I am here because I choose to be, and because he chooses to let me. When one or both of us tire of the situation, I will go. It has nothing to do with *lordship*. I don't need a lord. And neither do you."

At this heresy, even Gilbert put down his knife. The poet's lips were curled in contempt. Tostig was staring straight at him in disbelief.

"What? Are you so ungrateful? So devoid of all decent feeling, all *honour*, all . . ."

"My honour," Hereward interrupted, "is quite intact."

Suddenly his voice was no longer mild, and it stopped Tostig in mid-breath.

"Robert?" Matilda said urgently. "Tell Wulfstan I want a sacred poem. Now." Robert tried to rise, and fell back. I didn't know if he could not or would not.

Hereward raised the cup to his lips.

"Why don't *you* stop whining?" he suggested, though whether to Tostig or Wulfstan was unclear. "Stop grovelling after the past and look about you. Look to the future; make your own ideas instead of dutifully trailing after those of your distant ancestors. Because if you keep on the way you're going, English Saxons – and Danes – will disappear up their own arses."

He smiled suddenly, dazzlingly, at Tostig. "But perhaps you already have."

There was no need for it. And no way of stopping Tostig from leaping across the table, sword drawn in murderous rage. And suddenly Hereward himself was no longer lounging. He was on his feet, dragging his sword free with a peculiar, exultant joy, as if some obscure and urgent need was about to be pleasurably, gloriously satisfied.

"Robert!" I whispered urgently. But Robert only shrugged tiredly. He knew a lost cause when he saw one. I didn't. I rose quickly, feeling Matilda's eyes hot on the back of my neck. No one else paid me any attention at all, for everything was focused inevitably on the confrontation between Tostig and Hereward. Wulfstan and some of the young men stood around them tensely, threateningly, hands on their swords and daggers. I had never seen Hereward provoke such unanimous hostility. Only Hrofgar and one or two of the other younger men moved protectively behind him, and even they looked unhappy about it.

"One at a time?" Hereward enquired. "Or all together?"

"Boastful little buffoon!" Tostig uttered with loathing, just as I got to them. He was about to lunge too, till I caught at his arm.

"You would do this here?" I scolded. "What are you thinking of?"

Tostig was staring at me, as if he hadn't a clue who or what I was.

"Outside," Hereward said gaily. I hated him.

The men were all ready to go with him, kill him, be killed by him. Because he didn't like poetry. Because he said he didn't.

"Sit down," I said severely. I think it was surprise that made them all gawp at me. Then, reluctantly, Tostig's sword wavered. I held my breath.

"Perhaps she is right. We can – sort this out later."

"Now would be best," Hereward disputed.

"No it wouldn't," I said definitely, and for the first time he spared me a glance. Quick, impatient, irritated; as if I were a fly in his soup.

"*You* sit down," he advised, and I had never heard that tone before, not to me. It froze my blood. I was a mere child, out of my depth and we both knew it, but I would not back down. Instead, I took a step nearer him, defying the repulsion in his wild, brilliant eyes.

"Hereward, stop it," I said warningly.

"I'm trying to, but you're in my way."

"Hereward, you are spoiling her day!" I said desperately.

He stared at me. For a second I saw loathing, hatred, fury in his eyes. And not for Tostig or Wulfstan. For me. Inside, I crumpled with fear and hurt. And then the long, golden lashes swept down, thankfully veiling what I could not bear. When they lifted, I saw only the familiar, impersonal storms.

Without even glancing at Tostig, he carelessly sheathed his sword. He was looking beyond all of us, to the high table where Gilbert and Matilda and Robert sat frozen like a church painting of the Last Supper.

"I'm behaving badly," he observed belatedly, a weird mixture of studied carelessness and bravado. "Lady, your forgiveness once more?"

And Matilda, scarcely believing it was over, could only nod. But by then his eyes had already left her and come back to the poet. Wulfstan would not be so easily placated. Supposing Hereward meant to try.

"I offered no insult to your skill," he said clearly, "which I acknowledge freely and unreservedly to be of the highest."

Wulfstan eyed him with grim suspicion. "But I think you meant to insult my calling."

"No, no, only your material."

"The lady," I said hastily, "would like a sacred poem." I glared at Hereward, because there was no other way I could bring myself to look at him. "Uninterrupted."

Hereward smiled at me, beatifically, as if there had never been any savagery in his eyes or his heart. I was at a distance, like Wulfstan and Tostig and Matilda. Like the rest of the world.

I turned on my heel and stomped back to my place. Behind me, the men were reseating themselves among a subdued rumble of talk and an occasional snigger. Wulfstan began to recite.

"What did you say to him?" It was Lucy, catching at my sleeve as I passed her, furiously whispering at me.

"I don't remember. What's the matter with him anyway?"

My voice shook slightly. I cleared my throat, but Lucy didn't appear to notice.

"It's nearly Christmas," she said expressionlessly. "We used to enjoy Christmas. At Bourne."

I met her gaze, suddenly fighting off a huge wave of my own desolation. We had used to enjoy Christmas too. At Bruges. "Ask the lady," I said abruptly. "She would not keep you here, knowing you to be unhappy. You can still be home in time."

"And leave *him* here? Quite alone?"

Involuntarily, I followed her gaze. He was seated again, a curiously isolated figure, idly pushing meat around with his knife. Quiet. His other hand reached blindly for his cup, raised it to his lips. I don't know why such a movement should have conveyed anguish, but it did. I wanted to cry, very badly, and it wasn't all for me.

Abruptly, I shook myself free and went back to Robert. He felt like a haven after several particularly nasty gales.

CHAPTER 10

"Yesterday," I said to Hereward.

It was early morning, the beginnings of light only just managing to peep through the bars of the bear's cage. I was sitting opposite the beast while Hereward stroked its great head and sang it rude songs in Norwegian.

I had first heard of it the day after our arrival when, summoned to the bedside of the injured Matilda, I had found her lecturing a restless Hereward, who sat astride a stool, drumming feet and fingers through her words.

"You know I am very pleased to see you here – the Lord knows Torfrida and I have every cause to be! But it won't do, you know!"

"I'll leave as soon as I have seen my godfather."

The words were not pettish or defiant, merely matter-of-fact. My eyes flew to his face – veiled and carefully expressionless – the morning sunlight making a halo of his shining gold hair.

Matilda sighed. "I do not mean that. I don't want you to go."

Neither did I. Dear God, neither did I . . .

"I want you to write to your poor mother and tell her where you are," Matilda said severely.

Abruptly, Hereward stood, swinging round to the table where a scattering of the lady's jewels lay on careless display.

"I can't," he said briefly. "I'm not allowed to, am I?"

"*Allowed* to? When has that ever influenced *you?*"

He smiled faintly at the necklace his fingers were examining. There was a pause, then: "How are they?" he asked politely, as if he was only asking because it was expected of him, as if he cared nothing for the answer.

"Devastated," Matilda said brutally.

His fingers threw down the necklace with a tiny clatter. "I warned him you know. 'Father,' I said, 'mind that temper of yours or apoplexy will carry you off.' But does he listen?"

"It is not temper; it is anxiety," Matilda said tartly. "And you know it."

Hereward shrugged, flicking the unfortunate necklace with one cruel finger. His feeling seemed all to be in that digit, for his voice was perfectly calm as he said drily, "He kicked me out. I doubt his anxiety is excessive."

"Do you? I don't. Do you doubt your mother's concern too? Or perhaps you consider it her own fault?"

There was another pause. I could not blame the lady for her brutality. It needed to be said. And yet I did not want to feel the tension this was provoking in him, the tautness of his stiff, ever-restless body.

Outside, in the yard, I could hear a roaring, like some wild beast, and nearer, over the top, the more familiar barking of dogs. I saw Hereward frown, as if the noise irritated him. Then his fingers reached out again, idly pushing a ring along the line of sun which beamed across the table.

At last he said, "No. Tell her I am safe. If you will."

"With what message?" Matilda asked, more gently, but Hereward's softening was apparently over.

"You decide," he said flippantly. He was pacing now across to the window – to discover, I thought, what the roaring was all about. Matilda and I both followed him with our eyes. After a moment, I saw him smile. His own eyes moved suddenly, intense mischief dancing in their depths, reminiscent at last of the stilt race, catching me in my observations.

"Torfrida," he had said happily. "Did you know there was a bear?"

And now, two months later, I was in the beast's cage with him. "Yesterday," I said, "you would have killed your friends without a second thought. Today you treat this bear as if he is your only child."

Hereward finished the song without pause. Then he said mildly, "I have already explained his ancestry to you. I have nothing whatever to do with it."

According to Hereward, the bear, whom he called Harold, was the King of Norway's brother. To the amusement of the other young men, he had invented a series of fantasies around it, claiming to have conversations with it and translating its often hilarious replies. It had begun, I think, with Gilbert's refusal to let him fight it in the Yuletide contests, on the grounds that he was too young and untried – thus giving the half-admiring, half-resentful Tostig a useful weapon against him. And so Hereward, with my occasional help, had tamed it. This far at least.

I said bleakly, "You're bored. You're going to leave."

His hand grew still on the bear's ear. It rubbed itself against his fingers instead.

"I'm bored," he agreed. "But I'm not going to leave. Not yet." His eyes swung round to me so that I had to look away to hide the flooding relief. There was a pause, then: "It's not me you would miss, Torfrida. You can have fun with anyone."

You can, I thought desperately. *You* can . . .

I stared at him. "I need you," I explained patiently, "to tame the bear."

"He is tame. Harold, turn your back."

The bear lumbered on to two feet and turned round.

"See?" said Hereward. "Harold, bow to the lady."

Harold glared at me balefully, and bobbed his head. Then he shook it. I edged my hand nearer the gate.

"Can you cast horoscopes for bears?" Hereward wondered.

"Without knowing his birth-time?" I said sarcastically.

"Hold on," said Hereward. "I'll ask him."

That was the day that Edith came.

We had been out hawking, Lucy and Robert and Gilbert and I, with several of the young aspiring knights, all of whom seemed to have forgiven Hereward, at least partially, for his outburst the previous night. And if there was still a modicum of distance in their camaraderie, I was cynically sure that even that would disappear under just a little more charm.

We rode back into the courtyard, tingling with cold and laughing at some clowning between Tostig and Hereward, to find the place full of servants and a carriage and Matilda, somewhat dazedly greeting an elegantly veiled lady. Naturally, they both turned as we rode in. Edith of Lincoln, Godric's beautiful wife, smiled.

She had a very pretty smile, I allowed, and its effect was devastating.

"Oh Jesus Christ," Robert muttered under his breath.

"Who," Tostig breathed reverently, "is that?"

Lucy sniffed disdainfully. Hereward said nothing at all. But I had heard the catch of excited laughter in his throat, and his eyes were blazing. Clearly, for whatever reason, his boredom was over.

"Did you bring her here?" That was Robert, holding him back as Gilbert and the others pressed forward. Nowadays, he never hid his conversations from me, however discreetly they were kept from others. And I confess I stayed deliberately beside them, with no excuse but curiosity, for I had no idea what they were talking about.

Hereward snapped, "How could I?"

"By letter. Or other messenger," said Robert drily.

Hereward glanced at him. "Well I didn't. Godric has a hall in York: is it so surprising she is here?"

"Without him? Oh yes," Robert said savagely. I looked at him in surprise. "Hereward, did she know you were here?"

Hereward stared at him. "Yes," he said defiantly. "I told her not to come. Unless she needed me."

It was only an hour later that I saw them from my window. Their greet-

59

ing in the yard had been decorous, like that of old acquaintances, but her eyes had begun to glow at the sight of him, and I thought, curiously, that her fingers had trembled when he held them and formally kissed her. That was when I began to feel the first unwilling, unwelcome suspicion; for the impatience in him had been shouting out from every angle of his tense, restless body as he had stood aside and civilly let her be taken from him by Matilda. The true root of his rivalry with Godric was not, it seemed, either dice or stilts.

"My fools took the wrong road!" she was explaining gaily to Gilbert. "And then some ceorl directed us here – I can only pray you do not mind too much! If I might just trouble you to send to Godric, I shall be out of your way in a day!"

Edith, I thought bleakly in the safe privacy of my own chamber, was going to spoil things. At the time I did not recognize the twisting discomfort as jealousy; I was simply aware that somehow she threatened my precarious friendship.

She appeared quite suddenly before my eyes, as if I had conjured her from my thoughts, tripping into the yard that separated my quarters from the women's guest house, as innocently as if she were going up to the hall – except that she had no attendant with her. And she had not taken two steps into the yard before Hereward leapt out of nowhere to catch her in his powerful arms, silencing her quick squeak of fright with his mouth.

I grimaced with sheer distaste.

She only allowed him a moment before she pushed him away, glancing nervously about her for watchers. I refused to budge, but neither of them looked in my direction. She was gazing towards the hall, talking very quickly while she disengaged all but her hand from his hold.

He didn't accept the rebuff. He didn't believe it any more than I did. At first he spoke seriously, frowning, until she gave some light reply, and then his face cleared. There was a smile on his lips, deep in his eyes behind the burning coercion. Even while she talked, he was drawing her with him, saying only, very softly, "Come." I didn't hear the word, but I saw his lips form it over and over until her feet began to follow him – almost involuntarily, I thought, for this was too quick, too easy for her. But still she came, her fingers grasping his convulsively as he turned and quickened his step into a run. And then she was running with him, hand-in-hand, beyond the stockade and down the hill to the friendly, concealing dark of the forest.

Now they had gone, I wished I hadn't seen it. I wished it quite a lot.

"You said *after* Christmas," Robert objected when I proposed bringing our little farce to a slightly premature end. He had been looking better over the last few days, become more active outside and in; but today, after hunting, he seemed tired again, and pale, like some weary ghost.

I said, "I know, but . . ."

"I think you owe my parents a peaceful Yuletide," he interrupted. "Whatever you think you owe your own."

I flushed. "I wasn't intending to *punish* them by coming home," I said frostily.

"Weren't you? And don't you think that's exactly what you *would* do? Whether now or later?"

"Why are you being so unreasonable?" I asked, bewildered. "I don't understand you."

He looked at me.

"No," he agreed. "You don't."

I stared at him, thinking ruefully how curious it was to resent someone for being right. I couldn't go home yet. It would be too unfair and unkind. And in the absence of any letters from home to tell me otherwise, I had to accept the possibility that my father had relapsed instead of recovered completely.

And there was still the bear.

I said abruptly, "Why did your father invite Godric and Edith to stay? Doesn't he know about her and—"

"Of course he knows," Robert interrupted hastily, looking uneasily about him.

"Isn't that carrying hospitality too far?" I said crudely.

"Torfrida!"

"Besides," I said, ignoring his outrage, as I usually did, "I thought he didn't want anyone here to know about Hereward's . . . past. Edith is a fool and Godric doesn't like him. One or other – or both – will blab. And God knows the others are curious enough about him . . ."

"I know," Robert sighed. "I imagine my father is keeping them here for just that reason. To contain the knowledge here. To make sure they cannot – er – blab – beyond our own household."

The hall was in uproar when we returned for dinner, and the cause of it – a slight, vague looking young lady richly clad in dark blue wool and furs, with a child at her knee – seemed quite unaware of it. Seated in the centre of a circle that included Gilbert, Matilda and Emma and a large array of baggage, she was sipping a cup of wine.

"Aethelthryth!" screamed Lucy, and launched herself across the floor between the trestle tables, sending stools flying and causing at least two servants to drop their loads.

"Hallo, Lucy," the older girl was saying affectionately, yet as if they had only parted yesterday. "I believe you have grown." Accepting Lucy's embrace, she kissed her briefly, and said, "This is Siward. Siward, your Aunt Lucy."

Siward, a somewhat mischievous looking child of perhaps nine years old, angelically, almost albino, fair, smiled at his aunt, accepting her kiss with all the disfavour that only a nine year old boy can display.

"Hallo, Aunt Lucy. Who is that?"

That was Hereward, standing with unusual quiet now behind Lucy. He said, "I am Grendel, and I am hungry."

A look of startlement sprang to Aethelthryth's face. Jerking her head to see better, her mouth actually fell open.

Siward grinned. "No, you're not; you're my bad uncle Hereward."

"I would rather," said Hereward plaintively, "be Grendel." But by then his elder sister was on her feet, seizing him by the shoulders.

"Hereward, you, you . . ."

Hereward laughed.

And yet the trouble, when it came, took us all by surprise.

The first I knew of it was the screeching of women. Not the silly squeals inspired by spiders or mice or the over-bold hands of men, but screams of genuine terror.

I was with Edith at the time – not that it was an encounter either of us had sought. I had nothing to say to her, and she, for whatever reason, had always avoided me like the plague.

That night, I astonished us both by jumping off the women's house roof – from where I observed the stars on most of these cold, clear nights – into her path. Yet though she squawked in a muffled sort of a way and leapt backwards, I had the distinct impression she was not remotely afraid. She wasn't; not until she realized I was not Hereward. It must, I thought with satisfaction, have been doubly galling for her, since their assignations had been so curtailed lately by the constant presence at his side of the worshipful young Siward.

My eyes had learned to see in the dark, and they saw only too well her beauty, her nerves, her too-careful dress, the long, soundless "oh" formed by her full, pretty lips. I laughed – I'm not very sure why – and would have brushed past without a word, except that something forced Edith into a flurry of speech.

"Oh my good . . . Why, it is you! What – dear child, what in the world were you doing up there?"

I regarded her disdainfully through my rising temper. Seeing it, her eyes narrowed, and I heard the faint hiss of her breath with some satisfaction as she took a step closer. Clearly her desire not to offend was at war with her basic dislike. Dislike was winning.

"Spying?" she suggested tightly.

I curled my lip. "Observing," I corrected, and she whipped away from me, muttering furiously.

"I observe the stars," I said contemptuously to her back. "Not the rather less than divine exploits of humanity." I brushed past her quite ungently, but her fingers caught at my arm, light, yet clinging like some importunate if lovely insect. I didn't know how Hereward could stand it.

"Torfrida. My dear child, I did not mean—"

"I am not," I said indisputably. But before the bafflement had perfectly formed in her face, the screaming began, briefly freezing us both in perfect stillness.

It came from the family's sleeping quarters on the other side of the yard.

"My God, what was that?" Edith whispered, but already I was running towards it – instinct acting before the fear could take hold. Sprinting across the yard, I was aware of the rising alarm from all sides, of other people emerging from the hall and the outbuildings; and then, at the family's house door, I collided with a man rushing from the other direction.

"Stand aside!" he barked. "Go back! Barricade yourself inside!"

It was Tostig, already wrenching open the door, his drawn sword held tightly before him in his other hand.

"What is it?" I demanded, uselessly bewildered; but I had my answer in the roar which heralded the eruption of Harold the bear, charging out of the house. It was Tostig who saved me, plucking me round behind him while he faced up to the beast. Carelessly, Harold cast him aside with one swipe of his massive paw, and lumbered off across the yard, his broken chain clanking behind him.

I had never seen him move so fast: he had sniffed his freedom, and we were less than nothing to a wild bear. But Tostig was already on his feet again, leaping after him. Then he paused, groaned, and turned back, dashing into the house.

My brain may have been dull, but it hadn't stopped working altogether. Neither had my limbs, which were carrying me after Tostig before I had consciously formed the intention.

"Tostig! Go after the bear – I'll see to them, and send to Hereward . . ."

"Hereward? What can he do that I cannot?"

I couldn't quite believe that even now their silly male jealousy was getting in the way. If I hadn't been so frightened, I would have been furious. And at least he pushed past me back into the yard, leaving me to go on by myself, to see what carnage the bear had wrought.

I took my courage in both hands, plunging across the chamber and throwing back the hanging beyond. Three heads jerked towards me in unmistakable terror. I blinked in the sudden glow of light.

Emma was on her knees by her little sister, who lay on the floor dementedly drumming both feet and emitting the terrifying noise I had heard even across the yard. Beside them, one of Matilda's women was wringing her hands and weeping out some incomprehensible prayer.

"It's you!" she gasped. "It's you!"

"Yes," I said prosaically. My voice didn't even shake. "Is Marion . . .?"

"Hysterical?" Emma interrupted over the din. "Most assuredly. Where is the animal?"

She stood as she spoke. Her gown vibrated with the trembling of her legs, but she was making an effort to pull herself together that I could only admire.

I said, "I don't know. Tostig has gone after it; and a hundred others by now, I should think. Where is Hereward?"

"That," said Emma grimly, "is what we would all like to know."

It whipped my breath away. I could feel my mouth dropping open. "*You mean he let it out?*"

"Who else finds the wretched beast so amusing? Who else resents not being allowed to fight it in the proper way?"

I closed my mouth, already turning away from them. Hereward was capable of it. Drunk. Bored. Destructive. *Self*-destructive. And more dangerous than any of us had known . . . I swallowed.

"I should throw a bucket of water over her," I advised coolly, and ducked back behind the hanging.

What have you done? What have you done?

CHAPTER 11

Those few minutes in the light had ruined my night-vision. All I could see in the dark were blurs and bobbing lanterns and torches, all of which seemed to be making noise of some kind. So I almost fell over Edith, still standing in the middle of the yard, gazing about her with bafflement. No one had told her what to do.

"Where is he?" I demanded, peering at her, willing the darkness to dissolve around her face at least.

"Who?" she asked stupidly.

"Hereward, of course!"

"Now why . . .?"

"Oh God, you're utterly useless! Why does he waste his *time* on you?" I almost flung her away from me. Scouring the darkness, I realized the blurs were forming into men, with swords and axes and spears. The noise too was resolving, so that I could distinguish the urgent voices, and even the words, of different men – and the roaring, of course; I could hear that too above and through everything else. Harold the bear was in a rage.

I didn't blame him. Drawn like some silly, enchanted creature towards the lights, he was being encircled. But he had tasted freedom and he was not about to be trapped again if he could possibly avoid it. One man lay still on the ground already, and even as I ran up, the bear charged another, its great paws mauling once, twice in quick succession before it trampled its victim and broke free of the circle.

Half blind, I think, with pain and fury, it fell straight into the wall of the hall. Roaring, the animal thumped his head against it, lumbered along the ground, pushing at it, facing his enemies with eyes that glowed with venom. Then, without further warning, it crashed through the hall door, his chain dragged clanking after him.

"Oh Christ." The desperate voice beside me made me jump. It was Hereward. He didn't see me, though; already he was running for the hall.

I don't know why I went too – some vague, pathetically optimistic idea, probably, of helping Hereward to recapture the beast before any more damage was done. Only, then, when I actually went in, even I could see that we were too late for that.

Maddened by discovering himself again within four walls, terrified by the unfamiliar objects he kept bumping into, Harold was wreaking carnage. Tables, benches, servants were overset, flying across the room in a mess of plate and mead and leftover food.

Matilda and Lucy were huddled at the far end, Robert before them with drawn sword. I couldn't remember ever seeing him in that position before; and I couldn't imagine him being any use whatever against the bear's fury. He looked desperate and insubstantial, and yet I knew that he would lay down his life in the attempt to save his mother and the girl he loved.

I saw then that the bear had to die, and unexpectedly my heart rose up in my throat with impotent, angry grief. For the bear as much as for whoever he would hurt first.

There was uproar in the hall, the young men falling over each other to get in, and calling incomprehensible instructions to those already there. And then, crashing over the top, came Hereward, the force of his passage skidding him forward into the space around the maddened bear.

Abruptly there was silence.

Then: "Step back, Hereward," Gilbert warned, walking slowly to help form a new circle around the bear. But Hereward was not looking at him, only at Harold.

He shook his head once. "No. Get everyone out. I'll bring the bear."

And the bear, hearing his voice, turned to face him.

"*Bring* it?" Gilbert exclaimed. "Stand aside and let us kill it! It's too dangerous now, it's running amok!"

But Hereward stepped closer. And closer. His sword was in his right hand, but I knew he would never use it. All he wanted was *permission* to kill the bear, acknowledgement of his ability, of his right; of the honour the two Leofrics had seemed to deny him in the summer.

Hereward crouched slowly down, one hand reaching unhurriedly for the end of the dangling chain.

The hall held its collective breath. All but Gilbert, who pushed his out in a rush.

"Hereward, get back!" he said harshly. "How will I tell your father . . .?"

"That even a bear loves me better?" said Hereward, with only sweetness in his voice, for the bear, the bitterness of his words might have had no meaning. "It will be easy. My lord, I cannot guarantee this; will you please take them out? The women, at least . . ."

Before anyone could move or speak, though, the bear had jerked aside, as if deliberately drawing the chain out of Hereward's reach. He began again, talking softly, while the watchers gazed on with confusion and amazement and bewilderment; and fear for him – that too.

But the bear seemed calmer. Perhaps I just wanted him to be. I began to believe again that he might be saved.

Harold moved. He made one lurching step towards Hereward, and all hell broke loose. I was sure – I am still sure – that the bear had no aggressive intent, towards him at least, but no one else saw it that way.

What sounded like a hundred cries of warning blasted around the hall; men surged forward and the bear, as if enraged by the interruption of his curious courtship, swung furiously, lunging at Godric. The sword was knocked from the young nobleman's hand, and he fell back quickly.

And then Tostig, in a surge of mad courage, came at the bear in a run, and actually leapt on his back, sword hacking. A woman's voice cried out through the bear's pain. I think it was mine, for Harold easily dislodged the foreign body by falling and rolling. And as men scattered for their lives, Tostig was trapped underneath, his sword lost, his other weapons useless, and he could expect no mercy.

He got none. As the bear rose up over him, both claws slashing with more fury than accuracy, he began to babble, "God forgive me; my God, my lord, forgive me for everything, but most of all for letting it out – I never meant . . . oh sweet Jesus!"

It made sudden, perfect sense to me, even while the great bear's paw came at him again. I felt the world about me recede, as if I could take myself out of this hell by mere will power. I knew, you see, that a frontal assault against those mauling claws would be suicidal, that the men hurling weapons were too ineffectual, the two leaping belatedly for its back just out of time. Tostig was going to die.

From the corner of my eye, I could still see Hereward, frozen to the spot by the same terrible knowledge, already living, it seemed, with the inevitable tragedy.

It was all over very fast after that.

At first there was just a blur of movement on the edge of my vision, a flash of flame on steel, a disembodied roar as a man ran at the bear, sword drawn in that impossible frontal attack we had all discounted. I had no time for surprise, or fear, or even recognition, only confusion in the suddenly deafening noise.

And then, through it all, almost like a stone carving, I saw Hereward, crouched protectively astride Tostig's prone body, his sword already buried to the hilt in the animal's heart.

It didn't even cry out.

I don't know if there was really silence. It felt like silence to me, as the bear and Hereward gazed at each other. Hereward's face never moved. Not one muscle. And then, with nightmarish lethargy, the bear slowly toppled and fell forward on top of him.

The silence began to break into a thousand different noises. Tostig was scrambling free, blood dripping, staring in horror at the bear who smothered his friend. Already there was a rush of men towards them, presumably to heave the bear clear. Yet so suddenly that several people cried out, the bear seemed to move of its own volition. Rising into the air so that nearly everyone fell back again with shouts of warning, it threw itself sideways with impossible force. Only then could I see that it was not the bear's own movement, but Hereward who had heaved it. And it had landed at Tostig's feet.

Hereward leapt up in one movement, a new jerkiness overlaying his usual grace. Without even glancing at Tostig, he was kneeling beside the bear, as if searching for life. My throat closed up.

And then they were upon him: Matilda crying, "Oh thank God! Thank God!" upon his neck; Lucy squeezing his hand convulsively and weeping; and Gilbert, slowly patting his head with a hand that shook, saying helplessly, "My boy, my boy."

Behind him, Robert was shouting furiously, "You fool! You great big, vainglorious fool!" And all around him, men were congratulating him, shouting and laughing with relief as well as awe.

For a moment, I could not even see him for the press of people.

Then, through the joyful din, I heard him say deliberately, "Stand up, you bastard."

Abruptly, everyone fell into amazed silence. Confused, I thought at first it was to the bear he had spoken – the poor, abused dead creature who had been his friend. But of course, it wasn't. And Tostig was already on his feet, swaying slightly, blood trickling still from his wounds, facing Hereward as the crowd between them fell back.

"You want my thanks?" Tostig gasped out. "For saving my life? Well, I hate you for it. But you can have my gratitude, all the same." His hand began to reach out, and oddly, I thought it pleaded.

"I don't want it," Hereward said insultingly.

Tostig's mouth dropped open. His hand fell slackly back to his side. Deliberately, Hereward pulled his sword free. I heard the sickening sound it made, saw the gore still attached. For an instant, he looked at it, and I thought he was going to hurl it at Tostig. Then, instead, his foot nudged the bear between them, drawing all eyes with it.

"There," he said contemptuously. "Your doing, I believe. Rest assured, you killed a better man than you will ever be."

And he turned his back with supreme scorn, already beginning to walk away. But even wounded, Tostig could not let that go; I doubt any man could have, even if he knew and understood . . .

Tostig's white face was suddenly suffused with colour. I thought he would fall over from loss of blood. But he managed to hurl after Hereward, "That's very fine talk – for an exile! An outlaw!"

So they knew. My heart came alive again with a new fear. At the same time, I saw Matilda's eyes close, as if in prayer.

Hereward had paused. Now his head turned slightly, not to Tostig, but to Godric, and his lips smiled. It wasn't a pleasant smile.

He said, "What an old gossip you are."

Godric flushed. "Did you think to hide your dishonour from decent people?"

"You hardly compliment your hosts. And what have I to hide? No one exiled me from Northumbria."

Gilbert stepped forward, his hand reaching out as if to protect his godson – from what? I wondered wildly. And then it fell back again, for like me, he had seen that Godric was smiling. Godric had found his moment at last.

"Wrong," he said gently. "The King has banished you from all his lands. At the request of my lord of Mercia. And your own father."

This wasn't fair. This was kicking a man already as wounded as Tostig, in his own way. And Godric knew it, even if he couldn't comprehend it.

Hereward's eyes didn't move at first. His lip twitched once. So did his hand. Then, almost involuntarily, his gaze shifted, seeking and finding Gilbert's. The older man shrugged helplessly.

Hereward said dully, "Then it is true."

"I wanted to keep it from you," Gilbert said painfully, "until I had spoken to your father . . ."

"And what difference, precisely," Hereward cut in, "would that make?"

Gilbert fell silent. Hereward lifted one hand to his forehead. I thought it shook, and the ache in my heart grew so intense that I could not ignore it. I could never ignore it again.

There was nothing more Gilbert could say; not now. Shrugging helplessly, he turned away and walked quietly out of his wrecked hall. Robert, following in his wake, paused only to place his hand briefly on Hereward's shoulder, and oddly, the younger man did not flinch; he even acknowledged the gesture with a faint, upward tug of the lips, gone before Robert even reached the door.

"I am sorry," Hereward said abruptly into the ensuing silence. "I am being ungracious. Again. I will go . . ."

"Go where?" Matilda asked quickly. And she was certainly quicker than I, although it gave me the first inkling of what he would do, of what he had to do now. One glance at his face, at Matilda's, told me the rest. Something inside me began to freeze and crumple. This was too sudden, impossibly immediate . . .

Slowly, he moved nearer to her, taking both her impulsively thrown out hands.

"No," she said pleadingly. "Oh no . . ."

"Lady, I have to now, and there is no point in putting it off. Here, I am fair game to any bravo, any bounty hunter – and as such, I will cut up your peace, your life. I would spare you that much. For your sake, and Gilbert's, I have to go."

"But you can't!" she cried, panicking afresh as she read the implacable, unreachable determination in his face. I knew how she felt: I could not deal with this either – not on my account, nor on his. "Not now! Not yet!"

With difficulty, he smiled. One after the other, he lifted her hands to his lips. They clung there, instinctively, desperately.

He said gently, "I can. My love and homage, lady, to you and my godfather."

And he dropped her hands, turning to Lucy and to Aethelthryth and Siward, who had come more slowly to stand by her side, some meaningless flippancy already forming on his lips to spare them all. The pain in my throat was growing unbearable.

But: "Don't go!" Matilda burst out, throwing herself at him, weeping uncontrollably. "In pity's name, Hereward, wait awhile!"

And suddenly the lady's very real anguish was more shocking than anything that had happened that night. Only now did I finally begin to understand what her feelings for Hereward had become. And he – he had known it all along. It was there now in his patience, as it had always been, in the tension of his discomfort around her.

Holding her by the wrists, he held her from him, his eyes avoiding hers with pity. "Take her, Lucy . . ."

Lucy tried, with her sister's aid. Forcing my breath back out, I went to help. But she was out of control, hysterical, so that she fell on her knees on the ground, crying to him that she could not bear him to go, that he should stay just a little longer, just to see Gilbert in the morning; just until

Robert was better. To all of it, Hereward simply shook his head. I knew he was wondering when this nightmare would end, and yet he was kind to her, trying his best to shield her from the rest of the gaping household. I had never seen him behave so well as when nothing could have persuaded him to stay.

Eventually, she cried out wildly, "But you *must* stay, Hereward! Gilbert will insist! He will make you his *heir*, Hereward, if you stay . . ."

And at that, Hereward's eyes widened into hers with such shock that she was silenced more effectively than a slap.

He said curtly, "Robert is your heir."

And she, desperate to avoid his new hostility, gasped pleadingly. "After Robert; I meant, of course . . ."

"You have other sons, lady. I do not want what is theirs, any more than I want what is Gilbert's. In God's name, what do you take me for?"

She was mute, at last, after her desperation had made her say what she had, to induce that expression of revulsion in his taut, young face and make him unwilling to look at her any longer.

Quietly, I took Lucy's place, holding the lady now as she collapsed under the weight of her need and her own folly. Yet Lucy, though she had the chance, stayed where she was, kneeling beside the lady. Only her eyes, full of unshed tears, met her brother's. I thought she had always known too. She tried to smile. So did he. I could not watch any more.

Just for a second I thought his gaze was on me, but I could not look. I could not bear this farewell. I could not bear his suffering, or being any tiny part of it. Like Lucy, I would spare him.

Only when I heard his footsteps turn, did I look up again. And catch my breath, for he was gazing straight at Edith, who had come in with the crowd and now stood by Godric; and there was no difficulty at all in his smile now. Lucy and Aethelthryth had lifted Matilda, still weeping, out of my arms, carrying her away to her own chamber; and in the silence which followed this departure, Edith became aware that Hereward's were not the only eyes watching.

Her delicate shoulders twitched once. She smiled back at him, nervously now, her gaze flickering to left and right.

"We wish you farewell, and good luck, wherever you go," she said hastily. "I am sure you will be back. One day . . ."

"Stop it," he said. Not rudely, or peremptorily, just conversationally. "There is no need any more. I am going far away, beyond the seas. Share my fortune with me. Come."

I closed my eyes. But not before the vision of Godric's frozen, rigid face, staring straight ahead, was already etched in my mind. It was not an image of surprise, but a man whose worst fear of scandal was coming true. Somebody groaned – Tostig?

Then, amazingly, Edith gave a tinkling little laugh; it sounded so inane that it set my teeth on edge.

Laughingly, she said, "Go with you? Whatever do you mean? To be frank, Godric does not even like you very much! I doubt you would induce him to share *any* fortune with you!"

It was clever, quite unexpectedly so.

Slowly, I opened my eyes again. She was gazing up at him with bright, indubitable innocence. Only the whiteness of her clenched little fists in her skirts gave her away.

Hereward said evenly, "Edith. I am offering you your way out. I am giving you what you want, everything I have, and will have."

Something like a spasm crossed Godric's expressionless face. His mouth opened, then closed again. Edith, after all, was doing everything necessary for him. Her fingers had released her skirt to reach out and take her husband's hand.

"Silly," she said playfully. "I already have the world. I think your troubles have addled your brains."

She might have struck him. He could have borne that more easily. For it had been love after all which had led him into adultery; she was just one more to betray him.

And the fact that her shallow little soul was quite unworthy of him would neither enter his head nor be of the remotest comfort to him if the thought were put there.

With one graceful, sardonic nod, she swept away from him on Godric's arm.

I could have struck her. Yet Hereward, with some superhuman effort, was smiling at the blind or tactful young men pressing about him, shaking hands, clapping backs, hurling friendly derision and insults, just as if the previous conversation had never been. His life and his torment went on.

When his restless gaze found the bright, accusing eyes of young Siward upon him, I could stand no more and crept away. I went to the darkness of the stables, where I could cry unseen, and watch him in secret as he rode out of my life.

There was no one about. The stable servants had all slipped off to watch the bear hunt and the subsequent theatre in the hall. Hereward's horse was in its usual stall. Almost blindly, I let myself in.

The horse looked at me, twitching his ears, but he was still tired after the day's hunt and contented with feeding, so he made no objection. I didn't even interest him a great deal. Moving past him with only a casual pat for his nose, I sank down on the clean heap of straw at the side, and waited for Martin.

I knew their routine, you see. Martin would saddle the beast, and lead him outside; Hereward would mount up just outside the stall; and I could creep forward and watch in the solitude I needed. I didn't worry about Martin. He was the least curious of creatures, except where his master was directly concerned. If he saw me, I doubted he would even mention the fact to Hereward.

My mind felt dull with grief and pity; and yet part of it was spinning still with speculation: whether he was even now saying farewell to Robert, where he would go, what he would do, how he could eventually be forgiven and come home, be happy; and where I would be while it all happened. In another country, with everyone here hating me. Even Robert. Even Robert.

The stall door swung open without warning. I hadn't even heard the footsteps approaching. I blinked as a flash of torchlight dazzled me, then the door crashed shut again, and Martin fixed the torch in the bracket and laid the saddle on the horse's back. The horse whinnied gently, snuffling at his neck. Martin came round to the other side – my side – adjusting straps. And I saw that it was not Martin at all.

I sat still, frozen. I had no time to feel guilt or embarrassment, only the hard fact of his nearness. His fingers reached up to the saddle, testing, then stilled, unmoving. The horse tossed its head, then nuzzled him again; and slowly, his head bent forward till it rested on the saddle, and his fingers gripped convulsively.

Now, now I wished not to be here. It would have been easier to stay completely still and pray for his unusual blindness to last; but some confused sense of chivalry made me blunder to my feet, rustling deliberately. I think I even coughed.

Of course, his head swung up, his whole body span round, his hand already finding and half-drawing the dagger from his belt. His mismatched eyes, wet and cloudy as if the tempest was about to begin, met mine.

There was a pregnant pause. Then his fingers loosened on the knife; his hand came upwards instead, dashing against his eyes. And the tears I had been holding back, seemingly for hours, began a fresh assault of their own.

"Torfrida," he said, without much interest. "What are you doing here?"

I swallowed determinedly, wishing in a detached sort of a way that it didn't hurt quite so much.

I said shakily, "I came to say farewell. I couldn't bear the scene in the hall; and I didn't think you could."

Amazingly, his lips stretched into a smile. "Well, you were wrong, weren't you? It seems I can bear anything."

My eyes fell away. It was a gesture of kindness, not cowardice.

"Where will you go?" I asked with difficulty. "To Alba, after all?"

"They say Macbeth is done for. It sounds like the cause for me."

"Hereward, don't!" I didn't mean to say it like that, with all the grief in my voice. I certainly didn't mean to burden him with my own tears, not now when he was almost free of us all; but they burst their banks without permission.

"Don't what?" he said quietly, coming towards me.

"Don't *torture* yourself!" I got out, and gasped in the effort to prevent the flood. I tried to turn away in some vain, belated effort to spare him the grizzly sight, but amazingly his arms had gone around me, and I felt his cheek rest briefly against my hair. Just for a moment, I knew the vibrant warmth of his body against mine, the hardness of the weapons at his belt, touching but not hurting me in the astounding tenderness of his hold. Giving *me* the comfort I so wanted for him.

And when he spoke, that was gentle too, surprisingly light, and quite without self-pity. So perhaps I had given as well as received.

"Don't weep for me, Torfrida. I made my bed, and I suspect I shall enjoy lying in it - in just a little. Now, before I go. . ."

Quietly still, he held me away from him. His fingers moved, wiping the tears from my cheeks. Astonishment, I think, was holding back the rest of the flood.

Almost casually, he said, "I know what you have done for me, looking out for me, averting the worst of my folly – for that, and for the fun of your friendship, I would do something for you. And for Rob, who is my gentlest and most enduring friend."

"He is the sweetest man I know," I said in a rush.

"So marry him, Torfrida. He loves you as you are, young as you are. And he will make you happy."

I was staring at him. "He loves Lucy . . ."

"Boyish infatuation," said Hereward dismissively. "Already over; and he knows it. Think about it, Torfrida. Give up your fight, and try a new one. I won't dance at your wedding, but I will come back one day, and I expect to find at least ten children plaguing your lives . . ."

"Oh don't!" I burst out, with an involuntary if watery laugh. "How long, precisely, are you planning to be gone?"

"Oh at least a month." His eyes and lips were answering my smile. There was a pause, while I watched the laughter die away. Then: "I shall miss you, difficult child. Kiss me, and let's get this over."

Blindly, mutely, I lifted my face, felt his lips press briefly, warmly on my mouth; and then his arms and his body had gone, and the tears were starting again. Through them, I saw him quickly mount up and ride out through the swinging door. Into cold and darkness. Into exile.

Present: March 1076

CHAPTER 12

My pillow was wet when the knock at the outside door disturbed me. For several moments, disoriented by the flood of long-suppressed memories, I lay still, listening to Lise's collected voice as she conversed familiarly with whoever sought admittance. Then, when her footfall began to cross the outer chamber to my door, I rose from the bed, wiping my face with my sleeve much as my son did. I told myself I had been weeping only for Robert.

"It's his nephews," Lise said bluntly from the doorway, "and the twins. Do you want them, or are you asleep?"

Since she had not troubled to lower her voice, they would have heard every word. Nevertheless, neither of us doubted her ability to keep them out if I desired it. I did not. There were more, and worse, memories.

"Let them come in," I said quickly.

They strode in with purpose, dressed for outdoors in warm cloaks and hoods, and fully armed, shields slung openly across their backs.

"You were not in the hall for supper," Outi said accusingly.

"I was not hungry. I take it you were?"

"Oh yes! We had a whole table to ourselves! The Norman dogs were afraid to come near us!"

I was fairly sure Gilbert's "dogs" had been strictly instructed to this effect, but I let it pass, for all four of them looked slightly flushed with wine to me. Not drunk, just ripe for a fight, especially one that might be seen as some sort of vengeance for their dead leader. Responsibility wrestled its way up through black indifference.

I said quietly, "Revenge will not be found in Gilbert of Ghent's hall."

"No? Though Taillebois himself is found there?"

"If Taillebois were guilty," I said reasonably, "would he have come back here?"

Siward the Red had an answer for that, but before he could give it, I was speaking again. "What is it you want? What do you want of me at this time of night?"

"Permission," said Siward the White after a short pause. "Permission to go after the guilty."

I looked at him. He did not need my permission for that. None of them did. But his eyes did not falter. They pitied, and pled. The permission they wanted was to leave me and the children unprotected.

I said slowly, "How can you? How can you when you don't know who they are?"

"But we do know!" Duti cried impetuously. "Asselin! Hugh of Evermouth, Ralf of Dol! Ivo de Taillebois!"

Into the silence that rang round the chamber after that speech, I heard another knock at the outside door. I said quickly, "You know no such thing. You know a fight broke out, begun by their servants and involving them, but beyond that you know nothing at all. None of you saw the fatal blow!"

Blows, I thought, suddenly shivering; blows in the plural, judging by the poor hacked and burned body. Wrenching aside, I walked away towards the window. The shutters were still open to the stars, the stars that had let me down again. Or had I just been looking in the wrong place? Again . . .

I took a deep breath. "Look," I began, and then the hanging moved and Lise was there once more.

"The lord Gilbert is here," she said to me, but her eyes flickered to my other visitors, giving me a moment's warning before Gilbert walked in behind her. And behind him, Ivo de Taillebois.

Tall, with his dark, curly hair and short, distinctive beard, he looked as comfortable and as arrogant as I had ever seen him. Even when his darting, black eyes took in the presence of the twins and the Siwards, they only danced, as though amused. For their part, as if they could not help it, the Englishmen started as one towards him.

I moved quickly between them.

"Gilbert," I said. "How can I help you?"

His sharp, kindly eyes searching mine, he said gently, "I came rather to see if I could help you."

"For instance," Ivo said insolently, "if these men are annoying you . . ."

"My kinsmen are not annoying me," I said quickly, restraining the twins by a hand on either cloak. "It is, rather, your own presence which I find – inexplicable."

"That too will be explained," Gilbert said calmly. "But first, since we are in your company, I suggest we all dispense with our weapons."

Beside me, the twins' mouths were dropping open. Behind, I imagined the Siwards in much the same condition.

Siward the Red said, "Why? So that he can murder the rest of us?"

Gilbert said wearily, "If by he you mean Ivo, he was not excluded from my command to lay down arms." The word command was lost on none of us. He may have been nearly sixty years old, but his characteristic, understated authority had lost nothing with the passage of the years. Slowly, the twins turned to look at me, but my eyes were on Ivo, deliberately unbuckling his sword-belt while he met my stare. The sword dropped to the floor with a loud clank.

I said, "Lise," and without a word, the maid came and picked it up under Ivo's amused gaze. For a moment, I thought Gilbert would intervene, well aware that my insult was deliberate. At best, he had done nothing to stop Hereward's murder. According to Wulric the Heron. But I did not insult him for my benefit, rather for that of Hereward's kinsmen.

Only when Lise had deposited Ivo's sword in the outer chamber, did I turn and nod to the others. They dropped their swords too, but Lise did not pick them up. Neither did I appear to notice the other weapons at their waists. And Gilbert, taking his lead from me, however reluctantly, said, "That is better. I am glad, in fact, to find Hereward's kinsmen here, for they have an obvious interest in what we are about to discuss. We all, after all, have one aim in common."

"We do?" said Siward the White, and his disbelief was barely polite.

"Don't we all want to discover one thing?" Gilbert said sharply. "Who it was who killed Hereward, my godson!"

My breath caught, drowning the sound of the others'. "No!" I said, and when all eyes turned upon me in surprise, I swung away from them and sat down on the bed where none would follow. For several moments, they were silent. Even Siward the Red's inevitable accusation against Ivo was not made.

Gilbert said carefully, "You don't?"

"No, I don't care," I said tiredly. "It will not bring him back. It will, if anything, only cause men like them" – I waved one hand vaguely in the direction of the Englishmen – "to suffer for any retribution they take."

Siward the White said, "But you cannot mean to leave it like that . . .?"

"Why shouldn't she?" said Ivo de Taillebois. "The man left her four years ago! She owes him nothing."

"What do you know?" said Siward contemptuously. "Torfrida, you can't pretend you do not care . . ."

"I am not going to pretend anything," I interrupted. "Nor do I forbid anything. Just don't involve me if you won't take my advice."

Gilbert, ignoring my repelling position, came anyway and sat on the bed beside me. "What?" he said, with just a little too much understanding in his voice. "Do you really not even want to know why Ivo de Taillebois is included in this pact?"

"I know that already. Out of all of us, he is the only one who was there."

"So you recognize that. You see, you have been thinking about it."

I said tightly, "I don't *want* to think about it. I don't want to think about anything." And yet I had to think of something, deliberately, or the thoughts already in my head would tear me apart.

"Did you? Did you see it?" That was Siward the White, two steps closer to Ivo de Taillebois, staring at him with an intensity that would have shrivelled a lesser man.

Ivo let a definite pause go by before he answered. "I saw something."

"But why should we believe you?" Duti demanded aggressively. "You were always his enemy! You would say anything to cast the blame away from you!"

Unhurriedly, Ivo transferred his gaze to the twin. "Not all your friends died at Bourne. Find one truthful one who will say that I so much as crossed swords with Hereward that day, and I will lie down and let you kill me."

And when I saw that, despite themselves, the Saxons were impressed, however grudgingly, I could not help observing mockingly, "Begging the question, Ivo. Why should you care who killed him, so long as he is safely dead?"

For a moment he did not answer. I thought he was not going to, for he did not even look at me. Then, seating himself on the bench under the window where he lounged and inspected the soles of his shoes, he said conversationally, "Because of you. Because of the lord Gilbert whose guest I am. Because whatever else I thought of *him*, Hereward, I never doubted his honour. Because treachery was involved, and I do not care for the imputation to my own honour." At last his eyes glanced up, directly at me although his head did not move. "Because of you."

I looked away.

"Do your worst," I said drearily to Hereward's kinsmen. "And don't get hanged."

"Don't you want to know what I saw?" Ivo asked.

"No," I said after a tiny pause.

Beside me, Gilbert said, "Torfrida, we need your help."

My lips tried to smile, but nothing happened. Those tears I had wept for gentle Robert were coming back again. I whispered, "Why don't you all leave me alone?" And yet if they did, if they left me, what in God's name would I do? I looked up at the ceiling beams, as if counting them. "Tell us your story, Ivo," I got out. "Tell us all, and then let Hereward's kinsmen get on with the butchery."

Ivo said, "Your men told Gilbert it was a conspiracy. I know nothing of that, and nothing of any poisoned ale. I do not, however," he added as Siward the Red jumped impetuously to his feet, "deny that any of it was so. By the speed with which it all began, I would say there had certainly been some – collusion between the other Norman guests, but it was nothing I was aware of until it occurred."

"You expect us to believe that?" Duti demanded.

"No, but I expect your lady to. I do not like Asselin. Nor the other two particularly, although they have a smattering of civilization about them."

"Why would they not include you?" asked Siward the White. Always more thoughtful than the others, he was making a serious effort to understand as well as to judge. "A man of your standing and reputation: I would have thought your – *participation* – necessary to them."

Ivo's lip curved, but it wasn't really a smile. "Use your imagination. Have you never been in the position of wanting – needing, even – to outshine a man the world considers inconceivably better? Did you never vie with each other, even, for Hereward's approval? To the point of keeping things from each other so that you could be the hero of the hour?"

He did not wait for an answer, but carried on. "I imagine those were the reasons why both Deda and I were kept in the dark. Certainly, the first either of us knew of it was when the men-at-arms burst through the door, and ran straight for us. I'll give Hereward credit, he certainly acted fastest. He was over that table, sword drawn, before Asselin knew what he was about. They actually had to chase him, by which time he had met the men-at-arms head-on, and his friends were with him: that clerk who fights more like a devil, and the short, hairy one . . ."

"Wynter," said Outi dangerously.

"Wynter," Ivo agreed gravely. "There was that insolent servant as well, and one other, a lesser man with an enormous nose, one of the ugliest beings I have ever had the misfortune to lay eyes upon."

None of us had any difficulty in recognizing Wulric the Heron from this description, and in fact Ivo's tale was much the same as Wulric's, telling how Deda tried at first to stop the fight and then, when that proved impossible, concentrated on getting Hereward's mother and sister out of the hall and away to Folkingham.

"And what did you do?" asked Siward the White, lifting his eyes suddenly to stare at the Norman. "What did you do while another man rescued your betrothed and her mother?"

"I sat down to watch," said Ivo blatantly. "It was a damned good fight – begging my lady's pardon. I think it took the concentrated efforts of four men to do for the fighting clerk, but they laid him out eventually – under the table, as I recall – and shortly afterwards, the ugly soldier managed to run off . . ."

"He went," Duti said coldly, "for us."

"So I supposed. Certainly it left only Hereward, his servant and the hairy one against everyone else, and though they had let a lot of blood, they didn't seem to have killed anyone. However, in no time now, the Normans formed a solid wall, advancing on the three Saxons. For a few moments they stood their ground, then quite suddenly, with a roar that quite pierced my ears, they charged. I couldn't make out what happened next, but somehow – from surprise, probably – they got through that Norman wall and out of the door. Most amazing thing I ever saw, I give you my word."

I looked at my hands, lying open in my lap. Siward the White said grimly, "A good time to have called a halt."

"Well, believe it or not, the same thought occurred to me. When I had stopped laughing, I even stood up with the intention of doing precisely that – only while my countrymen were still scrabbling to get out of the door after their quarry, I heard this odd rumbling and pattering on the roof above my head. And when eventually I went outside after the others, they were being assaulted by a hail of missiles from the roof."

In my lap, my fingers gripped each other and squeezed.

Ivo said, "Hereward was up there and his two minions were tossing him up boulders and branches and anything else they could lay their hands on. All three of them were actually singing while they did it – some extremely questionable French song as I recall. However, the Normans eventually decided that they should take out the servant and the hairy one and cut off the missile supply. But when pressed, they simply shinned up the wall to join Hereward, and then all of them leapt across the roofs like sprites, with our men tearing after them, yelling, on the ground. Now that," said Ivo with a genuine tug of his lips, "was the *funniest* thing I ever saw. Clever too, because he had reduced a deadly fight to a farce."

Something in that caught my attention. Of their own volition, my eyes lifted to his face. I could feel the frown on my brow.

Ivo said, "He was talking to them as well. I could hear his voice, not just mocking now but – *joking*." His brow was creased. "I moved closer, to find out, I think, what he was up to. I saw him, standing alone on one of the outbuilding roofs, sword in hand, gesticulating while he talked. Once or twice the Normans seemed to be answering him – I definitely heard Asselin's voice at least once. And some of our men were shamefacedly sniggering. Then, as I got nearer, there was silence, from them and him. For some reason, I halted. And then . . ."

He paused, looking at none of us. Siward the Red said impatiently, "Then what?"

Ivo drew in his breath. If I had not known better, I would have thought it shuddered. Slowly his eyes refocused on Siward. He said, "Then? Then he threw away his sword, high over their heads. And jumped in among them."

When they had gone, I sat under the open window staring sightlessly up at the stars. Tomorrow, I thought. Tomorrow I would tell my children that their father was dead. Exhausted by their journey, they had been asleep by the time I arrived at Folkingham, and I refused to wake them for such a purpose, so it was all to do tomorrow. After which I could watch and console Aediva's grief, and Lucy's, while my mind, my whole being, churned with what I knew and what I did not.

I had not meant to be disturbed, or even impressed by Ivo's story. But there had been a genuine admiration, a sneaking liking even in his tale, that made me remember other events and other men. Afterwards, when Siward the Red had accused him again of failing to stop the murder, he had risen to his feet with the first sign of anger I had seen in him that night.

"What did I owe the Outlaw?" he demanded savagely.

But that was not what truly disturbed me. It was the fact that Hereward had been *playing* on the roof-tops, reducing the fight, as Ivo said, to a farce, making his attackers talk and even laugh with him. Winning them over as he had won that disparate group of aggressive youths in Northumbria, and many more since . . . I could understand that. What I could not understand was why he then threw away his advantage with his sword, and jumped deliberately in among them. Had Hereward of all people finally committed suicide? And if he had, why the charade of the roof-top chase first? Would it not have been easier simply to run into somebody's sword?

Besides, could Hereward really have changed so much in four years? I did not know. There were parts of Hereward that lay buried for decades so that even I knew nothing about them till they burst out . . .

The sky was clear. I had an excellent view of Orion from where I sat. Perhaps it was time to look again at the stars. Perhaps. And perhaps I had first to learn as many facts as I could. My breath shuddered, scaring me.

My chances had all run out. Deliberately, not understanding that they would be the last, I had let them go.

CHAPTER 13

In the morning, despite Matilda's objections, I rode back over to Bourne, taking with me only the twins. The Siwards I let go with permission, if not downright instruction, to find Asselin, Ralf of Dol, Hugh of Evermouth or any of their servants and bring them back to talk to me. Unhurt.

Before I left, I marched into the hall in search of Ivo de Taillebois. He was there, standing by the high table with Gilbert, pouring over some document, and he was dressed for riding. I thought he was probably leaving, going back to the King or to his own estates, rather than staying here to give Lucy the comfort she needed. I saw her too, drooping in the corner by herself, bewildered, as if she still did not know what had happened. I didn't altogether blame her for that. We had all got into the habit of regarding Hereward as indestructible. Or nearly so . . .

It was Gilbert who straightened first when he heard my step.

"Torfrida. Don't go back there just yet," he said, and at once Ivo looked round too.

"It was you who wanted me to help," I pointed out without rancour, and looked directly at Ivo. "Which roof?" I asked curtly, and he understood at once.

"Lord, I don't know – a guest-house, I think . . ."

"Describe its position," I interrupted, and he did, although his eyes narrowed. Even now, he did not relish being addressed in such a way. I was beyond caring. And when he would have said more, I simply nodded and walked away.

I do not know what I expected to find by looking again around the yard. The mess made by the battle and Hereward's roof-fight had been cleared up, and though I stood amid the burned out guest-house and gazed up at what was left of the roof, and the grey sky beyond, forcing myself to imagine the scene described by Ivo de Taillebois, I could not learn anything. It had rained heavily the night it had happened, washing away the blood and the scuffling tracks of the ten or more Normans who had hacked my husband to death. And burned him.

Ivo, sickened in his heart, I think, by what he no longer stood any chance of stopping, had turned away, got on his horse and ridden away. But he thought that Hereward, weaponless now, had nevertheless broken free again; probably run into one of the outhouses which the Normans then set on fire.

"Outi," I said to the twin who still stood silently by my side; his brother had gone into the hall to find Leofric the Deacon. "Outi, were there fires still burning by the time you arrived?"

Outi frowned in an effort of remembrance. What had happened since had wiped just about everything else out of his mind.

"Smouldering," he said at last. "Here, and the store-house over there . . . We pulled him out of the guest-house here . . . The others we could not recognize at all. They must have shot burning arrows inside the houses, perhaps even right into their victims . . . Christ, I'm sorry, Torfrida . . ."

"Don't be," I said. My voice was steady, although my limbs had begun to shake. It doesn't matter, I kept telling myself. None of this matters, because he is dead. Nothing any of them say can make that worse.

But it could. It could.

Swallowing, forcing myself to think clearly, or at least more clearly than yesterday, I asked, "Were any of the Normans taken alive?"

"None," Outi replied with grim satisfaction.

I rephrased the question. "Did any of the Normans talk to you before you killed them?"

"There were none left to kill – seriously, Torfrida, the place was dead when we got here. They must have seen us coming and bolted."

"What of our people? The servants? Are they really all dead?"

"Except the women, who ran or escaped with Deda."

Desolation. Desolation. There should have been proper grief for these people who had served me faithfully, even after Hereward had gone, and perhaps there was, somewhere, buried under the desperate need to know what had happened to *him*.

Not all your friends died at Bourne.

"Leofric!" I said suddenly, and span round towards the hall. How could I have forgotten that Leofric alone had survived the battle?

"We pulled him out from under the table in the hall," Outi said apologetically. "He was still unconscious."

Frustrated once more, I stopped in my tracks and stared at him. Taking a deep breath, I said, "Outi, were you with him at all that day?"

"I saw him in the morning, at the camp," Outi said cautiously. "Why?"

"Did he seem – himself?"

Outi frowned. "Yes, I suppose so. A little preoccupied, perhaps. He seemed amused by the fact that Hugh of Evermouth wanted to marry Frida."

I felt my eyes widen. "He knew of that?"

"Hugh had told him apparently, the night before. I'm glad to say Hereward laughed in his face and told him to wait until one of them had grown up."

"Well, there's Hugh's motive," I said, just a little shakily. I could almost hear Hereward's voice saying the words, and extraordinarily, I wanted to laugh. "What was he up to, Outi?" I asked, forcing myself back to sobriety. "What were his plans?"

Outi met my gaze sombrely. "I don't know," he said. "I thought – we all thought – he had come home to be reconciled with you . . ."

"No no," I said impatiently, for that line of thought was unbearable. "His *plans* – for you, the gang, for his *place* in England . . ."

But Outi did not know that either. I hadn't really expected him to, but if anyone did, it was Leofric the Deacon.

Some servant girls had drifted back to the hall, silent and scared, and bringing with them their friends and sisters from the village. We ate dinner much in the old style, except that it was a silent meal, and a watchful one, served by clumsy, inexperienced servitors. Nobody cared.

Although he clearly wished to be lower down the hall, I made Leofric the Deacon sit next to me, and tried to find out from him the state of Hereward's mind. When I first asked, he looked curiously hunted, as though afraid of hurting me further, but after a moment, he said simply, "Odd."

"Odd," I repeated. "In what way, odd?"

Leofric shifted in his chair. "Well, *hopeful*, I think – and yet – sad."

"Hopeful of what?" I pounced.

He smiled slightly. "Of you. And peace, I thought."

"Did he tell you that?" I asked sceptically, and he shook his head. No, I didn't think so. I wondered if Aelfryth knew yet.

Leofric was looking hesitant. Under my unblinking gaze, he eventually said reluctantly, "I had the impression he had made some kind of decision, but he never shared it with me, nor with any of us so far as I know." *He would have shared it with you*, Leofric's eyes accused, silently. Soon, I thought drearily, it will all have been my fault. I will have driven him into Aelfryth's arms, and she will be his true wife, his true widow. Hereward is dead . . .

Abruptly, I stood up.

"Where is he?" I demanded, and for an instant Leofric regarded me with his mouth open. While he swallowed, it was Duti who answered: "In the chapel."

The body laid out in the chapel, in all its pitiful gore, might have been a stranger's.

I did not know what I was looking for. Perhaps some proof that he had been dead before the fire had burned his poor face. For it had always struck me as odd that only his face and head had been so damaged. It had struck me even yesterday that the Normans had done this deliberately, taking fright at their treachery when it was too late, and trying to cover it up. If there was no body, then nobody could say that Hereward was dead, nobody could accuse them, or raise the country against them . . .

Only they had not known about the ribbon. Only I and the Siwards had known about that.

Slowly, I reached out to the ribbon and carefully untied the knot. It came surprisingly easily. And while I was so close, I looked at the wound in his chest. A sword, I thought, and deep. I thought it had pierced his heart.

My eyes closed. *Rest in peace, Hereward. Rest now in peace . . .*

Something deep in my own chest threatened to choke me. Gasping, I swung away from the body. *Some things are beyond tears.* When had I said that? I thought I would never cry again, not for him.

Slowly still, I rubbed the faded piece of ribbon between my fingers. Many of the tiny jewels had fallen off over the years, and many washings had muted its once bright colour. Where the knot had been was twisted and creased and just as dirty now as the rest.

The discovery made me frown. Threading the ribbon through my fingers,

I found another less stiffly twisted area, and that was patchily clean, showing, surely, where the knot had been tied when the fighting went on. Turning back, I stared at the body. Why had he taken it off and retied it? I could think of no reason. And no reason why it should matter, but it did.

"Behold the grieving widow," mocked Ivo de Taillebois' voice from the doorway. I did not give him the satisfaction of starting. "Mourning her man."

"What are you doing here?" I asked without interest, and he began to walk towards me.

"I came to see you. To see what you have discovered. What is this? A token?"

"It was once," I said, and his face changed. "He wore it in battle, for luck. He must, I think, have been expecting something of this sort."

"He had many enemies," Ivo said steadily.

There was a pause. Then, "Yes," I said tonelessly.

"Torfrida, he has not been your husband for four years! Don't let his men talk you into a grief you cannot feel!"

Irritated, I jerked away from him, moving down the little chapel towards the door. Almost at once, his stride came after me. "Torfrida, I followed you to give you comfort!" he exclaimed. "Not to fight with you . . ."

I paused, turning back to look him in the eyes. I thought his were actually pleading. I said coldly, "It is Lucy who needs your comfort."

"It is not Lucy," he said deliberately, "that I want in my bed."

Not for the first time, he had taken me by surprise. For a second, I was not even sure I had heard him aright, in this place at this time, with my husband's body cold at the altar. Yet again, something stirred inside me, wicked and shameful. It made me move quickly, reaching out for the door and the fresh air before I answered him.

"Then you should not," I said with equal deliberation, "have betrothed yourself to her."

I went to my old chamber, partitioned off the main hall. I knew as soon as I went in that he had never slept here. No mess, no scattered shirts and buckles and weapons, no golden hairs on my pure pillow. Only my bare, barren chamber as it had been since I had left him. My books were here, though – my astrology books that I could never bear to part with, Bede and Formicus. Perhaps they would help me yet, once I had thought.

But lying down on the bed, the scrap of yellow ribbon still clutched in my fist, I found I could not think. I had heard the men talking once, when they had not known I was there, about the way battle and death made them feel. Some, when they had killed, wanted a woman immediately and with an urgency that could not be denied. Well, my mind, my spirit, were desolate with death, but my body, suddenly, wanted a man.

It was Ivo's fault. I had never been immune to his attraction, and the shock of his boldness in the chapel did nothing to dispel that. But it was an unclean lust, a need barely even acknowledged by the rest of me. All it was doing was forcing me to remember the past, when such desires had been new, unfulfilled and only half-understood. A cerebral, self-willed and laughably inexperienced woman of twenty-two, I had been conscious only that something magical was lacking in my life.

Past: Home: April – July 1066

CHAPTER 14

The African *was* a handsome man: no longer young, perhaps, but dark, tall, exotically unfamiliar in his loose, flowing robes. And more than this, intelligence burned deeply, enduringly in his shining brown eyes as they smiled understandingly into mine.

I said breathlessly, "May I see it?"

He got up at once and went to a trunk, the gentle weaving of the floor quite undisturbing to him. No wonder. So far as I could tell, he lived on this ship, anchored these several weeks in the port of Bruges. And this tented chamber was his house, his study, his hall and his sleeping quarters. I felt no embarrassment at that. It was his learning which excited me, not his manliness.

And yet there was something very beguiling, almost seductive – at least, I imagined they were seductive, though I had never actually been seduced – about these surroundings. For me. He had filled his tent with books and strange, beautiful objects from Italy and Spain, Persia, Africa and the East, and scattered soft, colourful rugs about its floor. His couch, low and comfortable, was decorously covered with bright silk and cushions. There were large cushions on the floor – on the deck – too, and it was here I had chosen to recline, to hear him talk of the mysterious knowledge of the Arab world, while the sweet, heavy incense filled the air, and my senses, with pleasure and excitement and a curiously heightened clarity of thought. For he had read the works of the great Greek Ptolemy, and spoke to me also of an Arab doctor long dead, called Abu Ma'shar, wise in the knowledge of India and Persia as well as of the ancient Greeks.

The African, whose name was Constantine, turned back to me with the instrument in his hands. My own were reaching up for it involuntarily, but he held it a little away from me, suspended from his fingers so that I could clearly see the frame, with its lines and figures and measurements, and the disk with its holes for observing the stars.

I understood at once the hugeness of this discovery, though the details took time.

"This is wonderful," I breathed. "With this, you can actually *measure* the distances between the stars . . ."

"And tell the time."

I was silent for a moment, drinking it in; but the words would not be kept back for long. They were bursting out of me.

"But this is the most marvellous thing I have heard of! When you said you had an astrolabe, I thought you meant one of those models of the universe, with spheres and rings to show the movements of the planets. But this . . .!"

Constantine smiled again. "It is useful, in observing the heavens as well as in calculating horoscopes. You see how accurately an astrological chart may be divided into the houses?"

Dragging my eyes away from the astrolabe, I looked directly into his. "I will not ask to borrow it. But may I use it some time?"

"Tonight, if you like. Tracing the comet's course across the sky will be fascinating."

I wondered if he knew how tempted I was. For a moment, I contemplated letting them all – my parents, my uncle and cousins and friends – survive the evening without me or any knowledge of me. After all, the comet which had appeared last night was a rare enough sight; if it came again, as all the wise men were predicting, surely I should not be expected to pass up this chance of actually measuring its passage . . .?"

My breath caught. I heard it. Then, smiling ruefully, I shook my head.

"I can't tonight. I am promised to my uncle."

The African only inclined his head. "Whatever pleases you."

"Will you not be there?" I asked a little anxiously. "At my uncle's house? Several of your friends are coming, and any number of people who would love to meet you." I paused then, honesty compelling me to admit that he could have no such desire to meet most of them. And at that he laughed.

"I have not been invited. And in truth, I can see more from here."

"Yes," I agreed regretfully. My eyes had strayed once more to the astrolabe. "Perhaps I could come the following evening?" I suggested hopefully. "Though I may have to bring an escort . . ."

It was slightly disconcerting that Constantine appeared to be listening to me with only half an ear. The rest of his attention was, I thought, on some noise outside on the quay – or perhaps on the deck of his own ship. He had already stepped back, dropping the astrolabe again into its trunk, flipping closed its heavy lid.

I opened my mouth to apologise somewhat sardonically for boring him, but before I could, he was speaking quite courteously.

"Of course you are welcome. My only stipulation is that your companions be as discreet as yourself – your father, perhaps? I am not known in this country, and neither is the astrolabe – I have no desire to be taken as a witch because of it."

"There will be no danger through us," I assured him, but abruptly he seemed to have lost interest in me altogether.

Seeing his eyes were fixed on the half-open tent-flap behind me, I turned quickly, just as an almighty, many-voiced yell rang in my ears like a thunder-clap, and some six or seven men burst into the tent, swords and daggers drawn, mouths open in their fierce shout.

Somehow, in the initial shock, I had stumbled to my feet. Constantine moved, stepping in front of me, although he carried no weapon that I had seen. The invaders held one of the ship's African crew by the hair.

The noise faded away as they gawped at their surroundings; suddenly they no longer seemed so *sure*. It was this impression – as well as sheer native curiosity – which made me peer round Constantine at our attackers.

At the same moment, their leader said harshly in French, "Stand away from the lady!" And I recognized face and voice at once. A man of power, acknowledged as a formidable foe, and dressed for battle. Yet if I had ever been afraid, the fear vanished now without a trace, for I understood at once what he was about. Only the extent of his blatancy was unexpected.

I said, "*Asselin!*"

"My lady," he returned tightly, yet with every respect. "Are you hurt?"

I stared at him grimly. "Why in the world should I be hurt? I am, however, confused. Have you taken to piracy in any official capacity?"

"Piracy?" Satisfyingly, it was he who seemed confused. His sword, which had been pointing at Constantine's heart, wavered distinctly. However, he recovered quickly, saying loudly. "We are here to rescue you."

I almost laughed. But in fact, it was not quite funny. So instead, I sat carelessly back down on my cushion.

"I have no need of rescue. Let that poor man go – *unhurt*, if you please. Try not to break anything as you leave."

Though I was pretending complete unconcern, and even less interest, I could see Asselin's men exchanging puzzled glances. Only the bold leader himself was still frowning ferociously, and at least half of that was anger at me for not behaving according to his plan. Abandoning me as unappreciative and unhelpful, he turned instead upon the African.

"I told you to get away from her!"

Constantine said mildly, "I shall stand away when she asks me to; and when you lower your sword."

Asselin stared, but since he was not a man to be repelled by the courage of others – however inconvenient to his own cause – he looked more admiring than angry.

Then: "You're mighty cool for an abductor," he observed.

Constantine did not respond. So I did.

"You," I stated without pity, "are a mighty ass. Did you follow me here with that nonsensical misconception stirring you to this feat of bravery? Ought I to be impressed? Flattered? Grateful?"

From his face, it was clear that I should have been all of those things. At least. This time I did laugh, and Asselin, though he did not lower the sword, began to bluster.

"Why else would you ride all the way out here? Alone?"

"I wasn't alone," I pointed out in the interests of truth, "I was with Constantine. Why are you still here?"

"To take you home to your father!"

"Stuff," I said rudely, reaching for the book lying open upon the couch. It was heavy, but I managed to bring it on to my lap and open it with exaggerated interest. Not unnaturally, this infuriated Asselin. I was spoiling his plan quite thoroughly. However, having gone this far, he was reluctant to give it up altogether.

Striding forward, he said firmly, "For your own good, you will come with me now!"

Constantine was pushed impatiently, contemptuously aside. That was good. My one fear had been that by goading him to rage with me, I would also induce him to injure the African from spite. Now, as he advanced so purposefully upon me, reaching down to pull me to my feet, I didn't even bother to struggle. In these days, I liked my dignity.

I just gazed at him, quickly dominating his blustering ferocity with my own icy contempt, as I had learned to do long since. Constantine, who had made one almost instinctive move towards us, was still.

"It is just possible," I uttered distinctly, "that if you lay hands upon me again, I shall regard *that* as abduction."

Asselin's fingers loosened on my arm, but his breathing was heavier, and his eyes had widened. He couldn't quite believe I would do that to him. Yet still it never seemed to enter his head that I could see straight through him.

He said stubbornly, "Lady, I have never meant you harm. You know that. It is rather my duty, my responsibility to return you safely to your father's house."

I regarded him sardonically. "Don't try to intimidate me with my father's name," I advised. "I am well aware he knows nothing of this venture of yours. If he did, he would have disabused you at once of your feeble-minded notions of guile! Constantine will take me home when I am ready."

"That is hardly suitable," Asselin ground out between his teeth. Then, visibly inspired, he added with dignity, "People will talk."

But I had had enough. "It would never enter their heads to *think*, let alone talk, without your drawing attention to me with this ridiculous stratagem! Yes, Asselin, I said stratagem. And believe me, it takes far more than this nonsense to impress me *or* my father! Don't you have an appointment elsewhere?"

A moment longer he stared down at me. He was a bully, I saw, regretfully for he would have made a wonderfully *careless* husband. Once I had had such hopes for him too. And he for me, of course. Perhaps he saw they were finally at an end, for abruptly he turned on his heels.

"Very well," he said, gathering the remnants of his dignity. "I shall go. But I go straight to your father, lady; be assured of that!"

I didn't deign to answer him. I was on my cushion again, turning the pages of the fallen book. They were astrological tables of some kind. I remember registering interest for the future. For the moment, I was too furious to read anything. I did not see Asselin's men stamp and clank their way out, nor the careless blow with which they felled Constantine's hapless sailor. But I heard them, and the African's footsteps across the deck, his low-voiced question and the sailor's rueful yet jaunty reply.

I realized I was trembling. But I would never, never admit it.

Preparing to leave the tent, and the ship, only a little later, Constantine said idly, "I am sure you are right to reject him, but tell me, since I am a curious fellow, why are you not married already?"

I regarded him quizzically. "Being so advanced in years?"

"Are you?"

I said calmly, "I am twenty-two years old. And I am not married because I have, so far, chosen not to be."

"Ever?" he persisted. I wondered what he had heard.

I said evenly, "I was betrothed in my youth. He died."

The African said, "A broken heart keeps you chaste? I never suspected you of such romantic – impracticality."

And at that I could smile. "I assure you I am extremely practical! I always know exactly whom I could and could not live with." Eventually. "Asselin falls into the latter category."

Almost, I expected him to enquire about his own. When he didn't, I think I was piqued. And yet I knew well the African would not stay. He had too many places to see, too much knowledge to acquire and to impart.

A passing friendship was all there could ever be between us.

Outside the tent, I paused a moment on the open deck, looking about me. These days, Bruges was a busy port. There were sailors on the quay, rough and colourful, tall, fair northerners mingling with exotically dark peoples from the south, all calling to each other, rolling barrels of fish and wine, loading boxes laden with Flemish cloth, unloading others bearing English wool. My father's real wealth came from just such trade.

All around us was bright, boisterous activity. Perhaps I had been foolish to come here alone. I had Constantine's physical protection, but blameless friendship could not protect a name.

Another ship had tied up close to ours. A large, rather magnificent vessel of war, with a tall, black-painted dragon's head. The dragon's green eyes seemed to sparkle, as though with some precious gems.

"You are dwarfed," I remarked.

"It is a fine ship," he allowed. "And there is another just like it, which must be sailing. They belong to the English mercenary, Harold."

I can't remember now, just when I first heard the mercenary's name. Some weeks before, I think. He had been ship-wrecked off St Omer with two richly-fitted ships – of which this black dragon was apparently one, refitted and repaired – and a company of fit, foreign fighting-men. All of which was enough to invite both interest and investigation, but it was said that the charismatic captain had talked himself out of house-arrest and into Count Baldwin's service, being trusted with military tasks which he performed with such dash and courage that he was rewarded with more. It kept him busy and therefore out of more idle society, but his name was constantly in the mouths of men and women who wondered at his wealth – apparently fabulous – and his beauty – devastating, by all accounts – as well as his much vaunted prowess. He was not the sort of man who interested me.

There was laughter as well as efficient-looking activity aboard the mercenary's ship. The sailors seemed to be of many races, as crews often were, and they looked to be better dressed than most. Good pay, presumably. Which meant better booty.

"He makes a good living," I observed, and giving the man no further thought, moved forward to go ashore.

Once, I had taken an interest in everything English. But it had been nine years now since I had come home, and interests fade with memories.

CHAPTER 15

I knew Asselin had been there by the time I joined my father in his chamber – the room where he conducted nearly all his business, where he played chess and even, occasionally, ate. My mother complained that she didn't know what the rest of the house was for. My father said it was for her. And me. At which she generally sniffed and pointed out that even we rattled about in it, and what was needed was grandchildren, which I seemed determined not to provide. I told her to buy more furniture.

My father was entering figures on a large scroll when I found him. But at once, he laid down his pen, and the parchment rolled itself back up on the desk.

"You should let me do that," I said mildly. "Or one of the clerks."

"I may be old," he replied drily, "but I still like to know what is going on."

It was true. Since recovering from his illness nine years ago, he was more than ever the captain of his own estates, and of the increasingly lucrative wool-trading empire which had so attracted Gilbert de Ghent. On the other hand, ever since I had come home from England, I had made it my business to become intimately acquainted with his affairs, so that by the time I was seventeen, I was universally acknowledged as his capable lieutenant. Never again would they feel obliged to marry me off just to run the business.

"So," said my father as I sat down opposite him, and laid my own rolled parchment on the table. "What *is* going on?"

"You mean Asselin?" I said bluntly, and told him succinctly and humorously enough to cause his lips to twitch.

When I had finished, he only said mildly, "Asselin is quite right about one thing though: such carelessness with your reputation can only harm you, Torfrida."

I bowed my head slightly. I had already acknowledged it to myself.

My father said, "And besides, it may have been a silly ploy, and quite unfair to poor Constantine, but one must admit he is doing his very best to win you."

I looked at him quickly. "He proposed after all? What did you say?"

"That in such matters, I always allowed you to follow your own choice. However, I am convinced he is genuinely devoted to you and I believe – I believe he would not – oppose – your intellectual interests. Will you consider him?"

I looked at my father apologetically. This time it was he who sighed. In

91

fact, he cared little about marrying me off, for since his illness he had developed a dislike of any change to his personal life; it was really duty rather than desire which caused him to receive proposals and, occasionally, urge them upon me. Not so my mother, who took it as a personal affront that I would not oblige her in such a small matter: "Wretched stars!" she would rage. "Do they never tell you whom you *should* marry?"

And I would quickly banish from my mind the face that tended to swim into it unbidden; the face of a brave soldier and a noble man, tongue-tied for love of me – or with desire for my fortune, or even fear of my learning. I was never sure. We had nothing to say to each other, of course, but for some reason he did move me. And most of all, the stars seemed to have no objections, not to Osbern de St Walericus . . .

"I have," I said now, "been casting Asselin's horoscope . . ."

"What is it this time?" my father interrupted wryly. "Drowned at sea before the age of thirty? Loss of all worldly possessions? Deformed or idiot children?"

"No," I said, with the grace to blush at this rehearsal of some of my previous works – all of which, I have to say, had some truth in them. It was all open to interpretation, although the drowning of Albert de St. Adrien off the French coast had certainly validated my credentials somewhat.

Unrolling the parchment I had brought with me for just this purpose, I pushed it across the table to him and stood up.

"Oh, I heard from Gilbert today," my father's voice stayed me. "He and Matilda plan to come next month. With a guest."

"Oh?"

"Siward, son of someone called – Aethelthryth? Gilbert thinks you know him."

"I did once," I said, just a little sadly.

When I finally left Robert's grieving family there had been quite a flurry of messages back and forth across the sea. Even Lucy wrote one day, an epistle dictated to Gilbert's clerk on the day she was betrothed to Tostig of Rothwell and left Matilda's service for good. But then Gilbert's family had returned to Flanders, unable to bear, they said, the insufferable supremacy of Harold of Wessex, who now actually aspired to the throne. Reading between the lines, I gathered Harold did not favour Gilbert, perhaps because of his connection with the Count of Flanders, and therefore with William of Normandy. At any rate, they had come home, giving up their English lands before they were deprived of them, and now sent occasional letters to my father from their chief house in Ghent.

I wore green silk and a necklet of garnets and peridots, in honour of my uncle's supper. Once, Matilda, affecting not to recognize me on their return four years ago, had called me beautiful. I wasn't, of course, but I had most people too flummoxed or even frightened to notice such a minor detail. In truth my features were still too strong and unevenly proportioned for prettiness, my nose too big, my forehead too high. But at least my lumps had largely disappeared, except where they were supposed to be, and my skinniness had obligingly filled out until my figure was actually quite elegant, if still a little on the thin side for true beauty.

My hair too, although nothing induced it to curl, seemed to have thickened and burnished, so that it shone sleek and black around my face and down my back as far as my waist. As for my face, most of the spots and blotches had vanished with pubescence until I was just a little proud of my creamy white skin. Inevitably, of course, I had let them pluck my eyebrow, although I defiantly maintained the two arches somewhat more thickly and more distinctly than my contemporaries. It all added to the slightly formidable character I had adopted. It suited me. I was comfortable at last.

Having arrived finally at my uncle's estate south of Bruges, my most pressing concern was to observe and discuss the comet with my learned friends. Yet the common courtesies, which even I had to maintain, demanded that I spend time first of all with my aunt and cousins.

"Have you hard about the Count of Guinnes?" Adele demanded.

"Not recently," I returned, my eyes wandering in search of my friends.

"He has submitted!" Adele said triumphantly, just as if it mattered to her. "Sent gifts and hostages to Baldwin, and come back to his peace."

I did raise an eyebrow at that, recalling the defiant bravado with which the lord of Guinnes had been opposing Count Baldwin for some time.

I said, "A trifle sudden, is it not?"

"They say it was all due to Harold the Englishman," Marie put in on my other side. Clearly they were both bursting with this news, so although the comet was calling me, I tried hard to be interested.

I said, "Single-handedly, this Harold defeated the lord of Guinnes' entire force at once?"

"You are sarcastic," Adele observed without rancour. "But not so far wrong! In fact, he defeated the old man's grandson in single combat behind his own lines . . .!"

"And took him prisoner!" Marie continued breathlessly. "Evading all the rebel pursuit to bring him back to our own camp!"

"He is obviously a great hero," I allowed kindly.

"I hear he is in Bruges tonight," Adele said, "with Count Baldwin, although my father . . ."

"I saw his ship," I recalled. "At the port this afternoon."

I gave them some token description, but distractedly, I am afraid, for my restless eyes had at last found Osbern de St. Walericus, tall, handsome, watching me broodingly from across the hall. I confess that my heart gave a pleasant little flutter. I even bestowed a smile and a bow upon him before I passed into the garden to join my friends, and forgot all about him.

All my usual friends – universally clever and mainly elderly – were present, together with a visiting doctor from Spain. By the time Osbern de St Walericus interrupted us, we had already discussed the comet's predecessors, its position in the sky last night and tonight, and its likely movements over the next few days. We had drifted rather more humorously on to its portends and political significance, particularly for England and for William the Bastard who would, everyone knew, invade that country any day now; and naturally we wondered how this would affect the balance of power around our own Flanders.

It was the kind of talk I most enjoyed – intelligent, perceptive and not overly serious; and yet, if I am honest, I should confess to an occasional distracting frisson, which I blamed on the eeriness of the mysterious visitor to our heavens. At any rate, I remember, just before Osbern's arrival, slipping out of the debate surrounding me. I lost the thread in gazing upwards at the bright, trailing star. The voices nearest me became briefly incomprehensible; and those farther away – chattering meaninglessly, mercilessly, about comet superstitions, or social gossip, or the latest daring and no doubt mythical exploits of the rich English mercenary – they seemed to rise up around me, filling my ears with a sudden babble of excitement.

That was when Osbern touched my shoulder, snapping my eyes and my attention back to Earth. I found him standing solicitously by my elbow, a silver cup full of wine in one hand and a cloak to protect me from the night's chills in the other.

He said humbly, "Lady."

For a moment I gazed back at him, contemplating the precise form of my set-down. He knew it was coming too; I could see the resignation in his liquid dark eyes. Only then I realized I had already lost my place in the debate of my erudite friends who were walking tactfully away from us, back towards the lights and the house. I felt a flicker of annoyance with them, for though I had managed long-since to win their intellectual respect, even they could not imagine that any spinster's first desire was not for the company of a gallant and highly marriageable man. But I have always been strange.

Under my gaze now, Osbern actually shifted from one foot to the other like a guilty school boy. For that reason, I took pity on him; or at least I chose to believe that was the reason. Accepting with a resigned sigh the cloak and the wine, I returned to my star-gazing.

Osbern said abruptly, "It makes my flesh crawl, that thing."

I lifted one humorous eyebrow at the comet, my spirit regretfully following the backs of my retreating friends. "Imagine how the King of England feels."

"You think it comes specially for him?" he mocked. Osbern would always ridicule what he could not understand. Unfortunately, he ridiculed a lot of things.

Unimpressed, I said, "What an odd mixture you are, Osbern, of cynicism and superstitious dread."

"Not at all," he argued, making a rare conversation out of the encounter. "I am just hoping it will smite *everyone* called Harold, and then we may also be rid of that English mountebank the Count is making such a pet of!"

"The mercenary?" I was amused, I think, by Osbern's attitude, so I asked tauntingly, "Why, has he put *your* nose out of joint too?"

"Certainly not," said Osbern stiffly. "I only met the man once."

"What happened? Did you challenge each other most valorously over trifles?"

"You mock me," he observed uncertainly, then much more abruptly: "Torfrida, how long do you mean to keep me at arm's length?"

"I hope never to come so close!"

"Then you have done it! You have accepted Asselin . . ."

"I have accepted no one," I said impatiently, deftly avoiding his reaching hands. "But I am still waiting to hear about this memorable meeting between you and the legendary Harold. What happened?"

Osbern blinked rapidly, as though thinking himself back as many steps. Then: "Nothing," he said impatiently. "We all but collided in a doorway, and he stood aside to let me pass."

"That was civil." My eyes were straying skywards once more.

Osbern said contemptuously, "Civil? Aye, that or timid! I expect he had heard of me."

"I expect he had," I agreed gravely. "He will be a paltry fellow."

Stung now by my mockery, he stepped to one side, saying tightly, "You may judge that for yourself! It was this doorway I met him in – he's over there right now!"

I was not really interested, but still I followed his gaze, discovering many others turned in the same direction, and becoming aware for the first time of the stir of excitement around the garden that had nothing to do with the comet.

"The fellow in the pretty jewelled cloak," Osbern sneered.

Of course it was. Even with his back to me, this mercenary was a magnificent specimen. The ostentatious cloak of some bright silk was heavily embroidered and encrusted all over with precious gems, so that even when it was too dark for the rest of his splendour to be properly appreciated, the cloak at least would ensure his distinction.

Tolerantly amused by my countrymen's fascination, I thought their hero looked more like some gaudy tumbler, especially in the flaming torchlight under which he stood. I wondered if he had placed himself so deliberately.

Still, it was effective, I allowed. Vulgar in the extreme, but effective. Especially when topped by a golden head that gleamed so brightly I strongly suspected he had jewels embedded in his hair too. In fact, it was amazing those nearest him were not blinded by his light.

Or perhaps they were; for in reality this gorgeous being was hardly the heroic figure my countrymen had been extolling for months. Where, I wondered – quite diverted now – was the beguiling combination of Viking warrior and Celtic god they had so vividly conjured up?

To begin with, he stood no higher than any of the men around him, and if his body held even half the strength attributed to it by legend, the fact was well hidden beneath his luxurious dress and his casual, almost slouching stance. Besides which, he looked so inert to me that if the preposterous cloak had not rippled occasionally in the breeze, I might have mistaken him for some painted statue.

"Oh dear," I said, amusement gurgling up in my throat. "Paltry indeed! But perhaps you are wrong and that is only our hero's little brother?"

Osbern snorted with delighted laughter.

And that was when I saw Asselin striding purposefully along the path from the house towards the mercenary's circle of fawning men and flattering women. Balked of his prey only this afternoon, I knew with a twinge of alarmed distaste that he was ripe for violence.

"Why," I murmured regretfully, "can people not just enjoy the sky?"

However, nobody else seemed to be paying Asselin any attention. That was all upon the Saxon, until Asselin, goaded by the Englishman's failure to notice his impressive advance, ferociously rattled his sword in it's scabbard.

The result was startling. I did not hear the sound above the babble but Harold obviously did, for before I had even seen it, the Saxon had acted, spinning around in a mass of golden hair shaken suddenly loose from inside the cloak. And in the same breathless movement, swift and sure and somehow shockingly graceful, he wrenched free his own massive, wicked-looking sword and dropped to one knee, the sword held shimmering above him, while the wondrous cloak and bright, golden hair settled themselves once more about his body, like angelic armour.

By now, all talk in the garden had ceased. I wasn't surprised, for the whole affair had sprung up with astonishing suddenness. Besides which, the mercenary's unexpected manoeuvre looked so highly practised that it spoke volumes for his past life, and the attempts which had been made upon it. Despite his gorgeous finery.

Yet it was none of these things that aroused my curiosity. It was that he chose to defend rather than attack. So what was this mercenary? A man who could not fight, whatever his reputation said to the contrary? Or that even rarer creature, the one who troubled to ask questions before despatching his fellows to their Maker?

That is what made me start towards him in the tense moment of silence; that is what made me look upon his face at last. And with the first step, I knew.

I had no warning. I had been so sure that if ever I saw him again, I would have time to prepare, that I would detect his coming first in the stars when I looked for him or for me. But I had seen nothing, and I had no time. One moment I was aware only of a half-despised stranger whom I had just found unexpectedly worthy of my intellectual interest. The next, the glare of the torch shifted and I was gazing upon a face of strange, irregular male beauty, the face of that infuriating, unmanageable youth who still troubled my dreams after ten years.

Not Harold.

That was his joke. I knew it for such even then with the blood singing in my ears and the stony path rocking beneath my feet.

Not Harold. Hereward.

CHAPTER 16

I could not breathe. The world was spinning upwards from my feet to my deafeningly singing ears. I was aware only of *him*, the mass of his golden hair just stilling about his body as he gazed steadily up at his attacker, prepared, fearless, and curiously unassailable, with that massive sword held unwaveringly above him like fire under the lantern lights.

Then, with recognition came a bolt of fear for him. On top of all the rest.

I don't know how long it took for the world to rock, and right itself, for me to see beyond the shock and realize that this could not be Hereward. Hereward was *young*; his eyes held all the turbulence of youthful storms, not the cool hardness I saw now. And Hereward, eternally restless, had never possessed the poise, the stillness, the sheer self-control of this seasoned warrior. No nonentity, no tumbler. I was mistaken, mistaken twice over.

Then: "Remind me," said Asselin casually, "never actually to draw steel on you. What do you fear? Assassins?"

"No," came the immediate response. "Bad manners. How are you, O great, brainless hulk?"

And before my own and many other open-mouthed stares, the mercenary rose gracefully, sheathing his sword with one hand while the other fended off a boisterous embrace.

"Enlivened, little Saxon!" beamed Asselin. I had never seen him so amiable. "Enlivened! What shall we do?"

The Englishman said something quizzical. He spoke in French, and the voice too was very different – clipped and deep and designed for distance. The men around laughed. So did Asselin.

Mentally, I was shaking my head at the strange games of the human male, trying not to think of the shock I had just had, or what I felt about it now. Then the mercenary's eyes – they *were* restless after all – shifted, scouring the garden, taking in the new and altered formations of people around him. They glanced over me, inevitably, and passed on, only to pause; and then, even as he spoke once more in reply to some other banter, his gaze came back to me.

I was not surprised by that: I have always been striking in one way or another. No, what stunned me was the colour in his eyes. Like different shades of the same sea, one was cool grey, the other dark, intensely blue.

No two men had eyes like that.

It knocked the breath out of my body all over again, to know it was really him, that he was *here*, within talking distance, almost touching distance; that he was gazing straight at me with a slow, peculiarly hungry admiration growing in his eyes.

It was the kind of look I had never expected to inspire in him. It was like all the secret dreams of my plain, despised childhood coming true. I think I began to smile from sheer happiness. Certainly, I saw an answer in his own eyes, in the faint curving of his full, expressive lips. With a wild sort of excitement I had never known before, I waited for him to speak to me, to say my name, to come to me.

And then someone else entirely spoke beside me. "There you are, sweet lady. I have been looking all over for you! What means this strange star, do you think?"

It was Tostig, Earl of Northumbria, smiling into my blank, still bemused eyes. I didn't like Tostig. From all I could discover, no one liked him. Even his own brother, England's new King, had kicked him out of Northumbria when the people had expressed a somewhat forceful preference for Aelfgar of Mercia. So Earl Tostig had rolled up here, as so many English exiles seemed to, biding his time and fomenting more trouble. It was clear he meant to go back, and meant his brother the King no good. I didn't really mind that. Their family squabbles were no concern of mine. But I did object to the way he flirted with me so that no one would suspect the real reason he sought me out – which was to pick my brains about the stars. The stars relating to Earl Tostig, needless to say. I wished someone would tell this to his wife, for the lady Judith clearly did not like me at all.

Now, most inopportunely, his eyes bored into mine with a fierce antici-pation of their own, almost desperate in their desire to be told what he needed to hear. I should have had an answer ready; I *did* have an answer ready, only I had forgotten it. And I didn't want to see him. I wanted to see Hereward again, with the glow of desire for me in his strange, intense eyes.

I think I had even begun to turn back towards him, when Osbern reap-peared on my other side, saying jealously, "So what do you think of the little hero? Doesn't he glitter?"

"No," I said without thought. "He shines. My lord Tostig, you must excuse me . . ."

And since the other man's presence made it impossible for Tostig to detain me further, I quickly took Osbern's arm – because I didn't know if I could walk on my own – and walked away.

Emotions, conflicting thoughts and ideas were crashing into me and through me with such force now that the only thing I knew was that I had to escape, to deal with this astounding event on my own, until I was *ready* to meet him.

Yet I was sure I felt Hereward's eyes watching me; and as we stood aside to let the lady Judith pass, I took the opportunity of checking.

He had gone.

He was no longer there. Only Asselin and the group of men and women who had once surrounded him. For a second, I wondered wildly if I had dreamed the whole thing.

And then I saw him again.

He was quite close, with only a handful of people between us. He had clearly crossed the garden with us, on a parallel course; and his eyes were on me, only on me.

Stumbling as Osbern drew me on, I felt choked. I could not understand this. I could not like this. I felt *hunted*; yet I felt exultant, as never before in my whole life. How many times, for how many years had I imagined this scenario? That he, Hereward, would somehow come to Flanders, that when we met again he would fall immediately and madly in love with me?

And now, dear God, it might not have been love, but I certainly had his attention! And it was a hundred times more overwhelming, more *frighten-ing* than the silly dreams I had never truly expected to be fulfilled. Because his sheer physical presence was so much more powerful than I remem-bered; surely more than it had ever been when he was a boy . . .?

I couldn't deny my pleasure in it, fierce, triumphant, terrifying.

So why, I wondered with peculiar bewilderment, why in the midst of this joy, should I be eaten up with such strange, galloping grief?

Because he does not know me. He does not know me.

A glance I could not prevent found him again, still following, still watching, still *prowling*. I looked into his eyes, and recognized the shaming truth there. He was seeing only the striking, elegant, slightly strange woman I had become; I supposed the novelty of that strangeness was bound to attract him, just as the weird child I had once been had occasionally commanded his erratic attention in the past. But he did not know me. He did not know Torfrida, his friend.

And as the harsh reality of that fact began to break through my foolish, flattered joy, my dazed brain began to work again, to see the rest of the story.

He had been here in Flanders for weeks, months even; yet he had made no effort to communicate with me. Or with Gilbert, so far as I knew, for there had been no mention of Hereward in that letter. I could find excuses for the latter, of course, but not for me, not for me.

And so, finally, I saw his look of desire for what it was: shallow, animal, utterly impersonal. And more devastating than anything was the fact that I had welcomed it. Was I really no different from Edith of Lincoln after all? Were we sisters after all?

No, for I believed he had truly loved Edith.

A wave of self-loathing surged over me, through me, making me gasp aloud. Osbern glanced at me solicitously.

"Are you well?" he asked with curt anxiety.

"Cold," I said with difficulty. "I'm sorry. It was only a shiver . . ."

Osbern was saying, "I'll take you inside," but against my will my eyes were straying again to *him*. And he smiled at me, deliberately enchanting me; and I hated him for the way it made me feel. What price now the mild frisson of Osbern's touch, when a man who did not know me could do this to me with a smile?

Wrenching my eyes free, I saw my cousins rushing towards us, forcing us to stop civilly in front of them. From the corner of my eye, I saw Hereward stop too. One of his hands reached up to a tree bough above him; his forehead rested against his arm, his eyes unblinkingly upon me, not recognizing even yet, just hungering; hunting a stranger.

"Harold is here!" Marie burst out. "The Englishman! Mama has met him, Torfrida, I swear it!"

I swallowed a hysterical choke of laughter.

Osbern said drily, "We know. We saw him too."

"Where? Oh where?"

"You can't miss him. His cloak rivals that evil star up there."

I could not bear this. Muttering that I had to go inside, I bolted for the hall, a faint smile fixed to my lips as I threaded swiftly among friends and family and acquaintances without pausing to speak to any. I didn't even look to see if he was still following.

Fortune smiled upon me. I encountered no obstacles in my headlong flight, until the hall door itself, when a broad, silken black back blocked my way in. Even so, I would have brushed and squeezed my way past, had the back not suddenly turned and become a powerful silk-covered chest with a bright golden head above.

Swinging the jewelled cloak over one shoulder, Hereward smiled at me, and snatched away the last of my breath.

My foot faltered. Inane words of apology died on my lips unsaid. His companion had melted away, leaving him free to gaze down on me. From somewhere, I acknowledged that I was going to have to deal with this now after all. A thousand beginnings raced through my head, instantly forgettable and as quickly forgotten.

What came out in the end, bluntly, was, "How did you get there?"

At once the smile intensified, spreading to his eyes, and the blend of the remembered and the unfamiliar in him was painful and bewildering to me.

He said gravely, "I am good at games. I always out-think the opposition."

"Games?" I repeated at once. "Did you imagine I was playing one?"

"Weren't you?"

"No!" I uttered, with such revulsion that his eyebrows flew up, inevitably recalling his uncle Brand. He moved down the single step to me, and I backed instinctively away before I realized he had thus effectively separated me from the rest of the guests. His body shielded me, and I could not see beyond him. I made one quick movement, as if to brush him aside, and then, with conscious bravery, I forced myself to be still.

He said, "You are vehement. Don't you like games?"

I lifted my chin. He should have recognized that, at least.

I said, "I love games. What I don't like is being stared at."

"I could not help it; I still can't."

"Let me recommend you a good physician," I offered, beginning at last, in spite of myself, to enjoy it. I saw the laughter in his eyes too. Once it would have been vocal, joyous; I could not help wondering what had quelled that seemingly endless well of high spirits.

He said reproachfully, "I mean, as you well know, that it is your beauty which snares my eyes."

"Oh, well said," I approved, according him a tiny, mocking clap. "Most practised flattery! Only – it does not quite ring true."

His eyebrows rose again. I thought he wasn't sure whether or not to be amused, and was grimly glad to have thrown him.

Then he said steadily, almost as if surprised that I could doubt it: "But I have never seen a woman as lovely as you."

Oh he was good at this; very, very good. Not so much in the words he used, but in the *way* he said them. How I hated him . . . To my annoyance, I could feel myself blushing. I never blushed.

Grateful for the shadows, I said, "Too blunt. Try for more poetry."

"Later," he said gently, "when I'm convinced that you like it." His recovery was good too; and he was still disconcerting.

"There will be no later," I said flatly. "I have nothing to say to you. Excuse me." I took a bold step towards him, but he made no move to accommodate me. Osbern, even Asselin, would have fallen over their feet to let me through. *He* just gazed at me until I had no idea whether or not he was still playing. There was a small scar, jagged and white on his weathered forehead; I found that, but I could not find my old friend. He had disappeared completely, it seemed, under all the layers of his later life. Whatever that entailed – unlikely adventures with warrior kings and beautiful Irish princesses, according to rumour . . .

He said, "I don't even know your name."

"No," I agreed; he would never know how bitterly.

"Mine is Harold," he offered.

"Is it?" I said drily, and the laughter was back in his eyes.

"Don't you believe me?" The prospect, clearly, neither surprised nor appalled him.

"It is the name of princes and great noblemen," I said significantly. *And bears*. But I would not say that. I waited for him to. He didn't.

I gave a short, contemptuous laugh. Suddenly my rigid self-control was in tatters. I no longer knew what I was doing or saying. I only knew the urge towards recklessness, and an urge to hurt.

"Very well, *my lord Harold*," I mocked. "Since you like games, try this one. Discover my name, if you can, without asking me or anyone else what it is."

"Simple," he said blandly.

"You must not question anyone about me, directly or indirectly, and you must not follow me when I leave here. Nor must you come near me again while I *am* here."

"You are a hard task-mistress," he observed. "But of course I accept – on one condition."

"What?" I asked warily, made suddenly uneasy by my own behaviour. The spurt of recklessness was dying quickly. I was, after all, rather older than twelve now. I don't know what I thought I was doing, except punishing him obscurely: I think I was looking forward to the time when I would reveal my own name and cast all this back at him.

"That you make it more of a wager," he said. "I need a prize to motivate me. What would you like if I lose?"

"Your absence. And if you win?"

He smiled. "A kiss," he said steadily, "of course."

I should have been prepared for that, but I think my laugh was slightly shaky as I said dismissively, "Whatever. If you stick to the rules, you *cannot* win."

"How long do I have?"

"A week," I said generously. I could afford to be. After all, when I left here, I had no intention of going anywhere near him, or anywhere I was remotely likely to meet him, for considerably more than seven days.

"Done," said Hereward, holding out his hand. For a moment I gazed at it blankly: large and strong as I remembered it, yet now it looked hard, positively leathery, and scars criss-crossed along its back to the knuckles. A solitary, thick gold ring banded the middle finger; carved with dragons and crosses, it looked Celtic.

Slowly, with a reluctance I could not bear to examine, I laid my own hand inside it. His fingers closed around me, warm, firm, yet curiously gentle. Another memory stirred and was squashed. Harshly.

Hereward said, "A tough challenge, but as I told you, I *am* good at games. I don't suppose I could have the kiss in advance?"

I tore my hand free with a tiny gasp. And that time, ignoring my own dignity, I stepped into the vegetable patch in order to get round him. In an instant, I was away from him, although I could have sworn I heard his mocking laughter following me. Had he always laughed at me?

On the hall step, I could not resist looking back once more – just to see if he was coming after me. He was, it seemed, but only so far; and catching my surreptitious glance, he bowed with what I can only describe as insolence. I considered him well-served when Earl Tostig walked into him.

Naturally, the Earl rounded on him with one of his more dangerous snarls. Hereward, interestingly, merely looked amused, an unexpected reaction which clearly infuriated Tostig further. He was even reaching for his sword before one of his companions quickly hustled him away, talking urgently, as though explaining just who and what the object of his ire was.

Hereward had not even troubled to twitch his right hand. There was contempt, of course, in such indifference, but also, I thought from nowhere, a clear understanding of what and who represented a danger to him. Somewhere along the years, he seemed also to have lost his joy in battle.

I saw his lips move, asking for the identity of his would-be assailant. I heard his voice, and it still sounded only amused. Oddly, it was Osbern who answered.

"Your own Earl Tostig," he said contemptuously.

"He's no Earl of mine," Hereward said at once. Again, his voice was light; the faint smile still lurked upon his lips. Yet I could have sworn a shadow had crossed his face just as the name was spoken, a shadow so fleeting that only an obsessive observer could possibly have spotted it before it melted back into the poised, confident contours of his new face.

CHAPTER 17

Although my hopes that the mercenary's ship would already have sailed were doomed to disappointment, it did look as if all were quiet aboard her. Two sailors talked desultorily on the deck under gently swinging lanterns, while the black dragon banner, matching the ship's splendid head, fluttered peacefully in the breeze. I could ignore it with every appearance of serenity as my father and I dismounted in the midst of our own men, and Constantine welcomed us on to his own vessel.

It was dusk by then, the eerie light of the comet just beginning to be visible for the third night in a row. It had never been so difficult to concentrate on my chosen art. My eyes kept flitting around the harbour, absorbing the light and the movement, the sources of the occasional shouting and altercations on the quay.

Inside the African's lamp-lit tent it was easier, but I felt torn between an uncharacteristic urge to hide, and a much more comprehensible one to get my eyes and hands on his astrolabe.

Of course, when the instrument finally was produced, curiosity got the better of good manners as well as residual unease. I was able to extract it from my sardonic parent in no time at all, and Constantine, his dark eyes laughing at me, took me courteously out of the tent and suspended the astrolabe from what must have been its usual place when sailing in other waters.

He had thought it out. The tenting hid it – and me – from the shore and from the ships on either side. Only from the sea itself could anyone have seen what I was doing, and all was quiet out there. I could see a ship in the distance, sailing outwards on the tide, and something that might have been a small boat splashing some distance away, too far, certainly, to observe me with any clarity.

Impatiently, I stood on tip-toe to look. With far greater patience, Constantine made the necessary adjustments, while I gasped at what I could now discern. Swiftly, I got the comet in my sight, demanding to know where it had been last night and the night before, and then, almost before he had answered, the precise meaning of some of the instrument's markings.

The African answered all without fuss, and then, as I grew silent, left me to it and went to show my father his books instead. At least, that was what he said, but I, knowing Constantine rather well by now, realized he would also be picking my father's own not inconsiderable store of knowledge.

And I – I could measure the sky! For its own sake, and for the sake of horoscope predictions. I was enraptured.

I think at least a whole hour must have passed before I realized I loved my life again. I liked the pleasant, distant chatter of the sailors on watch, and of our own men waiting patiently for us to be done; the closer, more refined speech of my father and Constantine within the tent. I liked the gentle lapping of the sea against the side of the ship, and the way I had to brace my legs against its faint roll. I didn't even mind the singing and the increasingly raucous noise of a busy port at night. I knew it should be so; it was why we had our own men-at-arms.

My ears absorbed it all without troubling to analyse any, for I was busy, my brain was calculating, committing to memory, and my heart was simply enjoying the beauty of the heavens. For you see, in some things, I had changed very little from the child who had used to sit shivering on English roofs in the clearest, coldest of nights, just to enjoy the stars. Even then, it had not been all study.

So it was only when Constantine came out of the tent and walked across to the seaward side of the ship, that I became aware that the loudest singing was really quite close, that it was accompanied by the splashing of oars and the most raucous laugher I had ever heard in my life.

Consigning Saturn and its precise position to my capacious memory, I reluctantly took my eye from the sight. Rowing towards us through the still, smoky water of the harbour, was a small boat full of men and even a couple of women, in a tangled sort of a crowd, roaring out a song that was a mixture of languages and impossible – fortunately, I suspect – to follow. I saw flasks and drinking horns, many raised to mouths. The rest spoke for itself.

Reaching up quietly, I unhooked the astrolabe and took it into the tent, generously allowing my father another look while I stood at the tent door and waited for the boat to pass.

It was almost upon us now. And suddenly, over the top of the ridiculous song, a voice boomed out.

"Constantine, my learned friend! How are you? May I come aboard?"

"No," said Constantine equably, "You're too drunk."

I could see the speaker in the boat, because he had leapt precariously to his feet to address the African. Even in the dark he looked familiar, and his voice surely . . .

He called wheedlingly, "I've brought my own party."

"That's the other reason," said Constantine with mild amusement. "I have, you see, one of my own choosing here already."

"Oh well, I'll leave these villains behind, and I shall drink no more if you're going to be such a fastidious bastard."

The boat had rowed its erratic way out of my view into the ship's side – but not before our lights had glanced off the drunk's bright, golden head.

My heart was thumping, thumping. Was this not really what I had wanted, even while I went through the motions of avoiding it? Was this not why I had dressed with such care in my newest gown? Why else, for so informal a visit, would I be decked out in these glorious shades of golden silk, with the sparkling yellow braid around my forehead?

If it was Hereward – it *was* Hereward, I knew it . . .

My thoughts veered off into confusion and chaos. Even so, I was conscious of fury at myself. How was it that I was so incapable of *dealing* with this? With him?

Because I could not keep still, I was moving along the side of the tent, back to where the astrolabe had been, but my eyes all the while were on Constantine, waiting with an intense anticipation that held still some severe apprehension.

He may have been as drunk as Constantine said, but he swarmed over the side of the ship with all the agility of the lad I had used to watch swinging through the trees in Northumbrian forests.

Constantine said drily, "Welcome aboard."

Hereward grinned, and that, surely, was the grin of his childhood. My heart yearned suddenly, impossibly, until I took it severely to task. Leaning over the side now, Hereward appeared to be instructing his boat to row across to the red dragon ship. Then he stepped back and gave another slightly rueful smile to the African.

"Your pardon. I shan't stay for long if you choose to throw me off. When I saw you there, it struck me that I had not told you about that fellow of mine who gave you such trouble. I have . . ."

At this point, my father stepped out of the tent, for courtesy's sake, and caught Hereward's restless eyes.

The Saxon blinked.

"You never said it was a gentlemen's party," he said reproachfully. "Should I have brought the girls after all?"

"My friend, you are incorrigible!" Constantine observed, but abruptly my brain was working again. Because of our wager, I could not let my father be introduced to Hereward by name.

I said calmly, "There *is* a girl," and walked forward into the lantern-light.

Three pairs of eyes swung on me at once, but I, God help me, cared only for the pair that did not match. They widened slightly; I thought he even went still again, as he had been last night; and then I heard the breath of laughter catch in his throat.

"Oh, White Christ and Woden," he said impartially. "I believe I wish I were sober."

"Don't we all," said Constantine drily.

Hereward, I saw, was waiting expectantly for the inevitable introductions. His face was serious, but his eyes were dancing. I knew why.

Constantine sighed. "My lady, allow me, reluctantly, to introduce to you Harold the Saxon. Normally, he is a decent enough fellow. Harold . . ."

"We have met already," I interrupted smoothly, and his eyes regarded me with brief reproach before turning with rather more triumph towards my father. "And this," I added quickly, "is my father. Don't let us keep you . . ."

Hereward did not blink at this blatant rudeness, though it won me surprised glances from the other two.

"No, no," said Hereward. "I would not miss this opportunity for the world. Constantine will let me stay."

"Only because it would be more trouble to get rid of you," said Constantine hospitably. "Please, go in."

I went first into the tent, because I didn't know what my father had done with the astrolabe. He had left it on the couch where he had been sitting. Seeing it at once, I went quickly to perch in front of it. It pressed uncomfortably into my hip.

The others came in more slowly. Almost, I expected Hereward to sit beside me; when he chose instead to lounge on the deck cushions, I didn't know whether I was more relieved or disappointed. For now, in the more focused light of the lamps in the tent, he looked less like the Hereward of the past, more like the seasoned mercenary of last night.

"So," he said to my father. "I take it you are another inveterate seeker after knowledge?"

"Aren't we all?" said my father lightly.

"Lord no. I only come for the food." So saying, he reached across and helped himself from the inevitable dish of sweetmeats. Constantine watched tolerantly. They seemed, in fact, to be friends, though I could not imagine what on Earth they had in common.

"But why," I wondered aloud, "does Constantine let you?"

"He thinks he can pick my brains about Ireland," Hereward said at once, and I felt again the shock of his full, direct gaze. "Don't tell him, but I never went near any seats of Celtic learning. The only monks I met were fighting men, and possessed no more interesting knowledge than the best place to stick various weapons for maximum effect. Anatomy," he observed, transferring his gaze to Constantine. "Do you know about anatomy?"

Constantine said, "Enough to know what is happening to yours right now."

"Oh, I doubt that," said Hereward with a fleeting glance at me.

Because I could not bear it, my fingers gripped the astrolabe behind my back, and I stood up. Infuriatingly, his eyes followed me. Carefully, I slid the astrolabe round to the side farthest away from him.

"I shall leave you all for a little," I said lightly, and walked towards the opening. Constantine held it back for me. Meeting his eyes pleadingly as I passed, I breathed, "Don't tell him my name; don't let my father . . ."

His dark eyes widened into mine, uncomprehendingly, and then I was past, back into the sharp evening air. Rehanging the astrolabe with care, I returned to my observations. But my heart was not in it. My mind was not on it. My brief peace was gone again.

Yet though I was scarcely lost in my study this time, I still jumped when he said beside me, "I have heard of such things, but I have never seen one before."

I stared at him. He was alone; but his eyes were not threatening, merely politely enquiring. "May I?"

There was nothing to do but stand aside. I watched him look through the sight and thoroughly examine the instrument. It surprised me that he should, until he observed, "It must make navigating somewhat easier."

Before I could help it, I had asked what sprang into my mind. "You have travelled far?"

"Not very," he said regretfully. "I keep being washed up where I have little wish to be. And then things conspire to keep me." He cast me a glance. "Like you."

"What a pity," I said. "You were doing better too, for a drunk. Just for a moment, I almost liked you."

His eyes came back to me. His hands left the astrolabe and fell back to his sides. He said, "What a curious girl you are. Don't you like compliments?"

"Only those which are true. And meant."

"But I have never, to my knowledge, said anything to you that I have not meant."

I swallowed. I wished I was not quite so pleased to hear that. I wished I could believe it. Blindly, I tried to walk away, tried to radiate scorn – it seemed my only protection – but he stepped back, not touching me, but still in my way.

He said ruefully, "I would have sailed tonight if I had not met you yesterday."

"Or if the Count had not made you an offer you could not refuse?" It was a shot in the dark, but I saw at once that it had gone home. It was in his eyes. I laughed, striving to keep bitterness at bay.

"You are wasting your time on me," I said. "I see straight through you. You would do far better to pester one of the poor foolish little girls who were drooling over you last night."

And I walked around him back to the tent. I think I was disappointed when he did not try to stop me. I *know* I was disappointed ten minutes later when Constantine went to look for him and saw him waving from the deck of the black dragon ship.

I have shaken him off, I thought in wonder. I have.

And then: *Dear God, if I never see him again, what have I done? What have I done?*

CHAPTER 18

Over both bridges, the people poured into Bruges. From far and wide, they came to watch the contests of arms held in the field below the Count's castle. My parents and I were among the favoured few who watched the knights and soldiers gather from the Count's platform.

For a time, the three of us were silent among the gushing throng, each thinking our own, not necessarily pleasant thoughts while we pretended to take in the colourful scene below. For those who liked such spectacles, it was an impressive sight: martial, splendid, and to me, barbaric. Bright, swirling cloaks and glinting helmets swept together, mingling with the great war-horses and the running squires and servants who sprang between groups, eternally busy. The tension and excitement grew with the numbers of contenders gathering below, and for once, I was not immune to it.

Over the last three days I had reached new levels of self-contempt, for with every footstep that made its way to our hall, I found myself waiting eagerly for it to be Hereward's. It never was. And now – now when I had ruined it all – I found excuses for his neglect, his failure to recognize. I could no longer even complain because he looked no further than my skin: had I given him cause to? Had I even tried to talk to him, to impress him by my worth or to learn his?

Writhing with lost opportunity, I had tried feverishly to go on with my life. Then, yesterday, as I sat in my flower garden in the late afternoon sun, surrounded by charts and parchment and piles of books borrowed from Constantine, dementedly trying to work out whether or not I should attend the tournament, Osbern de St. Walericus had come to me, with his secret, fatal request . . .

"They tell me," my father observed, trying not to sound too much like a man who took no interest in such things, which he didn't, "that the clever money is all on your new man this year."

"Harold?" If the Count had been a lesser person, he would have smirked. "Well, mine certainly is! Watch out for him . . . Though they say young Osbern is vastly improved, and he did very well last year. Indeed, he performed outstandingly only last month . . ."

I saw Osbern myself at that moment, riding in from the town on a proud, white stallion, surrounded by his lesser men and servants. Though not yet in full armour, he looked splendid, tall, straight and handsome, and armed to the teeth. A bright, jewelled yellow ribbon was tied around the spear he carried in his right hand.

"Torfrida?" said my mother in my ear. "Is that not . . .?"

I knew what she meant at once. The ribbon was just too – *recognizable*. "A moment of madness?" I suggested.

"I believe it was," she said, a trifle grimly. It did not add to my comfort. Nor did Osbern's own manner, for despite his magnificence I could not like the way he swaggered about, encouraging his men to rile and abuse other contenders, as if he was already trying to pick a fight. I wasn't the only one who noticed either.

The Count said tolerantly, "I suppose it is hard on him to have come upon one of Harold's calibre at just this time."

"Speak of the Devil," said his son, young Baldwin, somewhat sardonically; and quickly following his eyes, I saw the mercenary ride out of the castle gate into the field.

At once a larger, more excited stir began among the contenders. I found my hand at my throat, as though loosening clothing that was too tight. I had to force my fingers to be still.

It was natural for the Count to be rooting for him: he wore the Count's colours, carried his banner, and was leading, presumably, the Count's own men.

"Has he no better than that?" someone mocked behind me.

"The men?" said the Count, neither offended nor cast down. "They are new recruits for the most part. But see if he does not get them to fight with greater valour than the most experienced company present . . ."

"No one doubts their valour," said the lady Judith wryly. "But I understand some skill is also necessary."

Earl Tostig, her husband, grunted with amusement at that.

Baldwin, already somewhat tired of his brother-in-law, said only, "Watch and learn. This is the second bunch of recruits he has trained for me, and in all my years I have seen nothing like the way he changes them, not just into efficient fighting men, but into that far more elusive entity, the fighting *unit*."

"That is hardly unique in a captain," protested Tostig, still presumably smarting from his encounter with the mercenary at my uncle's house.

"No, but the speed of it is," Baldwin insisted. "*And* the fact that he gets them to fight, and think, as one with his own men – those he landed with, I mean. There is no 'us' and 'them' in Harold's company. Look at these men now! They would die for him."

"Let's hope they don't have to," Tostig said drily.

I didn't want to hear this. I didn't want to think of his employment. I wanted to go on disapproving. Yet my eyes were fixed on the spectacle below only because I could not take my eyes off him. This was the use he had made of his talent, the unique quality that I had seen in him as a boy, when he had bound his godfather's men to him to the extent that, had he stayed, he would have become the natural leader of men much older and more experienced than he.

As yet, he wore no armour at all; but with his wild, gold hair streaming out behind him in the wind, he looked, for a moment, like some warrior angel of legend. I could see a bow slung over his left shoulder, a sword hanging at his left leg and a long dagger and battle-axe at his right. And yet he rode among the aggressive contestants with supreme ease, as casually as if at some party of Matilda's, reins held in one hand, the other hanging gracefully at his side, or lifted in salute to some acquaintance.

It was odd, but there was nothing provocative about him. The turbulent youth, I saw with a scorn that somehow did not please me, had learned how to appease. Perhaps he had needed to, to survive all those difficult years; and yet I felt I could not bear the loss of that wild, challenging spirit. I wanted my friend back.

Yet still my eyes clung to the stranger, secretly willing him to look at me, shamefully longing to inspire again what I had read in his eyes once before. For some dark, barely understood part of me wanted to be pursued and hunted and won – although what it all entailed was still blessedly hazy.

Of much, you see, I was still woefully ignorant, especially for a girl of my years who had had so many suitors. But the truth was, I had never *permitted* any of them to pursue me, and they had all been too frightened of me to try.

Attempting somewhat desperately now not to think of these things, to concentrate with my usual, superior dispassion on the rest of the scene, I only knew that I was far too excited to trust myself, that my body felt taut as the bow-strings being stretched and tested below.

He had halted now, his men behind him; and he was looking inevitably at Osbern, because Osbern was hurling some insult at him. I was, abruptly, appalled, shocked out of my daze.

Hereward laughed, throwing back his head in amusement which was surely genuine. Some of the angry frowns of his own men faded into grins, while the sniggers of Osbern's followers turned instead into glowers.

"Young Osbern still wants a fight," the Count observed, with something approaching compassion.

"He has come to the right place," said Earl Tostig drily. "Though it does not seem his man will play . . ."

"The Englishman will save himself for the contests," said the Count contentedly. "He is big enough to wait an hour to avenge the insults of jealous sprigs . . ."

"I think he is frightened," said young Baldwin, as Hereward went on ignoring Osbern's taunts, even turning his head away to tell some apparently funny story to the man at his shoulder. There, I thought, always looking for it, was a glimpse of the old Hereward.

"You have not seen him fight," said the Count irritably.

"Few of us have," said Tostig wryly.

And then Osbern put spurs to his horse, pushing him through the rest of his men so that he faced Hereward in a challenge no one could ignore or turn from. My breath had disappeared altogether. Suddenly I wanted to be anywhere but here. And yet the insatiable curiosity in me insisted on seeing how he would respond. I could not even turn my head away.

Hereward's black horse was trotting forward too, with no sign of slowing as he drew nearer Osbern. I saw the younger man's hand grip his sword, even begin to pull it free – and then, without warning, Hereward slewed to the left, as if he had intended all along to go that way; and yet they were so close that the horses almost touched noses before he veered off.

Someone laughed beside me. It was the Count, and several others joined in. The field below, or at least the part of it which had witnessed this scene was in an uproar of mirth – or outrage, depending on allegiance, for it had been quite deliberate ridicule on Hereward's part. And while I was bound to acknowledge that Osbern's behaviour had probably merited it, I did know an instant of pity for his proud soul. He was out of his depth, well out, I realized, and he did not even know it yet.

I saw stunned fury cross his face, had no doubt it was leaping and spitting out of his eyes. Poor Osbern: he had never had any idea how to deal with the unexpected, or the humorous. A wise man could and would have turned Hereward's little lesson into horseplay, at least in the eyes of the spectators, but Osbern was not wise. He had only one solution – to fight, and he didn't even know how to do that to a man riding in a diagonal line away from him while people were laughing all about him.

And then that was taken out of his hands too, for Hereward suddenly halted, even as a quick grin acknowledged the jeering laughter in his support. Again my breath caught in my throat.

He sat perfectly still in the saddle, his hand easily holding the big, restive horse in check. His head was slightly turned towards Osbern. His eyes, surely, were on the jewelled, yellow ribbon around Osbern's spear . . .?

The ribbon I had worn around my head the night we visited Constantine's ship.

He recognizes it, I thought, wonder warring with exaltation. He knows it is mine.

Osbern realized it too. That was clear from the sudden smile of triumph dawning on his lips. With exaggerated courtesy, he wheeled his horse about to face the platform, and looking straight at me, he bowed from the waist.

Hereward's head turned quickly. I saw it from the corner of my eye, although I looked only at Osbern, inclined my head only to him. My heart was thundering so hard it made me tremble.

"Torfrida?" hissed my astounded mother. "What in the Holy Virgin's name are you doing?"

What I had never done before, that was sure. Osbern had turned from me to Hereward, throwing words at him that I could not hear, but the men about them quite clearly could. For a moment, Hereward merely regarded him thoughtfully. I could not read the expression on his face; perhaps I was too far away, but I had the feeling no one was meant to. Then his lips moved.

"He objects to Osbern's token," Tostig said in surprise. He glanced at me quizzically, but I kept my eyes firmly on the field.

Someone else said, "I think he is saying one has to *win* such a reward."

He might have said that; certainly his lips moved. And suddenly, so did his whole body, twisting the horse into position with his legs, seizing loose the sword at his belt. His head was thrown back so that the golden mass of his hair swung, and just for an instant, I glimpsed the intense joy of the boy who had so provoked Tostig of Rothwell. Then it was gone.

Even on the platform, we all heard his curt command to his men to stay back, an order tossed out even as he rode straight at the other man.

Osbern was ready. The spear with my token was held straight out for Hereward to ride into. And he, Hereward, wore no armour at all. He had not even troubled to don the helmet one of his men had held out to him.

Oh sweet Jesus, I never meant this . . . But I had given the token, knowing it was wrong. And now somebody had to pay the price.

It was over before it had begun, so speedily that I barely registered the moves. Hereward galloped straight past the spear, missing it by a hairsbreadth, or so it seemed to me. And then, before I could so much as draw relieved breath, he had wheeled round, reading the other's comparatively slow turn, galloping in on the sword-side instead, away from the lethal spear. He closed. I heard the clash of steel on steel, a shout, the brief, wild encouragement of many male voices, and then Osbern tumbled from his horse, and the spear was in Hereward's hand, ribbon and all.

"My God," said young Baldwin softly. "He is quick . . ."

"And courteous," said his father, amused but unsurprised, for Hereward even troubled to bow ironically to the fallen figure, before leaning down to catch the reins of his riderless horse, now Hereward's own, and leading it forward with him towards the platform.

I thought he would come right out of the field, right up to the platform, and for a moment I was suffocated. I was shaking so much I dared not show my hands. My whole body felt as if it was spinning in a morass of shame and exultation, relief and awe, dread and longing.

But he only made his way through the obligingly parting crowd to the edge of the field, never looking at me. At the timber fence, he stopped, and bowed to the platform in general. A smile, an apology for beginning the contest early, without permission. The Count lifted one tolerant hand in forgiveness, and then, at last, the strange, miss-matched eyes moved and found me.

Dear God, the storms *were* still there, rushing, furious, violent; and behind it all, something so intense I could not read it.

Slowly, he lowered Osbern's spear until the ribbon was in his big, deft fingers. A twitch and it was free. Then, deliberately, he lifted it to his lips – and I felt hot from head to toe, as if it was me they had touched. Then my eyes were free, and he was galloping back to his men.

The excited babble closed around me like a blanket, allowing me a blessed moment to breathe, to gather my suspended wits, to wonder who had seen what.

I could not pretend. Everyone must have gathered that the token belonged to some lady on the platform; and some, particularly those beside me, must have seen the precise direction of his gaze. Even if they had, earlier, missed Osbern's and my own deliberately betraying reply.

As the Count stood to open the contests formally, I stepped back, my cheeks burning, and wondered when I could escape.

"Don't you dare," breathed my mother, who knew me very well. It was all I needed. I dared.

Looking neither to right nor left, I walked to the back of the platform, and edged to the right hand side, where I crouched down and dropped off, just as if I were a child again, and began to move sublimely through the soldiers and the lesser nobility gathered about the platform's foot. Until a voice hailed me.

"Lady?"

It was a soldier, wearing the Count's colours. That would not have surprised me. What dragged my jaw to my knees – metaphorically, of course – was the soldier's face.

"Martin?" I said disbelievingly. Martin 'Lightfoot', Hereward's friend and servant who had once shared our stilt race, and who had, inevitably, shared his exile. In retrospect, I don't know why it should have been so astonishing.

The man looked faintly surprised to be called by name, but hardly flabbergasted. Nor could I trace recognition in his dark, secretive eyes.

"Don't you know me?" I said unwisely, even as I wondered why he should when his master did not.

He said, "I know you are the lady my master sent me to."

My lips closed. My heart thudded once, then seemed to stop altogether. I acknowledged, distantly, that it could not do that. But I could think of nothing to say.

I didn't need to. Martin was pressing something into my fingers. My ribbon, my yellow ribbon. And something colder and harder. A ring. His ring, the one he had worn at my uncle's house and on Constantine's ship – gold carved with linked animal heads and tiny Celtic crosses.

From nowhere, something soft and warm was winding about my heart. I looked at Martin. Taking my token from Osbern, that could have been bravado, sheer male pride; giving it back to me in this way meant surely that the hunt had resumed. And on a different level, because he gave me his ring, his gift.

I went to see Osbern because I felt guilty. His injuries were my fault. I should never have given him that token and I should never have sunk so low as to use him for such a purpose. On top of which, I had not so much as spared him a glancing thought since Hereward had unhorsed him.

So, with Hereward's ring dangling on the notorious yellow ribbon (which I had tied around my neck, nestling warmly between my breasts, a sweet, dark secret) I followed Osbern's man to a tent on the far side of the field. Leaving the flap tied up for modesty, I went in.

Osbern lay on a mattress, his arm bound interestingly across his chest. His eyes, large and morose, brightened perceptibly when they saw me enter. He hadn't believed I would come.

I said, "Are you badly hurt?"

"I cannot hold a spear, or a sword. And if I could, I have no horse. My day is ruined."

"Well, you shouldn't have picked a fight before the contests had even begun!" I said unkindly.

"I know it, and I am well-served. I have lost your token, Torfrida. He took it from me."

I said, "I know. The whole of Bruges knows."

His eyes closed in shame; and relenting as I remembered my own unwholesome part in all of this, I added, "I am sorry, Osbern. It was my fault. I should never have let you wear the ribbon. I don't know why I did."

His eyes opened at once. "I hoped it was because you wanted me to win."

"Perhaps it was," I said ruefully. "Can I do anything for you? I shall send you an infusion and some ointment in the morning . . ."

"Thank you," he said with difficulty, torn between gruff sheepishness and delight in my care.

I bolted, feeling I had done my duty very ill. He still thought he had a chance with me. For myself, I knew nothing any more.

I paid more attention to the contests as I made my way back. Earl Tostig had left the platform and entered the field, leading his own men against Asselin's. Hereward's raw recruits seemed to have defeated at least one group in general battle, and were boisterously awaiting their next opponents. I hoped it would not be Tostig, but of course it was. Asselin, furiously unhorsed, was forced to surrender, and the next moment, with barely a pause for rest, the Englishmen faced each other.

It was always, I suppose, an unequal fight. Tostig, still in his prime, had greater tournament experience than any man in the field, and his men were veterans. Hereward could not even allow himself the luxury of concentrating on their leader, for his presence was needed everywhere by his own young, inexperienced men. With a feverish sort of fascination I had never felt for such a contest before, I watched him darting from man to man, helping those in greatest trouble, bolstering confidence, issuing quick instruction, encouraging and binding his men in their common goal. Three times I saw him break off a short bout with Earl Tostig to go to the aid of another.

It seemed he did not want the glory for himself; he wanted it for his company. And that was a maturity I had never expected in him. However, I reminded myself hastily, those were the rules of this contest, and Hereward had always fought to win.

I saw Count Baldwin leaning forward in his chair, a faint smile on his face. He had not given up hope of his man winning.

Now Tostig was pushing men aside in his efforts to get at Hereward again. But Hereward was already engaged with two of Tostig's company, his own man, whom he had been helping, having fallen and left both opponents to his captain. Suddenly, fear for him invaded me again, for he was not invincible or untouchable, whatever impression he was busy giving to his men. And it was not his losing I minded, it was the possibility of his injury, even death, for the contests were rough. And Earl Tostig was probably the roughest, even without a grudge to encourage him.

Hereward saw him coming. His eyes flickered, looking for support and finding none. The few of his troop still left were fully occupied. And then I saw something else in his face: the sudden, ferocious longing to take Tostig on.

Was it simply desire for the glory of defeating the opposing leader? Or was it because Tostig was the old enemy of Mercia? But there was little time to debate motives, for Tostig was thundering up, and the other two were pressing in for the 'kill', refusing to stand back and give the rightful honour to their leader.

I am no expert in matters of combat. I was even less so then. Yet even I could see that he must fall either to Earl Tostig or to one or both of the others. It was a matter of choice, Hereward's choice.

I had halted altogether by then, my fingers gripping the timber boundary as others tried rudely to press in around me. I wondered if he could bring himself to surrender to Tostig, for there was more honour in that than in defeat by lesser men. He was leaving it late to decide. The constant twisting and turning from one man to another must have made him dizzy. He held the long dagger in his left hand, and it seemed to be this he was preparing to use against Tostig while taking the blows of the other two on his sword. It was all defence. He *could* not attack. Gallantly, but infuriatingly, he had lost the last fight.

Then, even as I acknowledged it, he moved. Suddenly both his legs were on one side of the saddle, and he had launched himself off, almost flying through the air, with such force that when he crashed into Earl Tostig, they both hurtled to the ground among the horses' hooves, with a thud that seemed to shake the entire field.

The crowd went wild. I found I was biting my finger as it gripped the fence, and had to force myself to desist. Suddenly everyone left in the field seemed to be in a huddle around the two fallen men. Hereward's two erstwhile opponents threw themselves after him, but then, from nowhere, Hereward's recruits were upon them and the melee was indistinguishable to me.

Without conscious intention I was moving rapidly back the way I had come, the better to see. Anxiety was sharp in my stomach. To lose him when I had only just found him again, made friends again – if indeed I had . . .

The group was breaking up with a roar that spread around the field. I thought they were acknowledging Hereward's company as victors, but this I barely noticed, for both Tostig and Hereward were being carried off the field.

I wished my feet had wings; they had never seemed so slow. I did not even pause to consider how this would look, flying to his side; I did not consciously think at all.

I found them at last, the huddle of his men around the fallen body. Someone, catching sight of me, gasped and fell back, and then I saw him lying perfectly still, a red ring around his head where his helmet had been, a black, swollen bruise on the side of his jaw. Martin, at his shoulder, glanced up and saw me.

I heard him say, "The lady is here."

And Hereward actually opened his eyes, dazzlingly blue, intensely grey. I think it was sheer surprise that made me sink to my knees in Martin's place, as if my legs would no longer support me. I think, probably, they wouldn't. Vaguely, I heard someone saying, "He's fine. He was only out for a minute, winded and knocked on the head . . ."

And Hereward looked up into my eyes and smiled suddenly, confidingly, inviting me to share the joke I had not yet seen, assuming that I would. And teasing, that too.

He said, "Torfrida."

And I laughed, because I had lost, because he had found out my name

117

and yet still never connected it with *me*. It didn't matter; it was just funny. And he had won.

I leaned forward so that my hair fell over us, streaking black among his own. Quickly, I bent my head, touched my lips to his so lightly that I barely felt the flutter of his instant response – or was it astonishment? I gave neither of us time to find out which. I had risen to my feet with a speed worthy of Hereward himself. And that was when I saw beyond Hereward's men, to the figure of Osbern de St. Walericus, standing like a statue at the door of his tent, watching with hatred in his dark, unforgiving eyes.

And then Hereward began to sit up, speaking urgently. "Tonight. I must see you tonight."

My face flamed. His men were pretending not to hear. Cravenly poised for flight, I realized suddenly that I could not run from this. That I did not want to.

Breathless words tumbled out, giving him directions, instructions to go to the servants' house and ask for Lise. And then, avoiding the blazing of his eyes, I encountered in the distance, Osbern's.

"And be careful," I breathed. "Of *him* . . ."

Hereward's head turned, inevitably, to look, but I had already gone.

CHAPTER 19

I could not expect him before sunset. And refusing to appear over eager, I allowed him two hours after that to extricate himself from the celebrations and ride across the city.

It was the hardest two hours I had ever spent, desperately trying to occupy myself, alternately plaguing my surprised parents for conversation they were too tired to give, and seeking solitude or study in my own chamber. By the time I allowed myself to go warily down to the garden, I hated my pleasant chamber with its warm hangings, its heavily curtained window looking down onto the street below and its unusual carved figures in gold and wood, and the scattering of rare books and papers upon my table. None of it could keep my mind for longer than half a minute.

I walked slowly, seeing no one on the way, although I heard the servants talking, quarrelling and laughing in the kitchens. Was Lise there? Almost, I expected her to be in the garden, with him, waiting for me. But no one was there.

I sat down quietly on the bench, laying the book I had brought in my lap. I meant to be reading it when he came, to impress him by my superior wit and learning. That it was superior to his, I never doubted. Hereward had always been drawn to action, not letters.

My hand resting on the book, I took time first to gaze up at the moon, new and clear, with light, wispy clouds scudding across and behind, and at the comet, still with us but fading. I thought it would soon be gone, and I mourned it, not just for its beauty or its scientific interest, but because it seemed to me it had brought me the magic of Hereward's appearance here. And everything that went with that.

For the tiniest instant then, I think I did actually wish for a return to the quiet contentment of the days before he came, before I was changed into this silly, unrecognizable creature consumed with confused passions and excitements. And yet they were like some eastern drug to which I was already addicted. I would not have wished them away if I could.

So, I watched the sky, without calculation, breathing in the night scents of the earth. And I waited for him.

I don't know when it began to dawn on me that he was not coming. I'm not even sure how long I sat there before I realized that nothing could have kept him this long if he had truly wanted to come. My lamp had burned itself out. Had he been teasing me then? Punishing me for my harshness on Constantine's ship? Or had he just forgotten, lost interest, found something or someone better?

Either way, I was rejected, and no pain had ever been quite like it.

I closed my eyes to shut out the moon, and the lying comet. I felt tears squeeze out under my lashes and wondered, with that part of me that was still thinking, how I had let this insanity happen to me. In a matter of *days* . . .

"Lady? My lady, you will be freezing!"

My eyes snapped open. Lise was beside me, leaning over me in concern.

"I'm fine; I have my cloak," I said, drawing it around me with a shiver. "Go to bed, Lise. I'm just watching the stars a little longer. I shall manage on my own for once . . ."

"Lady, the man is here."

My eyes flew up to hers, forgetting the wetness still on my lashes. It didn't matter; she could not see in the dark.

I swallowed. "Harold?"

"Well, no; his man. He has word of him though. He bade me leave him at the far end, in case he disturbed you."

"A timorous servant for such a soldier," I observed sardonically.

Did I want to hear the servant's excuses? Did I want to become a bigger fool than I had already made myself in my own eyes and in his? No, I didn't. But still I found myself walking away from Lise with legs grown stiff from sitting so long in the chilled night air. I crossed the path, passed the sundial and went forward to the little willow at the far end.

A figure leaned there against the trunk, his hand holding on to one of the branches, as if he was tired from running a great distance. He straightened slightly when he saw me approach through the darkness, his hand falling quickly to his side.

"Lady," he said, when I was still quite distant – and his voice sounded breathless too, quiet, almost whispering, as if he were afraid to wake trouble. Decidedly an odd servant for the old Hereward. "I bring my master's homage, and his apologies."

"Martin?" I said uncertainly, for though he had never struck me as timorous before, there was a definite inflection of English in his accent. "What ails your master?"

"A little trouble on the road," Martin said sardonically. "I believe an admirer of yours objects to competition. Of any sort."

"Osbern!" I uttered, starting forward with contrition. "Martin, are you hurt? Is he?"

"No, no, it is nothing." He fended me off with one raised hand. "But it made him reluctant to come to you in all his dirt and rather less than respectable dress. He bade me give you these gifts in his absence, as tokens of his earnestness."

"*Earnestness*," I repeated, distracted from the form of speech that had brought a frown of unlikely suspicion to my brow. "Him?"

A breath of unexpected laughter escaped Martin's lips. "He can be earnest," he assured me, holding out a little leather pouch. I took it wordlessly. I felt both soothed and more anxious than ever. And I reviled the stars as base liars and myself as an unskilled hack. I didn't care what he had given me, only that he had . . .

"My master," said Martin, stepping back again against the tree, "begs some slight token of yours in return. If you care to give it."

"I have nothing out here," I said worriedly. Really, I was hopeless at this game. I had no experience of dalliance . . . Then I remembered. Quickly loosening the yellow ribbon at my neck, I took his ring off it, slipping it on to my finger instead, and scrunched the braided silk into my fist, holding it out. "There is only this. It is worthless, but I believe he won it."

"I believe he did," said Martin, although he could not have seen what it was. Reaching out, he took it, his fingers briefly touching mine, large, rough fingers like his master's; and then he stumbled, his other hand grabbing blindly out for the tree to steady himself.

"You *are* hurt!" I exclaimed, catching his other arm. "Come inside and let me see. I have some little skill with wounds . . ."

"It is nothing. I am just tired . . ."

But I had his big hand in mine, and my fingers were aware of scars across the knuckles. Like Hereward's. The unlikely suspicion returned. I stared up at him, wishing the moon were brighter, wishing Lise had brought a lamp to leave with me.

I was so close now I could smell the wine on his breath. Not ale. Wine. Slowly, I reached up to his head. There was a lot of hair, tucked into the collar of his cloak. There was something wet and sticky that might have been blood. I heard his breath catch as my fingers touched his skin.

"Lady . . ." he protested; but it was too late. I had discovered the scar on his forehead, short and jagged. I knew.

"Hereward," I whispered.

"You are mistaken . . ." Surely his voice was shaking?

"You are a liar."

"You are unkind. Does the whole world know me now for Hereward? I harboured the fond belief that it was only the Count who knew. Or cared."

"I have always known you. *I* am neither blind nor stupid."

"Yes you are."

Suddenly, while I tried to grasp this, his arms had gone around me, as if for support; yet I felt their strength, their warmth. And even more amazingly, his cheek was resting against my hair so that I could feel his smile.

"Yes you are, yes you are. Did you really think *I* did not know *you*?"

My head jerked away, staring at him. I saw his teeth gleam in the darkness. One arm left me, his fingers touched my face, the bridge of my nose, from which, only this morning, I had plucked returning unsightly hairs.

He said thoughtfully, a wealth of gentle laughter lurking behind his voice, "It was the eyebrows that threw me, just at first. It was a vanity I never expected in you . . . Kiss me."

He did not wait for permission. I was still trying to think what to say, how to be clever, when his mouth found mine uninvited, in the sort of kiss I had never known, and never imagined: invasive, consuming, overwhelming. And I realized with a burst of joyous relief that this was what my obscure longings had been about: his powerful arms around me, holding me close in against his body, his mouth lost in mine, at once tender and determined.

And then, when the world was dark and spinning in my new wonder, his lips left mine and buried themselves in my hair. Numbly, I realized he was laughing again.

"Oh, you witch, you witch . . . I was going to be so good, so honourable. I never meant to come to you like this, covered in blood and dirt, so tired I can barely stand . . . I meant to leave you my gifts and go; I meant to leave you pure and unsullied, and now I am doing this because you are an enchantress and I can't help myself . . ."

He was kissing me again, my neck, my face, my mouth, and I could do nothing but cling to him, gasping, so weak I should not have been able to stand, let alone strain into him as I seemed to be doing by no conscious volition of my own.

121

"Hereward," I kept whispering into his lips, his chest, his hair. "Hereward." Somewhere, I could not believe it.

I could not quite believe what his fingers were doing either, loosening my gown, letting it fall down my arms so that the night air briefly chilled the skin of my shoulders and breasts, until he had them covered with lips and hands.

I gasped and gasped again, so befuddled I had no clue and less care where this was leading. For once, I had no thought for the future, so wondrous was the present. Until, at last, he lifted his head, his hands, holding my face while he gazed down at me, breathlessly, urgently. The stranger in the dark I could barely see. My friend.

He said unsteadily, "Torfrida, will you take me to your chamber? Or may we lie together here in the earth? Under this excellent tree . . ." He was leaning against the tree; I supposed vaguely that here lay the source of its excellence. Then gradually the meaning of his words, of the whole scene in which I had been participating so enthusiastically, began to seep through.

"Oh God," I whispered. "Oh God, what are we doing? What am *I* doing? Hereward, stop," I pleaded, catching his face. "This is madness! You are wounded and I – I think I am insane!"

Briefly, I buried my face in his shoulder, squeezing shut my eyes, gripping his arms with tight, white fingers. Then I released him, hastily pulling my gown back up over my shoulders.

"Listen," I said shakily, while his hands fell to his sides and he watched me, unmoving. "Listen. I *will* take you into the house. I will tend your hurts, with the aid of the servants, and you will sleep tonight in the guest house."

There was a pause. Then: "As you wish." His hand reached out, taking mine, lifting it to his lips. He said, "I never meant to offend you."

"I don't believe I am offended," I said honestly. "Though I suppose I should be . . ."

I saw his lips stretch, the brief gleam of his teeth. "No," he said. "No. Take me inside then, and teach me to be good."

Hand-in-hand, we walked together towards the hall. Belatedly, I asked, "What happened to you? What did Osbern do? He swore to me he could not even hold a sword after you took it from him this morning."

"He probably couldn't." I felt him shrug. "I heeded your warning, for God knows I wanted no trouble tonight. So I left the contest surreptitiously, leaving one of my men behind in my most distinctive cloak, and set out here alone. The streets were empty since the entire population was up at the castle. I was – ah – set upon."

"Robbers?" I said without much hope.

"Strange robbers who stole nothing but were prepared to take the sort of punishment they got. Lest you think me immodest, let me explain that Martin and one of the others followed me, having heard that Osbern's men left the castle early too."

"They were Osbern's? I should never have given him that ribbon . . ."

"Well, he does seem to take his duties very seriously. There were men positioned all over the city, covering any route I could possibly take."

"You mean you were attacked *again*?"

"We rounded them all up in the end," he said casually. "And sent those that were left back to their master. Torfrida . . .?"

I frowned, trying not to think of the implications of *those that were left*. "Yes?"

He had halted, standing before the light that hung by the hall door, so that our faces were still in shadow.

He said, "One last kiss before you bring me out of the darkness . . ." He took it with, I have to say, considerable cooperation on my part. Then, reluctantly, determinedly, I led him inside. The hall was empty.

He paused, blinking in the sudden light, as I turned slowly to face him. His hair was tangled and matted with streaks of darkness, his swollen face blotched with dirt and bruises. There was a trickle of dried blood on his cheek, and more blood seeping through his sleeve.

Under my scrutiny, he gave an odd, lopsided smile. "Am I not a handsome fellow?" he said sardonically. "I did try to warn you."

"Oh Hereward, why did you not *truly* let Martin come instead?"

"And have missed this half-hour in your garden? Not for the world." His hand lifted, bruised and scarred, to touch my cheek, so lightly that I barely felt it. Yet my breath caught, for here in the light, his physical presence was more overwhelming than ever. He said, "Besides, I wanted to see your face again."

It was as if he said what he knew I wanted most to hear. My eyes fell. I led him to the cushioned bench nearest the dying fire, pressed him lightly into it, and unfastened his cloak. He watched me while I examined his hurts, even obligingly tore his shirt sleeve when I asked to see the wound in his arm. I had seen worse. It was, I thought, the blows to his head and sheer exhaustion that had made him dizzy. He would live. I had no anxiety on that score. Rather it was his intense, unblinking gaze upon me that was making me nervous.

Hiding it, I went to the door and called for Lise. I didn't need to; she was right there, waiting. I closed my mouth with the short syllable only half out.

"He is hurt," I said curtly. "Bring water and the salves."

"Send him to the kitchen, lady," she said indignantly. "It is not fitting for you to attend the servant—"

"It is not," I interrupted, "the servant."

"Oh." It was soundless. She almost jumped up to see over my shoulder. I said severely, "You could have looked at him more thoroughly, Lise. Are my parents still up?"

"The lady is abed. Your father *might* still be in his chamber, I don't know . . ."

"Fetch the salves," I said again and went back to my patient. He was sitting back on the cushions, his eyes closed. There was a frown on his brow, and that, together with the dirt and the bruises and the new lines of age and pain and experience brought a fresh rush of grief for the boy I had used to know.

I thought he was asleep, so I just looked and looked; until I realized his eyes were open – calm seas with the storms all blown out. Temporarily. I felt trapped, caught in my over-keen observation, and I could think of nothing to say.

He said lazily, "What are you looking for?"

"I don't know," I said truthfully. "I want to know where you have been, what you have done, how you come to be here . . ."

His lips curved. "I likewise," he said softly. And I felt so much gladness, it was an ache.

Fortunately, perhaps, Lise came in with the tray of salves and a water bowl and towels. Her eyes wide with curiosity, she managed several sidelong gawps at our guest. I didn't mind that. I did object to the giggle when, turning his head he caught her stare and smiled tolerantly.

"Lise," I said patiently; and she sobered at once and fled. I sat on the edge of his bench, soaked the cloth and began to bathe his face and head. For a little, he let me, then I felt his fingers close around my wrist.

"Torfrida. I can wash my own face. Be at peace."

"Don't be a baby," I said, and gazed into the strange eyes until his fingers released me. I think I was surprised. I may even have been disappointed, but at last I finished my task, cleaning his wounds, anointing them, binding his arm.

Towards the end, he seemed to lose interest, and just watched my face again. I finished tying the bandage.

"There," I said, just a little too briskly.

"Don't go away," he said when I stood up.

"I have to," I said lightly. "You put me out of countenance by staring."

"I can't help staring. I told you so before. Nor can I help congratulating myself for realizing all these years ago that you would be beautiful one day. Or reviling myself for a fool that I did not understand just *how* beautiful."

My eyes fell away from his again. "You don't have to say these things to me," I said awkwardly. "I may pluck my eyebrows these days, but I still have no need of flattery."

"Flattery is lies. I only ever speak the truth to you. If I make you uncomfortable, I'm sorry, but my head, my heart, is full of things I want to say to you."

My own heart turned over in my breast. I raised my eyes to his and he smiled slightly, holding out his less injured hand. I took it, sinking back down beside him.

I said, "Did you know me all along then? Was *that* your game?"

"Not all along," he said apologetically. "I was aware of some exotic creature watching me – while Asselin was clowning about – and when I could spare attention to look, and saw you, I was – lost. I had never – I have never – seen anything so lovely. All white skin and black hair and those enchantress's green eyes. And you were smiling at *me*. I could not believe my luck. And then you were surrounded by other men, taking you away from me. I could do nothing but follow."

"I felt hunted," I remembered.

"I *was* hunting. I could not let you out of my sight. And then, when I had caught you, you seemed to resent me for something. And those green eyes began to seem familiar to me. And there had to be a reason you would not tell me your name."

"Then you knew me on Constantine's ship?" I said indignantly.

He shrugged slightly. "Well, it confirmed what I already believed. I did play your game by all your rules. But no other woman looks at stars as you do."

My hand was carried to his lips again. I felt the persuasive tug, drawing me to him, and abruptly I was afraid again, pulling free and flitting away from him. In the darkness I had been all emotion, spirit, yearning; and so had he. Here, the unkind light of the lamps and candles made everything too real. *He* was too real, too strange, yet too tantalizingly reminiscent of the boy I had adored as a child. Too big, too *physical*.

I heard him say politely, "This is a handsome house."

"Thank you," I said, relief at the impersonal nature of the remark flooding me. "We had excellent craftsmen. And the lace cloths are English. The tapestries from France, mainly . . . The swords and shield upon the wall were my grandfather's, gifts from the Count when he was a young man."

He had risen, followed me to the hearth. Reaching above me, his fingers touched the sword-hilt, felt its blade.

"It is a fine weapon," he observed, apparently genuinely, but then his eyes dropped to mine and the thoughts there were not of swords or shields or handsome houses. His breath brushed my cheek; my own caught in my throat.

I ducked quickly under his arm. "Come. I'll show you the smaller hall. My mother and I use it to be private, or to entertain small numbers, close friends . . ."

Obediently, he followed me across the hall and through the inner door to the next. I was aware of his eyes and his head, moving, taking in his surroundings at last. I was glad. Suddenly it was very important that he understand my position, that I was someone; of my reasons for emphasizing this, or the dangers of doing so, I was at the time quite unaware.

I let him look. I pointed out things I thought would interest him, never pausing to look at *him*, or to sense the change in his mood.

When he picked up the golden dragon, I said eagerly, "If you like it, take it. Everything on that table is my own." It was on my mind, you see, that I had given him nothing but the ribbon in exchange for his own gifts. But I was unused to dalliance. Or to tact.

He laid the dragon down again with a faint air of deliberation.

Then, his eyes slowly lifting to mine as I stood beside him, he said, "Yes, Torfrida, I do take the point."

"What point?" I asked, genuinely surprised.

His eyebrows lifted. He said sardonically, "That you are rich and well-born, and immeasurably above me, even if I were still a noble land-owner, which I am not. I understand all that perfectly. All that eludes me is why the point is being made."

I blinked stupidly. "I don't understand."

"Oh come, Torfrida. Where is this much vaunted quickness of wit? All right, I'll spell it out for you. Am I being made aware of your mind-boggling superiority to show me that I need never think of marrying you? Or to remind me that next time I should bring a really spectacular present instead of those trinkets I so naively pressed upon you today?"

His fingers plucked the little pouch he had given me off my girdle, where it had been hanging, and threw it contemptuously on the floor. I felt my eyes widen uncontrollably with shock.

"What are you telling me, Torfrida?" he asked deliberately. "That I must buy you as a wife? Or just as a mistress, since I cannot aspire to your greatness?"

For three long beats of my heart, I could only stare up at him, stupefied. I had forgotten his dreadful tongue, his power to hurt. Then I felt the blood surge into my face as pride and sheer anger saved me from the gnawing shame sliding up from my toes.

"Your *wife?*" I uttered with loathing. "I cannot believe your conceit! I would as soon marry the lowliest soldier of your company! As for the rest, the truth is simple – *you disgust me!*"

He had turned casually back to the table while I ranted, his fingers picking up the dragon again, tossing it thoughtfully up and down in his palm. When I had finished, he glanced at me beatifically through his hair.

"I suppose then, that bedding you is out of the question? Yes, I thought so. Never mind. If I might trouble you to call back that pretty girl of yours to show me the way to my quarters, perhaps I can prevail upon her instead."

With one final toss of the dragon, he slid it into the purse at his belt, and grinned at me.

"For my time," he explained. "After all, I went to considerable trouble to get here."

The blood had drained from my head so fast that I could not speak. I felt kicked and trampled; for an instant, I actually wanted to die. My fingers gripped the table, just to stop myself falling over, and then I saw his eyes drop, observing it. At that, some pride, the pride that had begun this sudden nightmare, came back to my rescue.

Forcing my fingers to let go, I turned from him, walking steadily across the room.

"I shall send Lise to you," I said distantly, and closed the door behind me. I didn't think he had moved, but I was physically and mentally incapable of looking. In fact, it seemed doubtful that I could reach my own chamber without help.

The human body is amazing. It seemed I could. I did.

CHAPTER 20

I woke from a sleep that seemed like that of the dead, feeling still heavy, drained, quite unrested. The events of last night seemed now like a nightmare. Yet if I touched my lips, I could still feel his kisses; and there were streaks of blood, his blood, on the gown lying where I had cast it on the rushes.

On top of which, my deathly tired brain had been aware of some disturbance in the night. Of course, if *he* was here, there would be disturbance. What had he done? Insulted the servants? Fought with our men-at-arms? Broken *out* of the house with my grandfather's sword?

Abruptly, I leapt out of bed. I was dressed by the time Lise came in, wide-eyed and big with news. I wondered if he had truly prevailed upon her virtue; I wondered if he had truly had the strength.

"Have you heard?" she demanded, without explaining how I possibly could. "They tried to murder him in his bed!"

I paused, my hand still resting on the brush I had just laid down.

"Who? Who did?" I didn't even ask who the intended victim had been. There was no point.

"Some man of Osbern's. He broke in when he thought the Englishman was asleep and brought his axe down on the pillow. Only the Englishman was awake, and dived aside at the last moment, wrestling the man on to the bed. Then some of the Englishman's people were there too, though *I* never admitted them, and our own men at the last. It was a terrible to-do!"

I closed my eyes. "Does my father know?"

"Of course! He was there when they got the truth out of the murdering rascal and cut off his hand . . . ."

"Oh Jesus Christ and all His saints . . .!"

I was across the chamber and through the door, running, ignoring the servants I met on the way. Bursting at last into my father's chamber, the words were already tumbling off my lips."

"Father, this of last night has got to be . . . Oh!"

I broke off, for my father was regarding me mildly across his table. The figure seated opposite him turned its golden head in an interested sort of a way, and I saw they were playing chess.

Unbidden, unwanted and quite unexpected, the laughter fought its way up from my stomach and came out in a choke.

"My dear?" said my father, and I shook my head, wiping one slightly unsteady hand across my forehead.

"Nothing. Absolutely nothing. Forgive the intrusion."

And I closed the door again before flattening myself against the wall beside it and letting the laughter silently, convulsively out. Only when the tears began to pour with it, did I come back to myself and search out some greater privacy.

When Constantine came to say farewell, I felt it as another blow. He was returning to Salerno, to important employment with the Duke which would, he said, provide ample resources to write the treatises currently only in his head. I began to feel very lonely.

A week later, I attended the Count's banquet with the same determined pleasure I had brought to every other social event that month. Except that this time I actually expected the pleasure to be genuine, for Gilbert of Ghent was to be there, and Matilda. And, of course, so was William of Normandy, arrived on one of his lightning visits to his father-in-law, for reasons I could only guess at.

I wore red that day, deep, startling scarlet – and no jewellery at all to detract from the effect.

I saw Gilbert almost as soon as we entered the great banqueting hall, deep in conversation with Duke William himself, although a spontaneous smile broke out on his face when his eyes found me. When I was able to go to him, I was hugged with the sort of affection which had never existed between us in England.

"You are lovelier every time I see you!" he exclaimed. "So how is it you are never married?"

"Married, I would shrivel up like a damp rag under my husband's feet,"

I said lightly. "I have some vanity."

And then Matilda was there – Gilbert's wife, not William's – embracing me, introducing me to two tall young men, one so fair he was almost albino, the other with hair of a spiky, shocking orange. Dragging my dazzled eyes back to the former, I had little difficulty in recalling his name.

"Siward?" I hazarded, and the youth grinned, bowing with exaggerated courtliness.

"I bring you my mother's love, and my aunt's," he observed. "And mine. This is my cousin – on my father's side," he added dismissively. "He is called Siward too. They call us Red and White to distinguish us."

"I noticed when I was there, the English lack of imagination in names. Then, everybody was called Leofric."

"They still are," said Siward the White, skilfully drawing me away from the others. I chose to let him.

"And what brings you so far from home?" I enquired. "Do you seek fame and fortune in Flanders? Or service with the great man of Normandy, perhaps?"

Siward smiled. "My mother says you read the future in the stars. Do I have any with you?" The mischievous boy, I perceived, had become a somewhat over-confident youth.

"For you," I said tartly, "I prophesy a bad end and damnation to follow. For myself, I prefer the company of adults."

He looked slightly flummoxed at that, which was just what I had intended, so I turned to go back to Matilda, only vaguely conscious of the commotion arising at the door.

And then the other Siward was there, staring past me, demanding, "Who is that man?" I turned my head, my eyes weaving among the glittering throng, to find the source.

I should not have been surprised. But I had never expected to come across the English mercenary in this company. Yet there he was, large as life and twice as bright, swaggering in with a tail of men behind him, and that preposterous jewelled cloak hanging negligently from one shoulder. He was grinning, shouting some witty response to a friend in the company.

I turned away quickly as he made his obeisance to the Count. Then, becoming aware of both Siwards eyeing me enquiringly, with an effort, I remembered to speak.

"That?" I said carelessly. "That is the Count's English mercenary."

"Hereward," said a quiet voice thoughtfully behind me. I turned. William of Normandy was watching the Englishman, his eyes considering, his face unreadable.

"Hereward," Siward the White repeated softly, and I remembered the adoration of the boy for his uncle. I wondered what he thought of him now,

129

this gaudy, swaggering mercenary. And then, unexpectedly, Hereward's face jerked round, and I could swear his eyes actually met the Duke's.

Hereward. Dear God they – Matilda! – did not know! Had they seen him?

"Where is the lady Matilda?" I demanded, and they shrugged infuriatingly, looking about them vaguely as people do who do not really care about the answer. I left them abruptly, easing through people until I saw my mother with Gilbert; and some distance away, Matilda making her way towards them. And Hereward, coming the other way, from the Count, his eyes fixedly on Gilbert.

It was like one of those dreams when your legs just won't move fast enough, where your goal keeps retreating. But eventually I reached her, catching her arm.

"Matilda? Matilda, do you know he is here? Hereward?"

Her skin flushed. But her eyes came down to mine calm and clear. My hand fell away. I breathed, with relief. She knew. Or over the years she had learned to deal with it.

"Sir."

It was Hereward's voice, and it was spoken to Gilbert. He turned, a faint, interrogative smile on his lips, which fixed and slowly died as he looked at the young man before him.

He hadn't known. He hadn't known at all.

His lips formed one word, almost soundless. "You."

And suddenly Hereward was on his knees, in one of those startlingly swift, unconsciously graceful movements common to him since boyhood. He had Gilbert's hand, pressing it hard to his forehead. Then he raised his eyes, and spoke in Saxon.

"Forgive me."

"Oh get up, boy," Gilbert whispered. "Get up."

Hereward rose, not quite smiling. "I have made it difficult for you to repudiate me. I have always made it difficult for you."

"Oh you fool . . .! Why have you been so *silent*?"

Hereward spread his hands ruefully. "Look at me. Soldier of fortune, swaggart-in-chief. I am not a friend to be proud of."

Was that it? Was that really it? Was it the same proud reserve that had kept him from me? If so, how doubly tactless was my display of wealth that evening . . . Or was it merely that he could never work up much genuine interest in the plain child who had, occasionally, relieved the worst of his boredom ten years ago?

Gilbert embraced him. There was no doubt there, no loss of love, no possibility of repudiation. And over Gilbert's shoulder, he saw Matilda. Not me. I had moved aside.

Released, he came to her wordlessly, laid his hands lightly on her shoulders as he should, and kissed her lips. She bore it, smiling. Only I saw her eyes close at the touch of his mouth, and knew we still shared the same obsession. I supposed mine had always been as ridiculous as hers.

Gilbert said, "I don't suppose you recognize your nephew. And his cousin. They call themselves Siward the White and Siward the Red."

Hereward's fingers curled swiftly in shock. He could not help the quick movement towards the young men. But then, having looked, he made no effort to embrace them. Instead, he said in tones of casual amusement, "I won't ask which is which. Have you come to help William the Bastard kick Harold Godwinson out of England?"

"Hereward!" Matilda exclaimed, hushing him fiercely, ignoring, if she noticed it, his rudeness to his kinsmen. "Don't you know how he feels about that name?"

"Harold?" said Hereward innocently, but the storms were back in his eyes; they had brought back the storms. "Or Bastard? I don't care for either myself. When do you suppose one gets fed at these affairs?"

"Torfrida, take him in hand," Gilbert begged. "I hope you still can."

The violent eyes, full now of mocking laughter, came at last to me. He had known, he had always known I was there.

He said, "Oh she can. Either hand will do. The world knows I am at Torfrida's feet. Exquisite feet," he added, gazing admiringly at my toes. I tapped one significantly.

"Kicking feet," I corrected sweetly, and became aware of my mother's outrage. Hereward laughed.

Matilda said severely, "Ignore them, Joanna. The scenes these two can cause would curl your hair."

"Oh no," I assured her. "*I* am quite grown up now."

I wanted to know, I needed to know, if he had meant the things he had said to me. *Which* of them he had meant. Nothing had ever seemed so intolerable as all those people between us, or the fact that I was forced to walk away from him without one meaningful word. To sit and smile and talk and eat and eat and eat.

The feast was finished before I saw my chance and took it. He left the main hall whistling casually, as if in some barracks, his rich, silken tunic having falling open at the throat as the wine went down and the formality of the occasion relaxed.

Excusing myself to Matilda, I followed him. There was only one door off that passage, and it was open, revealing a bare chamber with damp walls, containing a rough looking table and one stool.

Only Hereward was there, gazing out of the slit window at the gathering dusk. He was humming to himself, swinging constantly from side to side as if he could not bear to be still. Torchlight from the bracket above his head lit up his hair like a beacon.

131

Hearing me, he turned. The song cut off as if by a knife. I knew at once I was unexpected.

"Torfrida. Are you looking for me or passing by?"

"For you," I said honestly

"You want to marry me after all?" he said insolently, taking a flask from his belt and unstopping it.

"No!"

He took a gulp from the flask and laughed. "Just as well. Like as not I'd be dead by Christmas, like poor old Rob."

I gasped at that, because there was no need for it, just no need. It wasn't only the implicit accusation that I had driven Robert to death, it was the upsurge of my old, very real grief. Stricken, I stared at him. He lowered the flask. And oddly, what I could see in his eyes was defiance.

I could do nothing with him. I should never have tried.

Again, I swung away from him. It seemed I was always turning away from him. And that was when Duke William walked into the room. He halted at sight of me. Hereward, it appeared, was not unexpected.

"Ah," he said interrogatively. "A previous engagement?"

"A future one," said Hereward obscurely, and laughed. "Don't mind Torfrida. She was only passing after all."

William shrugged. "I don't, if you don't," he said, inevitably missing the point, and came further into the room. But I found I was rooted to the spot; I itched physically for my charts and tables; and then, relieved that I could still think beyond what he said to me, I settled down to eavesdrop.

"You are a man of action," William said abruptly, "as am I; so I will come straight to the point. I intend, as the world knows, to take the crown of England which was promised to me. For this, I need as many good, experienced men as I can muster. Of you, and yours, I hear nothing but good.

"Rumour is sometimes too kind," Hereward said, but courteously now, as he had once faced Leofric of Mercia. Respect, I thought. William had his respect, whatever outrageous banter he had come out with earlier.

The Duke said drily, "My father-in-law, however, is not. He is prepared to release you to me at your request. The risks of my venture are great; the rewards of success much greater. Will you come?"

Hereward was looking at him directly, unblinkingly. At last his eyes fell. He moved, again as if he could not keep still, walking across the floor, three paces, four. Then he turned and looked again at the Duke.

"It is a flattering offer, courteously made; and I thank you for it. In other circumstances I would be glad of the honour to serve you."

"Other circumstances?" said William quickly. "You mean you balk at invading England? And yet I heard that they exiled you, and that your family regard Harold Godwinson as the enemy."

"My family regard *me* as the enemy. They are confused," said Hereward cynically. "The point is, I am promised to Count Baldwin this year and next. And though he has offered to release me, I could not in honour ask him to do so."

William looked at him closely. "Your godfather, Gilbert de Ghent, is coming with me."

Hereward's eyes flickered. "I thought he might. I wish him all success."

"Then you will not change your mind?"

Again, his eyes fell. "Don't ask it of me. I can't."

Before I could properly grasp the simple honesty of those curt words, another voice was speaking from the doorway.

"Why not?" said Earl Tostig. Really this little room was overcrowded now . . . "Afraid of my brother?"

Hereward looked at him and actually laughed. "Not so afraid as you are. When I do go, I won't need a Viking fleet to protect me."

Tostig blanched, his eyes flickering to William and away.

"Thank you," said the Duke softly.

"Don't mention it," said Hereward. "I throw it your way as a gift, in case nobody else has done so. But I doubt it will make much difference to the final outcome. You see, Torfrida? We all dabble in the future. Come, let us return to the jollity, and leave this family squabble – er – council . . ."

"You will hang," I said positively as he pushed me out of the door, "at the very least."

"But not for a long – a very long – time," he promised. "Was there anything else, or can I go back to drinking myself under the table?"

"Did you ever stop?" I enquired politely, indicating the flask at his belt.

"Thank you," he said, apparently pleased to be reminded of its existence, and lifted it to his lips. I turned away yet again.

"I know," his voice followed me with mock soulfulness. "I disgust you."

That made me pause, because he had brought it up again. Because I knew, now, that it had rankled. And because, after all, I still knew him.

"Perhaps," I agreed, without looking. "But that isn't the problem, is it, Hereward? You disgust yourself."

And I walked in stately silence back into the hall. Almost, I expected a rude belch to blow me in the door. But there was nothing. Perhaps he had grown up too.

Oddly, Gilbert's was the first face I recognized as I made my way through the hall, among the dancers and the increasingly lively revellers. I thought it was probably time to go home.

"Torfrida? Did you see Hereward out there?"

"He was in the passage," I said calmly. "Why?"

133

"Is he all right?"

"He was drinking," I said wryly.

Gilbert sighed. "I had better go to him."

"I shouldn't. He seemed quite intent on falling over."

"He would do," said Gilbert grimly, with just a hint of reproach in his eyes. "You see, I just gave him the news that his father is dead."

CHAPTER 21

"He's here again," said my mother, sinking on to the bench beside me. She had bearded me in the garden where I had been ensconced for hours, busily drawing up charts and frowning over the possible interpretations. Mostly impersonal ones. They involved Duke William and Earl Tostig and Harold of England. And Hereward, a little. Of course.

"Who is here?" I asked, without interest, pulling ungently at the rolls squashed under her careless rear. She shifted impatiently.

"What is all this stuff anyway? What are you about now? Why can you not marry and have children like normal girls? Your father has indulged you far too much in this matter, and so I have told him. Many times."

"Have you finished?" I asked, replacing the papers on my other side.

She sniffed. "Of course I have. There is no point in saying *anything* to you. The mercenary."

I blinked. "What about him? *Which* mercenary?" I added belatedly.

"Harold, of course. Hereward. Whatever his heathen name is. He is here."

I laid down my pen slowly. "Is he? Why?"

"God knows. He is with your father."

"They play chess," I said as much to myself as to her. "Or did. Once."

I thought about it as carefully as I could. I owed him – and I owed old Leofric who had been my unlikely friend in the end – a debt of apology. And I was not, of course, averse to another battle of wills in my father's protective presence.

I stood up. "I believe," I said firmly, "I will just go in and offer them some wine."

"And cakes?" said my mother sarcastically.

"And cakes," I agreed pacifically, and went.

I think she actually snorted.

They were not playing chess. My father was sitting behind his table, nodding thoughtfully as if to himself. Hereward stood by the window, all flowing silk and gold armbands, and the incongruously clanking belts of weapons at his hip. Though his fathomless eyes were now on me, I thought he had been watching my father. Certainly I had heard his voice talking as I approached the door.

"Ah," said Hereward blandly when I went in. "Ganymede in a frock."

My father blinked slightly, though whether at this mode of greeting or at my chosen task I was not perfectly sure.

"Don't we have servants any more?" he asked with unusual irritability.

"Lise," said Hereward provokingly. "Pretty brunette."

I said calmly, "She had hysterics when I asked her to do it. She was afraid of ravishment." My father choked. I patted him kindly on the back. "Let me pour you some wine."

Hereward said, "Well, she needn't fear it of me, not any more."

"No?" I said politely. "You have, perhaps, taken a vow of celibacy?"

"Almost," said Hereward surprisingly. "I have made an offer of marriage." He smiled at me, so dazzlingly it could have deprived the unwary of breath. "For you."

The wine slopped over the cup's edge, onto the silver tray, onto my father's table. I stared at it stupidly, till Hereward's fingers took the cup from me.

"Let me," he said, and I backed away from him as if he had offered me violence.

"Why?" I said.

"Torfrida!" exclaimed my father. "Your behaviour gets odder and odder! What is the matter with you? Go away and cast his horoscope – we'll let him dispute it later."

"Is that how she does it?" Hereward asked, apparently vastly entertained. "So it was the stars that did for poor old Asselin? And Osbern and Bauduin and Albert and all the others?"

I felt my eyes dilate. I was actually frightened. I panted. "You have been busy!"

"I told you," he said carelessly, following me to give me a cup of wine. "I always out-think the opposition."

"I am not playing this game!" I cried wildly. "*Why are you doing this, Hereward?*"

Accusation as well as pleading must have been spitting out of my eyes, but although I held his gaze, I could not even be sure I held his attention, let alone his understanding. Then he reached out and took my hand, and I wondered desperately if there was hope after all. In front of my father's eyes, he raised my fingers to his lips and kissed them, before wrapping them around the cup and holding them there.

"Why?" he said softly. "Because the world knows I am at your feet."

It was too soft, too bland, and it gave me an instant's warning. One eye shut, he leaned just a little closer, and whispered, "And because I want your lands, and your riches, and your beautiful golden dragon."

I gasped. My hand jerked, as if of its own accord, to throw the wine in his face. But he was prepared for that; it was why he was still holding my fingers around the cup, so steadily that the liquid barely slopped to the brim.

"Don't," he said. "You'll shock your father."

"I won't do it, Hereward."

"Why not? You would have done it for Rob. In the end."

"For Robert, yes. Not for you. Never for you."

He only smiled. "You say it with too much excitement," he mocked. "Remember, unlike Robert, I have held you in my arms."

He might as well have been doing so again; God knew he was close enough.

"That doesn't matter," I said wildly, seeking desperately for ammunition. With a gasp of relief, I found it. "Go home, Hereward. Leave me alone and go home. Because it is not my lands you want, is it? It's your own. Go home; be with your mother; and *grieve for your father.*"

His eyes had stopped mocking. They had gone black. For a moment he was still, perfectly still. Then his fingers loosened on mine and the wine slopped after all on the floor. Because I was trembling. And sorry.

"As I do," I whispered. "As I do."

He swung away from me before I could see anything else. I had invaded. I was intolerable. Well, good; then he would force this no further . . .

My father said anxiously, "Has she agreed?"

There was a pause. Surely, surely it was going on too long . . .?

Then Hereward said lightly, "It doesn't matter. You have." He picked up the other two cups and gave one to my father before turning and smiling back into my eyes. "A toast," he said blandly. "To our future wealth. And happiness, of course."

And drank.

He had a way, he always had a way, of depriving one of breath. When I had got mine back, I walked across the room to the jug, and deliberately poured my wine back into it.

"On this occasion," I said to my astounded parent, "I have no need of astrology. I will not marry Hereward. No, and no, and no."

And I walked out of the room, not even troubling to close the door behind me.

Over the next few days it seemed the whole of Bruges beat its way to our hall to offer felicitations on my very odd betrothal. My mother took to receiving them in stony silence, my father with smiling complaisance only just touched by nervousness when he caught sight of me. Needless to say, my own denials were treated with infuriatingly arch disbelief.

The last straw was when Gilbert and Matilda came. And Matilda was smiling the fixed smile I had not seen aimed at me since our carriage had tumbled down a Northumbrian hillside.

"Brave Torfrida!" Gilbert grinned openly. "So you have finally taken on my gracelessI said tiredly, "No. No, I have not."

My father said quickly, "I rather think it is Hereward who has his work cut out in husbanding my daughter."

"They were always well matched in respect of trouble," Gilbert recalled, amusement glinting and slowly dying in his eyes. "I know one thing, though: Robert would approve."

This was intolerable.

"No!" I said harshly, springing up from my stool and beginning to pace the room like some caged beast; like him. "No, he would not approve! You are all mistaken in this – there will be no marriage between Hereward and me. It is just some tasteless joke he has put about for his own amusement . . ."

Gilbert blinked. "Even for Hereward, that would be rather too much! What is this secrecy of yours? Are you afraid *we* will not approve? When you know we have arranged other matches for our sons? We do wish you well, Torfrida."

"Yes," said Matilda with difficulty. "We wish you well."

I looked at her helplessly; and cursed him over and over. When they had gone, I went at once to my chamber. Lise was there, sewing.

I said tightly, "This has gone far enough. Bring him to me, Lise. Now."

She must have been gone an hour, perhaps two. During all that time I never moved, until at last I heard the door open and leapt to my feet.

"Is he here?" I demanded. "Where is he? What did he say?"

Lise said flatly, "I couldn't deliver your message, lady. He left this morning. Something to do with horses – the Count's business."

"It had better be," I said viciously, and hurled my pillow to the floor.

There was nowhere I could go, nothing I could do to escape it. I did not even consult the stars. There seemed no point. At last I sat down and wrote to him. I hoped he would trouble to read it himself, for it was not the sort of letter one would want read by clerks or anyone else. I expressed myself clearly and forcibly, stating quite categorically that even supposing it got as far as the church porch, I would still refuse him.

I was clever. I took it to the Count himself to be delivered, and the Count, indulgent and arch in the belief that he was relaying a love-letter, happily obliged.

After that I cheered up a little, for there was nothing else to do until I had some reply from him. It never came. But I realized the preparations for the wedding were proceeding to the degree that even my mother was treacherously organizing things to her better liking.

Discovering her in close confabulation with several cooks on the subject of wedding feasts, I stormed into my father's chamber – fortunately unbolted – and turned out the poor clerk who was there with him.

My father permitted it, but as usual he remained calm under my furious gaze.

"Where," I demanded, "is Hereward?"

"He has not yet returned . . ."

"Have you heard from him? Recently?"

"But the other day. He is busy, but will still manage to return in time for the wedding. In fact, he said nothing could keep him from it."

"Oh this is miserable!" I burst out in a stifled sort of a way, throwing myself into the chair opposite him. "Father, I *will* not, I *cannot* do this. Why do you force me to it?"

He smiled, just a touch ruefully. "For your own good, my dear."

"My *good?*" I stared at him. "But . . . can't you see you are ruining both of us by this?"

He looked startled, as well he might. "Ruin? Torfrida, what *is* this?"

"I have told you."

"No." He stood up, coming round the table to peer at me more closely. "I am your father," he observed. "And I know you. I have waited a long time to see you look at a man as you look at Hereward. I want this chance of happiness for you."

"There will be no happiness from this." My voice was small and bleak.

"Yet you are not indifferent, Torfrida; you cannot pretend that."

I closed my eyes. "It is not," I said carefully, "my indifference which matters in this."

When I opened my eyes again, I found him staring at me. "You believe *he* is indifferent?"

"Not to my wealth. That is what will ruin him. Between us, we are leaving him no honour."

"No honour?" My father's mouth fell open and closed again on his convulsive swallow. "No honour in marrying *you?*"

"Oh, you do not understand!"

"No, I don't," he said frankly. "And I don't think you do either. Trust me, Torfrida: it is for the best."

I stared at him. I was running out of time. The wedding was barely three days away. For the first time, I let the possibility of actually reaching the ceremony enter my head. I tried to imagine my stark refusal in the church porch, and what would happen afterwards; but for once I had no answers.

And then I remembered Constantine, and Osbern de St Walericus.

CHAPTER 22

I rose before dawn – which was easy because I had not slept all night – dressed myself and crept across to the kitchens, where I stepped over the recumbent bodies until I found Lise wrapped in the arms of the muscular servitor who was her latest conquest. Very rarely did she sleep in my quarters.

I shook her urgently. The servitor groaned. Lise sat up with a jolt.

"Hush," I said as her mouth opened. Taking her hand, I put the letter into it. "You will tell my mother, should she ask, that I have gone out for the day and that I shall return for supper. You don't know where I have gone. You will give them this in the evening – *not before*. Do you understand?"

She gave several nods, talking urgently at the same time. "But lady, where *are* you going? May I not come with you?"

I smiled slightly at that, touched by this rare evidence of devotion.

"No," I said, more gently. "No, but you may take whatever you wish from my chamber. That is in the letter too."

"Lady, wait!" she wailed, at the finality of that, I suppose. "Are you not coming back?"

"One day," I said lightly. "Take care, Lise."

And I left quickly, closing the door on her frightened face with some relief.

Osbern's carriage, cumbersome and hardly new, stood as arranged by the church at the corner of the street. A dull but villainous looking individual in a large, floppy hat held the reins. Osbern himself stood by the door, the hood of his cloak preserving his identity from all who did not know him well. And four men-at-arms stood ready to escort us.

Wordlessly, Osbern handed me into the carriage, gave a brief word of instruction to the driver, and followed me inside. Then we were moving, and I could not quite believe I had done it. I had run away. I was going to Salerno to seek Constantine's help, to see the world without constrictions of family, or betrothal or any of the irritating conventions which had always tried to hem me in.

So why did I only feel sad and dreary? The knot in my stomach that should have been excitement at the start of my greatest adventure, I knew now was only grief. And I had the horrible feeling it would only grow larger and deeper and much, much sharper.

It was a bumpy journey. As soon as we were well clear of Bruges, I thought, I would ride in the open. That would cheer me up.

In the meantime we breakfasted on what Osbern had brought with him, and bumped and trundled our way through the marshy forests outside the city. I was glad of all the hours before dinnertime, to put distance between us and Bruges.

Conversation was not lively. I had nothing to say, and Osbern seldom did, so mostly I sat with my eyes shut trying to think of philosophical and astronomical things. Osbern gazed out of the window or down at his feet. Before mid-day, I think he was asleep.

Certainly the morning passed without greater incident than odd encounters with passers-by, all of which were taken care of by Osbern's men – even the slight contretemps with the peasant demanding right of way for his cart. There may even have been a brief fight then, for the carriage was thumped once, making it rock precariously enough for me to open my eyes. But then it moved forward again and all was quiet.

An hour or so after mid-day, we trundled through a village of some size. I opened my eyes and saw a man in leather trousers chopping wood while chickens ran and clucked about his feet. Two boys ran past the carriage, yelling, while two wrinkled women tutted in the doorway of a sunken hut. On the other side, a blacksmith was at work at his forge.

"This seems a big place," I remarked idly. "Where is it?"

"St. Walericus," said Osbern. He was looking at me; I had the impression he had been doing so for some time, and the thought made me unaccountably uncomfortable.

Surprised, I said, "I did not know our road went through St Walericus . . . Osbern, you do not intend to go to your grandfather? He will detain us for sure until my parents arrive!"

"Oh, don't worry, we shan't go near the old crow; but I need a decent meal and you must be hungry yourself. My own quarters are private enough . . ." So saying, ignoring my denials of hunger or discomfort, he leaned out of the window and shouted. A moment later the carriage came to a halt outside one of many buildings within a stockade. What looked to be the main hall was some distance away, but the yards were busy with people hurrying about their business, many glancing across at us though none paused for a thoroughgoing stare.

"Is this wise?" I said uncomfortably. "We do not wish to be seen, not yet . . ."

"They are my people," he said casually.

"They are your grandfather's people," I said significantly.

He only smiled and repeated, "Mine." He was already moving, opening the door and jumping down. It came to me, with uncharacteristically craven instincts, that I would prefer to wait here. But, forcing myself, I rose and took his hand to be helped into the mud.

The men-at-arms sat motionless upon their mounts, staring straight ahead. I wondered what misconceptions they had of this scene, and if I had been given to blushing, I would have blushed. As it was, I lifted my head a little superciliously, though I could not help the nervous flicker of my eyes. The villainous driver tipped his great, filthy hat to me. Under it, his face looked as black as Constantine's.

Osbern glanced at no one, except me. Keeping hold of my hand, although I made one effort to withdraw it, he led me across the mud and into the house. Behind us, a flurry of activity spoke of dismounting soldiers and feeding horses.

At first glance, Osbern's quarters were not even clean, but a respectable enough servant bowed us quickly through the outer mess of fallen cups and flasks and old dinners into a chamber beyond, and that was better. A table was carefully set with food and wine and two high-backed chairs. Osbern, it seemed, was used to taking his meals in private. I wondered how many women had been here before me, and wished he had shown me just a little more tact.

However, I let him remove the cloak from my shoulders and lead me to the table. As if sensing my unease, he said smoothly, "You see, I am prepared for your comfort."

"You are very kind to me," I said contritely, because try as I might, I could not make myself grateful for it. He held the chair for me and I sat. He sat in the chair opposite and, since no servants appeared, served me himself. Then, tucking in with some fervour, while I toyed with bread and chicken wings and cheese, he spoke with his mouth full.

"You know, I think it is time you considered your position, Torfrida. And your future."

"What do you mean?" I said, frowning. "I *have* considered it. It is why I am here."

"With me," he observed, swallowing the last of his mouthful.

"With you," I agreed warily, and he sat back for a moment.

"It won't do, you know," he said gently. "You cannot go all the way to Salerno in company with a man to whom you are not married, nor even distantly related."

"I shall hire a girl when we have left Flanders," I explained, for I had worked all this out earlier.

"Too little too late. Don't you care for your reputation at all?"

Head on one side, I considered it quite seriously. "I suppose I would mind if no one ever spoke to me again, and the Church excommunicated me, but since I don't think either of these catastrophes will befall me – no, I don't really think I do."

He smiled. "You are a glorious creature," he remarked.

"I am a desperate one," I said ruefully.

"Come here."

I blinked. His eyes had narrowed, his lids grown oddly heavy. Warning bells, belatedly, were beginning to sound inside my head. I started to wonder if I was quite so much in command of him as I had assumed. On top of which, remembering his occasional lunges of the past, a little wariness was clearly called for.

I said tartly, "I can converse with you well enough from here."

But his face had changed. The side of him he had always kept hidden from me was struggling to get out. With just the hint of a sneer, he said, "It was not conversation I had in mind. I cannot wait for the loving cup . . ."

And suddenly he had leapt round the table, pulling me to my feet against him.

"If you care nothing for your reputation, why, I do! Love me now, and I will marry you in the morning. By sunset tomorrow we can be back in Bruges, and no one, not even the English man, can take you, or deny me . . ."

I could feel his lips, wet and rough on my neck, and even as my brain grasped his treachery and my own muddled foolishness, I remember wondering how I had ever *liked* his touch. It was clumsy, clammy, revolting to me and, as he searched, panting, for my mouth, I decided, for once, to forego my dignity.

A sharp slap on the head, coinciding with a rather nastier kick in the shin, brought him back to himself quite vocally.

Shaking myself free, I said contemptuously, "Thank you for your trouble. I shall go myself to Salerno."

But he was angry. I had never seen his anger directed at me before and it was, I suppose, quite impressive – all snarling lips and flashing eyes.

"You?" he uttered, reaching for me again. "I don't think so! You imagine yourself so clever, but you are too naive even to get out of Bruges in one piece! Without me, what do you imagine would happen to you? Forget it! You go nowhere that I do not choose to let you. You put yourself in my hands, and there you stay!"

"And make you my father's heir?" I said with revulsion. "I would as soon be known to the world as your cast-off trollop!"

That did not help. I was seized convulsively into his arms again.

Between his teeth, he said, "I have said I will marry you. There is no question of anything else."

"Of course not," I said with contempt. "My father is a rich man. If I wished to be married for such a reason, I would marry Hereward. My mind, as you pointed out, is set on loftier planes. Let me go."

"Never," he said, with the sort of fervent exaggeration that would have been funny if it were not accompanied by a rather frightening strength. "It is time you learned who is master here . . ."

Inevitably, it was an unequal struggle. I could hurt him, but I could not stop him, and the result was never really in question. But from pride – and sheer animal fear following closely on its heels – I fought hard, refusing to give up, praying for some outside intervention to give me new opportunity.

I remember, kicking and biting, grimly forcing the fear back. Even then the cool, thinking part of my brain that was never quite silent, knew I could not do so for ever, but in the end I didn't have to. I don't think it had actually gone on for very long before a loud voice spoke vacantly, somewhere in the room.

"Horse is lame," it uttered in guttural Flemish.

Over Osbern's arm, which I was biting, I saw a large, dirty hat, and then I was released so quickly I nearly fell over; certainly it detached my teeth from Osbern's arm, somewhat painfully for both of us, I suspect.

I heard Osbern swear. He was striding towards the carriage-driver, saying savagely, "Get out, imbecile, till you are called!"

"Call now," said the hat, and hit him, so unexpectedly and so hard that he fell over.

I felt my eyes widen with the shock of that, but already edging towards the window and escape, I did not really have either the time or the inclination to sort out insubordinate servants – not on anyone's behalf, and certainly not on Osbern's.

The hat loomed over his recumbent body, and laughed. Then it said in Saxon, "Use the door, Torfrida. That is what it's for."

And my eyes closed. For a second, several seconds, all I could hear was the beat of my own heart. I did not even wonder how it was possible. Like everything else concerning him, it just seemed, suddenly, inevitable.

Why was I even trying to fight this marriage?

"Now would probably be a good time," said Hereward, and my eyes snapped open to see him walking quickly towards me. "This place is crawling with his people."

"No," I panted, as he seized me by the hand, pulling me urgently across the floor.

"No?" He let me go at once, and pushed at Osbern ungently with his toe. "Stay here then, and be raped by that. He shouldn't take long to wake up. But the choice is, as always, your own."

He went forward without even looking at me. But he held the door open as if he knew perfectly well that I would go through it before him. I did. I held my head high but I felt about three years old, and naughty.

I walked swiftly across the outer chamber, ignoring the gawps of the two servants sprawling there in the straw, aware only of Hereward shambling after me. He said something, leeringly, to the girl we encountered at the door, making her laugh.

Then the fresh air hit me, almost like a slap. The carriage was waiting where it had been left – but so were the men-at-arms. Bewildered, I wondered where Osbern had planned to take me after this – to a tame priest? I stopped dead, trying rather wildly to think what to do; and then Hereward was in front of me, bowing me grotesquely towards the carriage.

"This way, lady. Mind the puddles and turds now."

Laughter, unexpected and unwanted, sprang up from my stomach, and was squashed. Leeringly, he handed me up to the carriage.

I said breathlessly – because the laughter had not quite gone away – "You have an unlikely gift for mummery."

"Thank you."

"But what," I asked pointedly, "are you going to do about the soldiers? Send them inside to tend Osbern's head?"

He looked surprised. "Take them with us," he said, and closed the door on me.

He did take them, without any argument. We drove off, in fact, as we had come; back the same way, through the village and the trees beyond, and on, and on, leaving my poor brain seething with speculation and self-recriminations. And fear of what he was doing. What he *would* do.

When the carriage stopped at last, I was still trembling. We were at a crossroads. I knew it. The north road led to Bruges. Did that mean he was really taking me home? I had two other possible routes to contend with . . .

The door opened and Hereward stood there. When I looked at him – haughtily, I hoped – he removed the filthy hat – grudgingly, it seemed to my over-sensitive observations.

I swallowed. "Where are you taking me?"

The eyebrows twitched. "I'm not taking you anywhere. Someone else will. Home," he added mockingly, as if I had still looked unsure. "My men have to take the carriage," he said pointedly.

I rose wordlessly, and jumped down without his aid. Two of the men had dismounted, and one, laughing at some quip of his friend's, was climbing up to the box-seat.

"Your men," I said stupidly.

"A change of personnel," he said blandly.

My eyes widened, remembering. "The cart," I blurted. "Blocking the road . . ."

"You have quick wits," he approved. "Just not quick enough. Osbern indeed: could you not have picked me a worthier opponent?"

I ignored that. "And you – were you there – here – all the time?"

"Oh no, I arrived with the rest. But I liked that fellow's hat so much I had to have it. Would you like it? As yet another token of my esteem?"

"No," I said baldly, and he laughed, already walking away from me. I stared at the broad, casual back, the easily held, powerful shoulders. Humiliated beyond belief, I said in a stifled voice, "You would have driven me all the way to Salerno? With him?"

"Hardly," said Hereward, and his contempt cut into me like a knife. "Were you content with your sorry lot, I'd just have passed on the hat to another. Your value is high, my sweet, but not beyond price."

He was walking again, tossing me aside. I felt flattened, and yet I stayed him, because I had to know. "Hereward? How . . .?"

This time, he did actually deign to glance back at me, but quizzically, refusing to help. His face was still black with dirt. I wished it hid his beauty more. And I saw suddenly that he was tired, deathly tired to the point of exhaustion, worse even than on the night he had come to the garden.

I swallowed. "How did you know?"

"You left a letter," he said, surprised.

"But Lise was not to give it to them before this evening!"

"She didn't. She gave it to me." I closed my mouth. "I asked for it," he said kindly, "when I called upon my betrothed – having ridden all night without pause, I assure you – and discovered her absence. I hope you are grateful?"

Suddenly I just wanted to cry. But I wouldn't. I looked him straight in the eye, and saw, belatedly, the storms beneath the banter and the exhaustion. He was angry.

The discovery threw me. Why was he angry? Because I had preferred Osbern? Because I had tried to humiliate him? Or just because I had obliged him to turn out and rescue me when he had wanted only to relax and drink with his friends after an arduous campaign?

And why had he ridden all night to see me? Was that true, or just mockery? And dear God, I could not afford to pity him now . . .

"Grateful?" I repeated scornfully. "For a necessary evil? It was your own face you saved. Or think you did. As for myself – don't you have a saying in England? Out of the fat . . .?"

He smiled, an angelic, wintry smile. "But I have not dropped you in the fire. Yet. Till the wedding, my sweet. Unless I choose to see you before . . ."

And he strode off, leaping lightly into the saddle of the nearest horse. The horse wheeled round. Golden hair whipped across his face as he rode off into the woods at a gallop. The carriage lumbered after him more slowly.

The two men left with me waited at some distance, looking expressionlessly along the northern road. I followed their gaze because there was nothing else to do. I felt as if I had been punched when I was already down, already dying. I had never felt so alone, not since I had been twelve years old and sent away to England to marry a despised stranger . . .

A group of riders was coming along the road towards us. Men-at-arms, servants, and a lady. I peered, shading my eyes against the sun. Now I thought I would really weep.

It was Matilda. He had brought me Matilda.

CHAPTER 23

There was no great rejoicing at my return. No one understood that I had meant to go. My mother was just irritated that I had not said I was going to be with Matilda. And Matilda herself asked me nothing. Her eyes probed, understanding that I had been in trouble, but tactfully she refrained from demanding the details. It was enough for her that I was clearly unhurt.

Clearly.

Only Lise – with an expression so ludicrously combining joy and guilt that I would have laughed if I had been able – seemed likely for a moment to give the game away. But in the end, she was uncharacteristically silent too.

So, I ate my supper and writhed inside, and went early to bed, throwing Lise out before she had even closed the shutters. I needed the air and the sheer largeness of the sky in order to stay sane inside my own tiny, all-consuming problem. So I lay awake and stared at the ceiling until it was dark.

But I could not even see the moon from where I lay, and the other stars were obscured by cloud. Everything was conspiring against me.

Turning my face to the wall, I wondered quite seriously about running away on my own. I had enough money, enough things to sell, so that I could live on my own in France, or Germany, perhaps. I could pretend to be a widow . . .

It was not a loud noise, just a gentle brushing sound, like leaves blowing against the shutters. Only the shutters were open.

My head jerked round. I sat up with a gasp to see the figure of a man sitting on my window-sill.

"Hallo," said Hereward easily. "Don't cry out or you'll spoil everything. Is there a lamp?"

I was lighting it already. The shock kept my fingers steady enough. Only when it was done, and I fell back against the pillows, pulling the covers up over my chemise, did I start to tremble.

Hereward, dressed now in some old but clean dark tunic, without even a cloak, walked across the chamber towards me. For once, he wore no sword; I only saw his purse and a gold-hilted dagger at his belt. The shadows were still there around his eyes, but they seemed less intrusive, as if he had slept or at least rested. He was lucky. I thought I would never sleep again.

I said aggressively, "Spoil what? What do you want? Have you come to claim what you fondly imagine to be your pre-conjugal rights?"

"Are they on offer?" he asked interestedly, coming to a halt beside my bed and looking down at me with raised eyebrows. I curled my lip. "No, I thought not. I understand you want to talk to me."

I blinked at that.

"Awe-inspiring," I marvelled. "Messages to you only take three weeks."

"It took three days," he said apologetically. "But I was up to my ears in blood. Not my own, before your wifely concern impresses by its absence."

"Am I supposed to be grateful that you came at all?"

"I doubt it," he said, sitting casually on the bed. I moved distastefully as far away from him as I could get. He smiled beatifically. "Well?" he prompted.

"I believe," I said frostily, "that I put it all in the letter."

"Did you? You must forgive my not replying." He shifted position uncomfortably, then stood up. "What do you keep in this bed? Apples?"

"Stones," I said. "To beat intruders."

I actually saw his lips curve slightly at that, and had time to realize, rather wildly, how peculiar this encounter was, in terms of just about everything. But he was walking again, idly looking about the chamber.

"This is better," he approved.

"Better than what?"

He shrugged. "Your treasure halls. This is more like you. Bookish, but pretty. And definitely weird. I have come," he added, turning amiably back to me, "to make you a rather different offer."

I blinked again, struggling with the confusion his presence and his manner were managing to reduce me to. Then, as he began to move back to the bed, I frowned.

"In the light of the day's event's, you wish to downgrade your offer to exclude the respectability of marriage?" I said lightly, yet with more than a hint of suspicion. "My father would not buy it."

"Would you?"

"I didn't even buy the other one. I'm tired, Hereward. Make your offer and leave."

It had struck me by then, you see, that he was in fact, avoiding the point of his outrageous visit. I did not truly fear for my virtue, but I *was* somewhat uneasy; because, in spite of his shocking casualness, *he* was.

Under my frowning gaze, he folded his legs, gracefully, like a horse, and sat on the rushes beside the bed, knees up, his back resting against the wall. He took something from his purse.

"Do you want a cherry?"

"Hereward . . .!"

He put one in his mouth and smiled at me, as if he was teasing. He wasn't though, not quite.

"All right." He swallowed the cherry and removed the pip, lifting his eyes at last to mine. "Answer me this, Torfrida: do you want to marry me?"

I closed my mouth. It was difficult under that gaze, but I managed it. "How many different ways do I have to say it?"

"Oh I know what you *say*. Sometimes I even know why you say it. What I want to know now is what you *feel*, what the truth actually is. Do you want to marry me?"

I felt my tongue licking at my dry lips, and stopped it.

At last, I said tensely, "And if I don't? Truthfully?"

He shrugged, eating another cherry. "Then I'll cry off."

There was another pause. This time I had no clue how to fill it, and he did not seem inclined to help me. He blew the cherry stone out of his mouth into the air, and caught it in one hand. He seemed pleased.

I said, "Why?"

"Well, I was thinking," he said, reaching for another cherry, "and I came to the conclusion that a reluctant bride was probably worse than no bride at all. Even if she was disgustingly wealthy. So, if you want me, I'll marry you. If you don't, I'll cry off."

"*You'll* cry off?" Did I actually sound indignant?

"Well," he said reasonably. "Your efforts to do so were hardly marked by a high degree of success."

I leaned forward, staring at him to see, I think, if he meant it. He met my gaze steadily, peacefully. I could see no storms in his eyes, yet for some reason I was sure they were there. Over the years he had learned massive self-control. In fact, when I remembered what he had been, it was formidable.

I said, "To break your vow would not leave you with much honour. In the eyes of the world."

"I can live with that. I do already. There has not been a great deal of that particular commodity clinging to my person since I left England. One more notch against me will make no difference. I thank you for your concern."

"Don't mock me. Why are you doing this?" I paused, and then an answer struck me, with relief and appalling pain. "You are going back to England."

"I am never going back," he said steadily. "With or without you. No – I forced you into this. Perhaps I didn't bargain for an attack of conscience. I am not subject to them. Your father will hate my guts, of course."

"I rather think Gilbert will too."

This time his smile was definitely brittle as well as rueful. "Oh well, who cares? Gilbert *is* going back to England. Do I gather from these observations that you would like to take up my offer of rejection?"

I swallowed. Suddenly the hugeness of this conversation, of what I was doing, assailed me with force. My determination wobbled, precariously, not least because since the night in the garden, I had never known him so approachable . . . as now when he was, gracefully, unloading me again.

I said firmly, "Yes please."

And he nodded, as if it meant nothing, sweeping up the cherry stones from the floor with one hand and dropping them into his purse. It was an unexpected tidiness. Then, almost in the same movement, he rose to his feet, saying casually, "I'll do it tomorrow. You might like to be out."

"I might like to be in Africa."

His lips quirked slightly at that, not quite amused, not quite paying attention. It made me say, "Hereward?" And when his eyes eventually refocused on me, I swallowed and said in a rush, "The night of the contest, I did not mean to insult you by pointing out my own wealth. I was confused, a little ashamed, I think, of my own behaviour, not of you . . . I was not promoting my status in your eyes so much as restoring it in my own. I'm sorry."

His eyes stared at me. I could not read them, until the slow, rueful smile crept into them.

"A handsome apology, Torfrida. Once, I was good at them myself. I had to be. But there is nothing I can say to you, is there, for what I have done? And of all the things, all the good things, I have ever destroyed in my life, God knows the one I should most have welcomed and kept and nurtured, was you."

His words, gentle, bearable, healing, soaked into me, warming me so unexpectedly that he was already at the window again before I realized he was leaving. And then, along with the pity, panic rushed in on me. He had saved us, at some cost, from the awful sin that this marriage would have been; but suddenly the fact of his leaving over-rode everything else. Because this time he was walking away from me for ever. He could never come back to me from this.

"I am not destroyed!"

The words burst from me, panting, even as I leapt out of bed, running after him like a child.

"Hereward, I am not!"

He had half-turned back to me; I had caught at his hand, pleadingly, and suddenly I was crushed in his arms and his face was buried in my hair.

"Torfrida, I am tearing apart . . .!" he whispered. "Jesus, Jesus . . . If you had gone willingly to Osbern's arms today, I swear before God I would have killed him in cold blood . . . Did you really think I wanted your wealth? I don't give a fig for your lands or your money or your bloody ugly golden dragon. The truth is only this: I love you; I would die for you. Right now, I *want* to die for you . . ."

My fingers were in his tangled gold hair, tugging insistently that I might see in his face confirmation of his astounding words, till, abruptly, he moved, seizing my mouth fiercely in his; the last kiss, surely, he would ever give me.

And it was he who ended it. His cheek pressed briefly to mine, rough, warm, he said unsteadily, "After such an extravagant claim, you might think it would be an easy thing just to leave you. But it isn't. It isn't."

And then his warmth had gone. I felt the night breeze through the window, around my shoulders, stirring my chemise about my legs. And he already had one leg over the windowsill.

I said desperately, clearly, "Then don't."

He paused, very still, staring down at his big hands, gripping hard on the sill. I saw his eyes close briefly. I heard him breathing as though he had just climbed a mountain.

He said carefully, "Don't what?"

"Don't leave," I whispered. I was shaking so much I was vaguely surprised I could still speak. "Stay. Stay with me, Hereward. Hereward!"

The last was a muffled cry as he seemed suddenly to launch himself on me from the window. I was back in his arms, relief and gladness flooding me, straining me to him as we stumbled back against the wall and his mouth devoured mine, and his hands, his whole body invaded.

I was lost in this fire. There was nothing else. Only, as my shift fell around my feet and the caress of his body became unimaginably intimate, a sudden, sharp pain, did I wrench my mouth free, staring up at his wild, clouded eyes for one, two galloping beats of my heart.

"What have you done?" I whispered, although I was surely his accomplice.

"I have made you mine," he said unsteadily. "And now I will make you love me."

And he lifted me in his arms, just as I was, making me gasp and gasp again. I was swung through the air, laid softly on the bed with him above me, leading me, guiding me, moving me with unstoppable pace through the stages of passion I had never dreamed of. Until something truly astounding began to happen inside me, part of all the rest and yet curiously separate.

His lips were smiling now as he whispered against mine, "I believe . . . I believe I have taught you the song. Sing it to me, Torfrida. Sing it . . ."

I sang.

"I suppose it comes of being a soldier," I said.

He was lying on his back, one arm thrown up on the pillow above his head, the other around me as I cradled my face on his broad, powerful chest. His breathing was calm now, even and contented, for he had sung his own song, in perfect harmony with mine, and that had seemed almost more wonderful, more awesome than all the rest.

He said lazily, "What comes of being a soldier?"

"Assaulting a lady up against a wall, as though she were some dockside trollop . . ."

150

I felt his body begin to shake with laughter. "What do you know of dock-side trollops? And from where I was standing, you did not appear to feel – er – assaulted!"

Since I could not with any conviction deny that, I decided circumspectly to let it lie.

"Besides," he added, moving suddenly, rolling me on to my back and looming over me in a way that made my eager heart begin to gallop again. "Besides – for what it is worth, my wicked enchantress – I cannot recall any one else ever filling me with quite such. . . urgency!" The smile began to die in his eyes. "Did I shock you?"

I considered. "I don't know," I said candidly. I rather thought I might *still* be shocked, but I didn't care about that either.

He said ruefully, "I suppose it was no way to treat a virgin. In my defence, I can only say I was not perfectly sure I would find one."

My eyes widened. I struggled, but he caught my hands, bearing my arms back down on either side of my head, laughing at me till the genuine outrage began to melt away.

I said severely, "Have you any ways left in which to insult me?"

"Oh, I'll think of something," he promised, while his fingers made me gasp. His eyes were growing cloudy again. There were, I was learning, many kinds of storm. Some of them I was certainly not averse to provoking again.

He said, "I suppose I ought not to do this either to one I have so recently deflowered; but unless you have some particularly strong objection, I'm afraid I am going to do it again."

"I don't believe," I said breathlessly, "that one can be deflowered twice."

"Oh well," he murmured against my lips, "that's all right then."

When I woke, the lamp had gone out and the first light of dawn was seeping through my window. The tousled head on the pillow beside me still slept, its brow clear and untroubled like the boy Hereward. For some time, I just lay still beside him, inhaling the warm, elusive smell of him, listening to his deep, even breathing while I tried to come to terms with the intensity of this unexpected happiness. It was difficult to believe it was real.

I understood perfectly that whatever had happened between us now, still I scarcely knew him. Yet it no longer frightened me. It was a discovery, a voyage, that I was looking forward to, not with any urgency, but with quiet patience. And excitement; that too.

As if he felt it, he stirred, and smiled, his eyes still closed.

He said, "Torfrida."

And I leaned over quite naturally and kissed him.

151

After a moment, a long moment, I said uncertainly, "Hereward, it is dawn . . ."

"Three," he said softly, with unmistakable meaning, and the laughter of pure joy gurgled up in my throat.

"We can't," I said regretfully. "Lise will be here soon and . . ."

"We can," he interrupted, by which time things had reached such a pass that I elected to give in gracefully and admit that we could. Which was a mistake, for Lise, knowing I had retired early, came early to attend me.

Tripping blithely into the chamber with the latest news upon her tongue.

"Lady, did you know I – oh . . .!"

I fell back on the pillows, dragging the sheet up over my head. I didn't know whether to laugh or cry. I think the former was winning when I felt Hereward get out of bed, heard Lise's giggle as he pushed her out of the room. Then he came back to me, his eyes rueful.

"Sorry," he said, sitting down on the edge of the bed. "I should listen to you. I am a careless lover." His fingers caressed my hair, my face, came to rest at last on my lips, but his eyes were fixed on mine, unmoving. He said, "Do I take it from this night's astonishing work that you have elected after all for my original offer?"

I said, "I am keeping the golden dragon."

"Give it to Lise."

"All right," I said pacifically. I sat up and put my arms around his neck and he held me for a moment, almost like a vow. I accepted it as such. I had ceased to be surprised by anything. Then he released me and bent to gather up his scattered clothes.

He dressed quickly, going over to the window to pull on his boots.

"Do you think I can make it unobserved?" he asked humorously.

"Well if you can't, they'll only make you marry me."

"A rough punishment, but I'll take it like a man."

With the sheet around me – I could not find my poor discarded chemise – I went to him. He held me loosely, his eyes clear and faintly smiling.

"I shall see you in church," he observed. "And you had better come."

I said, "I will," and lifted my face for his kiss. It was light and brief, and followed by another somewhat deeper. My arms crept around his neck.

"Hereward?" I whispered in his ear. "Three?"

And his laughter soared up with his passion, so that in the end it was quite some time before he finally slung his leg over the window-sill. Even then he paused, moving his head from side to side as if to clear it, and I realized his shoulders were shaking again with laughter.

"Do you know, it was so much easier on the way up? You are sapping my strength, witch!"

"Not noticeably," I said, still breathlessly, and he seized me round the waist for one last, boisterous kiss. And then, still grinning like a boy, he dropped downwards. I watched him sprint across the yard, leaping over buckets and chickens and even one open-mouthed kitchen-boy, before he scaled the back wall and was gone out of my life for two whole days.

My first and most unlikely soul-friend; my lover; my husband.

Present: March 1076

CHAPTER 24

Soul-friend, lover, husband. I had lost all of them four years ago, along with my belief in any of them. There should have been no grief left, now that he was merely dead, and yet at this moment I wanted his physical presence so badly that I felt sick. Driven to my window, in an effort to escape the memories that fed my sickness, I saw I had dropped the yellow ribbon on the floor. Slowly stooping, I picked it up, staring sightlessly at the stained and worn rag.

It was the lover I missed most. I could confess that to myself. And in my vulnerability I also admitted for the first time that it could not all have been lies, our early life together. I put my head out of the window, cooling my desperately flushed skin, wondering yet again exactly when it was he had ceased to love me.

But I had no pride now. If he walked through the door this instant, I knew I would forgive him anything he had ever done or would do, if only he would lie with me for one hour. I could realize that now, even say it aloud now, now that he was dead and never could touch me again.

My eyes were blurred. Somewhere I knew that if even one tear fell, I would never be able to stop. Resolutely, I drew in my breath, tucked the ribbon into the neck of my gown, and sallied forth to find the others.

The twins were kicking their heels in the hall and looking grim.

"Where is Leofric?" I asked.

"Church," was the succinct answer. I could not grudge him that. It was where he got his strength.

I said, "You found Hereward's body in the guest-house. Were Wynter and Martin there too?"

Duti shook his head. "He was alone."

"Then where *did* you find their bodies?"

Somewhere, behind the calmness of my questions, I was shocked at my own ability to discuss so callously the deaths of those who had been so close. We had suffered tragedies over the years. But nothing ever like this . . . Fortunately, my distraction was halted by the realization that the twins were exchanging glances before they replied.

At last, reluctantly, Duti said, "We didn't. We didn't find their bodies. At least, we could not identify them." He paused, to see how I would take this, and when I kept my expression deliberately unchanged, he added, "There were four charred corpses in the store-house. Two of them were the right shape and size to be Wynter and Martin. The others we think, were servants."

"Has anyone claimed them?" I asked, and when they blinked at me, added impatiently, "Their families, I mean. Has anyone claimed the two servants?"

Wynter's family were all dead now, and if Martin had ever had any, I had never heard of them. The twins shook their heads in perfect unison. Four men, unidentified, unclaimed, unmourned by any save us, who had no real idea who they were anyway . . .

I said, "Have you buried the bodies?"

Again they exchanged glances. "No," Outi said at last. "We thought – perhaps – they should be – could be – interred with Hereward."

Their eyes were anxious on mine, as though I would refuse. As though I could. Who had a better right to lie beside him through eternity?

I managed to say, "Since they died with him, it would be fitting," before pausing to add, "But we should try to establish that they are indeed Wynter and Martin. Are the bodies still in the storehouse?"

"It's cold enough in there," Duti said apologetically. "And there's plenty of room since the fire burned most of our stores. We took most of what was left into the kitchen."

I nodded and left them.

In the yard, Ivo de Taillebois was mounting his restive grey stallion without noticeable difficulty. My step faltered, and then paused, hesitantly. I had absolutely no desire to see or speak to him again, and yet I had thought of another question to ask him. In the end, refusing to bow to either timidity or lust – either of which I despised in myself – I changed direction and was marching to meet him before he could have seen my hesitation.

I took him by surprise. I could see that in his eyes when they finally glanced up from the skittish horse and took in my advance.

"Lady," he said carefully. "Do you require my escort to Folkingham after all?"

"No thank you," I said politely, for I knew if I antagonized him too far, he would not answer. "But I have another question for you . . ."

He nodded, his dark, watchful eyes unblinkingly on mine.

I said, "You told me last night that Wynter and Martin ran across the roof-tops with Hereward." Again, he nodded. "Yet, when you followed to find out what he was saying to make the Normans laugh, you saw him standing alone on the roof."

"That is correct." His bow was a trifle ironic. However, I was not going to take offence.

I said directly, "Did you see what happened to them? To Wynter and Martin, the servant?"

At least he did me the honour of thinking about it. I decided again that he had been honest last night in his willingness to help, whatever his behaviour to me, and I awaited his answer with some sense of anticipation.

Several seconds went by before he spoke, and then: "No," he said regretfully. "In fact, I did not see them at all after they leapt after Hereward. I stopped watching – through shame of my countrymen, I am quite prepared to admit – until I heard Hereward talking. And by the time I got there, Hereward was alone. They might have been on the ground, in among the Normans. I suppose he might have jumped to help them in some way . . ."

"After throwing away his sword?" I said sceptically.

"You are right, of course. It does not make sense."

I sighed. "Never mind. Thank you." He was inclining his head, not altogether seriously, but I had already turned away, retracing my steps back towards the storehouse.

I emerged discontented, displeased that I could learn no more than anyone else, and concentrating on that rather than on the very real sickness in my stomach. I had seen burned bodies before, including my husband's, but these were far more badly injured and, as the twins had said, quite unrecognizable. If the short, stocky one was Wynter, his own mother would not have known him, and neither that nor the body which was probably Martin Lightfoot's, bore any identifying ornament or clothing. When I could force myself, I again tried to examine their wounds, but the fire had left little enough even of those. It was probably wishful thinking, but because I made out a large sword cut in Wynter's neck, I could believe they had all been dead before the fire took them.

And yet the storehouse itself, the actual building, was relatively intact. As though somebody had put the fire out when it had done the work required of it.

I spent some time gazing at the men whom the twins believed to be servants. But if they were, I could not place them. They could even have been Normans, fighting perhaps with Wynter and Martin when their masters foolishly fired the house . . .

Speculation. I had nothing else. Not a shoe, not a boot or a glove undestroyed, not so much as a ring left on a clenched fist . . .

155

Halting abruptly under the icy rain which had come out of nowhere, I frowned. The wiry corpse of Martin Lightfoot had had a clenched fist.

I did not want to go back into that place; but I did, after several deep and rather desperate breaths. Going straight past the other three laid out, what was left of them, on the mud floor, I knelt, dripping slightly, by the fourth. He lay on his back with his right hand curled, palm downwards on the ground beside his thigh. Trying not to breathe now, I made myself touch the blackened, almost skinless fingers, and force them apart.

Something metallic fell tinkling on to the floor. Quickly, I stooped, feeling for it in the rushes at my feet until my hand closed over something cold and small. Staring at it, I rose more slowly to my feet.

Torfrida, did you know there was a bear?

It was a man's brooch, not large but rather fine. Certainly it was not Saxon craftsmanship, although there was an animal carved into the gold. The animal, rearing on its hind legs, was unmistakably a bear.

I was wringing wet by the time I burst into the village church in search of Leofric, and I must have looked like a mad woman, with my veil askew and my hair escaping from it, tangled and bedraggled around my face and shoulders. Slamming the door shut behind me, I was vaguely aware of two figures, men, standing up near the altar. One moved immediately, and when I had wiped the drips out of my eyes, I recognized him.

"Leofric!" I exclaimed, starting towards him. "I have found the most astonishing thing, and I need your help to . . ." Abruptly, uncertainly, I broke off, because Leofric's other visitor in the church was gazing wildly around him, as if for escape, at the same time trying to slink into the shadows. I nodded significantly towards these antics.

"Leofric?" I said enquiringly, and the Deacon smiled slightly, uncomfortably.

"It is all right," he said. I think he meant it to be soothing. "He is – shy."

But something else had caught my eye now, something in the fellow's desperate movements that was more than a little familiar; a quickness, a deftness that sat ill with such sidling. Leofric had taken my arm, as if to lead me back out of the church, but at the first pressure of his fingers I shook him off and started towards the other man quite fearlessly – and he, seeing the game was up, stopped sidling and stood stock still. Since there was very little light, I could not properly make out his features or the expression on his face; all I could see was his eyes gleaming at me, startlingly blue and full of pain.

"Lady," he whispered. "I am so sorry . . ."

And my voice was hoarse with a hundred different emotions as I helplessly spoke his name.

"Wynter."

Past: Journeys: 1068-1070

CHAPTER 25

The feast was magnificent, the company jollier than any since the old Count had died. Young Baldwin, Count in his father's stead, beamed upon us all with condescension and complaisance. He was making a point. And of course, he was not the first man to believe that a bigger and better banquet made him a bigger and better man than his father.

"I can't make up my mind," said the man beside me, "whether we are celebrating the Count's new cook or the final capitulation of the Zealanders."

Since the words appeared to be directed at me, I turned my head to regard the speaker. I saw a handsome, well-made man, fit and strong, in his thirties perhaps, with short, dark hair just fading to iron grey at the temples. He was looking at me, faintly smiling.

I said, "Certainly both are notable victories for him, not least because of the complete absence of effort required of himself."

His smile broadened. "Hush, lady, you will loose your head!"

I tilted it forward experimentally, and he laughed.

"My name is Drogo, by the way. Of St. Matieu."

"I am Torfrida."

"I know. Your beauty as much as your learning, ensures that everyone knows you."

Lifting one sceptical and slightly bored eyebrow, I returned to my lamb and its excellent rosemary sauce. He said, "You don't believe me? Yet I had to bribe the steward to place me here. The price was necessarily high to beat all the others."

"You have been tricked," I said wryly, "by a steward quite experienced in taking advantage of strangers."

"Oh I am not a stranger. It is some time since I have attended the court, certainly, but it is hardly a first visit. I believe no one could accuse me of naivety! No, I have spent the intervening years in the Holy Land."

"Jerusalem?" I said quickly, glancing at him with rather more attention. "You have been to Jerusalem?"

His lips twitched, very faintly, and yet it was enough to show me I had fallen into his trap. Someone had told him how to interest me. Intrigued that he had taken the trouble, I sat back and watched him for a moment.

His eyes continued to gaze at me with frank admiration – I wasn't entirely surprised, for I knew I looked well. I had dressed with great care in shimmering green silk and gold and garnets, partly to maintain my role as hero's wife, but mostly to pass the time. I was here for the same reasons.

It was a shame – I would have liked to hear about Jerusalem from such a man – but I really could not let him away with such blatant manipulation.

I said carelessly, "How unfortunate that this meat is so tough . . ."

"Who is tough?" asked Bauduin, one of my old suitors, from across the table, having extracted himself from my cousin Marie's lively conversation in time to eavesdrop on the end of ours.

"Who is tough?" my new acquaintance repeated in amused tones. "The lady's husband, by all I hear!"

Bauduin's face changed. "Indeed yes. He is to be congratulated on a noble victory in Zealand."

I inclined my head calmly. "I shall pass on your kind words."

"When do you expect his return?" asked Drogo de St. Matieu.

"Soon." *But when? When?*

Drogo was smiling. "Fortunate man again. I must confess that had I the honour to be your husband, I would have ridden night and day from the moment of victory to stand by your side."

Bauduin said sardonically, "But then I doubt many of us, finding ourselves with that singular honour, would find it easy to ride away quite so often in the first place."

It was said with lightness, robbing the words of insult if not barb. Well, I didn't mind that – I expected revenge tasted quite sweet after several years. And if it touched a raw edge in me, that was my problem alone, and I would not let them see it. I looked mockingly from one to the other.

"Then it is no wonder," I said dulcetly, "that it is my husband who collects all the laurels."

I wondered sardonically if they had been speaking to my mother, who said regularly – impossibly regularly – "If you take my advice, Torfrida – which you never have yet! – you will keep him a little closer to you. Give him a reason to stay. Give him a son." This was generally part of conversations which began: "If your marriage is troubled, Torfrida . . ."

Drogo smiled, summoning a servant with a minuscule flicker of one eyebrow. My cup was refilled with dark red wine.

I stepped into the unexpectedly sharp night air, flanked by the two courteous escorts I had recklessly favoured over the unbearable alternative. After all, there was safety in numbers. In my ears was a faint, ignorable rumbling, as of people and horses passing in the distance. Perhaps it was not so late as I was imagining.

Looking upwards from habit, I registered the clarity of the sky, the size of the new moon, the rough positions of the constellations. Tomorrow, I would draw up another chart for him. And perhaps cast one for myself . . .

Here, I brought myself up short, blinking as reality finally pierced my confusion. I had drunk too much wine. For during my dwalm – which surely cannot have lasted beyond a few seconds – the yard had somehow filled with lights, blazing torches and lanterns, the muffled thud of hooves in the mud, the snorting of horses and the disciplined shouting of men. Shadows flared against the walls as horses trotted in an unending stream, swinging around the yard in a wide arc.

"Well," Drogo was saying slowly. "Either we are in the middle of an unlikely coup d'etat . . ."

It was odd that I could speak, for I could not breathe.

I finished the sentence for him, my voice admirably calm. "Or my husband has come home."

My eyes, inevitably, were fixed on the rider in front, trotting swiftly in our direction. Even with the torch-light blinding me, I knew who he was. He wore helmet and breast-plate and a bright, scarlet cloak hanging from one shoulder, the flame of his golden hair falling over it, for he had never adopted the French fashions. His hair, I had begun to think, was the only English thing left of him . . .

I would not shade my eyes from their torches, so it was not until his own helmet blocked the light from me, that I saw his face: cold and hard and unyielding; a heavy frown between eyes that glanced neither left nor right, controlled eyes betraying nothing but exhaustion; and his lips set and thinned.

It wasn't much, but it was enough to fear for him again, enough for my heart to reach up to him at once in pity and helpless desire to comfort. And he rode past me. He neither looked nor saw.

It was quite another's voice which attracted him. Siward the Red's, smiling just a shade uneasily from the horse directly behind.

"Hereward! Your lady . . ."

And at that, he did glance quickly over his shoulder at Siward, and then, almost at once, to me. His horse halted. There was a pause, while his face adjusted, painfully. That is, it was painful to me, whatever he felt. And yet it barely lasted an instant, for he turned away almost immediately, calling out some order over his shoulder which set off a stream of them all around the yard; and then he had dismounted, was walking back towards me, without lameness, I saw, anxiously, or even excessive stiffness from long riding.

All around me, men were dismounting and moving, and more kept coming in, on foot now, and I had begun to tremble uncontrollably, because the reunion was here, now.

It was only when I saw his eyes move, that I recalled my silent companions. Desperately, I wished them elsewhere, anywhere but here, now . . .

Hereward ignored them. He came to a halt before me, his body taut from some inner storm or equally silent exhaustion of body or spirit, or both. And I saw he did not want me here.

I was impeding something, whatever he had come here at this hour to do. There was shock in that, and a far stronger hurt than there should have been, now that I knew him, and understood.

After a tiny moment, I saw his lips quirk slightly. He had made the effort. His arms moved; I felt his hands heavy and warm on my shoulders. Then he bent and kissed my mouth in formal greeting.

His lips were cold; yet the strength, the life in them, snatched my breath away.

He said, "Torfrida. Are you coming or going?" As if we had parted only a little earlier in the day.

"Going," I managed.

His eyebrows twitched. "Dull party?"

"Good sauces," I said judiciously

"That old trick: covering the indifference of the meat."

"And of the company."

"Present companions excepted?" Drogo de St. Matieu broke in beside me. I had forgotten about him again.

My shoulders were cold. Hereward turned civilly towards my escort.

"Drogo de St. Matieu," I said quickly. "And Bauduin, whom you will remember."

"I remember the name." Hereward nodded somewhat curtly to each. "I'm afraid you must excuse me now, however . . ."

"Of course," Drogo broke in again, but smoothly. "You have your report to make to the Count. And his heartfelt thanks to receive, I have no doubt."

"Have you not?" said Hereward.

"Along with ours; it was a noble victory," Bauduin said genuinely. Yet Hereward barely spared him a glance.

I said, "Shall I come back in and wait for you?"

"No," he returned without any deliberation whatsoever. He was not even tempted. "I shall be home shortly. Do you need men?"

"Of course not," Drogo answered for me. Then, ignoring the fact that I had my own men-at-arms, he added, "Yours are tired, my lord. Mine have had nothing to do for hours. And here is the lady's carriage at last . . ."

As if he had not spoken, Hereward continued to look at me. Yet there was nothing personal in it. Merely, he wanted to know my answer. Drogo was nothing to him – in this matter at least.

I said, "I believe we need not trouble them further. Go in, Hereward; get it over with."

A smile did touch his eyes at that, although he was already turning away from me. I began to walk, quickly, towards the carriage which was fighting its way among Hereward's men, still pouring into the yard.

Almost, I wished I had not met him. The waiting would have been easier if I had not known he was back; if I had not seen the trouble in his closed, preoccupied face.

We had a big house, for Hereward had luxurious tastes and was not averse to using his wealth to indulge them. Of my own riches, which were now his, he was rather more wary, though he would live on my estates, organize and make improvements. But the presents for his men, the extravagant decoration of our house in Bruges, his gifts to me or Frida – those were all his, or bought with his gold, given by princes in Orkney and Alba, Cornwall and Ireland, and by our own Counts of Flanders.

Our hall was spacious, as it had to be for the extent of our hospitality, with excellently carved tables and large, tasteful hangings from France and Flanders itself. Drogo de St. Matieu wandered around it, silver cup in hand as he inspected my husband's treasures and mine. I thought seriously about ejecting him. And then, as before, I thought of waiting alone for ten minutes or one hour or five, and again made the decision to pass the difficult time as easily as possible.

Easy for me; I did not make it easy for him. Since Bauduin had deserted me after encountering Hereward, I had installed Lise as chaperone in the corner of the hall, glowering at us over her needle. I made Drogo work to entertain me with his natural wit and his knowledge of distant lands, until I realized he was watching me sardonically.

Then: "I cannot be palmed off so easily, you know," he said softly.

I lifted one eyebrow. "You are welcome to stay if you wish to. My husband is of a hospitable nature."

"I had already gathered," Drogo said, walking towards me, "that your husband was indifferent."

He was a stranger; it should not have hurt, for I knew Hereward. I knew him, a little, but I did not know whom he saw, who else knew him when he was away from me.

I said, "You malign him. The word I used, deliberately, was hospitable."

Drogo sat down on the stool at my feet. His arm brushed against my knee. He said, "He would welcome *me?*"

"When he comes," I said sweetly, "I shall ask him to allay your fears."

Drogo's face changed. Unbearably, I actually saw pity there. "Torfrida, he is not coming. Not tonight."

I had no reply to that, so I stared at him.

He said, "Get rid of the girl and we can talk properly." His finger, unexpectedly smooth and soft, touched my cheek. "*If* you wish to talk . . ."

I stood up, moving restlessly towards the harp, wondering how soon, now, I should get rid of him. "I always wish to talk." And then, instead, I played, and sang French songs and Celtic ones; and then, in a moment of nostalgia, my favourite one from the Fens that I had first heard Hereward and Martin singing the day after our marriage. He had taught me it in the end, although at first he had pretended not to remember it. His instinctive, quite untutored musical skill was still one of my most treasured discoveries.

Drogo sat on a stool beside me, either rapt or asleep – I didn't bother to look to find out which. The song haunted me sometimes; it had become the music inside my head when Hereward lay with me. So it seemed perfectly natural, at first, when his voice rose up and joined with mine in the last line.

It was Drogo's ungraceful jerking which spoiled it, as he jumped to his feet to face the returning husband he had been trying to wrong.

"All that," said Drogo as our voices died away, "and musical too. I congratulate you afresh."

He said, "Spare yourself. It is one of the many things I cannot help."

I opened my eyes, rising more slowly, turning at last to face him. He stood well into the hall, casually unfastening his red cloak, throwing it over the carved, high-backed chair beside him. The lamp-light flickered across his face as he moved, leaving it shadowed, frighteningly unfamiliar.

He was my husband.

I went to him. "Sit down; rest. Let me pour you some wine . . ."

"I have wine," he said, picking up my abandoned cup and raising it to me. "I always have wine, as you have often pointed out." Then, although, achingly, I could see his eyes were cold, his body taut from some inner storm or equally silent exhaustion of body or spirit, or both, he turned civilly to Drogo. "Welcome to my house."

Laughter bubbled up in me quickly then, though not quite easily. "There," I said, "he even spoke the word! You are welcomed."

"I have been keeping the lady company," Drogo said smoothly.

"You are all goodness," said Hereward civilly. The sardonic glint in his mismatched eyes was not invisible, but it had to be looked for. "May I get you anything else? More wine, perhaps? A bed for the night?"

"Thank you," said Drogo smiling, "but your wife has already been more than generous."

I paused, unmoving for a second, my hand resting on the back of the chair.

It was subtle, you see. The voice of a man who believed he was safely mocking a blunt-witted husband; yet he meant Hereward to understand it. He had been riling him, or trying to, even in the castle yard. Turning my eyes slowly up to his face, with an odd, dispassionate curiosity, I realized the man meant me ill.

But why? Bad temper because his plans had been interrupted? Or just because I had refused to be seduced? Well, you should not play such games if you are not prepared to lose to one who plays them better . . .

And dear God, what had I become to be playing them at all? Admittedly some men cried out to be taught a lesson, but was this despised game not beneath me? Had I no better way to waste time?

Or was it not I, but Hereward he sought to hurt? By provoking him to violence over me . . . Now I had truly frightened myself.

Yet Hereward was looking at Drogo, and his eyes were openly mocking now. "I would expect nothing less of my wife," he said gently, and dropped casually into the high-backed chair I was gripping. The lord's chair. "Please, sit down," he invited.

But again Drogo seemed to challenge Hereward's humorous confidence.

"I believe I have completed my task here, and must take leave of your kind lady."

Hereward smiled, an angelic smile; he made sure it touched his eyes. "Don't let us keep you longer from your bed. I thank you for your care of her, of course."

Drogo smiled back, took his leave gracefully. Yet although he made a point of kissing my fingers, it struck me that he was baffled, unsure whether Hereward's failure to rise to his baiting was due to doltishness or indifference. I don't think the truth ever entered his head.

Unaccustomedly silent, Lise followed him. Hereward watched with apparently benign interest. Then, his eyes still thoughtfully on the closed door, he enquired, "Who did you say that was?"

"Drogo de St. Matieu."

"Is he amusing? Do you like him?"

His eyes moved round to me, unexpectedly serious, yet not with suspicion. It was Drogo, I thought, astounded, who interested him, not me. Was he *really* indifferent at last? Was two years as long as anyone could hope to keep him?

I licked my lips, answering distractedly, "I don't know. I thought so at first, but he seems to mean some pointless mischief . . ."

"Not pointless," Hereward said vaguely. "I doubt it is pointless."

One hand rubbed tiredly at his forehead, and at that curiously childish gesture, I forgot my own selfish fears in purely instinctive concern for him. Dropping to my knees, I took the empty cup from his hand.

"Come," I said gently. "You need to sleep."

The hard, serious eyes refocused on me, and slowly began to lighten. It seemed there was some hope for me.

"I do," he confessed, "more than anything in the world. Almost." His lips moved, nearly smiling. "A little more of that wine first, however, if you would?"

"I would."

Calmly, I poured the wine, gave him back the cup. Our fingers touched, and I wondered if he noticed the inevitable leaping of my pulse. I wondered if I still had power to move him. And yet while my own thousand fears and insecurities span round my head, overlaid by anxiety about him, about whatever trouble was churning and disturbing him, some part of me was still functioning sensibly, seeking to soothe because I could do no less.

I said, "Were you given a hero's welcome?"

"By Baldwin? I think he said hallo."

Indignation rose swiftly once more, but I only said wryly, "He is not the man his father was. Everyone was talking at the feast, about the sheer cleverness of your victory, admiring your battle plan, your whole strategy."

"So they should. I stole it from William the Bastard. I'm sure they told you that too."

I said carefully, "Some slight similarity to the Battle of Hastings was noted. Any who detract from your victory, though, do so only through jealousy. You know that."

"I don't really care. I only need work, to keep us."

We didn't need his work. He knew that. It was he who needed it. "After Zealand," I said gently, "I don't think you need fear for work."

"You think not?" He was looking down at me properly now. "You were there today, probably several times too before today?" I nodded. "Did you see no evidence of – coldness at my name?"

"From Baldwin, yes," I said truthfully. "He never liked you. I believe he was jealous of his father's affection for you – or his favour at any rate. But he needs you."

"Only as much as he is told to need me. If I moved on, would you come with me?"

My eyes widened. Abruptly, with unexpected hope as well as inevitable unease, I remembered the letter from England. I said, "I am your wife."

And he smiled, a gentler, more personal smile. He even reached down, touching my hair, lifting a strand in his fingers. "That is the least of what you are to me. My anchor. My conscience. My brain, even."

Not *my love* . . .

"Forgive me," he said. "I am tired, sulking like a child because my master does not give me the adulation I think I deserve."

I had found my way now, remembering other home-comings, other reunions, none of which had been easy; and if this – difficulty – was more pronounced than ever, yet still we were going through the same stages – a

164

nervous, tense encounter, fraught with possibilities and anticipations; then talking, talking him back to peace, to a point where we could remember what we were to each other.

I said, "I think it was hard in Zealand. For all of you."

"The hardest yet," he confessed. "For me."

He never told me the details of campaigns; unlike other men, he never boasted of killings or maimings or the extent of his depredations. Only the politics behind it, or the thoughts and ideas he needed to straighten out in his head. Often, he asked my opinion on those; more than once he had acted upon my answer.

He said now, "And that is the odd thing. You know me – I like a few problems to keep me interested, and God knows the Zealanders gave me plenty. It wasn't that; it wasn't even the lengths they went to, wasting their own land rather than leaving it to us, or the carnage of the bitterest battles. The hardest part was just as we went into the final battle, and the truth came to me like a somewhat untimely light on the road to Damascus."

I frowned. "What truth?"

His lips stretched. "That I really didn't give a damn whether the Zealanders paid their tribute to Flanders or not. On the whole, I even believed not."

It was a mercenary's problem. Gold was not always enough. He needed to go home. Relief flooded me from the old anxiety. I had done the right thing there at least.

Slowly, I bent my head until my forehead touched his knee. I said, "Then your victory was all the more admirable."

"Was it? I thought the Zealanders' resistance rather more so."

Like the English resistance to the Normans. Such as it was . . . For, of course, it had happened by then, what everyone had been waiting for since Edward the Confessor's death: William of Normandy's swift and efficient conquest of England. Gilbert of Ghent had been part of it, along with many of Flanders, including Asselin, my erstwhile suitor. But though the English were subdued, for the most part, my letter had told me they were increasingly unhappy . . .

Hereward's hand was in my hair, gently stroking. I wondered if he knew it was me.

I said, "You did the only thing you could. If you cannot go on with Baldwin now, then let us go somewhere else."

"So simple," he said wryly. "I should take you on campaign with me, to guard against – everything."

I smiled into his knee, then straightened, rising to my feet, drawing him with me.

"Come to bed."

I had his hand, but it suddenly left mine, catching me in his arms instead, close in to his body, his face buried in my hair. "I have missed you," he whispered. "God, how I have missed you . . ."

I closed my eyes, letting the intensity of gladness soak in and surround me. It was all right. It was going to be all right after all. With new joy, only partly composed of relief, I lifted up my face to receive his kiss, but by then his mouth was on mine already, and I wanted to weep.

His mouth loosened. He said, "Well? Are you not meant to return the compliment? How much have you missed me?"

I swallowed. "Not at all," I said shakily. "You might find tears on my pillow still, but they were my lover's when he heard of your imminent return."

He smiled against my lips, kissing me again. In the end it was he who led me to the privacy of our own chamber.

I remember saying, "What would you do if I had meant it? About the lover?"

And he considered with apparent gravity. Then: "I like to think I would not care. Provided you still loved me best. But in reality, I'd probably slit his gizzard and feed it to the dogs. What *is* a gizzard?"

"I really have no idea."

"So much learning; so little use . . ."

CHAPTER 26

Torfrida, my daughter, was awake when I went to her, alternately gurgling and imperious as she made her many demands for cuddles, toys, food and freedom to stagger about the nursery. She had just started to walk, and the novelty clearly pleased her as she came at me with her funny, uneven weave. Laughing, I caught her in my arms.

"Guess who is here?"

"She knows," said Sigrid the nurse, and I frowned, wanting to have been the bearer of such news myself. But Sigrid was nodding to the cot, and when I looked I saw a carved, wooden horse standing up on the mattress. It was curiously life-like, yet all its points and edges were blunt and rounded. I knew the work; I knew the style. I had one just like it, only with sharper edges.

He had been here already. Last night, before he had come to the hall to find me. The knowledge pleased me. I even felt an unfilial smugness when I thought of my mother's advice about sons. Hereward, at least, was happy with his daughter.

So I was smiling when I returned to our chamber. And Hereward, although he had been sound asleep when I left him, was now up, standing by the window table, dressed in his leggings and a rather richly embroidered tunic. He wore two gold armbands and a slightly barbaric chain of golden figures around his throat; and his hair, bright and shining in the morning sun-light, fell forward across his face, hiding it from me.

It was the second awakening of the morning, but it did not matter: my pulses were racing again. I said, "I like the horse."

There was a pause.

Without moving, Hereward said, "Why is Aediva writing to you?"

My heart thumped once and was still. I realized the object of his attention was that letter from England, and ruefully cursed myself for not moving it. I had never intended him to discover it in this way.

I said lightly, "Why don't you read it and find out?" For as I moved, I saw that it still lay folded upon the table. He did not reply to that. Instead, his eyes lifted to mine, clearly waiting for an answer to his own question.

I said deliberately, "*Your mother* writes to me because I wrote first to her."

"Why?"

One word, curt and uncivil. I began to feel like one of his soldiers caught out in some transgression, and the guilt at my secrecy twisting still in my stomach did not help. But I would not be intimidated.

"Because she is my husband's mother!" I retorted. "Because I liked her. Because I was anxious. Because I pitied her the loss of her husband on top of that of her eldest son. Do you need any more?"

"No. You had no reason, in effect, and certainly no right."

"What?" I stared at him. "In this matter, and in this matter alone, you are prepared to be the heavy-handed husband?"

"This matter certainly," he said deliberately.

I went to him, taking his icy hand in mine. It lay there, unresponsive.

I said, "Hereward, it is time you thought again about this."

"Why should I?" he retorted. "When you clearly consider yourself capable of thinking for me?"

"Then let me! Listen: I want to reconcile you. You both need it; and there is Alfred, and Lucy, and Aethelthryth whose own son now follows you . . . I thought at first she – they – would come to us here, avoid the troubles in England for a while at least. But what you said last night about moving on has made me think that if you decided to leave the Count's service, we could go to England."

His hand jerked free as though I had burned him. "I could not. You may, of course, go if you wish – I daresay Gilbert will have you if Aediva balks at the prospect. But I should point out that my daughter will not go with you."

167

"What is the *matter* with you?" I interrupted with sudden anger. "Why does Aediva deserve this special loathing?"

He turned away from me abruptly, but not so fast that I did not see the barb go home. I pressed it harder. "I remember you saying once, in England, that Aediva did not deserve your treatment of her."

"That was before . . ." An impetuous beginning, half-swinging towards me, before he cut it off with a quick, unamused breath of laughter, and walked away from me. But I would not let him.

"Before they exiled you? What had she to do with that? Because she did not, could not, prevent it? *No one* could prevent it; this silly quarrel between you and your father that could have been mended merely by a word from you and from him, a word you were both too proud – and stupid – to say!"

He had reached the end of the chamber, with nowhere else to go and nothing to distract him, so he came back, his step prowling, restless, his eyes dark with the storms he didn't even try to hide. These days, that was rare.

More gently now, for I did understand and pity him, I said, "You never used to be so unforgiving. You who were so frequently forgiven yourself."

He had come to a halt in front of me. Almost as if he could not help it, his eyes closed against the old memory, the old pain I was churning up. This was why he would not think of Aediva; this was what he had never really confronted in himself over the long years of exile.

Then, self-taught, his control came back. His eyes opened directly, fearlessly into mine.

"Ah," he said sardonically, "But that was when I was young and soft. Betrayal and exile make you harder."

"No, Hereward," I said deliberately. "They make you self-pitying."

He had passed me again, shrugging as if it did not matter; but his whole body said it did. Quickly, I snatched up the letter, following him, thrusting it into his face.

"Take it! Read it, Hereward . . .!"

With sudden violence, he struck the paper from my hand.

I watched it stupidly for a moment, dazed, I think by the speed of movement as much as by the physical threat which he had never even implied before. Then, slowly, I lifted my eyes back to his.

"Don't," he said warningly. "Just – don't."

But being me, I did.

"What are you afraid of, Hereward?" I taunted. And suddenly fury was blazing out of his face, startling and vicious, forcing me backwards by its power.

"Of your *damnable* interference!" he said harshly. "What qualifies you, Torfrida, to poke into this? I suppose the flatterers have called you clever for so long that you believe it yourself! But you know nothing about this, Torfrida, and you will leave it alone – do you understand me?"

He did not wait for an answer, or even a reaction. Already he was away from me again, snatching up his cloak from the chest.

Ignoring my suddenly unquiet stomach, I said relentlessly, "Don't you care? That they are in trouble? That some Norman soldier is trying to take Bourne from them?"

His hand stilled on the cloak. For a moment, I thought I had won after all. I could not see his face, but I saw his fingers grip convulsively.

"Who?" he got out.

"Warenne. Frederic de Warenne. Does it matter?"

There was another pause. Then, slowly, his tense shoulders relaxed. He was forcing them to, and I saw it with a sinking heart. His fingers slackened, lifting the cloak and throwing it around his shoulders.

"Well," he observed carelessly. "It is Alfred's problem, not mine."

"Alfred needs you," I said desperately. "He has always needed you!"

He came back to me swiftly, so swiftly that I had to force myself not to back away from him.

"I'm not afraid of you, Hereward," I said determinedly. One of us had to believe it.

He smiled, the cruel smile I had seen so little of, while his fingers quickly pushed up my chin. "You should be," he said softly. "Sometimes, Torfrida, you should be." Unexpectedly he swooped, briefly kissing my lips. "As for the rest, I have but one word in reply: rot."

And he let me go, strolling towards the door.

Bewildered now, I called after him like a child, "Where are you going? Are you going out? Where are you going?"

He glanced back over his shoulder. He looked surprised.

"Going? To the Count, of course. To collect my pay."

A peaceful smile, belied only by the tempest still raging behind his eyes, and then he was gone, the door closing behind him with a definite, somehow insolent click.

I collected Frida, and went to see my parents. With my father, I came rather abruptly to the point: "Have you encountered a man called Drogo de St. Matieu?"

His eyes, from laughing at Frida's antics, rose quickly to mine, unexpectedly searching and quite, quite serious. Nameless anxiety flooded up again.

My father said slowly, "Not personally. I have heard of him though."

I licked my lips. "He has returned, I believe, from Jerusalem."

"Via Byzantium and Germany and Italy," said my father drily.

I felt my eyes widen. "What was he doing there?" But I knew the answer before my father spoke.

"Soldiering, of course. He is a mercenary, Torfrida. A Flemish one. And the word is that he wants Hereward's position."

My brain was seething on the way home, with indignation at Drogo's behaviour to me, to us, at my own foolishness and blindness. Lost only in my need of Hereward's return, I had failed signally to recognize a danger the rest of the world must have seen. But Hereward had been away – did he know?

"Not pointless," he had said, when I had accused Drogo of mischievous intent. *"I doubt it is pointless."* So, if he had not known, he had suspected something. He had at least recognized his own kind.

But no, I would not allow that Hereward and Drogo *were* the same kind. The world might think so, but there had always been more to Hereward . . . He was nearly twenty-nine years old, though; perhaps he was running out of time to make for himself the sort of fame he truly wanted. And he did want it, I had always known that, even as a child listening to him reviling all the old Saxon virtues, the chief of which, surely, was eternal fame, living on in the memories and stories of one's deeds, passed on through the generations.

No. He was twenty-nine, not fifty-nine. He had time. But I realized suddenly that part of his trouble now was the *fear* that he had not.

"I didn't give a damn whether the Zealanders paid their tribute to Flanders or not."

And Drogo – Drogo was older, more experienced in the warfare of two great Empires, had fought with the Normans, presumably, in Italy. And he was a native of Flanders. It was conceivable that Baldwin would prefer him to Hereward. And though part of Hereward clearly yearned for change, it was not in his nature to give in to this sort of challenge. I knew, despairingly, that he would stay to fight it. And whatever bridges I had built with his mother would perish again.

And Hereward's salvation – was I really trying to save him still, after all these years? – was further away than ever . . .

And over all these worries was still the one of how long he would bear a grudge over my secret correspondence with his mother. And my joy, despite it all, of having him home.

My litter was dropped with a bump, jolting me back to reality. Frida laughed. And a group of soldiers flashed past us, shouting joyously. And the name they were shouting was *Hereward.*

In fact, from all sides now, I could hear commotion, galloping horses, running soldiers, chanting; and they all seemed to be pouring in our direction. Craning my head out of the litter, I watched with curiosity; oddly there was no fear – and there should have been – of soldiers running wild. Especially soldiers just returned from campaign, as they were. They were

Hereward's soldiers.

And then I saw Hereward himself, borne aloft on the shoulders of his men, the whole group of them swarming down the street towards our house. He had his back to me, but there was little doubt of his acquiescence.

"What have you done?" I said aloud. "What have you done?"

"Don't be frightened, lady – it's all good humoured," said a voice beside me. Siward the White, Aethelthryth's son who had come here with every intention of serving the great soldier William of Normandy in order to oust the upstart Harold of Wessex; and who had stayed instead with Hereward, he and Siward the Red, his cousin. Now Hereward called them both his nephews quite impartially.

"Good humoured," I repeated vaguely. "Yes . . ."

It was too. The soldiers were happy, and however riotous, they were still under Hereward's influence.

"But why? What is going on?"

I saw Hereward turn and shout something over his shoulder. And that one glimpse of his face suddenly snatched my breath away. Blazing with some fierce vitality, a pure, wild joy in life, it reminded me almost unbearably of the stilt-race in Lincoln. And yet there was more than a hint too of the suppressed energy, dying for release, that led him into fights – serious fights. The soldiers might have been loyal and obedient, but Hereward himself, in this mood, was dangerous.

I saw that at once, and knew that I was the catalyst. Because I had stirred it all up again, the memories he could not bear and the present which he would not.

The question was not after all about what he had done, but rather, what had I done? Nevertheless, I found myself repeating, "What has he done, Siward?" And when no reply came – again – I dragged my eyes away from the soldiers' hero to young Siward, and found his expression an odd mixture of guilt and pride and ruefulness. It didn't help.

Siward said reluctantly, "We went with him to the castle to receive the Count's formal thanks. He – Hereward – reminded the Count, quite courteously, of what his father had promised in the event of success in Zealand. Because, if you remember, the old Count promised considerable bonuses on top of our usual pay."

I nodded impatiently.

"Baldwin waffled around it for some time, offering words of thanks, and praise even, though I thought that stilted enough, considering. Anyway, it was soon clear we'd get nothing, that the Count would neither honour nor even acknowledge his father's promises."

"He really is a little rat," I said furiously, and Siward laughed.

"That is, more or less, what Hereward implied! In the end, he smiled, and I heard him say, "Well, my lord, it is your choice, and I must gratefully concur. You keep what you have, and we keep what we have!' Then he gave a great, sweeping bow – you know the way he does, contriving to make the deepest insolence out of the greatest courtesy! – and then he just turned and walked out, with us, as usual, at his heels."

"What did he mean?" I asked with dread. "What did he do?" But I thought I knew already.

I did. After all, he had done it before.

"Well," said Siward uncomfortably. "We brought the tribute back from Zealand – twice over, in fact, for that was the price we won by our victory – and we were still guarding it. So Hereward just – er – he – ah . . ."

I closed my eyes. After a moment, I opened them again, delicately touching my upper lip with my tongue.

I said, "He gave it to the men. He distributed the Zealanders' tribute among his own people."

Siward nodded, and grinned, and clutched his head. "I don't know if he is mad or magnificent, but I know which the men believe."

"So do I . . ."

They were disappearing, hoards of them, into our house. I wondered if there would be any room for me.

"Only one thing bothers me," said Siward. "Well, one more than all the others! That fellow Drogo de St. Matieu, who was with you last night, was at the Count's side throughout the interview. And the word is that he – Drogo – would supplant Hereward if he could. As captain of the Count's soldiers."

Dragging my eyes back to Siward, I said flatly, "Well, I rather think Hereward has handed him that one on a platter, don't you? I believe we may count this . . ." I waved my hand at the soldiers still streaming in twos and fours up the street, "as a fairly spectacular resignation."

They lined my path all the way into my hall, Hereward's devoted and suddenly wealthy troops.

And as I entered, flanked by the two Siwards, I was confronted by a loud, solid sea of men, sitting and standing, drinking ale out of silver cups, tin ones, drinking horns and bowls and jugs and vessels of any kind. And our servants scurried between them, offering food, looking both awed and frightened. And at the head of them, Hereward lounged in the high-backed chair, a smile playing on his lips, his fingers curled round the stem of a golden cup I had never seen before. Zealand tribute, or booty? It all seemed to be the same now.

Gradually, yet fairly swiftly, the noise began to die away, as all heads turned to me, and the soldiers respectfully stood and parted to let me through. I went forward mainly because I didn't know what else to do. Hereward saw me.

Our eyes met; his smile was fixed for the smallest second, and then he rose to his feet, showing again the curiously uncontrolled grace of his boyhood rather than the sure poise of the man I had married. Something rose up in my throat: emotion, dread, excitement – I had no name for it, it was all confusion.

He was walking towards me, and I barely heard Siward's casual words about finding me outside in the melee. I was aware only of Hereward, and of his need for my approval. It was there in the unquiet eyes, a plea which only I could read.

He *knew* I would not approve of this. I was his conscience.

And the men looked on, *his* men who idolized him, and not just for this act of defiance. These men had gone to Zealand prepared to die, not for gold or for a cause or for the Count their true master, but for him, for Hereward. What he had done this morning was their reward.

And I could spoil it with one word of disapproval. Not destroy, or take away, but sully. As it deserved to be sullied.

And I thought, for his sake, I probably should speak that word. It was, after all, stealing from his father all over again.

He stopped in front of me. I could feel the Siwards' tension, the silence, the sudden unease of the troops communicated from I know not where. But I could see only Hereward, and the strange, understanding twist of his lips. Almost a smile. Already, he forgave me the betrayal he could read in my eyes.

I said, "You will not be happy, will you, my lord? Until you have a rope around your neck?"

And taking his massive arms in my hands, I stood on tip-toe and kissed him.

The soldiers roared. The Siwards shouted with laughter, and Hereward's arms closed around me, hugging me. I felt his lips in my hair, smiling. And then I was released and led more decorously to join him in the other high-backed chair.

Hereward drank from the golden cup, watching me over the top, then passed it to me.

He said, "Thank you."

I sipped the wine. For public show, I smiled, but I said intensely, "You are insane, Hereward. Baldwin will never forgive you for this. You will truly have to watch your back now . . ."

"No I won't," he interrupted.

And I put down the cup. Intuition, foreknowledge, whatever it was, rose up like a sudden wind chilling my bones, muddling up the rest of the nameless emotion I had been fighting since I had come in.

"I won't have time," he said. He reached for my hands, folding both of them around the cup again before lifting it to his own mouth. Under my

173

petrified gaze, he drank and lowered the cup without releasing me. I could see a droplet of wine on his lip.

He said, "I sail tonight, for England."

CHAPTER 27

When I had taken in his words, I said stupidly, "But that is too soon. I can never have everything ready for Frida and myself . . ."

"You and Frida are not coming."

That shut my mouth. Even now, the shock, the unspeakable hurt of it, still rocks me. But he continued to hold my hands around the cup, a strange, sad little smile on his lips.

"Don't look like that," he said softly. "How can I take you to England when I cannot protect you? I need to go secretly first, to find out what is happening at Bourne. Later, if it is safe, I shall send for you."

I whispered, "I did not marry you to be safe."

"Torfrida . . ."

"If you insist, I will leave Frida with my mother . . ."

"I won't take you."

"You are leaving me."

The words came out before I could stop them, still a whisper, but suddenly hard, accusing, incredulous. And then that old, patient look came into his eyes, the one that had dealt so gently with Matilda's importunate pleas the night he had left England. The recognition struck me like a blow, silencing me with new pain.

His voice said quietly, "I could never leave you. Not in the way you mean. You are my soul."

"And you are a liar. You have always been a liar."

I tried to snatch my hands free, but he held onto them. Had this not happened somewhere, some time, before?

He said, "Don't make it harder, Torfrida."

"I make it nothing. I am sure your followers will understand my departure now. I have done what you wanted."

A second longer, he looked at me; I could not read his eyes, but then I was too angry, too drowned in hurt to try. Slowly, his hands released mine, falling to the table. The cup sat there, untouched.

Later, he came to our chamber to put some things in a bundle to take away. I would not even look at him. I was sewing execrable stitches in a new tapestry – blatantly, systematically destroying everything I had done before.

He said quietly, "I am taking Martin, no one else. The Siwards have orders to care for you."

I curled my lip at that. "I care for myself. I always have."

There was a pause. Then, slowly, he picked up the bundle and slung it over his shoulder. I felt him walk towards me and crouch down by my stool. His hand reached up, lifting a strand of my hair.

"Will you not at least wish me well?"

And in a cold, careless voice I answered, "What is the point? My wishes do not concern you."

His hand fell away. He gave me another moment that I would not take, and then he rose to his feet.

When the door closed, I went on sewing, and sewing, and sewing, large, ugly, obliterating stitches, until I heard the sound of his voice outside, and the clip-clop of his horse trotting away, and I realized I could no longer see the work in front of me.

My head fell forward till it rested on the frame, and the wetness destroyed whatever my iconoclastic stitches had left.

In the end, it was my search for Constantine's Ptolemy that forced me to the hall three days later. The household had eaten. The only people left in the hall were my parents and the two Siwards, who all seemed to be living here.

The men stumbled to their feet as I drifted in. I waved them vaguely back to their seats, looking about me until my father's eye caught mine.

"My dear, you are a casual hostess," he observed humorously; but I could neither laugh nor appreciate it.

"I'm looking for a book," I said, rummaging behind the plate on the side table.

"To tell you what to do?" sneered my mother. There was a pause while my father sighed and the Siwards looked appalled.

"Yes," I said. "To tell me what to do."

"*I* can tell you that!"

"Don't," murmured my father apprehensively.

But: "Tell me," I invited.

Instead, she rose and came across to me. She looked angry, but I knew that nothing she could say would touch me. Her eyes raked me from head to toe.

"Look at you!" she said contemptuously, although she did keep her voice low so that the others would not hear. "Your husband has gone without you to another country, and you spend your time gazing at the stars! Have you any idea how *pathetic* that is?"

I blinked. No one had ever called me pathetic before.

I said, "What would you have me do? Go on as if nothing had happened?"

"No! I'd have you take a long, hard look at yourself! I tried to warn you that you were driving him away, and now you have."

"This is different," I said tiredly. "You were wrong about before: that was just Hereward's – need. Of action."

"And this?"

I had no words for this, so I offered none. It seemed to infuriate her further.

"Might I remind you, Torfrida, that it was you who wanted him to go back? Who *nagged* him to it?"

"Not . . .!" I began impetuously, and broke off, spinning away from her with more vivacity than I had shown for two days. Now none of them could see my face.

"Not without you?" guessed my mother who, underneath it all, was no fool. "That is what this is all about? He has not cast you off, thrown you out of his house or even beaten you? No; he left his kinsmen here to look after you and your child, and went away to his own country. And so you are still here – my brave and spirited daughter – neglecting your child, weeping into your wine and looking to the *stars* to tell you what to do!"

That penetrated, probably because I didn't like it; I didn't like it at all.

I said coldly, "I have never wept into my wine. Or anyone else's."

"Well, perhaps there is hope for you," she said sarcastically.

I looked at her. "Where?"

I meant it to be dry, sardonic. Instead, it was pleading, a child to its mother: tell me where.

She cast her eyes to heaven. "Oh, in the name of the Blessed Virgin! Where do you *want* to be?"

"With him," I said hoarsely.

"Then go to him."

Almost, I smiled at her simplicity. Only surprise that she had suggested such a thing at all kept my face straight.

I managed, "Do you think I have not thought of it?"

And she stared at me, not for the first time failing to understand. "Then what in God's name keeps you here?"

"He does not want me."

She blinked once, whether at the stark tragedy of the sentence, or the fact that I had said it, I did not know. She reached out, pushing me on to the nearest bench, and sat down beside me.

"Torfrida. Does he take you on campaign with him?"

"No . . ."

"Then why should he take you into England, where his own people have only recently been reduced to obedience by a foreign invader? Where, from all we hear, insurrection is imminent once more? I never liked this marriage of yours, Torfrida, but I think more of him for leaving you behind."

I looked at her helplessly.

"Mother, it is not as simple as that. I cannot explain it all to you; just believe he does not want me."

She gave me the sort of glance that mothers have been casting at their children throughout the ages.

"For one so learned, Torfrida, you are a great fool," she observed. Her hand waved back towards the table. "I have, in the last few days, spent enough time with these two nincompoops to know fairly exactly how he feels about you."

I looked at my hands, threaded tightly together. I did not think I could bear this. Yet for once she had all my own arguments marshalled and ready to be knocked down.

"Oh yes, I know they are his kinsmen and I your mother. There are platitudes they feel obliged to utter, and things they would never tell me in a million years, however true they were. But other things, things that need never have been said to placate or please me, or to turn the direction of my curiosity – these *were* said."

She had my attention now. But my throat had dried up; I could not ask. Again she answered the unspoken question.

"Such as what he wears under his shirt every night he is away from you, and ties around his arm in every battle – a yellow, silken ribbon, sewn with gems. Does that mean anything?"

My mouth opened and closed uselessly. Something seemed to shatter around my heart.

"Or that he writes letters to you that he never sends."

"Does he?" I whispered achingly to my hands. "Does he do that?"

My eyes closed. What had I done? I had sent him away, without love, when he needed me. Not with him, perhaps, in this case, but the need was there all the same, and as great, surely, as my own . . .

"They told me these things," she went on relentlessly, "because they cannot tell you; and yet they see your trouble. I don't know whether it is you or he they love – both, maybe. Certainly, they wish you well. Now, Torfrida, wake up. What are you going to do?"

I stood abruptly, staring out at the dark window. I had been studying star positions for days, and now all I saw was the moon, large and round and full, and exactly the colour of Hereward's hair. Laughter fought its way up from my stomach until, frightened of its wildness, I choked it back.

My head cleared and I felt my eyes had too as I turned them upon her. Some force in my gaze made her step backwards.

"I am going to England," I breathed.

Part of the road was the same. The countryside was familiar in its shapes and its colours and its unvarying, flat vastness, broken only by stretches of green wood and a few depressed villages. But it had been twelve years since I had first come here, a scared and furious child, determined to be sent home with the next tide. I was different now, a wife and mother who had left her own child in her desperation to get here.

And the people I met were different too. They looked suspicious of strangers; their eyes were deliberately dull when they were forced to speak to me; and one couple, of theignly rank, I thought, definitely muttered behind my back as we drove on in the direction they gave us.

It was my accent. I sounded foreign, French like their new masters, some of whom I observed swaggering along the road or making loud, imperious demands in alehouse yards, martial and arrogant, as if they had always been there.

I supposed, as we drove along the bumpy forest track to Bourne, that it was no wonder the country seemed unwelcoming, unwholesome, unfamiliar to me. I had arrived yesterday in a trading vessel, and set out first thing this morning in a horrible old hired cart. The driver was hired too, but the available men-at-arms had looked so villainous that I had hastily declined to employ them. As a result, I arrived in something less than state, with only Lise for companion.

The road was quiet here. Emerging from the woods, I didn't meet a soul. Even the fields looked empty. Along with everything else, it caused a twinge of anxiety in my breast, adding to my guilt, my sense of loss because Frida was not with me. I had abandoned her in Bruges to my mother's tender mercies, with the Siwards to guard her. And yet my strongest worry was still reserved for Hereward's reaction to my presence.

"What's that?" Lise said suddenly, and I followed her finger. She was pointing to the gates of Bourne. Something dark was flapping in the breeze against the right-hand gatepost.

The cart could go no further.

It came to a halt at the gates, and I saw that the flapping object was a large piece of black silk, tied with a rope around something solid and round. But I did not have time to ponder its purpose. My driver was shouting impatiently. In fact, he was already climbing down to try the gates himself – presumably he was in a hurry to return to the tavern from which we had hired him – when a large, grumpy individual began to make his way down the hill from the hall.

He was dressed a little like a soldier, in a leather tunic, though there were no weapons at his belt, only keys. He was scowling ferociously.

"What do you want?" he shouted through the gate in Saxon.

"The lady wants to go in," said my man laconically.

"What lady?" was the only aggressive response.

Grasping the side, I jumped down, splashing mud up on my skirts, and walked round the cart towards the gates. I spoke in the man's own tongue. "You may address your remarks to me; but I have no intention of shouting like a fish-wife, so if you expect a reply you had better either come out here or let me in."

Rather to my surprise, he unfastened the gate and came out, securing it again behind him. I frowned. Was this Hereward's influence?

"My name is Torfrida," I said shortly. "I have come to see your lady, and the lord Hereward of Bourne."

At this, the man's frown disappeared, but only to dissolve into not very amused laughter. "*Hereward* of Bourne? Love you, lady; you're twelve years too late for him! Pity, in its way, but there it stands."

Something in the easy confidence of that disparagement rang rather *un*easily true in my ears. Nevertheless, I said decidedly enough, "Very well, at least take me to his mother, the lady Aediva."

He glared at me frowningly, neither impressed nor pleased. Then his eyes took in Lise, clearly the tirewoman of a respectable lady, and the broken-down state of the old cart she sat in. They came slowly back to me, as if hopeful but doubtful of finding there the solution to this apparent paradox.

I was ready to fight, but he said grudgingly, "I'll ask her."

"Tell her Torfrida is here," I shouted irritably after his swiftly retreating back. "The lady Torfrida, of Flanders . . ."

"Friendly," Lise observed sarcastically. "Isn't the master here then? Is this not his house?"

I said brightly, "I'm sure he is here. His people are just keeping it a secret until they know it is safe to reveal it. I suppose . . ."

Lise sniffed, a trick she seemed to have learned somewhat irritatingly from my mother. I walked up and down the length of the cart in silence, speculations multiplying in my head, warring with anticipation, the excitement of seeing him. Even for us, the last reunion had been brief. And I knew how to get around any grudges he might still be bearing . . .

"Lady."

At Lise's significantly spoken word, I looked up quickly. A woman was coming down the hill towards us, her linen veil and dark skirts blowing out in the breeze, and she was accompanied by a Norman nobleman. The type was unmistakable: short, black hair, long, loose tunic, sword swinging easily at his belt; a seasoned soldier, comfortable and confident; it was there in his every slightest movement and expression, in the arrogant stride that would have been called a swagger in anyone less at ease.

My heart thumped uncomfortably. Why was he with Aediva? For it was

Aediva; I recognized her easily now, a little older, a lot tireder, more faded, and puffy about the face from weeping.

But where was Hereward? Had I really angered him so much that he would not show me this tiny courtesy? Or was he away from home?

Suddenly, the thought of spending another night without him, without putting things right between us, was *intolerable*.

Anxious to be rid of us, the driver was already climbing back up to his box, pushing my trunk somewhat unceremoniously to the ground. I didn't care. Aediva was rushing at me, both hands outstretched, but though her lips were smiling, something in her urgency bothered me, and not just because I sensed some peculiar reluctance behind her welcome. Close to, I could see that her dark gown was old and much mended, that about her whole person hung an indescribable air of neglect.

"Torfrida?" she almost gasped. "Torfrida, is it really you?"

I forced myself to smile easily. "Why, I'm afraid it is. Forgive my coming unannounced. It is just that . . ."

"Of course. I am so glad you have come to bear me company! This is the lord Frederic de Warenne," she added suddenly, introducing me to the man at her side, whose eyes I now found on me with an expression I had learned to read very easily. Only in his case it was overlaid with a kind of insolent consideration, as if he was weighing up the precise qualities of a piece of meat.

I had, of course, ways of dealing with such insolence, but the sound of his name on Aediva's lips kept me uncharacteristically silent.

Frederic de Warenne. The Norman who was claiming Bourne as his own.

I chose to smile distantly, inclining my head very slightly.

"My kinswoman," Aediva explained to him quickly – and unaccountably vaguely. "The lady Torfrida, of Flanders."

"Welcome to Bourne," said Frederic de Warenne, his voice soft and smooth, with just an edge of steel. He smiled with even, white teeth. "The lady Aediva's kinswoman is, of course, most welcome in my house."

CHAPTER 28

At first, with relief, I thought the hall was just as I remembered it, large and gracious in the true Saxon style. On the few occasions I had been here as a child, it had been a place of warmth and hospitality, and whatever the tensions caused by Hereward, deliberately or otherwise, this atmosphere of welcome, of comfort, had never been touched. I had thought then that it spoke of past contented family life, and had wished more than ever that Hereward would sort out his quarrels and go home.

Frederic de Warenne waved me courteously to a bench, and shouted imperiously for wine while a nervous serving girl took my cloak. Aediva sat down close beside me. I could feel the tension in her.

I felt a shiver run through me, because it wasn't really as I remembered it at all. It was a cold and frightened place. The warmth and comfort had gone, as though they had been folded away with the trestle tables after a meal.

"Lady, where is he?" I whispered, because her manner seemed to demand whispers.

"He is not here," she breathed, and something inside me died again. "He was never here. Say *nothing* in front of the Norman."

"Never here," I repeated dully. Then, throwing my desolation off like a wet cloak, I lifted my head and demanded, "Then where is he? And has this Norman really supplanted Alfred?"

"He has killed Alfred."

The words were small and cold, and they chilled my blood. I could only stare at her helplessly, with the narrow hope that I had misunderstood. And then the Norman was back, sitting opposite us, the perfect host in Aediva's house, talking pleasantly – and infuriatingly – about nothing.

Beside me, I found Aediva's icy hand, and held it. It was all I could do.

And yet, when he stood up impatiently to take the wine from the serving girl, who was shaking too violently to pour without slopping, I breathed, "You mean *truly* killed?"

"You passed him on the way in," she said bitterly. "Whose head did you think was under the black silk on the gatepost? My people cover it regularly, his as regularly expose it again . . ."

A *head*. Alfred's young, vital head . . . The grief came at last, overwhelmingly for her and for *him*. And for myself.

"Sweet Jesus," I whispered.

"Jesus was no help at all," she said in a curiously detached sort of way. "No one can help me now." Her desolation swamped me, so that I struggled to think.

At last I said urgently, "And the Norman? What does he mean by you?"

She shrugged. "Dishonour, I suppose. I am old, but he plays with me as with a mouse."

Struggling, I stared at her averted face.

"Does he mean to marry you?"

"I doubt it." She looked at me clearly. "Why should he?"

And then he was back again, bearing wine for us. Watching him carefully, with growing indignation, I saw that his perfect courtesy to Aediva was secretly – in fact not so very secretly – mocking, as if he had promoted a kitchen slave for a day, for his own amusement. Perhaps I was not meant to have seen that; not, at least, until he had discovered who I was.

Seating himself on the stool beside me, he smiled at me with deliberate charm but not much effort. Frederic de Warenne considered himself irresistible. And he was handsome, I thought dispassionately, with his broad brow and long, aquiline nose and strong, even white teeth. Like a horse, but less than half as trustworthy.

I squeezed Aediva's clutching fingers comfortingly.

But where in God's name was Hereward? Had he been shipwrecked again? Or – and this had a far greater ring of truth – had he allowed himself to be distracted from his purpose? Because he did not, at heart, want to know all this.

I doubted he could bear it.

"From Flanders?" Frederic's chief lieutenant said to me. I think his name was Humphrey. "They say the lady's son is in Flanders."

It was the nastiest moment so far. My attempt to eat quietly with Aediva had been thwarted by Frederic's insistence – smiling but implacable – that we both come to the hall with the rest of the household. I could have made an issue of it; there was something about his smugness that made me itch to wipe it from his handsome face. But in the end discretion won out, for I wanted no open antagonism, not until I knew where we stood. I needed a chance to speak to Gilbert of Ghent, to find out about the King's views and Hereward's precise whereabouts.

Now I wondered if I should not have pleaded any excuse to stay away from this gathering. For lower down the tables the soldiers were clearly allowed a degree of licence that was degrading to us to have to witness. I rather thought it also degraded the local girls at their side, some of whom laughed and cavorted with enthusiasm, pretended or otherwise, but a few of whom were clearly distressed and frightened. To make matters worse, we were entertained by a jester, whose songs and jokes were in highly questionable taste.

And finally this remark by the Norman officer, which seemed to link Hereward and me as clearly as the priest himself had done two years ago.

"Some peasant told me so the other day," Humphrey went on, grinning. "And in what I can only describe as a threatening manner too! Though what the man is meant to do to me from the other side of the sea – or indeed from this side – I cannot begin to imagine!"

There was general laughter among the Normans. Aediva looked at her food. I smiled faintly, trying not to display the flood of relief which Humphrey's merely crass bravado had brought me.

Frederic, following the mocking style of his underling, said, "Perhaps you even know him, lady?"

"Hereward?" I said boldly, and Aediva jumped quite visibly, although at least her veil fell further across her face. "I have met him, of course. He is quite a great man in my country."

Frederic's eyes widened. I had the doubtful satisfaction of actually surprising him.

"Do you say so?" he murmured softly. "That her son is the same Hereward who captains the Count of Flanders' army?"

I inclined my head patiently. There was a brief pause while I wondered uneasily if I was being too clever. And then Frederic gave a shout of laughter. His men joined in.

"Then it is he who has just thrashed the Zealanders back into the Count's obedience?"

I realized Aediva's women were exchanging glances of triumph which they didn't even trouble to hide. Well, no one was paying them much attention. One of them, the elder, I actually remembered from before. The other was young, intense looking, and her violet eyes, when they swung back to the importunate Norman beside her, were full of loathing.

I was sitting in the midst of a maelstrom of hatred and contempt.

Across the table, I watched the lips of the Saxon who served them. I could not hear him, but it looked suspiciously like: "Would he'd thrash *them* back to Normandy."

I had the feeling it was a familiar pattern at meal times. They met, Norman and Saxon, the former loud and arrogant, the latter silent and sullen, except for the trollops at the lower tables. Now, with the flowing of the wine and ale, the Normans grew louder but less attentive, and the English could revile them quietly among themselves. It was probably a release for them. For Aediva, who was aware of it too, I realized, it only added to the tension – I suppose she felt she should be able to help them and could do nothing.

But at least while this odd peace lasted, the Normans argued and joked with each other, more or less ignoring us. And as Frederic and Humphrey leaned forward to shout at each other, elbows among the slopped wine and fish-bones, Aediva and I were able to converse in low tones behind their backs.

"They have made no friends here," I observed.

"They are too distant from any supervision. They squeeze the people, taxing them repeatedly, and quite illegally, abusing them beyond endurance simply because they can. And on top of that – *this*. In short, they are out of control."

"But Gilbert, you say, is at Folkingham again. How can he stand by and condone this?"

She shrugged tiredly. "He does not, of course. If he visits, they behave better. But he is not here often. To be frank, my dear, invasion and conquest stretch friendship."

I swallowed that.

After another pause, I said humbly, "And Alfred? May I ask you about him?"

And to my surprise, she smiled, though the tears swam into her eyes almost immediately.

"Oh you may," she whispered. "I cannot speak of him to anyone here – it would only make things worse, riling our own people by my grief, or *them* by my anger – and Torfrida, my heart is bursting . . .!"

"When did he – die?" I asked, low.

She said calmly now, "Not a week ago. He finally gave them the excuse, rushing upon some of *his* men who were insulting me and my women. He even killed one. Inevitably he – Frederic – arrived to avenge it, and killed my son. It wasn't even a proper contest because, he said later, Alfred was no knight and therefore unworthy of knightly consideration. He just attacked him and slaughtered him."

Her lips twisted with pain. "He was brave, you see, but he never had his brother's skills. He was a sweet-natured boy always – except for those few months just after Hereward left . . .

"There was no need to kill him. It was not vengeance. It was not justice. It was greed. Because as soon as my boy lay dead at his feet, he said, 'Well, I think that settles it. Bourne is mine.' And no one can deny him."

Her eyes closed.

I said helplessly, "Aediva, don't . . ."

"He cut off my son's head and. . . stuck it on the gatepost, to tell everyone Alfred was no longer their lord. Our people took away the rest of his body, tried to keep the head decently covered to avoid distressing me further . . ."

I glanced at the arrogant, aggressive back of Frederic de Warenne, as supremely confident in his unforgivable position as in his argument with his lieutenant.

I said intensely, "He cannot get away with this."

"He has got away with it."

"To a point," I allowed. "Nothing will restore Alfred. But I promise you I will bring this to the King's attention. My friends here, and in Flanders, will force it upon his notice and on those who can and must redress it."

Until *he* comes, as he must now, in the end . . .

"You believe anyone will care." It was not a question; it was a statement of fact.

"I will make them care."

A faint warmth entered her red, grieving eyes. "You are a sweet girl, Torfrida. You always were, even under the prickles. My children all saw that. I am glad he married you."

I swallowed, but before I could say what I needed to, I saw that Frederic was turning to us, regarding us thoughtfully over his shoulder.

"Such old friends," he observed sardonically, "clearly have much to discuss."

"Clearly," I agreed. "And as clearly, we are poor company at your feast. Perhaps you would excuse us, to go and discuss our silly women's things, and let your – ah – jollity proceed unconfined."

If I had hoped to shame him by this – after all the jollity was pretty unconfined as it was – I was again doomed to disappointment.

"I would not hear of it," Frederic said gently, and I thought his smile had grown . . . wolfish. "We *like* silly women's things – don't we, Humphrey?"

"Love them," Humphrey confirmed.

I almost jumped, for his breath actually tickled my ear as he spoke. Turning unhurriedly, I gave him the long, clear look of scorn that had repelled numerous over-familiar suitors in the past.

His smile did fade slightly; he even leaned back to a more decorous distance; but I wondered how long my tried and trusted methods would last in this place. Aediva was right; they were out of control. And with this knowledge came an inkling of what it meant for me, personally. Only a fool, I thought, would not have been frightened.

But Frederic was laughing, and before that smug arrogance, I would not give in to timidity. I stared at him glacially.

He said, "Why, I believe this lady has cast a spell on all of us. I forgive you willingly, lady, since you cheer up this drab company so dazzlingly."

"You must forgive them the odd, drab tear," I uttered, before I could stop myself. "They are, after all, in mourning."

The meal was finished but the wine still flowed. I wondered when we would be allowed to leave, for tension and ill-behaviour were galloping towards levels unbearable.

When one of the Normans, taking his cue from Frederic's contemptuous manner, dared to touch Aediva, the servitor I had seen complaining of them before upset a jug of wine over the man's lap. He was struck to the floor for his stupidity, and would, I think, have died under the Norman's sword had I not sharply requested Frederic to intervene.

He did so laconically, watching me the whole time, as he commanded his man to leave the fool alone or serve the wine himself. So the soldier – called Alain, apparently – contenting himself with a kick and a shrug, sat back down and groped at Aediva's younger woman instead.

But Humphrey was breathing in my ear again. "I suppose you must miss your husband."

"I suppose I must," I said, shifting my face distastefully away.

This turned out to be a mistake, for it brought the back of my head into unexpected contact with Frederic's shoulder. Before I could move again, his hand had come up, trapping me there while his fingers began actually to rub my lips.

Never had I known such blatant discourtesy.

"Well," he said softly, "we must see what we can do about that . . ."

And for the first time, I was truly afraid. My previous tense unease, the fear I had been repressing, seemed all to explode into revulsion, into something akin to terror. Because I saw finally that I could not deal with this.

Every instinct was screaming at me to struggle, to bite and hit and throw the loathsome creature off. But all my life, my inner, thinking self has been strong enough, for good or ill, to compete with raw feeling. Now it let me lie still for a moment; then smile at him and gently reach up to take his hand in mine, remove it and sit back in my chair.

He permitted it. And I felt I had overcome another huge hurdle. And made myself more for the future. I began to wonder seriously if we could ever get out of this hall. And how safe we would be if we did . . .

Frederic was saying mockingly to Humphrey, "Right of lordship, my friend!"

"Why don't you stick to the old woman? She was good enough for you before!" Humphrey said rudely.

"This is intolerable," I said to Aediva in swift Saxon. It had to be swift or they would have heard the tremble in my voice.

"Bear up, my dear," she said pityingly. "They will fall over soon. Only a little longer."

It was obviously the way things had gone in the past. But looking about me, I thought she was wrong to be so sure this time. Certainly they were drunk, and some among the simple soldiery were clearly about to slip down under the tables. But there were many semi-alert faces among the drunkards. Alain, drinking noisily from Leofric's silver cup, was far from incapable, it seemed to me; and neither Humphrey nor Frederic himself had let their wine flow too fast.

I had changed the pattern, I saw with dread. A new face, a new defender for the lady, a new challenge to be overcome by one or other of them. By now the jester had left off his bawdy song and began to caper about the room in a heavy-footed parody of an English dance, grunting out some guttural nonsense as he went.

The Normans roared with laughter. The table-servants and Aediva's women stared at the table. Aediva herself only shrugged. Their mockery was nothing to her. It harmed no one.

Suddenly Alain slammed down the big, silver cup so that wine slopped out of it and shouted over the noise to his lord.

"You know, I *like* this cup! Comfortable on the lips, like a very old wine, or a very young woman! May I keep it?"

"Of course you may," said Frederic generously.

"And the girl too?"

The girl's eyes flashed venom at the table. Then, as the English all eyed him with quite overt hatred, Frederic added, "You may *all* choose something. And if there's nothing civilized enough for your tastes – hell, pick something gold or silver and melt it down!"

"My lord!" Aediva broke into the cheering as if she could bear no more. "These are my husband's *personal* things, and my own. They belong to my son!"

"Your son is dead," Frederic said with casual brutality. And Aediva closed her eyes again. Unexpectedly, her women spoke up.

The elder said flatly, "Hereward is not dead." And won a sudden silence that folded about her with scorn and dislike.

I found myself counting the beats of my heart.

"If *he* were here," added the younger with intense hatred, "you would plunder none of these things."

"What, would he spirit them away by magic?" Humphrey mocked. "Or bring the Flemish army over to help him?"

The Normans howled with glee.

"He wouldn't need to," said the young woman, lifting her head with pride and peculiar longing. "Even as a boy he could beat *anyone*. None of you would stand a chance against him!"

Alain seized her round the waist. "What nonsense these pretty lips jabber!"

"It is not nonsense," Aediva said quietly.

But Frederic suddenly had had enough. He laughed unpleasantly, and his insulting hands were suddenly upon her, so that I jumped to my feet, aware that the crisis had come at last. I think I meant to hit him with my wine cup.

But before I could act, Humphrey had me by the waist, and Frederic was saying cruelly, "Not nonsense? You are a silly old woman and you know nothing! *I* have heard of this heroic son of yours! The great man who stole from his own lord to pay his men! He's naught but a mercenary and a brigand! Aye and a coward too, else he'd be here. But can he protect his own mother from this – or this – or this? Dare he so much as lift a finger against me, or Humphrey or any of my lesser men?"

"Ask him."

CHAPTER 29

The words seemed to be blown in by a sudden wind, ruffling around the hall. No one had heard the door open, but we all heard it close. Paralysed, everyone stared towards it, and I, peering over Humphrey's suddenly limp arm, felt my heart try to jump out of my strangling throat.

He wore a helmet glinting red and orange from the flaming torch above his head. His wild, gold hair streamed out from under it like a warrior angel's train over leather tunic and breastplate. His arms and legs were barbarically bare, bulging with muscle. He held an axe loosely in one hand; the other held a sword, just as casually, to a Norman soldier's neck, while his arm held the man, still choking, below his chest.

He smiled around the silence; a dazzling, dangerous smile. They never guessed how dangerous until it was too late.

"Hallo," he said, and with monstrous carelessness drew his sword across his captive's throat.

Released, the man fell gurgling from Hereward's relaxed arm. I felt sick with shock. But then we were meant to.

Frederic pushed Aediva aside, still trying to recover. For the first time, I felt some sympathy for him.

"Who the devil are you?" he sputtered, reaching angrily for his sword.

"I am Hereward of Bourne. And you . . ." The sword lifted, pointing straight across the hall at Frederic's heart, every vestige of a smile gone from his face and his soft, deadly voice. ". . .you are dead."

There was a pause, more of shock than of fear, I think.

But then: "Spit him," said Frederic briefly.

And Humphrey leapt across the table, sword in hand. Alain was ahead of him, cheek-by-jowl with another, both running at Hereward together, while the lesser soldiers stumbled to their feet, fighting loose of their women and their ale, and struggling to reach their weapons.

Aediva sat down abruptly with a piteous cry, burying her face in her hands at this, the loss of all she had left. But I, backing several involuntary paces away from her until I encountered the wall, the wine-cup still useless in my hand, could not take my eyes off *him*. Not even when his axe half-cut off Alain's head, and his sword took the other officer in the stomach.

There was no time for triumph. They were all upon him, drunk and not so drunk, and he in their midst, hacking, thrusting, spinning, cutting, his mouth open in some searing, continuous battle-cry which I could hear over all the rest of the hellish noise.

I had never seen him fight before, not like this. No tournament could have prepared me for it. Often, it was not even fighting, but simple slaughter. It was vicious, brutal, pitiless, and yet it was magnificent too, barbarically splendid. In its own way, it was even beautiful; and I, as shamefully entranced by that beauty as I was appalled by the violence, could not even close my eyes.

He was like some shining, vengeful god, untouchable and unbeatable, and they fell under his whirling axe and bloody sword, under his feet and elbows and head, like so many giant insects.

Of course, he took blows too, when, occasionally, they got near enough for long enough; but they never stayed his hand, nor slowed him in the slightest. He never even winced, so I did not. Not then.

Slowly, Aediva raised her head, and looked. And looked, and looked. And the Saxon servants, clinging along the walls with the women, kicked out at the fallen within their reach. Aediva's women were open-mouthed, round-eyed with fear and excitement and slow, unbelieving triumph.

"Is it him?" the girl kept saying. "Is it really him?"

Nothing, nothing could stop this pitiless death-bringer. He was like the berserkers of the old Viking tales. As the bodies fell around him, so fast that I could not quite believe it was real, I wondered wildly where it would stop . . . if he *could* stop.

Evidently, Frederic wondered the same thing. Or perhaps he assumed no Saxon would dare enter a hall so full of Normans without plenty of men to back him up. At all events, seeing the direction of events, he took no chances but strode the four long paces to the window, leapt upwards and squeezed himself through.

And Hereward, even in the midst of his endless slaughter, saw him go. His cry rose up and up, became words, orders as he hacked his way ruthlessly forward through screams and blood and vicious blows.

"Martin! The window!"

So Martin at least was somewhere near – guarding the door? Watching outside? Whatever his role, it was a relief to know there was someone else, for even yet I could not quite see how he could win his way out of this. Mostly drunk and rapidly decreasing in numbers as they were, it was surely only a matter of time . . .

None of it can have taken long, but after Frederic's escape, it was quickly finished.

The Normans lay dead or dying across the tables, in tangles upon the floor, among the fallen plate and scraps and pools of blood and spilled ale. All of them.

In the midst of it, Hereward stood, breathing deeply, audibly, in the sudden, eerie silence, his sword still held before him, ready. Blood oozed from a gash in his bulging arm, from another wound in his face. But his eyes were on Aediva, his mother, who had risen as if she could not help it, her hands half-lifted towards him.

"Hereward," she whispered. "Hereward . . ."

And then, it seemed, despite the years of dread, it was easy after all. She had stumbled round the table somehow and he had come for her, dropping his weapons on the floor with a resounding clank, crushing her in his powerful, bloody arms, his eyes closed tight over her shoulder, his lips moving in words even she can scarcely have heard.

"Forgive me. Forgive me." Over and over. "Forgive me."

It appeared she did hear.

"Hereward. You did this – *this* – for me!"

And he moved at last so that he could look into her face.

"For you," he said clearly, like a vow, "and for my brother. And for my father who would have done no less."

I thought I would weep then. It was the shock, I told myself; but it wasn't, or not entirely. There was a great sorrow for him, for the years he had wasted, and pride too, high and soaring because he was making it right at last. What should have been said to Leofric was said to her; and I believed, I had to believe, he heard it too.

I saw Aediva's hand lift, touching his hair, his wounded face, and her lips smiled tremulously.

"Leofric would have tried, God bless him for it. But even in his youth, he could not have done *this* . . ."

He probably couldn't, I reflected. But it was doubtful he would even have tried. No one but Hereward would have been mad enough. Or bad enough to wait until the Normans were drunk enough to slaughter . . .

Hereward said flippantly, "Behold my unexpectedly righteous arm. Late and guilty and far from unsullied, but strong at least." He stopped, folding his lips over the inappropriate levity he could not help. "And yours to serve. As it should always have been."

"Oh Hereward . . ." She clutched him to her once more. But he was a soldier, eternally alert for danger, and over her shoulder, his eyes were moving again, scouring the hall. And inevitably, they came to me.

I could think of nothing to say. Neither could he.

I read the sheer astonishment in his face. God knows what he read in mine. There was a short, pregnant pause, while the whole world seemed to stand still. I had the awful feeling it was about to collapse around my ears. I was praying for some pleasure in his eyes.

Then, gently putting Aediva aside, he parted his lips to speak, and I melted.

I never discovered if the words were to be harsh or loving, for his face gave me no clue, and he never said them.

At the crucial moment, a sudden movement behind him caught my eye: it was Humphrey, risen bleeding to his feet, sword in hand, and close enough to kill him before he could fully turn, let alone pick up his fallen sword.

A voice from the door – Martin's – cried warningly, "Hereward! Behind you!"

With the first syllable, Hereward span instinctively to face the danger, just as I threw my wine cup with the unerring accuracy I had boasted since childhood. It met Humphrey's temple with an audible thud that was at least partly *crack*.

Humphrey looked surprised. His eyes gazed widely at Hereward, as if wondering just how he had managed that, and then he crumpled silently to the floor and was still.

Hereward watched him without excitement.

"Thank you," he said mildly.

Gratefully, I recognized that tone, knew how to respond without thought.

"Don't mention it," I said politely.

Retrieving his sword, he turned back to me more slowly. "Torfrida. Did I pack you by mistake?"

"No. You forgot to pack me altogether. I have remedied the oversight."

He said evenly, "I seem to remember there was a child."

"There still is. Tyrannizing over its grandparents and cousins."

Throughout this brief exchange, his eyes were on mine, all the terrible violence of the recent storms still there; yet I could see him wondering detachedly how to deal with this additional problem. I felt sick again.

Then Martin was beside him, breathlessly.

"It's all clear. No one else around. Leofric's gone after the one who jumped."

"He couldn't find him though," said a pale, lanky man quickly, coming into the hall. Sword in hand, it took me a moment to recognize Leofric the Black, the dreamy youth who had been Hereward's boyhood friend. The sword somewhat casually saluted Aediva, and those Saxons just beginning to close in, with awe and doubt, upon their saviour.

Hereward rubbed his forehead once with the back of the hand that held his own sword. Impatiently, he sheathed it.

"Never mind. We'll get him later. You remember Torfrida, don't you, Leofric? Now my wife."

"*Torfrida?*" He stared at me. "*Little* Torfrida?"

"I grew. It happens to most children."

A slow smile broke out on his deceptively gentle face. "You did. And most charmingly."

"I told you," said Martin philosophically.

Hereward said wryly, "I thought you were meant to be a priest these days."

"Deacon," Leofric amended peacefully. "And even deacons may look."

His smile was singularly sweet, but Hereward seemed to have lost interest. His task was not over. I knew from his posture – carefully, tensely still – that he was consciously doing what had to be done, saying what had to be said. Standing once more by his mother's side, he turned to face his people.

"Elfwyth," he said to the elder of his mother's women, and took her by the shoulders and kissed her.

I was the only one denied his affection.

191

She wept as he put her aside and turned to the others, his eyes banishing the storms as he had learned to do, while he spoke quietly and sincerely.

"Some of you know me already. The rest – who were probably children when I left – must have guessed who I am. Hereward, son of Leofric. In his name and in my own, I thank you for your loyalty to my mother, in what must have been intolerable circumstances."

He held up one quick, self-deprecating hand against the surge towards him.

"No. I am aware you neither wish for nor expect thanks – that too is part of your goodness. But I who have been far away and useless in her trouble and in yours, must thank you anyway."

He looked directly at the chief of the English servants, or at least the man who had acted as such, and added, "I take it this evening has cleared up the matter of the disputed lordship of Bourne?"

The man grinned. A spontaneous, still breathless cheer broke out. Imaginary weapons were raised aloft in salute.

Hereward did not even smile, although Aediva and Leofric did, and even Martin leaned on his sword with smugly twisted lips.

"Good. I have taken back what is ours, but it is not over yet. There will be retaliation for what I have done. We may well have to fight to keep it. I have been here only three days, but long enough to know the strength of Norman power in these parts. So . . ." His eyes moved around them again, frank, friendly, uncoercive. "If any of you wish to leave this house, to disassociate yourself from my actions, you are free to do so. No harm will come to you from me, unless you raise a hand against me or mine. It is not necessary to tell me, just go before morning.

"Now, there is work to do."

His shoulders relaxed slightly in relief, because he had got this part over with; now he could turn back to action.

"I am going out with Leofric and Martin, to make things secure, maybe even to meet up with the one who got away. What was his name? He of the big nose."

The English howled with glee. I watched with a strange, half-sardonic pride as he began the binding process – making them his, even though he had just returned from prolonged desertion to land them, probably, in even greater trouble.

"I'll send Ordred in to help, but I want these bodies disposed of. My brother . . ." He looked with difficulty at Aediva. "My brother will be made whole in death. I believe we have more fitting decorations for our gates now."

"Hereward, no," Aediva whispered, echoing my own sudden revulsion.

"It is necessary," he said briefly, implacably. He was already beginning

192

to move away, leaving me again with nothing righted nor even acknowledged. "Look away if you don't like it. Dispose of the rest, and I'll be back in an hour or so."

"What if any of them are alive?" Aediva protested, as the serving men began to heave the dead towards the door. Despite everything, she was still astounded by the brutality of her soldier son. Hereward half-turned back to her, a first, wry smile beginning on his lips.

"Give them to Torfrida," he said flippantly. "That should either finish them off or scare them back to health."

I dreamed.

I know I did, but I could never afterwards remember of what, just that it was interrupted abruptly. Not by a shout or a bump, or even the click of the closing door, but suddenly I was awake, sitting bolt upright in the big bed. And a figure was standing, leaning against the chamber door.

I had time – an instant – for fear; and then it moved, coming towards me, and I said, "Hereward."

"May I light the lamp?"

"I will do it."

His voice was still distant, curiously formal as it thanked me; and his face, when my clumsy fingers finally managed their task, was white and shadowed, tired beyond belief in the flaring flame.

Filled suddenly with only overwhelming pity, the words I had planned died in my throat. He had removed his helmet and breast-plate, but the weapons at his belt still clanked ominously as he sat on the bed, not touching me, just looking down at his big, scarred hands which had so recently done such dreadful and efficient violence. But that could not have been his trouble: he was a soldier.

No, it was grief and guilt which bore him down now in the peace of the night; and perhaps confusion as to where it was leading him. I could tell nothing else, only that for some reason the strong, powerful man on my bed had never seemed so far from me.

So I could not speak of the things I had meant to.

What came out was: "What did they say? Those letters you never sent me?"

There was a moment's blankness. Then his lips curved slightly into a faint smile, and his eyes lifted at last to mine.

"All that I never said in your presence. All my impossible dreams of finding a fitting place for us; all I needed to clear in my head. Nothing. And everything. Who told you?"

"My mother. The Siwards."

"How did they know I never sent them?" he wondered wryly.

"Why didn't you?"

193

His eyes fell away. I had lost him again.

After a pause, he said, "I don't know."

Because he was strong and despised the weakness of his need. Partly, perhaps. And now, now he was soul-weary, and I was just another task to face.

I said, "Lie down; let me see to your wounds . . ."

"There is no need," he said politely. "I bound my arm and nothing else is serious . . ."

"With some dirty rag," I interrupted, eyeing the object in question with disfavour, for genuine wifely concern was able to overcome the last of my hesitance. I even reached up to the cloth, but abruptly, he caught my hand, bearing it downwards so fast that I gasped.

He said, "No. There will be time for that later. There are things I have to say now."

He let go of my hands almost at once and did not touch me further. Bewildered, fighting a new dread that this time I truly did not know how to get round him, even how to *reach* him, I simply gazed at his averted profile, beautiful still, but stern as I had never seen it, without either the softening fun of youth or the later sardonic flippancy which had so intrigued me. There were the beginnings of a beard on his jaw – after all these years, would he finally grow a full, Saxon beard? Such small, unimportant thoughts kept me sane in the interval before he spoke.

Then: "I did not want you here. Not until I had seen what to do and made things safe. But you are here now, and there is only one way to deal with that. If you cannot agree, I shall send you back."

I closed my eyes because I could not bear it, and the quiet, relentless voice went on with a strange, determined sort of dispassion.

"Don't misunderstand me. I *want* your cool, thinking mind with me. I want your advice, your laughter, your daily presence at my side. I want your beauty to soothe me when I'm tired, to confound my enemies and win round my friends. And I want you – God knows I want you! – in my bed. These are truths I cannot change. But none of it matters, Torfrida, if I cannot rely on you to do exactly what I say."

My eyes had opened into his with new, startled wonder. And I saw that his unquiet eyes were not dispassionate at all.

"If I am to do this, I need to know you are where I left you, or where I bade you to be, doing what we agreed you would do. I cannot have any more wild starts across the country. Do you understand me?"

Slowly, I shook my head.

"No. I am here. I cannot come again. And I don't know what it is you are planning to do."

The ghost of a smile passed across his face and vanished. "Why, neither do I, but I need your promise, Torfrida."

Still slowly, so as not to force him from me again, I reached out, slid my hand into his. His fingers curled around mine and held. Relief flooded me.

I said unsteadily, "You have it. I promise. But I need one from you too: you must tell me what you are doing, what you are planning, otherwise I am floundering in the dark, unable to help you. And I *can* help."

His eyes searched mine for a moment. Then he nodded once, and opened his mouth to speak. But I knew now that the task was over. Anything else could wait for morning. So it was I, this time, who placed a finger on his lips.

"Hush. That is for another day. Come to bed. You need to sleep."

His fingers helped me loosen his belts, with all their bloody weaponry. I did not look at them. Together we removed the tattered, scarred tunic, and when we came to the stained, still yellow ribbon tied around his shoulder, he tried quickly to hide it with his hand, like a little boy, as if he had forgotten about it. And I wanted to weep, because he really did wear it, because he had never seemed so vulnerable to me before. Wordlessly, I let him hide it in his violent fist while I gently pressed him back on to the pillows.

CHAPTER 30

Brand – he of the amazing eyebrows and appalling table manners – was now Abbot of Peterborough. And he had closed the gates against us.

We had set out early in the morning, Hereward and I, with a stream of his higher-ranked followers: Leofric the Black – now the Deacon; a stockier, hairier Wynter than I remembered; and two identical youths who were apparently his cousins and who answered to the unlikely names of Outi and Duti.

Behind the monastery gates, the monks jostled each other and chattered as excitedly as their less religious brethren. From the town, the wealthy "Golden Borough" itself, a sizeable crowd of observers had followed us at a safe distance, and now stood around us, gawping.

"It must be Hereward! Look at the size of his following – and every one English!"

"Which one is Hereward then?"

"Which one do you think?"

"Does he mean us ill? Plunder?"

"Why else would he have come here?"

"The reverend Abbot is his uncle!"

"Would you go on a family visit with such an army at your back?"

"No, but I haven't just killed fifteen Normans . . ."

"Fifteen? I heard it was fifty . . ."

Hereward smiled amiably at them. I wondered if they found it comforting. "I am Hereward of Bourne," he observed, not loudly, yet the monks within the gates all fell silent. There was a slight flurry as one pushed his way to the front, a man of middle years, still vigorous, a man not easily intimidated. He bowed his head courteously.

"My name is Ivor. I had the honour of acquaintance with your late father."

Hereward gazed at him with bland civility.

He cleared his throat. "I am the sacrist here. I believe I may speak for my brethren when . . ."

"It would give me great pleasure to speak with you," Hereward interrupted gravely. "And to them. Perhaps later we may indulge ourselves. First, though, I am afraid I must see the Abbot my uncle."

"If you will dismount, my lord, Brother Porter will admit you – and your lady wife?"

The question in his voice was unmistakable. I had the feeling he would have liked to have been able to insult me with a different title, but Hereward introduced me quite seriously, adding, "Your caution is understandable – admirable even – but in this case unnecessary. I know they look a ferocious set of brigands, but I assure you they are as gentle as lambs. We come in peace."

A loud, distinctive snort of derision rent the air. The brothers fell back. A large man in stained clerical garb stood revealed. I knew him at once, but after twelve years, the sudden rush of affection took me by surprise.

"You, Hereward? In *peace?* There is, of course, a first time for everything, but in this case, I take leave to doubt it!"

"Uncle Monk," said Hereward fondly. "How are you?"

"I *was* very well. What do you do here?"

Hereward looked hurt. "I came to visit you, of course. And after twelve years, I had hoped for a little more enthusiasm."

"I have been grateful for those twelve years," Brand said drily. "It is the twelve before which bother me."

Hereward grinned, properly this time. "Just let me in, my uncle! I am a changed man, I promise you – a man of peace . . ."

"It's not what I hear."

". . . a married man and a father," Hereward finished undeterred. "And I thought you might like to renew your acquaintance with my wife. Now, would I bring my wife on a mission of violence?"

"I don't know," Brand said frankly, eyeing me with considerable doubt.

"Saving the lady's presence, my mind boggles at the idea of what sort of female you can have induced to marry you. What do you mean, renew my acquaintance?"

The question followed so quickly on top of the insults, as if the significance of Hereward's words had only just registered, that I laughed aloud. And the iron-grey eyebrows shot upwards like some creature unexpectedly disturbed in the undergrowth. His startled eyes were scrutinizing me again, with more care this time.

I smiled at him.

Hereward said, "Don't you recognize her?"

And abruptly, Brand rattled the gate.

"Open it!" he roared, and before anyone could get in, he had come striding out, a walking monument to his last several meals. Laughter, sudden joy, rose up in my throat, together with some un-named emotion which catapulted me off my horse and into his arms to be hugged to his dubious habit.

"Torfrida, Torfrida, is it really you? How can you have done such a thing as to marry this – this . . ."

"Nephew," said Hereward obligingly. I could feel the calculation in his eyes. I had not been brought along for my company. He was doing more, far more, I suspected, than just testing, or even seeking, Peterborough's allegiance.

"Well, you are a monk," I said excusingly. "And besides, you were not there! No one else in Flanders would have me."

"I tried to warn you about the stilts!"

Releasing me, his eyes moved uneasily once more over the men, over Hereward, dismounting now in leisurely fashion.

"And these?" he asked. His eyes looked directly into mine. He knew I would not lie. Fortunately, I did not need to.

I said steadily, "He does come with peaceful intent. He would never hurt you; you must know that."

And he relaxed. "Of course I know it," he sighed, holding out his arms. "Come here, you reprobate. Kiss your uncle."

Hereward eyed his uncle's chest with disfavour.

"I'm not sure I care to come so close," he said outrageously. But since he had already embraced the Abbot, his insolence was robbed at once of offence. With interest, I saw genuine affection flash briefly, intensely across the old man's face. I had never been sure of their odd relationship before, but now I saw that whatever else, there was love. On Brand's side at least.

"Come in then, come in," he said gruffly. "But I hold you responsible, Hereward!"

"You always did."

"How is your mother? I have not seen her in nearly two years . . . I gather you have come home to harry her into an early grave?" And then, as we began to walk together into the abbey grounds, his face changed. "About Alfred – I am sorry. There is no more I can say."

Hereward nodded quickly. He had not come to speak of Alfred, and he did not want to. The wound, like the guilt, was still too raw.

"Is it dinner time?" he asked.

Brand swiped a hand across his eyes and sighed. "I suppose it can be. Do you want to be private?"

"No," said Hereward surprisingly. "Or not yet. There is something I wish you to do for me. I'll tell you when we are inside. Where do you want the horses?"

We repaired to the refectory, where we were seated with honour among some scared and awed looking monks.

"I heard he was in Flanders," Brand said to me. "I even wondered if you had come upon him and were able to exercise some benevolent influence upon him. Yet it never entered my head you would *marry* him!"

I regarded him with a touch of sardonic humour. "I rather think it never entered your head either that he could ever be induced to marry plain little Torfrida."

"You were never plain," he said flatly. "You may have scowled and had spots and dull hair, but you were never plain. Precisely. There was always something about you." He nodded derisively at his difficult nephew. "Even *he* saw that."

"I thank you," I said gravely. "I think."

"So what does he want? Has he really retaken Bourne?"

"Yes, and his other estates, and most of the illegally stolen lands round about too. There is, I believe, scarcely a Norman left in the district – apart from Gilbert of Ghent. As to what he wants – I'm not sure. We could ask him."

"I asked already," he said, glaring at the back of Hereward's head. And my husband, who had been issuing some low-voiced instruction to his men, turned unexpectedly and caught the baleful glare.

He smiled beatifically. "Pin down your eyebrows, Uncle Monk. I want you to knight me."

It wasn't only the eyebrows that threatened to fly off Brand's face. His jaw too seemed to drop down to the floor. I had some sympathy; this I had never expected.

"You are astounded," Hereward observed, while his men and the monks looked on in silent expectation. "Do you doubt my deserving it, or my wanting it, or your own ability to grant it?"

Brand's brow had crashed back over his eyes in one enormous frown.

"None of these," he said at last. "Merely your motive. You have made your own way in the world – and most successfully by what I hear – without this honour. Why now?"

Hereward's eyes fell briefly, then lifted to his uncle's again, open and direct. "A so-called knight with a big nose insulted my mother; and murdered my brother without granting him even the courtesy of a fair fight. Because he claimed Alfred was not a knight."

Of course.

Brand blinked once. "You are going after Warenne. He is the Earl of Surrey's brother, you know, and close to the King. How ever you kill him, it will be called murder."

"Let me worry about that. He and I will know."

"The Normans," Brand went on, "do not recognize knights made by churchmen."

"They will recognize this one."

Brand sat back in his chair. "Fair enough. Now tell me why I should do it; why I should risk myself and my abbey and all it contains of wealth and godly men, just to let you kill another Norman?"

He had a powerful point, but Hereward never even blinked.

He said quietly, "From what I hear, you risked all these things two years ago when you gave your support to the Aethling against King William."

"True. I bought myself out of trouble that time. I doubt it will work twice. Besides I have little desire to facilitate your brawls, nephew."

It was more, much more than a brawl, and Brand knew it. Glancing at him with some indignation, I found his eyes locked with Hereward's, looking for the truer explanation. And my husband was not mocking now.

He said quietly, "Look beyond this brawl, uncle."

And I felt at last a glimmering of understanding, a dawning wonder that was terribly close to fear. This was not just for Frederic or for Alfred. Not any more.

He said steadily, "Our people are being reduced, enslaved till they are little better than the beasts. In time, they will disappear like the ancients. I cannot let it happen, not without a fight . . ."

And as a knight, he would gain greater standing with his own people as well as with the Normans; by obtaining the honour from the Church, he provided himself with righteousness as well as with evidence of the Church's support. It was certainly clever. Often, in Flanders, it had been I who had helped him to see the larger story in which he played. Now, just a little dizzyingly, I had the feeling he had gone beyond me, that he was seeing far more than I.

Brand said, "God help me, I'll do it."

Hereward left Peterborough a knight, solemnly presented with his own belt and his father's sword as symbols of his new status. In the Abbey's

richly gilded and decorated chapel, where the relics were encased in sparkling jewelled boxes and the ornate altar table and chalices were made of
solid gold, Brand performed the ceremony for Hereward and his chief followers. Then, when they had fallen back closer to me, Hereward held old
Leofric's sword hilt in his hand, gazing down at it, his face carefully neutral.

Brand said, "Aediva gave it to me for safe-keeping when your father
died. She said Leofric would have wanted me to have it. But we both knew
she intended it for you. Because *he* did."

Hereward's lips twisted in a quick spasm of pain, then straightened. His
eyes lifted to his uncle's.

"Thank you."

"Use it well, Hereward. Please."

The abbot's voice was uncharacteristically serious. I thought Hereward
would shrug it off with mockery or flippancy to cover the very real feeling he could never deal with. But after a pause, he only nodded.

"I will," he said. Like the vow he had once given me. Emotion that was
part unease, rose up into my throat. Driven, I slid my hand into his, felt his
fingers close at once, and took comfort. Comfort and a proper pride in him.

Outi and Duti were teasing one of their fellow knights by the chapel
door, calling for Hereward's collaboration. He was already turning towards them, thought not, I noticed, with his usual avoidance of intolerable
scenes of emotion; just because he had taken it upon himself to keep his
men happy. I had the oddest notion that something was happening to
Hereward. For better or for worse, he seemed almost to be *growing*. Or
just, finally, beginning to fill the growth that had always been there . . .

"Hereward."

Unexpectedly, it was Brand, calling him back. Glancing back over his
shoulder, Hereward must have seen, as I did, the war raging indecisively
across his uncle's face.

He said, "You began it; you had better finish."

Brand sighed. "Warenne," he said reluctantly, and I felt an unpleasant
jolt back to reality. "Frederic de Warenne was here yesterday, looking for
you. He thinks you would not have the nerve to stay at Bourne, but would
hide in the forest and scrounge from your friends and family."

Hereward's face never changed. "What did you tell him?"

"Nothing. I said I did not even know you were in the country; that I had
not seen you and did not want to."

"Just the truth then," said Hereward.

"Just the truth," Brand agreed. "He is headed into Norfolk to gather
support."

Only as we approached the Norman column of some thirty men did

Hereward slow to a more leisurely pace; and that was deliberate, so that we appeared to swagger out of the trees with contemptuous unconcern.

Reaction among the Normans was immediate, a flurry of talk and pointing fingers and closing ranks while they assessed the danger. They must have seen a wild looking band of Saxons, all long, flowing locks and barbaric beards, ominously and audibly armed with clanking steel and wooden spears. And at the forefront, the bright, commanding figure of Hereward himself, wearing neither helmet nor protective armour of any kind; yet his whole appearance, his whole demeanour, was uncompromisingly dangerous.

I recognized Warenne easily at the front of his own men. I saw his thick lips move, giving the order that led to thirty drawn swords.

Hereward laughed loudly, and whistled.

Duti and the other half of our men came trotting out of the trees behind the Normans, who jerked round in understandable alarm, causing their animals to rear and whinny. Warenne ignored them, for he had recognized Hereward, and his eyes had grown wide and fixed. I really don't think it had ever entered his head that the hunter could so easily become the hunted.

"*You?*" The word was wrung from him, more in doubt than astonishment.

"I," Hereward agreed mildly enough, pulling up with some distance still between them. "You – ah – left my house so precipitously that we could not finish our business."

Frederic de Warenne's lips curled with contempt. "So you think to ambush me with your brigands? I warn you, my men sell themselves dear!"

Peering round Gaenoch, I saw Hereward's brows lift with lazy amusement. "Well, for the sake of their own self-respect, I hope they do. Your last set certainly didn't. However, my quarrel is not with them. If they stand aside from us, they will not be harmed."

"Then it is just myself you intend to cut to pieces with fifty swords?"

"One sword," Hereward corrected gently.

And Frederic actually laughed. I had to give him credit for courage – of a sort.

"You wish to fight me in single-combat? My good Saxon peasant, I only fight such duels with knights of my own rank."

"So you told my gentle brother," Hereward said evenly. "Before you hacked off his head."

"What, you seek *revenge?* Come, come. Don't your people accept blood-money in lieu? Consider Bourne your brother's – wirgeld. Only . . ." He smiled faintly. ". . .make the most of it, for I'll be back."

Hereward rested one brawny forearm on the pommel of his saddle, regarding his enemy with patience. But he wasn't patient: that much was obvious to me from every taut line of his body.

201

He said gently, "I don't think you quite understand. You are not going anywhere until I lie dead under your feet."

"I shall not sully my sword—"

"On one unknighted. I know," Hereward interrupted, apparently bored. "I have remedied that problem. You may consider me worthy of your sword."

Warenne's eyes flickered. He was, I saw with growing alarm, hoping to keep us here, as if he expected some kind of help soon . . .

Warenne said, "I don't believe you."

Swiftly, I urged my horse around Gaenoch, picking my way deliberately to Hereward's side.

"Then believe me," I said lightly. "I was there."

The Norman's impatient eyes flashed over me and away, then sprang back, and stared.

"I believe you have met the lady of Bourne," Hereward said sardonically.

And Warenne said, "*He* is your husband?"

"Oh he is," confirmed one of his men unexpectedly, and Warenne's head jerked half-round towards him. The speaker, under his conical helmet, looked faintly familiar to me. He was grinning, and at Hereward. "I danced at their wedding. In fact, I was mad as fire, for I wanted the girl myself. How are you, little Saxon?"

"*Asselin?*" said Hereward, staring. Well, so was I.

Warenne said suspiciously, "You *know* this Saxon?"

Asselin's grin broadened even further. "*Know* him? I know things about him that would curl your hair. Curl *his* too if I told them in front of his wife." His teeth flashed briefly in my direction; his hand, sword and all, crossed his heart in a salute that was not quite impudent.

But Hereward was impatient now. He said briskly, "Bid your men stand aside, or mine will force them."

Warenne stared at him, down his long nose, with all the black, stern authority of a conquering people.

"And if I refuse to fight you?"

"It won't be an option," said Hereward, "when I pull you from your horse – but you'd loose all your advantage that way."

"Don't try such stratagems on me! I too know something of your past," said Frederic contemptuously, already beginning to dismount. Hereward smiled. With a jerk of his head, Warenne banished his uneasy following to a more circumspect distance. Before he obeyed, I saw Asselin speak quietly to Warenne. To my anxious, suspicious eyes, it looked like, "Watch him. His left hand is no weaker than his right." Unnecessary advice, surely, after Bourne . . .

Several of our own men followed the Normans, standing between them and the combatants.

Hereward dismounted too, with swift, easy grace. Yet there was a tense, almost desperate will in him, and he did not so much as glance at me. Or at Asselin, a mere inconvenience from his past.

Outi, his hand on my mare's saddle, urged me out of the way.

With drawn swords, they circled each other. But only for a moment. Hereward could not afford to waste time, and he didn't. "I *will* kill the bastard," he had said savagely to me this morning. "I have never wanted to kill anyone so much in my life!" But it was not just his own desire; I knew this was expected of him.

Hereward made the first attack – so suddenly that I gasped with fright – and was repelled; and after that the fight was fast, furious and brutal.

Warenne was no novice. Nor was he a coward. At Bourne, I suspected, he had fled an imagined mob, to regroup and fight another day. And here, rather sooner than expected, was the day.

I forced myself to watch, to keep my appalled eyes open, but curiously this was far harder to take than Hereward's swift slaughter of sixteen men. This was concentrated, less blurry somehow. And the blows, the cuts, the deadly energy, were all horribly visible. There was nothing beautiful about this.

I tried to keep my gaze fixed only on Hereward's face, to see only the fierce concentration, the grim determination. There were no battle cries this time. It was fought in curious silence, save for the grunts and gasps of the fighters and the crashing of their weapons. The men of both sides were quiet too – even Asselin, oddly grim-faced – as though they were witnessing some religious ritual and not the ritual killing of one man by another.

And then, quite suddenly, it was over. Hereward was pushing and pushing, driving the Norman back until he was unable to do more than simply, desperately, defend himself. And then that too was taken from him. Hereward's sword sliced into Warenne's hand, forcing an involuntary scream. Then Hereward drew back so swiftly that I barely saw, and plunged the sword into his enemy's heart.

He is the Earl of Surrey's brother. However you kill him, it will be called murder.

I wanted to be sick.

Surrounded by the silent men, Hereward drew his sword free, watched Warenne fall. I thought he was already dead. A moment longer, Hereward gazed at him, breathing deeply. Then I saw his mouth close with decision, and he looked up quickly to find Asselin walking towards him between two of our men.

For a moment, their eyes held. In Asselin's, I could see the old admiration, the old envy, the old desire to impress and outdo; and yet there was calculation there too, an anxiety that this might rebound to his discredit, especially since he had admitted to previous intimacy with the perpetrator.

They were old roistering partners, these two, not soul-friends. And Hereward had been a mercenary then.

He said evenly, "Take your lord and give him a decent burial. It's more than he allowed my brother." I didn't know if he had allowed the distance, or made it. And he turned away briskly, issuing orders to Wynter as he went.

Martin Lightfoot was at his side now, handing him Swallow's reins, and Hereward mounted as lightly as if he had not just fought another man to the final standstill. A faint, grim smile even hovered on his lips as he glanced back at all the uncertainly muttering Normans, but it was to Asselin he spoke.

"My name, if anyone should ask, is Hereward *of Bourne*."

CHAPTER 31

When Lucy came, Easter had already passed.

By then, of course, Hereward was back from his trip to Flanders in search of men and money – although he had been gone six months rather than the one we had hoped for. That was the fault of Count Baldwin who had immediately clapped Hereward in prison for the theft of the Zealand tribute, until a combination of flattery, bribery and the threats of our friends had procured his release.

He returned with the first ship of the year, bringing the proceeds from the sale of some land, and more than thirty of his veteran soldiers, as well as the Siwards. I still like to think that we impressed them all by the scale and efficiency of our organization – myself, the twins, Leofric, and Wynter who, his stolen patrimony restored by Hereward, turned out to be one of the most sensible and capable of leaders.

For it had fallen out much as Hereward had foretold before his departure: our little band of malcontents and outlaws had swelled alarmingly over the winter, to include now such eccentric characters as filthy charcoal digger, Wulric the Black, who claimed to have single-handedly killed the ten Normans who had murdered his family; and his friend, the terrifyingly ugly Wulric the Heron who, by the speed of his attack, had swooped down upon an execution and saved several of his countrymen from the Norman hangman. This wild and motley army had already outgrown Bourne and had to be contained partly in a near-by camp in the forest. Restive without its nominal leader, it had nevertheless settled into the sort of obedience and strict training that Hereward had laid down. Yet with so many violent and individualistic men to control, it was a very anxious, exhausting and difficult six months for me, and for Hereward's lieutenants; only the glow of admiration in his eyes when he saw what we had done made up for that. It was, God help us, all the reward we needed.

My other reward for waiting, of course, was Frida, incredibly grown without me. Her shyness when she first saw me again almost broke my heart, and her fat little arms clung and clung every night when I put her to bed.

Inevitably, everything livened up with Hereward's return. Within a day, he had burned three villages above the forest which a band of Norman adventurers had occupied, and by the beacon of the flames many more had come in to join him. And while the north rose in rebellion, Hereward was opening lines of communication with their leaders, and with Edric the Wild who led a growing revolt along the Welsh marches and beyond. In fact, before Easter, things were looking so hopeful that I began to think, unbelievably, that we might succeed before the year was out.

At Easter, my mother surprised me beyond anything that had gone before by her decision to retire to a nunnery.

For Hereward had brought her, too, back to Bourne, clinging to him as to her only rock after the death of my father. I knew how she felt. Yet through my own grief, I was still secretly amazed that my life went on, that his death made so little practical difference to the life I now led: there was guilt in that too, and its own sorrow.

Being informed, quite casually, about my mother's astounding decision, I had stared at her open-mouthed, until she said calmly, "An English convent is as good as any other. Hereward was recommending Crowland."

Hereward would. He fought with the Abbot.

I had expected her to return in a week, but she was still there. So, when Lucy came, I was no longer feeling as defensive as I did in my mother's over-critical company.

She rode out of the forest's budding greenness like some fairy of the Celtic tales, her large husband and bristling escort incongruous companions for so ethereal a creature.

Or at least that was the original impression of my eyes, half-dazzled by the first blink of sun all week. But as she drew nearer, I saw that she was talking animatedly to her cousin Duti who led her escort. And judging by the expression on her husband's face, she had been doing so for some time.

Laughter bubbled up, nearly erupted when her mother fondly echoed my own more ambiguous thought.

"She is just the same . . ."

Only her husband, Tostig of Rothwell, looked older.

But she was undoubtedly the same Lucy, with the same impetuous charm, tumbling off her horse in the yard to cast herself into her mother's arms while Tostig observed proceedings somewhat grimly from the back of his own tired but magnificent grey stallion.

Leaving the mother and daughter to their long-awaited reunion, I went forward to greet him.

"Welcome to Bourne," I said civilly. "Will you not dismount and come inside?"

His eyes flew to mine, searching my face for signs he might recognize, dismissing his original idea that I was some kind of servant.

Then: "*Torfrida?*"

"Of course. Who else would have the gall to welcome you here?"

The frown vanished in a shout of laughter, and he dismounted to take me by the shoulders and kiss my lips with enthusiasm; after which he examined me in more detail.

"Why, little Torfrida," he said softly. "You have been busy in the years since we parted . . ."

"So have you," I returned, sliding neatly out of his embrace, but taking his arm in friendly fashion to lead him into the hall.

Tostig sighed. "One has to be busy, married into this family! So where is Hereward? I have been looking forward to meeting him again, now that he is the legend who slew fifteen Normans at one stroke -- or was if fifty Normans? Whatever, I suppose he must be as changed as you."

I shrugged, just a little warily, for there was more than a hint of mockery in his words. "We have all grown up, I suppose. But certainly he has more on his mind nowadays than merely competing with his friends." I smiled up at him. "Don't we all?"

Just for an instant, I thought he might take offence. Then, ruefully: "I don't know any more. What else is there to do? We seem to be running out of enemies we can beat."

"Then it is true?" I said quickly. "The Northumbrian rising is quelled?"

"Do you imagine anything less would bring me here, a supplicant for his alms?"

There was silence. Close by, I felt Lucy's eyes on me, staring, but the self-loathing in Tostig's voice was too distressing to ignore.

I said, "Don't be bitter. We are all in this fight. When it is over and won will be time enough to worry about who owes what to whom."

"It *is* you!" Lucy exclaimed suddenly, hurling herself at me like a puppy. She may have *looked* ethereal, but she was solid. I stumbled slightly, guarding myself with an instinctive gesture that caused her eyes to widen. "Are you . . .? Oh I'm sorry to be so rough; I did not know! But *look* at you! You are blooming!"

"And you still look fifteen years old," I retorted.

She laughed. "It's all artifice, I assure you! Where is my graceless brother?"

"I haven't a clue," I confessed. "But don't be offended: we only got the news of your coming after he had left. A messenger has gone to find him."

"Then he's still running wild? I don't know how you can bear it."

"The same way Tostig bears you, I expect."

"Dear Torfrida, I had almost forgotten you," she said affectionately, and then she was flitting round the hall, exclaiming over things she remembered, and things she did not, while I summoned serving girls to bring wine and spiced cakes.

It was a strange hour which followed, a mixture of family gossip and messages from Aethelthryth, and a rather harrowing tale of rebellion brutally squashed and a flight with nothing save what they could carry. Then, later, over supper, Lucy said, "So what is he doing now? Attacking some Norman stronghold?"

"Probably," said Aediva with a sigh of mingled pride and apology.

"But what does it achieve if he cannot hold it?" Tostig demanded. "And beyond a certain point, of course, he cannot!"

"Well, you must ask him . . ."

"It keeps the Normans busy and nervous," I said calmly, laying down my cup. "It reminds them to – ah – behave. And it inspires imitation. All over Kestevan and Lyndsey, and Holland, the Fens and beyond."

"So what?" said Tostig rudely. "Taken all together, such troubles don't amount to anything like the Northumbrian rising – and look what we achieved! Nothing!"

"I doubt that is true. And who is to say it is over? After all, William is no longer up there – is he?"

Tostig blinked. "I don't know where he is!"

"We heard he was on his way to Winchester. Well, any way, away from all of us." I lifted my cup to him. "You must talk to Hereward. He has a plan."

Involuntary laughter hissed through Tostig's teeth.

"Hereward always had a plan, rot him. God, Torfrida, do you remember that damned bear?"

"You ruined that particular plan," I said severely. "Hereward had trained him to bow to the lord Gilbert."

"And converse with the lady Matilda," Tostig grinned. "Yes, so he told me! They sing about it still in Northumbria, you know . . ."

"Your daughter is beautiful, by the way," Lucy said warmly, when she had pushed the remains of her meal away.

"Thank you."

"You will be hoping for a son this time?"

"I am hoping for anything at all that does not make me look and feel like a whale all summer."

Slightly shocked, she giggled. There was an obvious question to be asked about her own offspring, or rather lack of them, for Siward had told me she had not so far been blessed with children. But before I could ask it, Outi burst into the hall, his hair wild, his face white and taut. The door banged shut. Then, into the surprised outbreak of silence, Duti leapt to his feet.

But it was to me Outi came, crying out, "Lady, he's back!"

There was nothing in that to cause the consternation in his face, nor the sudden, dreadful thudding of my heart.

"He's hurt," Outi said, panting. "They're carrying him in . . ."

"Oh sweet Jesus and the Blessed Virgin . . ." Aediva whispered.

Somehow, I was on my feet, walking calmly towards the door, reminding myself over and over that I must show no fear for him, that the desperation trembling at my knees had to be held in check. I was conscious of Edric's messenger, standing, alert eyes darting from me to Outi. But there was time for no more.

The door was thrown open again, and Leofric backed in, half-carrying, half-wrestling a figure far from dead, judging by the energy in its voice as it commanded furiously, "For Christ's sake, let me alone! I can walk!"

"You can't even sit," Leofric panted. "Hold on to him there, Wynter! Martin . . ."

I thought vaguely that it must be relief, the dizziness I could not show either. I have the feeling I stood stock-still, like a statue, for several seconds until his voice hailed me into action.

He could not see me, but he knew I was there.

"Torfrida! Get that damned priest off me! I'm not dead yet!"

I moved forward. "Damned priest, be gone," I said shakily, laying my hand on Leofric's arm to deny the offence, to thank him.

But I could see Hereward now, throwing off Wynter and Martin with an anger that was frighteningly genuine. These days he generally controlled his temper absolutely, but this I understood. So much depended on *him*, on his reputation; he needed to be seen by his men, upright and whole, like old Siward, the ferocious Earl of Northumbria who had reputedly risen from his death-bed just so that he could die with his armour on.

Well, Hereward wore no armour, and he was not going to die. But his men needed to know that. Just for an instant, as our eyes met, he was still, and the pause was pregnant. Yet he stood alone now, and the storms were no longer so violent.

I said, "What is it?"

Leofric said, "He swooned. An hour ago. Just keeled over. There was blood."

There was still blood.

Hereward said dangerously, "I went to sleep. I was tired. Martin, get out of the way or open the damned door."

I moved quickly, careful not to touch him.

"Are you ready?" I asked low and urgently, so that no one else in the hall would hear, and when he nodded impatiently: "One minute, Hereward; no more, or you will undo any good from this, I promise you."

He didn't answer, just moved forward. We went together to face the frightened, anxious eyes of his men, scattered through the yard and the out-houses. And of course, he made it a joke.

While Martin held the lantern, to let them see that he stood whole and unaided, however bloody his tunic, he mocked his own weakness with such success that the yard was soon full of laughter – as much of relief as genuine amusement, I suspected.

"Now, Hereward," I warned.

We said good night in the midst of their mirth, and closed the door upon them. Some would come in later, of course, for they ate and slept in here; but by then I would have him safe and unseen in his own bed.

The door shut with a bump under my back. It was the force of his swaying. Somehow I refrained from catching at him, and as if he sensed the effort it cost me, he glanced down at me and smiled.

And then Aediva was there, squeezing his hands, tears standing out on her lashes, and he was saying something patient as, over her head, he saw his sister pushing through the tables towards him.

"Hallo, Lucy," he said casually, as if they had parted only yesterday.

She was laughing and crying at once. "How *dare* you greet us in such a way? We did not come here to be scared *witless* by your starts!"

"Sweet sister, you never needed to be scared."

His shoulders eased off the door. He was walking forward without aid to receive his sister's hug, and then he turned to face her husband.

There was an infinitesimal pause.

I understood it. Lucy had been easy, because they had always understood each other. Tostig – Tostig, I saw now, reminded him just a little too much of too many things he had chosen to forget. Hereward, in a word, was disconcerted. It was only an instant, and he would have got over it. But Tostig used it to look him up and down with just a hint of the old contempt I had seen before Hereward had troubled to win his friendship.

"So," he observed mockingly. "*This* is the living legend? It disappoints me."

Hereward's lips stretched slightly. "It is dog-tired and bleeding, whatever else it is. You must forgive the poor impression. I have better days."

"I would hope so."

"You were always an over critical bastard. I never meant to let you in my house. I shall beat Torfrida for this. After she has tended my wounds and gone to sleep."

Another of those involuntary hisses of laughter escaped Tostig, and

Hereward, realizing it would have to come from him, moved the distance between them and embraced his old friend.

Tostig gripped him hard. I tried not to wince for him.

Then, releasing him, Tostig said gruffly, "Take care of it," and nodded at the bloody tunic.

As soon as I closed the bedchamber door, my arm was at his waist, supporting, leading.

"It's very pleasant," he remarked, "but not necessary."

"I will be the judge of that. Sit."

Obediently, he sat on the bed, just a little faster than normal. I took no chances this time. I cut the tunic and the shirt, washing, anointing and binding the reopened wound while he, as had become the custom at such times, sat perfectly still and watched my face, not my hands.

I said conversationally, "A messenger has come from Edric."

There was a pause. "Did I disgrace myself?"

"Not irretrievably, I imagine. It is not a crime to be wounded. I daresay he is even impressed by the concern of your people."

"Have you spoken to him? Will Edric play?"

"I get the impression he is keen to. But Northumbria has collapsed."

"So I supposed from Lucy's descent."

"You'll have to take care with Tostig. His confidence has suffered."

He sighed. "I have always taken care with Tostig. It's a pity, in many ways, that I am now mature and responsible. Otherwise I would know precisely what to do."

"Fight each other to a standstill in some contest – preferably for a prize neither of you wants – and then get so drunk that you fall over together?"

"That's the one," said Hereward, pleased by my quick understanding.

"Well that won't work either – you're still wounded. But what of you? Where have you been?"

"Lincoln."

"I thought they liked you in Lincoln."

"Mostly. The wound opened after that, during a brief interchange of views with some Norman soldiers."

"So what were you doing in Lincoln?"

"Trading," said Hereward peacefully, lying back on the pillows under my insistent hands. His eyes closed. "Or at least arranging to trade . . ."

Removing his leggings, I said politely, "Trading what, exactly?"

"Gold. For men."

I paused. His eyes opened, lit fleetingly by his smile. I said, "What men?"

"Danes. I'm cold," he added plaintively.

I covered him, none too gently. "You are buying mercenaries? From the Danes? Are you mad?"

"No. I have parted with no gold, and won't until they earn it."

"Earn it how?" I demanded. "Hereward, you cannot let Viking freebooters loose on this country! Is it not suffering enough?"

"Most people in this part of the country are *descended* from Viking freebooters. They like Danes. They might even like another Danish king. Besides, say what you like about them, they are gallant fighters." His heavy, closing eyelids fluttered open again. "And useful allies."

I stared at him. "Can you control them?"

"I won't need to. King Swein will.".

"And when you want them to go? What then?"

"Pay them," said Hereward, sounding surprised. "It's an old custom, begun by our own noble Alfred a long time ago."

"They came back again," I said grimly.

"Things have changed since then," Hereward said comfortably, closing his eyes once more. "The Danes themselves have changed."

But I would not leave it there. "And if Swein wants to be King? He believes he has some claim, remember!"

This time, the eyes stayed closed. "I don't believe he has the stomach to risk his entire army against the Normans. We'll get allies, not new usurpers."

"When?" I demanded.

"Oh, late summer, I should think . . ."

Narrowing my eyes, I sat on the bed, gazing down at his angelic face. The frown of pain, the lines of tiredness, had vanished all together. I said dangerously, "How long have you been planning this, Hereward?"

He didn't answer. He might have been asleep, except that his lips were smiling.

CHAPTER 32

When the news came about Brand, we were celebrating (the first feast I had managed to attend from beginning to end since the birth of young Hereward, whom his proud father insisted on addressing as Prune) because our Danish allies were back in York, seizing their second opportunity while William dealt with Edric the Wild. And Edric himself, who had refused our help in this, remained defeated but untamed with a sizeable army still in the field. So we had plenty to celebrate, with the warm, slightly wild gaiety that seems to come with the longer, colder nights.

As far as poetry went, Hereward would only permit comic verse and riddles, none of the heroic epics so beloved by his people – the poetry he called maudlin drivel – yet he dismissed it in a way that only added to the hilarity and general jollity of the occasion.

The great haze of good will, overlaid with the great excitement of the times, reached out and caught me. Willingly, I sank into it; I thrilled to the slightest touch of the man beside me. For the first time since little Hereward's birth, I felt *well*. And I knew that tonight would end the long weeks of our abstinence. He felt it too; I could see it in his smile, in the moderation of his drinking, and the peculiarly lazy anticipation with which he lounged in his chair and exchanged banter with his people.

"And there is still the Aethling," Tostig was saying eagerly. "And Malcolm of Scotland: we cannot discount him . . ."

"I think we probably can," Hereward said drily. "He hardly has his troubles to seek in his own kingdom. William could buy him off fairly cheaply. In fact, I suspect he already has."

"And yet," I said with deceptive negligence, anxious to display my own powers of information gathering, "I hear that Malcolm is wild to marry the Aethling's sister."

Hereward blinked. "Is he, by God? I thought the Aethling's sisters were too holy to contemplate marriage with any save Christ; let alone a bigamous arrangement with a character of Malcolm's morality! Does he really plan to dismiss the daughter of the mighty Earl Thorfinn in favour of a dispossessed nun?"

"He doesn't need to," I said smugly. "The daughter of the mighty Earl Thorfinn is dead. Malcolm is a widower."

Hereward's lips twitched. "Well, if *that* comes off, it *will* put the wind up William. It might even put some backbone into Edgar!"

I didn't dispute it; my mind was on other things entirely.

Into this slightly decadent scene crept a monk, making his slightly nervous, dripping way between the tables, side-stepping some rollicking dancers on his long, obstruction-strewn route to the high table.

"For you, my deacon?" Hereward said to Leofric, observing this progress.

"Never seen him before."

"How can you tell? They all look the same to me . . . Brother, you are welcome in my hall. Will you sit and eat with us?"

"No, I thank you," was the surprising response. "I have not the time, and nor do you. I come from the Abbey of Peterborough. My lord Abbot has asked for you. He is dying."

For a moment, Hereward did not move. His smile, neglected, died slowly on his lips. His eyes did not leave the monk's face. To my shame, I knew an inner wail of rage, of frustration because this night, so long

212

awaited, had been stolen from us. But mostly, overwhelmingly, I felt grief, for the amiable clerk who had been my first English friend, my first instructor in the lore of the stars; and for his nephew, my husband, who had rarely shown him any affection, yet who had turned to him repeatedly both in need and in succour.

My hand stole into his. It felt cold, but it gripped mine hard.

Hereward said clearly, "How long does he have?"

"I cannot say. It is for the Lord . . ."

"Guess," Hereward interrupted unpleasantly.

"One day or two," said the monk hastily. "No more, we think. But he is . . ."

"I'll come," Hereward interrupted again. Standing abruptly, he pushed back his chair, barking out orders to Martin who leapt up to obey. I tried to stand with him, but his hand on my shoulder kept me seated. "Refresh yourself," he said to the monk. "Come back with me or stay here for the night; it is your choice. Torfrida . . ."

I met the gaze which swung on me, and summoned a smile. It wasn't a bad effort. I said, "I know."

The harsh face relaxed, ironing out the frown. He even smiled back, very slightly. "Yes, you do, don't you? Look after my mother."

I nodded, and swallowed. "And you will give Brand my love?"

"So!" roared Swein Estrithson, King of the Danes, appearing in our hall early that spring with his vast escort, somewhat sooner than we had anticipated from the warnings of our men. "So," he said again, fixing Hereward with his large, unblinking eyes. "You are the one who sends me such insolent messages."

I couldn't help my dismay. Could Hereward not be polite to anyone, even a King, even over hundreds of miles? A pace in front of me, yet beside me at the head of our extended household, he looked quite unabashed. In fact, he smiled.

"I am Hereward, son of Leofric," he acknowledged, somewhat casually. "But my letters intended no insolence."

"Did they not? Am I expected to believe that?" Swein seemed determined to introduce a little tension to the proceedings. Had he known Hereward as I did, he would have realized it was already there, though not from fear; rather from anticipation and a ruthlessly subdued excitement that he would have died rather than reveal. He looked, in fact, merely amused.

"You do believe it," he said wryly. "If it were otherwise, you would not be here."

"I might have come to cut off your head," Swein offered.

"We have better enemies than each other."

Now it was Swein who looked amused. Standing no taller than Hereward, his armour, the helmet he still wore, his sheer breadth, made him seem considerably larger. And, of course, he had the happy knack of looking down his royal nose with his beard jutted outwards in a blatantly intimidating manner. He kept this up for some time while our people and his began to look anxious.

Then: "You don't frighten easily," he observed.

Hereward's eyebrows twitched. "My lord King, I don't frighten at all. Not among friends. May I present to you my wife, the lady Torfrida."

I stepped forward and the old warrior's eyes, transferred with impatience as well as reluctance, widened flatteringly.

"You may," he said softly. "You may indeed . . ."

When I choose, I can be a perfect hostess. I saw to the King's comfort, and to that of his entourage, and supervised the laying out of the feast which, if not up to the standard generally considered worthy of a King, was still warmly appreciated. Of course, the liberal servings of wine and ale helped.

I sat at Hereward's side while the King talked to him and looked, mostly, at me. They had much to talk about, for William had swiftly re-taken York again, by the simple if brutal expedient of wasting the entire country around it. I won't speak of that. Everyone knows what William did to the north. And so the Danes, so very briefly glorious, had marched out of York once more, under conditions of a truce that allowed them to stay on the Humber over winter.

"To hell with them all," had said Hereward tiredly. "Is it bed-time?"

"It could be," I had said cautiously, "if you are prepared to keep Prior Aethelwold waiting."

"For you, I'd keep Jesus Christ waiting. Do I have to see him?"

"Not until you die – and even then only if you're lucky."

"Not Christ, provoking wife. Aethelwold."

It was not that he did not feel the blow, or the anger at what had happened; it was just that there were other plans to concentrate on, and that giving up never entered his head, not even when Edric the Wild finally submitted; not even when William appointed a Frenchman to succeed Brand at Peterborough.

And not just any Frenchman but Turold of Fecamp, who had already made himself a by-word for tyranny at Malmesbury. The monks of Peterborough were dismayed by the King's choice, made more on the grounds of the new abbot's abilities as a soldier than as a churchman. But Hereward had actually laughed, observing that this was William's tame way of dealing with our revolt, and that it was not yet out of fashion to roll such creatures as Turold off the highest roof he could find.

And now I had discovered the reason for his optimism. He had been in communication with Swein Estrithson all along.

Hereward said to him bluntly, "Have you come to replace the fleet your sons and your brother commanded?"

Swein blinked. "How many ships do you think I have?"

"More than you sent," said Hereward at once.

Swein smiled. "Did you expect me to risk everything for this throne? I have a perfectly good one of my own. No, I came to see what was happening."

"And what is?"

"Nothing," said Swein with undisguised dissatisfaction. "So I decided the men needed some occupation."

"You are bringing them all here?" Hereward said, carefully neutral. He did not look at me.

"Well, a good part of them."

"You know they agreed a truce with King William?"

Swein's eyes were not quite friendly. "If I hadn't known before, your message, as I recall, was quite – definite – on the subject."

Hereward smiled amiably.

Swein said, "I did not make the truce. The men are mine, and they'll do as I tell them. They need another base."

"The Isle of Ely," said Hereward at once. These days, Ely was often on his mind. He had even sent people there, refugees and fighting men who had originally come looking for him. "It's an excellent raiding base, and the safest natural stronghold in England. There is already a powerful force there – they will welcome your alliance."

I hoped he had asked them. I wasn't convinced, looking around me, that I would welcome such neighbours, and I rather thought the monks of Ely would have similar reservations.

"They are bored," Swein said flatly. "And have had no pay since autumn. We agreed, I think, that payment would come from England. Once they were here."

"You mean booty," Hereward said bluntly. "As I recall, they got pretty good pickings from York. Including my esteemed godfather who, I understand, fetched a mighty ransom on his own. But you don't get *paid* for declaring a truce and sitting on your backside in the Humber all winter."

Swein blinked, almost sleepily. He wasn't looking at me now. For a moment, I thought Hereward had gone too far.

Then: "What *do* you get paid for?" Swein enquired evenly.

Hereward reached for his cup. I knew from his passive face that he had an answer, that he was following a plan hatched some time ago. Warning bells rang inside my head.

He smiled at the King, the great, dazzling smile of his boyhood, seldom seen nowadays. It still took my breath away, and it certainly got Swein's attention.

"Have you ever," Hereward asked blandly, "been to Peterborough?"

Everyone knows what happened at Peterborough; everyone has their favourite version, their favourite tale of horror or heroics. I cannot tell you the truth of those stories, for I was not there. All I know is that after Hereward had visited, no one ever called it the Golden Borough again.

On the third night after his departure with the Danes, I lay alone in darkness, my insides twisting still because of what he had done, because he had given me no clue as to this particular, unforgivable venture. Because I could not sleep, I heard him come home, heard the excited welcome, the shouts of bravado and ale-induced laughter among the clop and whinny of the horses. I even heard his voice, light, almost careless, and my stomach churned all the harder.

They crashed loudly into the hall, and I listened for a long time to the sounds of their celebration. However, the men who had remained at Bourne were still half-asleep, and Hereward's companions were clearly exhausted. And drunk.

His voice was one of the last to give up.

I had never dreaded the sound of his footsteps before, crossing the hall to my door. I lay coldly, stilly, and waited.

The door opened and closed very quietly, as if in an excess of husbandly consideration he would not wake me. Unreasonably, I felt fresh anger rise. I could see the blacker darkness of his figure, quite still against the door, as if he were watching me. Then he bent. I heard the unmistakable sounds of him removing his boots.

"Don't bother on my account," I said politely. I thought he paused for an instant.

Then: "I don't care to sleep in my boots. I thought you were asleep."

I sat up, impatiently reaching for the tinder box to light the lamp. But before I even registered his movement, he was beside me, sitting on the bed, gripping my hands without gentleness.

He said, "Leave it."

"Why?" I demanded at once. "Are you afraid to face me after what you have done?"

"Why should I be?" said the angel's voice carelessly. "It's no different from anything that has gone before. You knew the worst of me before we ever married."

"No," I said harshly, pulling my hand free. "I did not. What you did at Peterborough is *sacrilege!*"

"Because I took a few baubles?" His voice in the darkness was still light, amused. I felt him lounge back on the bed, away from me. "I am not the greatest of Christians, of course, but I believe ownership by the Church does not make a thing *God's*. As I understand it, Christ reviled such wealth.

Was there not something about rich men and camels and the eye of a needle?"

"Rich *men*," I repeated pointedly.

He said, "Abbot Turold, I believe, is a man."

"These things did not belong to *him!*"

"He would have used them though."

Through the darkness, I stared at his shapeless face. In disbelief, I said,
"That is your justification? For sacking a monastery? And if Brand had
been alive . . .?"

"It would not have arisen," Hereward interrupted, his voice patient. It
struck me then that he was refusing to fight with me, and if I had been less
angry I would have realized before I did that his carelessness was deliberate, that despite my best efforts, the distance between us was achieved by
him, not by me. But I still had plenty to say.

"Do you imagine," I asked bitterly, "that Brand would have approved
of this?"

"What is your problem, Torfrida?" Hereward mocked, with just a slight
edge now. "I have paid the Danes and retained them; I have kept valuable
treasure from enemy hands. It was necessary."

"It was unworthy!"

The words were out, angry, accusing, desperate, before I had even
thought them; but saying them, I acknowledged the true root of my anguish. He had disappointed me.

Gasping to control the rush of emotion, I raged, "Is this what it has all
been for? All the months of watching and waiting and planning? To kill a
few monks and steal the Church's treasures?"

His head moved slightly, as though in consideration. Then, at last, he
said judiciously, "I burned the monastery as well."

Impulsively, almost involuntarily, I leaned forward, desperate to see his
face in the shrouding blackness.

"Are you *proud* of it, Hereward?" I whispered.

"Are you?"

Shocked, I could not answer for a moment. The lightness was still there
in those two tiny, deliberate words, but not the mockery, not the amusement; those he could not keep up. For he was serious, dangerously so. It
was a long time since I had been afraid of him.

At last I said, "What do you mean?"

He stirred. "I mean, I found no trace of Brother Ivor, the sacrist, at Peterborough. Or of many of the treasures I know best."

I am not stupid. "Someone warned them," I said wonderingly, then defiantly: "Good!"

"Was it you?" he asked casually.

And here, of course, was the source of his own problem, his strange manner towards me. Curiously calmed now, I said prosaically, "Let me light the lamp." But he moved, suddenly not relaxed at all, his hands staying me again.

"Was it you?" he repeated.

Forcing myself to stillness in his hold, I said, "I don't like Brother Ivor. But I probably would have told him, or anyone else, if I had thought you actually meant to do it."

I could feel him staring sightlessly through the silence. Slowly, deliberately, his hold on my hands slackened. Then he said, "What did you think I was going to do? Take the Danes to Mass?"

I would not laugh. I was still shivering inside. But though the danger of his suspicion had passed, I would not leave my own, far surer accusations.

In a small, cold voice, I said, "You could have done worse. You *did* much worse. You have debased your name and your cause. You have shamed them."

Abruptly, my hands were dropped, and I didn't want to feel the loneliness or the rejection it caused.

With the first hint of impatience, he said, "When you come back to the real world, Torfrida, we'll talk further. I did what had to be done, and neither of us should be ashamed of that."

I said clearly, "I am."

But he did not reply. He said nothing at all as he undressed and lay down beside me, neither touching nor avoiding. And as his breathing deepened and lengthened into sleep, I still lay awake, cold and churning with fears and furies; while the sane, cerebral part of me thought calmly, and with interest, about Ivor the sacrist.

"Lucy, will you help me with this?"

With what was never specified, but it was enough to keep her with me in the hall while the others went about their business. Lucy herself did not seem to mind much. If anything, she seemed relieved to stay with me. Sitting down on the stool beside me, her eyes flickered continually to the door.

"Are you looking for him?"

In Bourne, *him* tended to mean only one person, and Lucy did not pretend to misunderstand me. She said vaguely, "I know he is back."

"Yes, he is. And I don't think you have forgotten how he feels about betrayal."

Shocked, her wide eyes flew to mine. She swallowed visibly, knowing it was too late, but trying anyway.

"What can you mean? As if I would betray my own . . ."

"You mean you did not send a message to the sacrist at Peterborough, telling him of Hereward's plans?"

Her white face flooded with such sudden colour that I was surprised, in

218

a dispassionate sort of a way, that it did not make her dizzy. But of course she was guilty. Knowing her brother, it seemed, rather better than I, she had guessed what he would do.

Her hands gripped the edges of her stool as she gasped out, "He knows! Oh dear God, he knows . . .!"

"He will do, if I choose to tell him."

Remarkably quickly after that, Lucy returned to normal. Her gaze cleared into mine. She said, with no hint of defiance, "He was committing sacrilege. I did it to try to save his soul."

"And if you had managed at the expense of his life?" I asked politely.

The colour began to drain again, and seeing it, I pushed my point home.

"The monks had closed the gates and armed themselves against him. Worse, he knew Ivor had taken treasures to Turold, to keep them safe from *him*. The monks became his enemies, Lucy, when they did not need to be. If you had left things alone, he would have gone there in peace, taken what he wanted with their consent if not their goodwill, and left."

I felt a faint prick of conscience here. One did not take a pack of ruthless Vikings on a mission of peace. It would never have been quite like I described it to Lucy. But I had a point to make, and it was extremely important that Lucy understood.

She said, "Even you can't pretend that what he did was right. Nor even what you think he might have done if I had been silent."

I said evenly, because I did not believe it all myself, "He has done many things that would not be right in times of peace. But he is a soldier, engaged in a war. You took your side when you came here, if not before. Have the courage to stand by it, Lucy, or go."

Within a week, the monks of Peterborough had regrouped and were conducting normal service. Hereward remained at Bourne, though he spent most of his time at the forest camp, out of my way. However, he was actually in the hall, lying on the floor with bruised shadows under his laughing eyes and letting Frida crawl all over him, when Wulric the Heron, who had been sent in search of King Swein, came back. He was panting, and much too early.

Hereward stood, rolling Frida off like a puppy, and went towards his henchman, frowning. "Did you deliver my message?"

Wulric shook his head nervously. "No, my lord. I couldn't. I thought it best to return and tell you at once."

"Tell me what?" said Hereward. He had gone very still, almost as if he knew. "Where *was* King Swein?"

Wulric swallowed. "With King William."

He left almost at once, without saying where he was going or for how long. As things stood between us then, I was not surprised. So I did what I always did in such emergencies: I looked to the stars.

And having done that, and taken some comfort – for they foretold no immediate drop in our fortunes – I slipped outside alone, and walked a long, long way. It did me good, the solitude and the casual, accepting greetings of the people I met on the way. So, returning, I sat down on the sloping ground in the shadow of the hall and gazed upwards at the sky and outward at the vast darkness of the fen. Both seemed uncommonly clear and beautiful, and mysterious to me that night; both had occasional odd, elusive lights that I could not explain.

Hugging my knees under my chin, I still could not quite believe the unchanging message of the heavens. For common sense told me other-wise. This trouble between Hereward and me, stemming from his raid on Peterborough, was not like any other previous quarrel. I could cope with hot, hasty words, with temper and storms. It was the courteous silence which was breaking me down; the never touching; the fear of his con-tempt; the fear of my own.

"You used to smile," his voice observed above me, "when you looked at the stars."

I could not prevent my start, or the speed with which my eyes flew up to his face. He was standing beside me, his cloak blowing out from one shoulder. The star light winked on the large silver and agate brooch which fastened it there. I had the full moon and the torches outside the hall to help me this time: I could read something of his expression, and feel it too.

I said, "I used to smile at a lot of things."

"Even at me." It was not an accusation, it was a question; almost, I thought, an apology.

I looked away. "I might again, if you stayed long enough."

That was not accusation either. It was an invitation, and he took it as such. Silently, he sat beside me, close but not touching. Still not touching. Yet I felt as if my heart was trying to clamber out of my mouth, with fear of spoiling this moment, ruining this opportunity. They were so rare these days that I could not doubt the importance of this one.

Perhaps he felt it too, for the silence stretched out – each of us, it seemed, reluctant to break it. But I did not mind the silence with him. I never had.

At last he stirred. "What do the stars tell you?"

"You don't believe in their prophecies."

"No; but I believe in your perception."

I looked at him again. His voice was calm; so was his face, gazing up-wards, till his eyes moved unexpectedly and caught mine. They were – *unquiet.*

I said carefully, "Has something happened?"

"I have been to Ely. To watch the Danes sailing off."

The deliberately expressionless voice made me wince inside. Yet I answered in the same tone, "It was inevitable, if Swein has made peace with William."

"Been bought off by William," Hereward corrected drily. "Did your stars warn you of that?"

"They didn't need to. Common sense told me the Danes were not trustworthy allies."

"I knew that too. And yet I expected more of them than this."

I nodded slowly. Then, still holding his gaze, I said, "What will you do now? Submit?"

He blinked. "Why should I do that?"

"Because there is no one left but you," I said tartly. "And William will come for you next if you don't."

"That is probably true," he allowed. "However, he has paid off his mercenaries, so he doesn't have quite the force he used to. And I may not be worthy of his attention."

At that, I knew with immediate dread that he would *make* himself so. Yet I said calmly enough, "You have often said yourself that we cannot withstand an army . . ."

"Not at Bourne."

The words hung between us while my heart beat and beat, and our eyes still held. A burst of laughter came from the hall; some insubstantial insect of the night brushed past my cheek.

I tried not to swallow, but I found I could not speak unless I did.

"You want to leave here."

The words were flat, toneless. I didn't know what they meant, if they deserved the great wave of desolation which engulfed me as I spoke them. I dragged my eyes free, and waited.

Hereward moved, stretching out one leg. He said, "Abbot Thurstan is here. In the hall. He followed me back from Ely, with an invitation from the monks and soldiers there."

"To join them?"

"To lead them."

Present: March 1076

CHAPTER 33

Wynter said again, "Forgive me."

And while I stared and stared at him, while I forgave him for being alive when Hereward was not, while I went through the motions, the very real emotions, of welcoming such a friend back from the dead, while he told me his brief, reluctant story, I was remembering all that had gone before, when we had come back to England and Wynter had done so much to help him begin it. Yet through the bombardment of memory and confusion, I was painfully, uneasily aware that something was not right.

Wynter said, "When I saw it was all up, when he jumped in among them, I ran. There was nothing I could do, alone and injured. And ever since then, I have been – ashamed to come back."

He was sitting on the step that led up to the altar, his shaggy head in one dirty, bandaged hand, while a faint ray of pale sun shone unkindly through the little window above to show us his shame and his guilt. And I could not dispute it. This was the man who as a boy would have died gladly for Hereward; there was another unspeakable tragedy that in the end, after all they had been through together, Wynter had left him to die alone.

I said low, "Did Martin go with you?"

There was a pause, then: "I have not seen Martin."

"Then he at least is truly dead?"

"If he is," said Wynter tiredly, "he is a luckier man than I." Abruptly, he was on his feet again. Jerkily, he said, "Lady, there is nothing I can say . . ."

"No," Leofric agreed. "You need rest. Go now, while I . . ."

"But there is," I interrupted, staring from Wynter to Leofric and back. "There is something you can say. You can tell me if you saw who killed him."

Looking only at his boots, Wynter shook his head, violently. "I did not see," he said low.

"Where were you?" I demanded, just a little harshly now, for the pain of this betrayal was lashing at me all the harder because I could so easily understand and forgive it. "Where were you when he threw away his sword and jumped?"

"By the guest-house," Wynter muttered. "At the door . . ."

I turned away from him, seeing now only the altar cross. "Why did he do it?" I asked, of no one in particular. "Why did he do that?"

Wynter said low, "He trusted them. He thought he had them won over."

"Why in God's name should he have thought that? What did he *say* to them?"

Slowly, I turned my gaze back to him, but the brief blink of light was gone. Wynter's face was again in shadow. Yet I could have sworn his eyes flickered not to me but to Leofric. And though I refused to move my own eyes from Wynter's face, I felt Leofric's tiny, nervous twitch of the head. In the brief silence, fear and hurt grew and grew; along with vague, dispassionate surprise that amongst all this I was still capable of feeling.

Wynter said, "I don't know. He – they – spoke in French, very quickly."

I stared at him, quite hard, but he would not look at me. To the side, I felt all Leofric's discomfort which would not let him be still, and the thought came to me that I had as yet seen no real grief in the Deacon – care for me, for the people, yes, but no grief for his greatest friend.

And he no longer wore the bandage that had been on his head yesterday.

Had they turned against him too? Wynter *and* Leofric?

That, I could not bear. I felt I would die of pity.

Somehow, I managed to say, "I see you cannot help me," and walked away out of the church, while their eyes, sad and silent, watched my back. In my own clenched fist, I still held the golden brooch I had meant to show to Leofric.

I took it back to the hall, to my own chamber, and by the light of the window as well of a lamp lit behind me, I examined it again. I still could not recall ever seeing it before, although it was true I had scarcely seen Hereward or any of his men for four years. It looked more likely to belong to a Frenchman. And in fact, I would have paid it no attention at all were it not for the fact that I had found it in the hand of the man we thought was Martin.

To my knowledge, Martin had never owned anything like this; he had never shown any interest in gold or riches of any sort. Even if he had killed the brooch's owner, I could not imagine him taking it. But Martin *was* his messenger. He had always been his private messenger to *me*, and I could not lose the delusion that he had been trying to communicate something to me about his death.

Torfrida, did you know there was a bear?

I wanted to be important to him, of course, at the end. I knew that. And I knew that I was clutching at straws, associating him with this brooch just because he had once, in my presence, killed a bear. I knew that even if it *was* some cryptic message, it could as easily be intended for one of his men, or for Aelfryth. But I needed to know what it meant, not least because it had been untouched by the fire. None of Martin's charred skin stuck to it. It had been placed in Martin's hand after the fire for someone to find.

Could Wynter and Leofric really have betrayed him? His best and oldest friends? I had trusted them with my life and his, with my children's lives, more often than I could count. Up until an hour ago, I would still have done so. And yet the insidious thought was now in my head, that they had not only betrayed him but conspired with his Norman enemies. Leofric had not been so badly hurt as he had pretended. Wynter had not been dead. My whole being was outraged, consumed with guilt, because I could not really believe such dreadful suspicions. I did not *want* to believe them. And yet I had misjudged people before. I had misjudged Hereward himself. And the fact remained that they were keeping things from me, and not just to spare me distress. They were lying to me.

Because my children were there, I rode back to Folkingham at a pace that must have taken the twins by surprise. Everywhere, in every village and hamlet, there were groups of men, restless, arguing, suspicious; often they stopped to watch us ride by; some even tried to stop us to ask what they should do now that Hereward was dead. "Go home," I said. "Go home and wait . . ."

I could no longer trust my world. If Leofric and Wynter could betray Hereward, then nothing was solid, nothing certain, no one trustworthy. Had I not learned that long ago? Hereward himself was not what I had thought him . . . He and the Normans had spoken in swift French, according to Wynter: he could have been conspiring with them, making deals with them, though over what I could not imagine. Could Leofric and Wynter have killed Hereward because *he* had betrayed *them*?

Yet although it was again dusk before we reached Folkingham, I could make no sense of their actions, nor see the point of the bear brooch – unless it was something to do with Gilbert? With Matilda's secret feelings for Hereward? Yet surely, even if Gilbert had only just found out about her unlikely love, surely it was no reason for murder! Unless . . .

Unless I had been naive all those years ago. Was it not perfectly possible that Hereward had been Matilda's lover in Northumbria? Before – or even during! – Edith's visit. It would more easily explain his discomfort when they met in public, as well as the depth of Matilda's feeling when he left. Discovering such a betrayal by the godson he had helped so often, would Gilbert not have been compelled to act? Setting the jealous young Normans to pick a fight . . .

But when we entered the hall where the household was already at supper and Gilbert rose to greet me, my mind balked once more. Gilbert was subtle; he had stood aside once, consciously or unconsciously with his head in the sand, while his allies insulted and murdered his old friends. That was true. But through it all, ever since I had known him, he had held a deep and abiding love for his godson. If the bear was the man responsible for Hereward's death, or for the attack that had led to it, the bear could not be Gilbert. Could it?

Yet who else was remotely associated with that incident nearly twenty years ago? Everyone else was dead . . . Apart from Siward the White. And Lucy. And if nothing was impossible, could *she* not have betrayed her brother again, as she had done before to Ivor the sacrist of Peterborough? Especially since he stood in the way of her new marriage. Or had Ivo learned of the bear story from her? If he had, I could still see no purpose to the brooch . . .

Suddenly, the hall door burst open, jerking me out of the speculations I could not leave alone. A man, a Norman soldier, was propelled across the floor, narrowly missing the table at the foot of the hall. Behind him, into the stunned silence, strode the Siwards.

The Norman glared round us all, growling at his attackers; and I realized they had brought me Asselin.

Carefully, I put down my knife.

"My lord Gilbert!" Asselin fumed. "If you possess any influence over those barbarian dogs . . .!"

"If you refer to the young men behind you," Gilbert interrupted mildly, "they are simply obeying my order to find you and bring you here."

This was not strictly true, of course, since it was my orders the Siwards had obeyed, but at least Gilbert's claim had the effect of silencing Asselin, furiously kicking at a table leg while Siward the White enquired where he should put his prisoner. I thought Asselin would burst. Part of me wanted to rush at him immediately, force the truth out of his boastful, swaggering lips; I even rose quickly to my feet as though to do so. But in fact, there was a stronger part of me which feared the truth. Something was not straightforward about my husband's assassination, and at heart I did not want the rest of my past, of his, made to count for nothing. And it would, surely, be nothing, if the greatest and the best had betrayed him . . .

Past: Refuge: 1070-1072

CHAPTER 34

On the isle they called it Hereward's castle. In fact, it was little more than a shelter for the men, with a wooden tower in the middle from which I could see the long causeway, painstakingly and efficiently built by the King's soldiers. I could see right along it, from the men who had placed the last timbers and were now running back towards their own side, to the mass of knights and men-at-arms gathering at the far end, their conical helmets like some great, spiked lawn, their long shields curiously, dauntingly businesslike. This was an army that knew how to fight; the most experienced army, probably, in Europe. And it was commanded by William the Bastard himself.

There was a knot in my stomach, and my heart was beating too fast. But we had expected this ever since we arrived on the isle – Hereward and I and our servants and nearly all of his vast, swollen "gang", some of whom, taking their lead from Hereward, had even brought their wives and children. After the great Earl of Warenne had failed to capture us en route, William's coming to Ely had been inevitable. There was no point in panicking now.

I said, "A fine body of men he is sending for you." And my voice did not tremble at all. It was cool, holding just enough light mockery to make him smile. His eyes understood me perfectly, but we were playing our roles now, for those who observed.

"He'll hate to lose them," he said regretfully.

"They're about to attack, Hereward!" Tostig said urgently from behind us. "Look!"

"I am looking; and of course they are."

"Well, what are your orders? What should we do?"

Hereward cast an amused glance over his shoulder. "Nothing that is not done already. We have defences enough: trenches, earth-works, a few men in ambush . . ."

"Your presence down there would help!" Thorkell the Pure burst out. "Belly of God, it is *necessary!*"

"You over-rate me, my friend."

"Hereward, will you take this seriously?" That was Tostig again, his lips twisted with frustration, his eyes bright with anger. Seeing it, I touched Hereward's hand, and Hereward turned fully towards the others.

"I *am* serious," he protested. "I promise you, none of them will even reach this side."

Tostig stared at him. "You cannot know that."

"I know the marshes," Hereward said at once. "Go down there yourself. You won't find one Fenlander worried."

"Nothing worries *them*," Tostig said contemptuously, but just then some slight movement on the far side of the causeway distracted me: bright, autumn sunshine glinting on distant armour. Moving armour. My stomach twisted.

"Hereward," I breathed.

He looked too. They all did. Hereward nodded slowly.

Tostig said urgently, "It's about to begin!"

Thorkell said, "*Now* will you come down . . .?"

And Hereward looked surprised. "I can see much better from up here."

"You are imp—"

"Look," said Hereward.

We did not hear the enemy order; but we felt it as the horses suddenly exploded on to the causeway. It was the first charge of massed Norman knights I had seen, and the power, the force in it, was terrifying, even from this far away.

"They're going too fast," Hereward said. "They'll never keep it up over that distance."

"They're in a hurry," Thorkell said contemptuously. "William has promised great lands and riches to the first men on to the island."

"My God," said Tostig, awed. "They're actually jostling each other for position!"

"Do they think we are such easy meat?" Thorkell said angrily.

Hereward smiled lopsidedly. "I think they probably do. We ought to feel sorry for them."

Thorkell said something obscene below his breath. He was becoming adept, if not quite infallible, at minding his language in my presence. Some years older than Hereward, he was broad-shouldered, with a fierce, reddish-brown beard. I had first encountered him in the abbey's courtyard, surrounded by monks and lay brothers and soldiers of very varying repute, all cheering and chanting their welcome to their new leader. Thorkell had been objecting, volubly and vulgarly, to the Abbot's invitation to Hereward and me to join the monks at dinner – on the grounds that neither he nor his men had ever been so honoured.

Hereward had said coolly, "Torfrida, this is Thorkell, called The Pure by his sarcastic friends for the distinct *im*purity of his language. You will forgive him the odd indiscretion, for he is an excellent fighter. In fact, he is captain of those men already gathered here before us."

Thorkell's men had raised a ragged, laughing cheer. Somebody had thumped him on the back. Thorkell himself had been obliged to smile, although he had looked somewhat embarrassed as he greeted me gruffly and gazed suspiciously – and defiantly – at Hereward.

As if unaware of the hostility, my husband had nodded in a friendly sort of a way. "We'll talk later, Thorkell, for there's much to discuss. First, though, I am hungry, and would, Father, gladly accept your invitation, which is, I am sure, extended to my chief officers and to the captains already established here."

Abbot Thurstan had closed his lips. I could hear the caught breath of some of the startled soldiers, the odd amazed and delighted snort of muffled laughter. Only the monks themselves had looked dismayed. One of them was staring at his Abbot significantly, as if willing him to the right decision.

Sardonically, Hereward was looking round them all. "You don't like such changes, Brothers? You'll get used to them."

"My son," Thurstan had broken in at last. "You have not considered our calling, our requirement for solitude . . ."

"You gave up your solitude when you accepted the help of these men," Hereward had said bluntly. "And your independence, I'm afraid, when you put yourselves under my command. We are one community. We eat together." Suddenly he grinned, and clapped one of the still silently mouthing monks on the shoulder. The monk staggered, choking. "Cheer up," Hereward urged rallyingly. "They'll earn it, you know, when William comes! Shall we go in?"

It was not, perhaps, a propitious start. As we went inside to the refectory, I could see written clearly on the monks' faces their doubts about what they had done in delivering themselves up to such a man. But that had been many weeks ago. Now, no one doubted him. Or hadn't, until William's knights began to charge across the causeway towards us.

Tostig said excitedly, "It's weaving! Look! It's rocking like a boat in a storm!"

That snapped my attention back. He meant the causeway, of course, and making allowances for understandable exaggeration, he was right. The King's men had built their causeway from logs and stones which they had carried in from miles around. Whole trees were used in certain parts, and underneath they had floated inflated sheepskins. It was ingenious in its way.

But such foundations, it seemed, were not secure enough for this marsh, especially with the weight of a hundred thundering knights, even though the causeway was too narrow to permit more than two side-by-side.

It was a spectacular sight, now they were closer. More than half of the causeway was full of charging, thundering, fully armed knights. I could hear their battle cries swept across on the wind, and they chilled my blood.

228

Completely oblivious to the heaving of the ground under their horses' feet, they ignored the beasts' frightened stumbling, righting them, urging them on, careering in magnificent glory towards their goal.

"Brave men," said Hereward without emphasis.

I found I could make out the knight in front now, half a length ahead of his nearest companion. His long shield low, every effort concentrated on speed. This man was determined to be first, and his shining white horse was strong enough and eager enough to oblige.

With another overwhelming flood of despair, I realized we could not defeat such men, such strength. Not with all the courage and righteousness in the world. Not even with all the skills Hereward had instilled into our men. Not even with Hereward himself.

"It's breaking up," said Hereward quietly.

And I saw that it was. Somewhere in the middle, horses were floundering rather than stumbling. I could see water splashing up, hear the screaming of horses. Pieces of wood were floating loose, and men and horses began sliding and plunging into the water, helplessly drowning in their heavy armour. Behind them, the other knights tried desperately to pull up, to save themselves, but even those who managed to halt in time were pushed in anyway by the force of those behind.

The whole causeway was falling apart. At the far end, the foot soldiers who had begun to follow the knights were trying to surge back to avoid the fleeing knights as well as the damaged bridge. But not everyone seemed to know what was happening, and those retreating became tangled up with those still marching blindly, stolidly forwards. Everywhere they were shouting: with fear, with pain, or simply in warning to their comrades.

And I could see our own men now, archers firing from behind the island's defences, others appearing suddenly from out of the reeds on either side of the causeway. These people knew every hillock, every stone, every safe inch of this marsh. Hereward had seen to that. Their arrows fell in hails on the foremost knights, further thinning the once proud charge. But the leader, with a couple of others at his tail, was still coming on, even though the causeway had split in two across its breadth, so that an ever-widening chasm of stagnant water yawned before them.

Secret pity, outrage, welled up in me for these enemies. Those at the front – the bravest – or perhaps just the greediest – were about to go the way of their unfortunate fellows. Few had so much as glanced behind them, but they must have known something was badly wrong: the noise alone would have told them so. Now they too were pulling up, trying to turn away from the gaping hole, pushing each other off the side in their desperation, and struggling in the hold of the odd pieces of marshy ground that clung to them all the harder with each effort they made to free themselves.

Only two knights, the man who had led from the beginning, and one other on a black-tailed chestnut stallion, kept coming in our direction.

"They're going to jump it!" Tostig exclaimed.

They were too. Instead of slowing, of trying to escape, they were urging their surely terrified and exhausted horses to even greater efforts, until at last the leading destrier leapt, closely followed by its fellow, soaring above the watery gap.

"They'll never do it," said Thorkell positively.

The chestnut stallion didn't. It plunged, shrieking, into the murky water, the knight on its back helplessly flailing. But I'm afraid I scarcely noticed him, for by some miracle the white horse had landed on the other side, its hind legs slipping and scrabbling and recovering while its knight held grimly on and rode desperately towards us.

Only a few more lurching strides on that heaving, wandering floor, and then another leap for the island itself. And our men hurled themselves at him, cheering.

Hereward was laughing softly.

He said happily, "I owe you all an apology. One of them did make it."

Fascinated, I turned my gaze upon him.

He said, "Thorkell, have them bring him to me. At the abbey. And then make sure any close survivors and any reachable arms are retrieved."

Only a few weeks ago, if anyone had dared to so command Thorkell they would not have lived long. Yet today, Thorkell turned wordlessly to obey, as biddable as any to Hereward, if to no one else. It had taken time, many battles of will, and many more physical contests imperfectly disguised as training – leaving Hereward with several serious wounds which he admitted to no one; but it had been done.

Hereward said briskly, "Have you two taken root, or are you coming with me?"

"Coming where?" Tostig said irritably.

Hereward looked surprised. "The abbey. It's dinner time."

A breath of laughter rushed out of Tostig's mouth. "God, you're a cool bastard," he said admiringly. "You've just inflicted the first defeat on English soil of William the *Conqueror,* and you want to stuff your face?"

"Having just defeated William," Hereward observed, already heading for the stairs, "I have nothing else to do."

Having collected on the way a very vocal triumphal escort of islanders and soldiers and fighting monks, we arrived at the abbey in some style – to be greeted in the refectory itself by roars of approval and enthusiastic chants of Hereward's name.

Hereward smiled, lifting one closed fist both to acknowledge and quieten the uproar.

"Spare your cheers until the enemy has left!"

"*Are* there any of them left?" some one shouted out, and everyone howled with glee. Everyone, that is, except the upright figure standing stiffly between Thorkell the Pure and Abbot Thurstan. Disarmed, with neither helmet nor breast plate now, he stood in his mail shirt and leggings, his face grimy but still proud. The only Norman knight who had made it to the isle.

While all eyes were rooted to Hereward's face – including the knight's – I studied the knight himself, with considerable curiosity.

Did he know that the vast majority of his comrades were dead? Beneath the short, damp brown hair, his face was certainly white, where the dirt revealed it, but in the circumstances that was not surprising. He was not a particularly handsome man, I saw, but he was striking in a harsh, not unattractive way. Perhaps about Hereward's own age, he was, clearly, an experienced soldier who had no intention of revealing whatever grief he felt – or whatever fear regarding his own position; and that must have been considerable. Instead, he reserved his attention for Hereward, watching him with a clear, penetrating stare that contained, outwardly at least, only curiosity.

Silence had fallen in the refectory. Finally, Hereward allowed his gaze to alight on the captive. He smiled, though I doubted the Norman found the gesture reassuring, particularly since Thorkell poked him ungently in the back at the same moment to force him toward us. I saw the knight's eyes flicker briefly to me and away, then back for a longer look.

"The Norman you asked for," Thorkell said sardonically, as though he had caught a pike or a water-foul for Hereward's table.

"Thank you," Hereward said drily. His orders were obeyed, but he was not pleased at the discourtesy. Then, surprising everyone, he held out his hand to the enemy. He said frankly, "That lunacy of yours on the causeway was the bravest thing I ever saw."

There was a pause. I saw the Norman blink, then gaze at the outstretched hand as though searching for something to do with it.

"I am Hereward," said my husband helpfully, as if the other could have avoided knowing it by now. Then: "I believe it disgraces neither of us to take the hand of an enemy."

The Norman swallowed. It was the only sign of emotion he revealed and I wasn't quite sure what it signified, but his hand came up, briefly clasping Hereward's.

"I believe you are right. You must forgive me. I find you – unexpected."

"Because I speak French, or because I have not cut off your head?"

Another pause, then: "Because you speak French," the Norman agreed, "and because you have not *yet* cut off my head."

Hereward laughed, an easy sound of genuine amusement. "That's what I like! A man who never counts his chickens. Do you have a name?"

"Does it matter?" the knight asked lightly, by which I gathered it was a name of no significance and that he had, therefore, no wealthy kin to pay a ransom. No wonder he had been first across the causeway for William's reward.

"It does," said Hereward, "if I am to present you to my wife. This is my wife, the lady Torfrida."

The Norman's eyes came quickly to me. They were dark brown, direct and not harsh at all. I inclined my head, regarding him enquiringly until a flush began to mount to his cheeks.

"Deda," he said quickly. "My name is Deda."

He bowed to me with some grace, but then, straightening, he turned determinedly back to Hereward. "May I know your plans for me? Ransom will bring you little enough . . ."

"I never ransom gifts," Hereward interrupted.

"*Gifts?*"

Deda stared, but already Hereward was saying, "Shall we eat? Father Abbot, is there a place for our guest beside us?"

"No," said Thurstan uncompromisingly.

But Hereward only shrugged. "Then we'll make him one." And he led the way to the high table, unbuckling his belt as he went. I could see Deda further startled by this act, until he saw Hereward hang the weapons casually on a nail in the wall behind his place. There was a shield already there, painted bright red with a black dragon's head carved upon it. Its eyes were emeralds.

"You are prepared," Deda observed.

"We are all prepared," said Hereward, nodding significantly down the hall as the monks and laymen began to take their own places, each first hanging up weapons and shields, and dropping any armour on to the floor in front of the tables.

The Abbot himself said a short prayer of thanks for our repast, and, at more length, for the destruction of our enemies. Deda, casually placed between Hereward and me, sat through it in silence, his face still, as though carved in stone. And Hereward did nothing to intervene, to halt the Abbot or comfort the soldier, whose feelings he must have understood only too well. In fact, his thoughts seemed to be somewhere else all together, and I felt a not uncommon little spurt of irritation with him.

Through the raucous *amen*s and the noisy beginning to the meal, Deda still sat. There was an instant, when I looked at him, at his face gazing down so impassively at the table, when the depth of his grief rose up and hit me like a blow.

I said quietly, "In this place, you may pray too; for their souls if for nothing else." And he looked at me quickly.

"I already have."

232

"And I."

His eyes searched mine for a moment. Then: "You are a gentle creature to be among such – warlike surroundings."

"I am not gentle at all, but it was thought my presence would stop the men getting too vilely drunk."

He blinked; a faint, involuntary smile. "And does it?"

"All except the monks," said Hereward unexpectedly from his other side, "whom nothing can keep from the jug." A derisory clerical belch greeted that, and several hoots of laughter.

"That gentleman is Brother Acer the Hard," Hereward explained to Deda's slightly shocked expression. "So called, he tells us, for his endurance of hard labour. In fact, it is his head which is hard. He drinks us all under the table – regularly."

Acer grinned good-naturedly and raised his cup to us all in general toast. Under cover of the inevitable repartee, Deda turned back to me. He did not look amused.

A trifle grimly, he said, "Do they always behave so before you?"

And I smiled excusingly. "Where is the harm? There is no disrespect intended, and I believe I shall not go into a decline because somebody belches!"

"You find us unrefined?" Hereward enquired, re-entering the conversation without warning once more, and the Norman turned quickly to face him.

"I find your monks – unmonkly," he said boldly.

"You think they would benefit perhaps from the discipline of some French abbot? If my friend Bruman has not ducked them all in the sea. But you will have to forgive the Brothers their occasional levity. They have, you see, associated for some months with soldiers, living and training with them every day. But because their tongues are looser does not make them less godly, or their cause less just."

"I see. None of you are in this for personal gain."

The conversation had given Deda confidence: a faint sneer had entered his voice, and Hereward's fleeting smile acknowledged it.

"What gain could any of us have? Win or loose, the most I would have is what I started with. What gain is there for my wife and children who have exchanged the comfort of a home for an armed camp? Or for the monks who have lost their peace and solitude."

"And seek to protect their own wealth!"

"Wouldn't you?" Hereward countered. "But that is not the point at issue. They have an abbot; they don't need another."

Deda sat back. His eyes were openly mocking.

"So," he said largely. "you would have me believe that you are all here – all you exiles and outlaws – I beg your pardon, all you *soldiers* – just to protect the Abbot of Ely?"

"Of course we are," said Hereward, wide-eyed as any innocent. "Halting the tide of dispossession, righting the wrongs done to a thousand English men. That's us."

CHAPTER 35

"What do you think of Deda?"

We were alone in our chamber. When Hereward spoke, I was standing by the unshuttered window, looking into the darkness – not, for once, at the stars, but at the lesser lights of the campfires I could see on the opposite shore. Tonight, they were mourning their dead, while our men celebrated an effortless victory; and I brushed my hair as I did every night.

I said, "I like him."

"I imagine he would be glad to know it."

I cocked one eyebrow over my shoulder. "Jealous?"

"Oh no. Merely, I had thought of selling you."

"He has no money."

Hereward sighed, his breath unexpectedly close and warm on my neck. "True." His fingers took the brush from mine and tossed it aside. Then his arms folded around me and I leaned back into him.

I said, "Has he told you much?"

"Nothing I didn't know already. He was quite meticulous about that."

"But you have not given up on him," I observed.

"I never give up."

"You are wooing him," I accused. For I had seen it before, his deliberate display of flippancy, or idiocy or some other weakness, just to emphasize, when he chose to reveal it, his true gravity, or cleverness or strength. Hereward was out to impress the Norman.

"Well, if *you* don't want him, my sweet . . ."

But I did not want to play; there was too much on my mind. So I interrupted him without formality. "You want him to change allegiance, to stay with us."

There was a pause. Then, lightly: "It would be something of a coup, would it not? And an inspiration to others of his kind. And from that, new heart – and unity – to the English risings. Backed by the new might of righteous Normans. Don't you think?"

I said slowly, "He must stand high with William. He was in the forefront of the attack from the beginning. It *would* be a coup, with all the advantages you spoke of."

"I sense a *but*."

Turning in his arms, I threw back my head to look up at him. "*But*," I said frankly, "I don't think he will change."

Infuriatingly, Hereward appeared to have lost interest. My chemise was hanging off my elbows, and his fingers, stroking over and over with sensuous, sensitive rhythm, were melting me to distraction. I swallowed.

"What," I said with difficulty, "if you persuaded him of our justice *and sent him back?*" The relentless fingers stilled. His eyes lifted to mine. "What if he persuaded William to leave us alone? By proof, seen with Deda's own eyes, of our invulnerability? Combined with a fair view of our cause, would this not lead William to abandon us? For now, at least."

Hereward's breath held, then came out in a rush, stirring the hair at my ears.

He said softly, "A greater coup by far . . . If William left, it would be seen as our victory. Men would flock to us, even the most reluctant rebels, and surely that would be all we would need . . . If it came off, if it came off . . ."

Deda said slowly, "They have done this every day, from time immemorial. The siege has not interrupted their lives at all."

Standing beside him, watching the men at work in the fields, harvesting hay and wheat, as earlier we had watched the fishermen sorting their catch of eels and pikes and trout, I nodded.

I said mildly, "We have replaced any outside markets the islanders may have lost. They are self-sufficient here. There is no reason for their lives to be disturbed."

In the distance, a shepherd stamped across our wide vista, trailing a small white line of sheep. Beyond him, nearer the river, two men were cutting turves.

Deda said, "And *your* life?"

I looked up at him quickly. His eyes were watching me intently. I said lightly, "I like disturbance. In fact, I often cause it."

"I could believe that."

"Are you complimenting me, or censuring me?"

His eyes smiled back. "Guess."

"Shall we walk on?" I said modestly.

"If you wish. Tell me, though," he added as we moved away in the direction of Cratendune. "You are clearly a lady – a French lady – of great learning; out here in the marsh, you must miss the company of likeminds."

"No," I said truthfully. "Of certain friends, yes. But there are many learned men here, not least Abbot Thurstan himself. And my husband, you know, is not quite the simple, brutish soldier you are imagining."

His breath hissed out. "*Simple*? I should say there is nothing simple about him at all!"

"Now you make him sound many-faced and treacherous."

The Norman lifted his gaze to mine. "Is he?"

"No," I said evenly. "But why should you believe me? I am his wife. Use your own eyes, your own judgement."

"Is that what he wants?"

"Yes. Oh and he wants you to enjoy yourself." I laughed at his startlement, and for a few minutes we walked on in silence.

Then, a trifle grimly, Deda observed, "He is very confident. Over-confident, one might think."

"He is never unreasonably confident," I said judiciously.

"*You* make him sound invulnerable!"

"Perhaps he is," I said lightly.

"Nonsense, every man has a weakness."

"And what is yours?" I asked challengingly.

I saw the skin crease at the sides of his eyes as he smiled. "I don't think I shall tell you that." Again, his eyes lifted deliberately to my face. "But I rather think I know Hereward's."

"Over-confidence?" I hazarded, refusing to take him seriously. He shook his head.

"No. You. You are his weakness."

In spite of myself, I felt a rare flush mount to my cheeks. I'll not deny there was pleasure in hearing such words. But I did not want to be Hereward's weakness. I wanted to be his strength.

The mist came down the night before Deda's departure, and in the morning it hung about the marsh, drifting in suffocating swirls across the island. I imagined it clinging to my clothes, clawing at my hair as I pushed my way through it at Hereward's side. I shivered, and he cast one arm about my shoulders, briefly hugging me to his side before his hand slipped down and took mine. I was glad, although I would never admit it, for the mist was oddly isolating and I was afraid of losing him.

In front of us, I could just make out Acer the Hard in his ghostly habit, who was to take Deda across the marsh's secret paths to his own people. And on Hereward's other side, I could hear the muffled footsteps of Deda himself. Ever since his spectacular arrival, Hereward had taken the Norman about with him intermittently. The rest of the time he had been free to wander where he chose among the men and the islanders. I had observed him talking, even making friends with a lot of people, from the twins down to the most dubious looking soldier; and he had been among the ordinary folk too, asking questions – I knew this because Inge the fish wife had told me.

236

The Norman said suddenly, "We never did have that contest of arms."

"Well, I could not permit you to be hurt in a mere game," Hereward said at once.

"You count me so valuable?" Deda actually sounded curious. Looking beyond Hereward, I could just make out his face, faintly frowning, searching Hereward's strange, violent eyes. Then: "This gift is a double-edged weapon, Hereward. I may – I *will* – tell the King everything I have seen and learned, of your endurance and courage, your amazing organization and sheer invulnerability. I may even plead the justice of your cause. Up to a point. But in a fight, I will do everything in my power to use what I have learned against you. You may find you have been too generous."

Hereward called to Acer, who halted obediently. Then he said, "If there was generosity, it was not all calculated. Some things we just do – and say – from friendship."

Deda said, "You are bidding me farewell."

My hand was dropped. Offering his own quite casually to the Norman, Hereward said, "What do you expect? I'm not risking my neck in that swamp."

Surprised laughter caught at Deda's throat. He grasped Hereward's hand, then suddenly embraced him. "I shall miss you, Outlaw. Damn you." He stepped back. "I hope we meet again, in different times."

"If I can arrange it, we will."

Deda smiled. "I believe you are serious."

"He is always serious," I said, "if you know where to look."

Deda turned to me, the mirth dying slowly in his eyes. Disconcertingly, the silence stretched until even he became aware of it. Then, with a sudden, half-embarrassed laugh, he said, "Why, so am I, God help me! So am I . . ." And he was gone, striding after Acer as if he had lived all his life in the Fens. Later, Acer would blind-fold him, for though we counted him a friend, we were not stupid.

The Norman army vanished with the autumn leaves. Whether we had Deda to thank for that, or William's business elsewhere, nothing could have been better for our cause. We had conquered the Conqueror, temporarily at least, and the fame of Hereward's Camp of Refuge spread throughout the country. So much so that before the winter closed us in, drowning the secret paths and hampering our communications, we received all sorts of unlikely messages of support.

One afternoon, the usual comradely peace of our dinner was interrupted by Acer the Hard and Wulric the Heron, dragging some poor individual between them. The torches had just been lit against the failing light, and their shadows danced wildly around the refectory's rough walls.

"Release me!" the captive kept shrieking. "Release me!"

Hereward put down his knife.

"Er – release him," he said drily, through the din of the constant scream-ing. "What is it and what does it want?"

"We found him trying to sneak onto the isle by boat. He says he's serv-ant to Dolfin of Worcester."

The man was still shrieking his plaintive cry, "Release me! Release me!"

Hereward frowned. "We're eating, confound you! Take the wretch to Siward!"

"Siward sent him to you. He won't talk to Siward. He says he'll only talk to you."

"And – er – he has a letter," Acer said apologetically. "And that is ad-dressed to you."

"Is it, by God?" said Hereward, vaguely interested at last. "Bring it here then – but if the courier won't shut up, cut his head off."

The shrieking stopped abruptly. Several of the men sniggered.

Breaking the seal, Hereward said, "Who the devil is Dolfin of Worces-ter?" His eyes scanned the letter while I peered brazenly over his arm. I pointed to the signature, my lips twitching.

"It isn't from Dolfin; it's from his lady – Aelfryth."

At that the twins whistled and hooted with delight, and Hereward threw a walnut at them. "Ouch!" said Outi aggrieved, but Hereward ignored him, letting out a shout of laughter as he read.

"I believe it is a love-letter," I marvelled.

He cocked one eyebrow in my direction. "Aren't you jealous, wife?"

"Well, even she says you have never met. Which accounts, I suppose, for her affection."

"Shrew." He glanced over at the servant. "You, come here."

The fellow came, stumbling nervously. He had the shiny sort of appear-ance I most disliked.

"Your lady requires you to return with an answer?"

"Yes, my lord. Indeed. And I take the opportunity to say that I hope those ruffians of yours will bear suitable punishment for so abusing the servant of that great lady."

Hereward blinked. "Oh, most suitable. I'm only surprised they did not gag you. It could, of course, be remedied. Can you remember messages, or only carry them?"

"I remember everything that is said to me," the man insisted with dig-nity.

"Poor bastard," said Thorkell feelingly, to the accompaniment of more laughter.

Hereward picked up his knife. "Then tell the lady this: that we thank her for her unsought and undeservedly kind words; that I am, just at present, a little too occupied to visit in Worcester as she requests, though if she wishes to *send* the riches she offers, we shall receive them most gratefully; and finally, that if she really wishes to serve our country's cause, letters to me do rather less good than would a surgical detachment of her husband's lips from William's backside."

"I have just remembered," he added kindly to me as the men roared with laughter, and the lady Aelfryth's servant managed to look aggrieved, outraged and frightened all at once, "who Dolfin of Worcester is."

"Clearly. A Saxon collaborator?"

"A filthily rich one." With some surprise he regarded the servant's trembling hand outstretched towards him. "You want to be *paid?*"

"I want the letter, my lord. Were it to fall . . ."

"Oh no. The letter I keep. Go with Acer – he'll find you a bed for the night."

"The letter *I* keep," I corrected drily, twitching it out of his hand. Hereward sat back, smiling, watching me as I read the fulsome compliments, the slightly ridiculous phrases of love.

I said, "She must be a child. Dolfin's *daughter*, surely."

"Wife," said Hereward definitely.

"You are flattered," I accused him. "The wench has fallen madly in love with your reputation, and you are *flattered!*"

"I always wanted a reputation," he excused himself.

"You always had one," I returned ambiguously.

It was a harsh winter, surrounding us in icy mists and whirling snow, biting winds that caught at your chest and chilled you to the very bone. For several weeks we felt completely isolated from the rest of the world, and yet, despite the cold and the inevitable illnesses of the season, I think we regarded the winter as a welcome respite, savouring it because we did not know what the new year would hold.

By the time Earl Morcar arrived in a fine, cold, misty rain, the first signs of spring were in the air; the awful, chill seemed to have gone from the wind, and the odd flashes of white around the isle showed us the first, hardy flowers of the year. Before the rain had come on that morning, the birds had been singing quite merrily, as if they knew the trials of winter were over. And yet our trials were about to begin again, for although Morcar's coming in to us was a victory in itself, he brought disturbing news.

"The King is coming back to Ely. To try again to get you out."

Hereward took some more wine. I saw Morcar watching his hands, looking for the slightest tremor. There was none. "What makes you think so?" Hereward asked casually.

"You have too much support in the country; he can't let you go on. It was that soldier you captured who advised him to lift the siege last year, but it is other men, greater men, who do most of the advising. The Earl of Warenne whom I think you know. And Ivo de Taillebois, who already holds most of your lands, and who has been promised many more riches if he can get into the isle."

The irony was certainly not lost on Hereward, of Morcar, grandson of old Leofric of Mercia, placing himself so willingly under the command of the rebellious thegn whose lord he should have been. And yet Morcar was only the first of the great men who came in to us that spring. What we had achieved on Ely had given new hope to the native cause, inspiring Earls and Bishops to join us, to acknowledge Hereward as their undisputed leader. So by the time my third child was born – with breathtaking speed one windy March night – we were all buoyantly confident.

And the next day, as Morcar had warned us, the King came back.

CHAPTER 36

"She is a witch," said Brother Daniel.

Once, on the night I had first come to the isle, he had made the same accusation against me, when Hereward had boasted about my astronomical skills. The immediate reaction of the men, and the even more terrifying tongue-lashing of my husband had ensured that it was never repeated. And in fact, Daniel and I were now friends, since I had deliberately chosen to help him in the infirmary.

"She is a witch." This time there was amazement and genuine loathing, rather than mere disapproval in his voice. And Hereward only nodded. He was tight-lipped, as I had rarely seen him, and I could not blame him for that; I could not blame him at all.

We were standing on a minor hillock to the south-west of the isle, opposite the main concentration of the King's forces, as this second causeway neared completion. It was the little tower constructed at its nearest point to us that had first drawn us here, Hereward and me, together with Daniel and Acer and the Siwards. And as we watched, a bent, dirty old hag of a woman had been led across the causeway with considerable respect by the Norman soldiers, and helped up to the top of the tower.

It was then that Daniel had made the unnecessary observation. I had known as soon as I had seen her.

Vaguely, I was aware of Hereward's stillness beside me. He would not move a muscle; I could not, for I understood, and I was afraid – not of her, whether she was unholy or simply mad, but of Hereward.

240

Dramatically, the hag threw up her arms; the wind whipped at her scraggy, grey hair streaming it out behind her. The workers on the causeway, mostly Saxon slaves, put down their tools and gazed at her, open-mouthed. Our own men, down by the island's bulwarks, who had so bravely withstood the bombardment of the King's siege engines, put up their heads and gawped.

I felt shame begin to creep up from my toes; then, as she began to speak, it galloped and consumed me. A stream of verbal filth, long and loud and strident, issued from her toothless mouth, vile, shocking, reviling the monks and the inhabitants of the isle, cursing Hereward by name and predicting all kinds of perverse horrors for him and all who followed him. From there, while my eyes and ears refused to close, and my tongue seemed to have fused with the dry roof of my mouth, she actually progressed to spells which must have curled the monks' hair.

Filthy and stupid and probably insane; yet still she caused the icy tingle of evil in my spine.

And then, before anybody could lose that shock, she suddenly hiked up her foul skirts with a shriek of laughter and, turning her back, she stuck out her behind and urinated over the side of the tower.

I felt sick. It should have been funny. But nobody laughed, save the witch herself.

A shouted order from the causeway drifted back to us on the wind. Work resumed. They would be finished by this afternoon. I could not understand how William, so upright and conventionally pious, could bear somebody like her in his camp, let alone make use of her. But I knew why he did.

You are his weakness.

Slowly, I turned my gaze upon Hereward. Since he had cut his hair and shaved off his beard a weak ago, in order to mingle with the King's own workers and set fire to the first attempted bridge, there was little, physically, to hide his feelings from me. Even the sharp gusts of wind could not blow his short hair across his cold, set eyes.

Carefully, I prised open my lips, forced them to speak over my reasonless shame.

I said, "It is Deda. It is Deda's doing."

"Well," said Hereward, unexpectedly quiet and clipped – he was already beginning to stride off, away from me – "he won't do it again. Siward, we have work to do."

Norman horsemen were beginning to mount the causeway, forming up with quiet, ordered efficiency – so different from that first, mad charge that had brought us Deda, our double-edged gift . . .

William had learned by his previous mistake. Not only, this time, had he picked the best possible stretch of marsh on which to build, he was letting only a small assault force ride first across it in single file. The majority he kept on his own shore, formed up and ready. Whatever Hereward intended, I knew there would be no easy victory this time. Even the stars had remained impenetrable on the subject, so far as I could ascertain. I had only their incessant, unspecific message of tragedy to fear.

That and the nagging memory of Thorkell's observation: "This time, the King's got sodding Deda – and sodding Deda knows sodding everything!"

The third of the witch's tirades saw the causeway reach nearly to our shore. When she began, the labourers fled back towards the Norman side, the missiles of our defenders flying after them, mostly harmlessly, while the knights began to cross and the old hag on her tower reached a fever pitch of excitement. Her foul words screeched to the heavens, causing Daniel and Abbot Thurstan, who had grimly joined us on our hillock, to twist their lips in appalled distress. Daniel was praying as if to counteract her evil.

And then, foulest of all, when she lifted up her skirts for the third time to present her unsavoury rear, she actually defecated. It was a prelude to their charge. I knew that even before I saw the leading knight's hand lift in command – was it Deda? – and they came.

Thurstan said, "Dear God, lady, you should not . . ."

And that was when our men rose up out of the marsh, like giant, almost ghostly flies among the reeds, smoking, blazing arrows threaded and poised in their bows.

They shot. Not in perfect time, but in unstoppable, ever-increasing numbers. While the Normans, shocked by the unexpectedness of the attack, and confused no doubt by the sudden smoke screen, let them get away again, leaping and wading back to the isle by the routes they had all learned during the winter and early spring.

The arrows did not all reach the causeway. They didn't need to. The whole marsh was alight.

The wind swept the orange flames through the reeds and briers to the bridge, rushing them along the length of the causeway, stretching on and on, ever nearer the Norman camp. And even as panic broke out in the Norman ranks, and the fire forced the leading knights to flee or jump into the smouldering marsh with screams of piteous, astonished agony that reached easily as far as our hillock, I saw Hereward leading another group of archers out from the island in a quick, vicious dash. Their arrows carried no flames, but they left many more Normans dead. Bleakly, I wondered if it was easier than the fire.

He did that several times, from many unexpected directions, while from others I saw the Siwards and Leofric doing the same. All around them men screamed and died, losing their final dignity and their courage in pain and the primeval fear of fire. And the marsh burned and burned till the stink filled the air around me.

And above it, the old witch in her flaming tower shrieked and howled, just a terrified old woman anticipating an inevitable, horrible death. It came unexpectedly. Whether she stumbled or jumped, she was suddenly falling in a tangle of flailing legs and flapping skirts, the monstrous backside revealed for the last time before she hurtled into the burning causeway and the final silence.

Beside me, Daniel said wonderingly, "It has worked against her. The Lord has turned her own spells against her. Her evil is spreading the fire, keeping it alive . . ."

"No," I said prosaically, faintly surprised that my voice was still steady. "It is the peat. They can't escape it. Even under the solid-seeming ground, the peat is burning, waiting for them to step into it . . . Father, forgive me . . ."

Thurstan dragged his eyes to me in some surprise. "For what, my child?"

But I could not speak, let alone answer. Some of the Normans had organized a human chain, passing buckets of water towards the fire. When they threw the first, the ground spewed up angrily at them, sending the front two men falling backwards. I couldn't hear their screams, but I could imagine them.

Shaking my head at Thurstan's concerned enquiry, I took to my heels like the poor, burning soldiers, and fled.

How could I explain that I felt responsible? Because my knowledge was akin to forbidden knowledge, I had inspired this insulting comparison, and forced Hereward's pitiless reply.

For I was his weakness; and, it seemed, his strength. Victory, once more, was his.

I thought that when the dying was finished and the fires were all burned out, leaving only their acrid stench in the air for miles around, he would sleep apart from me, with the men who loved him all the more for this day's work.

As I soothed and comforted baby Leofric to sleep in our own quarters within the monastery, I imagined that over the celebratory singing and the roars of joyous laughter from our camps, I could still hear the crackle of burning briars, the cries of men in agony. I even felt the pain of the women who wept for them. I wallowed in that, writhing in the guilt of my own non-bereavement, and of my own fierce gladness which would not be silent, despite all the rest.

In such turmoil, I should have set the baby's nerves on edge till he screamed loud enough to wake the others, but for some reason he fell asleep in my arms, warm and cosy at my neck as only small babies can be. Sigrid and Lise breathed a sigh of relief. Lise scampered off to join the celebrations while I was still laying the baby in the cradle.

When I straightened, he was beside me, silently gazing down at the child.

He had learned to veil all kinds of storms, all kinds of hurts – all except the old one, which kept coming back.

I blurted, "It was not betrayal, Hereward. He was always your enemy."

His lips moved, forming a hushing gesture; and though the baby never stirred, he drew me away, beyond the hanging. I heard Sigrid flop down on her own mattress.

"He even warned you," I said more firmly, "that he would use all he had learned against you."

"I know. But I never thought he would stoop to insulting you." He smiled slightly. "The odd thing is, I rather thought he loved you."

"If he did, it was only because I am a more acceptable part of you."

Hereward closed the door with his shoulder, shutting us into the private world that had been my haven and my joy for a whole year. For a moment, he paused, leaning against the door, watching me as I unwound my veil and sat down on the bed.

At last he said, "I don't deserve your comfort, Torfrida. It is not Deda's acts which hurt – I would have done the same in his place. It is just the old wounds I thought had healed long ago."

"I know."

He smiled slightly, coming towards me. "Then kick me. Don't pity me."

"It's not you I pity. It's *them*. And me."

"You?" Now he did look startled. I was watching my hands as he sat beside me, and his big, rough fingers closed over them. "Did you care for him then?"

For a long time, I had vaguely hoped for a blameless opportunity to make him jealous. Yet now that it was here – I could tell by the carefully expressionless tone of his voice – I would not take it. It was too trivial for today.

I shook my head. "No. Not in the way you mean. It is being compared to that creature which wounds me."

Hereward said, "It is because there is no *real* comparison that he was able to do it."

I smiled, glancing up at his face. "Now who is comforting whom?"

"Was there not something in vows we once made?"

"He said I was your weakness," I blurted.

"So you are. And my joy, and my soul. Without you, there would be no reason in anything. Like it was before, only worse, because now I have known you."

There was sweetness in that, but it didn't take away the pain. With difficulty, I said, "I do not want to be the reason hundreds of men were burned to death."

For a long moment, he said nothing at all; so long a moment, in fact, that the warmth of his last words began to seep away into despair.

Then, evenly: "Torfrida, if there had been no witch to anger me, what precisely do you think I would have done when the Normans crossed that causeway?"

There was relief, so selfish and so huge that it was making me gasp; but I would not be pacified so easily.

I demanded challengingly, "What, precisely?"

And his lips twitched. "I had several plans for several contingencies. Perhaps I chose the most ruthless because I am too proud to stand my wife being slighted, however ridiculously. Perhaps I chose it because the wind was in the right direction and because the hag herself drew enough Norman attention to enable me to place my men. But whichever way it had been done, the Normans would have been no less dead. What else can you expect?"

I laid my head on his shoulder.

"We have had this conversation before," I observed. I felt his cheek, his lips against my hair, and closed my eyes. "When I saw them burning, I saw *you*. I imagined you as victim instead of victor."

The Normans retired to lick their wounds, but this time they did not lift the siege. Of course, the blockade was not absolute – Hereward and the fenmen knew too many secret and difficult paths for that – but it did make it somewhat harder to get messages in and out of the island.

However, we did hear that Bourne was now in the hands of one Oger, a follower of the great Ivo de Taillebois. Only the lands Hereward had disputed with the Abbot of Peterborough were denied him, and those were, inevitably, now in the grip of Abbot Turold. Also, the Aethling's sister, Margaret, had finally married King Malcolm. Earl Morcar got quite excited about that. Hereward said sardonically that he hoped Margaret had more influence over him than anybody else had ever been able to exert. Aethelwine, the Bishop of Durham, who had recently come to us from Alba, said surprisingly, that this was exactly what she did have. And Hereward, far from unhopeful already, began to make ever more optimistic plans. It was not unreasonable now to expect a general rising, with the Aethling to set it off.

Perhaps the King thought so too, for he sent us his messenger. An ordinary Breton knight named simply Ralf of Dol, he was received in the refectory by Hereward and me, together with Abbot Thurstan, Thorkell the Pure, Earl Morcar, the Bishop of Durham, and the chief officers of our army.

The knight, clearly following orders, marched forward and handed the folded paper to Hereward, who took it casually enough, although he did invite everyone to be seated while he broke the seal and read.

We waited. Ralf of Dol watched Hereward's face with unblinking, blatantly curious eyes. So many stories had grown up around his person that I suppose he was having trouble marrying them all together with the handsome, courteous, quietly authoritative figure unhurriedly scanning the letter of a King with carefully impassive countenance.

At last, Hereward glanced up at the knight who, misunderstanding, said tactfully, "Perhaps the lord Abbot should see it too."

Hereward smiled. "Not just the Abbot, but everyone here will hear what is in the letter and contribute to the decision we all reach. This is what the King says . . ."

It was not a contemptuous epistle. Far from it. It began by recalling their meeting in Bruges, and admiring the courage and skill with which Hereward had managed this and other earlier campaigns. It acknowledged frankly the difficulty of besieging Ely, and the failure of past assaults, for which he gave full credit to Hereward and his defenders. And then came the point, observing the uselessness of all those men of both sides, pinned down for no purpose. The King, therefore, proposed that the island be surrendered, the defenders to march out with all their arms and the full honours of war, to receive the King's peace and the return of most confiscated lands. The monastery would remain unmolested. The King even hinted at the possibility of important places in his own army for Hereward and his chief officers.

Ralf of Dol, who can hardly have expected to hear all this, twitched one eyebrow involuntarily, and then was still.

Hereward stopped, then read it all again, this time translating it into Saxon. When his voice finally stopped, there was silence in the hall.

Then he said, "Well, gentlemen?"

Thorkell the Pure said something obscene, then coughed and blushed and apologised to me, although it was Aethelwine of Durham and the Breton knight himself who looked most outraged. I hoped they were noting that the man knew at least some Saxon.

By which time, Abbot Thurstan was saying carefully, "It is something to consider. We would lose nothing by these terms."

"We'd gain nothing either," said Tostig quickly.

"Be fair," said Hereward mildly. "You and I and countless others would get our lands back – or some of them, anyway. Though no doubt countless Normans, thus dispossessed in our favour, would once more be on the rampage for land to replace it. And so it all begins again."

"You reject it?" said Thurstan.

"Do you?"

Thurstan sighed. "I'll be truthful, my son. I am weary of this. We are all weary."

"Weary enough to give up?" Thorkell exclaimed angrily. "Look carefully, Father! It is all too vague! There is nothing here to prevent your removal and replacement, nor to redress what has gone before elsewhere. I'm sorry, Father, but we are not children to tire of a game that has grown tedious! If this enterprise was just and right when we entered it, then it bloody well still is. None of us are here to get our sodding lands back! When we began it, we claimed a higher cause, a cause still not won!"

"Well spoken," Morcar said quietly. "This is not enough."

"I rather think," said Ralf delicately, "that it is all you will get." He spoke in French, but clearly he had understood at least part of this exchange. Hereward looked at him thoughtfully.

"And it's not so bad," the Prior pointed out. "After a year, I doubt very much that anyone else is following our example."

"There is still Malcolm of Scotland," said Siward the White.

"The King," said Ralf of Dol, "will be dealing with Malcolm of Scotland."

A fleeting, genuine amusement crossed Hereward's face. "If he can manage that, I'll kiss his boot myself. However, by all means, let us leave Malcolm – and Prince Edgar – out of the equation. As I see it, the King has few alternatives, or he would not offer us such apparently generous terms."

"The King," said Ralf of Dol, "always speaks well of you. He considers you an honourable, if misguided, man."

"Does he?" said Hereward ironically. An involuntary grin flashed into Ralf's face and was gone.

Then, gravely: "I assure you, my lord, I am no flatterer."

Thurstan said, "And if, next time, the terms are not so generous?"

Thorkell said impatiently, "Father, you asked *him* here to command the defence of this isle. If you want him to go, say so to his face. And mine, for I'll go with him, and so will every man here! At least," he amended in the interests of accuracy, "every man who has made no previous vows to God. If he still commands, then for Christ's sake listen to what he says!"

Thurstan turned slowly to face the still impassive Hereward. I hadn't realized before how old the Abbot had grown. Perhaps this was a young man's fight . . .

He said, "Well, my son? What is your recommendation? You have heard all our views and said little. Would you lead your men out to receive the honours of war?"

Hereward smiled and shook his head. "No. No, I would not."

He had said he needed me. I didn't know why. He had made the decision without so much as looking at me. I should have been hurt. Instead, I was proud. I didn't know if he was right or wrong. I saw another year of my life slipping away in this claustrophobic place when I could have had a proper home and peace with my husband and children. But he, he would not settle for anything so selfishly mundane.

Beneath the table, my fingers found his hand; it twisted in my hold and clasped hard. Relief. Relief that I was agreeing. He had needed me after all.

Morcar said, "Nor would I."

"Nor I."

"Nor I."

And so it went on, each of the soldiers rejecting surrender. Ralf of Dol, his eyes fixed once more to Hereward's face, caught his breath. With a sudden twinge of anxiety, I tried to analyze his expression: it was, I think, the pity which caused my alarm, but there was a relief too, as if anything less would have disappointed him now that he had met Hereward. Whatever else, Ralf was impressed.

The monks and lay-brothers, undecided, looked to their Abbot.

Hereward said quietly, "It began as your cause. You have more defenders than you ever dreamed of. It is up to you."

Thurstan looked unbearably unhappy. "My son, my sons, I would not have you waste your young lives . . ."

"They are not wasted. For my own, it has never been better spent."

He had always known how to get at men's hearts. Thurstan's drawn breath was shaky. He said, "Then I abide by your advice. What would you have us do?"

Now Hereward looked at me. He opened his mouth to speak.

I said calmly, "Ask for more."

CHAPTER 37

Is betrayal ever expected? If it were, I suppose, it would not bear the name. Certainly it was the last thing on my mind when I crossed the abbey courtyard that morning, with the first of the early autumn mists swirling about my skirts.

I remember feeling only mildly disgruntled that the wretched fog seemed to have brought back the cough which had not bothered me since spring. And I realized too that time was flying by again: another winter was approaching, and one with less to look forward to than last, since William's response to our terms had been to sequester the Abbey's lands outside Ely, leaving the monastery and its defenders considerably worse off. To counteract that, and the increasing boredom of the men, foraging expeditions were longer and more frequent, taking Hereward from me far oftener than I had grown used to. Once, on a solitary expedition more worthy of the wild boy than the responsible commander of two thousand men, he had even encountered Ivo de Taillebois. The Norman had come off worse, but with an added grudge to avenge . . .

He had been gone five days now, and I could not begin to look for him again until at least another seven had passed. But, refusing to let either that or the mist depress me, I stepped cheerfully into the infirmary and closed the door.

"At last!" cried Duti from his perch on the nearest bed. "A saviour! Torfrida, tell this over-cautious clerk that I am well and healed and have no more need of his tortuous physic!"

Brother Daniel, carefully measuring quantities of infused herbs on the central table, unexpectedly spilled some over his hand, turning so quickly to face me that he knocked the whole jar over with his sleeve.

Ignoring Duti, I went at once to help, while Brother Daniel muttered incoherently that he was sorry, he was clumsy and I should not worry, that he would clear it up, and much more in the same line until I interrupted curiously: "Daniel, is something wrong?"

"Why no, of course not," he said at once. "What could be wrong?"

"Has this prattling bully been annoying you?" I demanded, and Daniel shook his head, at last smiling through Duti's indignant protests.

Then, letting the cowl fall forward to hide his face in shadow once more, he said in an understated sort of way, "Though he is a restless patient."

Duti, his natural dislike of confinement presently being worsened by separation from his brother – who accompanied Hereward on his foraging – made a rude, schoolboy noise with his lips. He had cracked a rib falling from his horse during some training session, and Hereward had refused to take him.

Now, his bandages half-revealed under the rakishly open shirt, which was all he seemed to be wearing beneath a fur-lined cloak, he said to me persuasively, "Let me out of here, Torfrida. Truly, I shall not over-exert myself."

"You had better not if you expect to go on the next expedition," I said severely. "Daniel, I am looking for my lord Abbot, but I can find neither him nor anyone who knows where to look. I have promised some of the island women, you see, that I would speak to him about . . . Daniel?"

Here, explanation trailed off into question, for the monk was definitely agitated, turning his back to me with unprecedented rudeness, while his hands worried desperately and uselessly at the jars on the table.

I think that was my first inkling of disaster.

I found myself very still, listening to the suddenly loud beats of my heart, while I waited, straining for Daniel's response. It never came.

Dread was rising faster now.

I said, "Daniel, where is the Abbot?"

"He is not here," said Daniel quickly.

"Confound you, Brother, she can see that!" Duti expostulated.

"No; I mean he is not on the island."

"Not on the . . .!" Duti's eyes moved to mine, round with astonishment.

Not this. Please not this.

I touched Daniel's arm, and he let me, his fingers deliberately stilling on the jar they held, although he would not look at me even yet.

"Where has he gone, Daniel?" It came out almost whispered, pleading; and through the cowl's tunnel, I saw Daniel's eyes squeeze suddenly shut in anguish.

"To the King."

I had known before I asked; yet the shock of hearing it still deprived me of breath.

Daniel was yanked suddenly backwards as Duti seized him by the throat. I barely noticed. My brain was struggling to think beyond the shock, while Duti demanded, "When did he leave?"

"This morning, at first light . . ."

It was timed carefully, I realized, surprised by my own power to calculate. To make sure Hereward was too far away to return in time. But still . . . I looked at Duti. "Send the signal to Hereward. And to Tostig. It is still possible they'll get back in time. If Thurstan has to go all the way to Cambridge, negotiate, then bring William, with his army . . . Stop it!" I added, sharply, breaking off to wrench Duti's choking arm from Daniel's throat. "Leave him! Can't you see his *shame?*"

Slowly, Duti released his captive, who rubbed distractedly at his throat while his eyes, large and bleak, gazed helplessly into mine.

At last he said hoarsely, "Hereward would not allow it. With him here, the Abbot – we – would have had no support. I am a humble monk, lady. I am not party to the plans of the great. But he – the Abbot – seemed to believe it could be accomplished before your husband's return."

"The cowardly, treacherous . . ." Duti fumed.

"He means to save him," Daniel pleaded. "If he is not here, he cannot be taken."

"His children are here!" Duti snarled. "His *wife* is here! He would give up the isle for her, and the King knows it – thanks to Deda!"

"The Abbot means to plead for them. I swear he would let no harm . . ."

"Once we are in William's hands, the Abbot will not be able to control his own bowels, let alone . . .!"

"Enough," I interrupted quietly. I sounded slightly irritated, which, in fact, I was. There were too many things to do to indulge in this orgy of vindication and recrimination. "Duti – organize the signals. Now. We must send men as well to meet them and let them know how things stand here, lest they walk into a trap . . ."

The signals were sent, beacons of light from the isle's highest point, namely the top of the abbey itself. We knew they could be seen at the next signal points on distant islands because we had tested them – it had seemed a necessary precaution with so many men away for so long. I could only pray it would be seen through the heavy mist.

Wulric the Heron and Wulric the Black were sent out northwest to meet Hereward; two others to the northeast in search of Tostig. The monks, none of whom we could trust now, were herded inside the monastery and locked in the refectory, while Thorkell and the Siwards deployed what men they had left in preparing defences and observing any signs of movement.

It came before first light, far sooner than I had hoped.

The King's men were hard at work, swiftly repairing the causeway to Aldreth that had burned in the peat fire. Rousing the men, drawing them in from other parts of the island to where the trouble would clearly begin, Siward strengthened the bulwarks that had been so successful before against the royal siege machines. But looking from the same point as then, I could see no machines. Only men, forming up.

"They can't be going to risk it again," I said slowly. "Even without Hereward . . . Would the reeds light in this damp?"

"Perhaps," said Thorkell. "Underneath, where the peat is . . ."

He ran off, shouting some order to the archers. Sickened, I turned away. More burning, more death. And I had ordered it. For the first time, I felt the weight of Hereward's responsibilities on my own shoulders. I knew I would do what had to be done, at whatever cost; but I had no idea what sort of person would emerge when it was all over.

Leaving the war I was not fit for, I rode across to the camps, collecting the women and children to bring back to the abbey. It was the only possible place of safety for them if the royal army succeeded. Then, wrapping my cloak closer around me, I went alone this time to watch the rebuilding of the causeway. The spring fire, clearly, had not damaged it as much as we had imagined. The main foundations must have still been there, at least on the far side. Still, at this pace, and with Thorkell's continual harrying, I did not see how they could finish it before tomorrow night at the earliest.

A great shout went up – and I soon saw why. A flaming arrow had finally managed to set the reeds on fire. They smouldered rather feebly, though it was enough to send the enemy scuttling to put it out. This time, no one threw water on it. They had learned that much. They broke it up and smothered it with sticks and hides. And while they did so, our archers picked off some more men, and work had to stop.

I allowed myself to hope. I allowed myself to believe that Thurstan had misjudged the loyalty and determination of Hereward's men still left on the isle. I even smiled and waved encouragingly to the cheering men at the bulwarks. Grinning back, they lifted their bows to salute their captain's lady, and returned immediately to their work.

I wondered vaguely why William bothered. Why he needed Thurstan's betrayal just to try again what had failed in the past. Was it simply that he knew now how few men were left on the isle? That Hereward himself was not here to command . . .?

And then, while the old smile still faded on my lips, the new fear hit me like a blow.

The door of the refectory was unlocked. With Duti at my side, I stepped in. The babble of noise faded away. My eyes scanned the monks, standing and seated among the familiar tables, with all degrees of outrage and fear and shame quite visible to my eyes. I could smell their sweat, mingling sourly with old food.

Some, I recognized with relief. But there were over forty monks there, and I had no time to spare. I looked instead at Brother Daniel.

"Brother, who accompanied the Abbot on his journey?"

Daniel looked blank.

"I ask," I explained, "because I doubt very much that he went by boat. He would have been seen. I think he went by the secret paths, and I am afraid – I am afraid he did not rely on the fenmen to show him the way."

"What does it matter?" someone demanded. "He clearly got there!"

"It's the coming back that concerns me. Daniel, *who went with Thurstan?*"

Daniel swallowed. "Acer."

I closed my eyes.

Acer the Hard. Not afraid of hard work, or of the marshes, which he knew better even than Hereward. Nor even, it seemed, of betrayal.

I had barely turned my back on them before Thorkell came panting to the door. His furious, desperate eyes met mine, telling me even before his words did that my fears were founded.

"Torfrida – they're coming through the west paths. The fenmen have seen them."

They could not come quickly on to the island over the paths; but still, by the time our men were sent from Aldreth, there were enough of them to have fired the hamlets close by, and to drive our men back towards the abbey.

Our one hope, so Thorkell said, was in the returning mist, since it gave us, who knew the island, the advantage over strangers. Yet it seemed to me we were all floundering in darkness. I began to face the fact that we were losing the isle, and the despair was terrible.

When they started to pour over the causeway itself, I had to act. You see, with all our men pulled back to face the western intruders, the enemy had finished the bridge with remarkable speed. And the Siwards, gathering their men from the mists, swept back down to face the greater threat, the threat they could not conquer. They knew it, as I did, but it was not in their hearts to give up.

Weeping, because I had never known such courage in the face of such insurmountable odds, I went inside and fetched my children.

"You're never taking them out there!" Lise exclaimed.

"I cannot leave them here to be used against their father."

I spoke patiently, coolly, for my cool brain had worked this out long since. They, and I, had to go, at least try to escape. Lise stared at me. So did Sigrid. From their frightened, pitying eyes, I knew they understood. And I had to turn away from that, from the monster I was and had to be, to so risk my children against the dreadful crying of my own heart.

"Get your cloak," said Lise briskly to the nurse.

"Stay," I said quickly. "You are safe enough, I believe, if you go to the Church. Please, Lise, I cannot have you too . . ."

But it seemed I could, for when I ran out of the chamber, they were still at my heels and I had not the strength to send them back. And who knows? Perhaps we were all safer away from the isle: 'Saxon' women and children might well be considered legitimate prey by the invading Normans.

In the courtyard, by the abbey gate, we met Duti and Thorkell, arguing in the midst of chaos. The sounds of close battle slammed against my ears: screaming steel on steel and the shouts of men in fury and triumph and agony.

"Go with her!" Thorkell shouted angrily when his eyes fell on me. His forehead was grimy and wet with sweat, and there seemed to be a lump of gory skin hanging off his left arm. "Protect her, for Christ's sake! We are lost here – it's all you can bloody do, man!"

Duti's hand swept across his face, but it did not hide the tears or the tearing pain. Abruptly, the argument seemed to go out of him. His shoulders dropped.

"And you, my friend?" he said low. "You cannot take on all this alone . . ."

A strange, tiny smile curved Thorkell's thin lips. "Belly of God, I began it, remember? Before Hereward came. I'll see it finished, one way or another. Tell him that. Tell him – oh Christ, what does it matter? He'll know. Your duty is to your lady. Go quickly. In the mists you should be able to lose any bastard Normans still in the northwest, and find at least one of the paths. God bless you lady. And them."

I felt his touch, butterfly light on my cheek. For an instant, his eyes on my aching face were tender, and then he was gone, the most profane of men, with God's name on his lips at the last.

From the northern side of the abbey we could see the royal soldiers pouring up the slope from Aldreth. There seemed to be no resistance to them now. I thought my heart would break.

Until a roar of "Hereward! Hereward!" rent the already shrieking air, and Thorkell the Pure led his men in a suicidal charge from the abbey gate. Duti was pulling me on, because we had no time even to watch our friends be cut down like corn. There was always more, and worse, to bear. And the funny thing was that I could do it.

Silently, with each of us women carrying a child, and Duti in front with drawn sword and axe, and God knew what pain from his ribs, we slipped into the mist. It was only when young Hereward objected to the wetness on his head that I realized I was weeping.

I suppose it had always been a forlorn hope. The isle was too small, infested from at least two sides by swarms of invaders who vastly outnumbered the men we had left. We had never stood a chance of eluding them. Yet it was only when we came face to face in the mist with a Norman soldier that I felt the galloping, personal tragedy. Was this it? The brutal death of my children arising from my own, criminally wrong decision?

Duti leapt at the soldier – so quickly and so silently that I don't think the surprised Norman even saw him before he died. But already it was too late.

Rows of conical helmets were rising out of the mist, swinging about to surround us under clipped, confident orders. Duti was left with too great a choice of target. His body, poised, aggressive, turned and turned, looking for a gap, until at last, with something of his cousin's style, he grinned.

"Well? Who wants to be first to die?"

"You're not at a tournament, boy. Drop your weapons," said a commanding voice in French.

"Drop your own," said Duti at once. "I have nothing to lose."

"You have three women," said the Norman drily. "And – er – three babies. All yours?"

"I am a stallion," said Duti.

"You'll be a dead stallion," I said in low-voiced Saxon. "Surrender, Duti. The children can be Lise's . . ."

And he looked at me with the same despair and desperation in his face that I had seen so often that day, acknowledgement of failure, of failing *him.* And then, abruptly, he whirled and charged, screaming, at the nearest soldier.

I think he meant to die in the act of killing, but they chose to disarm him, brutally enough to make me turn aside. Meanwhile, the Norman commander strolled up to us and inspected us one by one, even placing one insolent finger under my chin. I stared at him, because for once I had nothing to say.

Then, suddenly, he reached up and plucked off my veil. My hair tumbled loose, cascading about my face and shoulders.

An odd silence fell. I stood unmoving under their stares. Then the commander smiled.

"Bagged," he observed. "Hereward's lady, or I'm an imbecile."

"You're certainly that," said another voice from the fog, making me gasp, while everyone span searching for its source. I heard the whine of an arrow in flight, a dull thud, and then the commander clapped a hand to the back of his neck. I had the forethought to step aside – the unbelievable, unbearable sound of that voice had given me back my instincts – before he fell like a stone, and hell broke out once more.

Duti, shaking his captors off easily as they turned to face some greater force, was again by my side, retrieving the fallen captain's sword just in time to defend himself.

The new attack seemed to be coming from all sides, arrows decimating and dividing the circle of Normans. And then finally I saw him, Hereward, riding hard out of the swirling fog like some great, mythical beast, his mouth open in that queer, animal yell I had heard only once before, when he had killed all those men at Bourne.

I think I cried out for sheer joy that he was alive, that my own fierce wish had not been responsible for conjuring an illusion. He did not pause. Nor did his companions. I saw Leofric the Deacon, and Wulric the Black and, amazingly, Siward the Red – how had he got there?

The fighting was quick and brutal and far from one-sided – but it was noisy enough to attract attention, and very soon my anxious, flitting gaze picked out more men in Norman armour, running down the slopes from the monastery into the mist hovering below.

"Hereward! From the abbey!" I called out desperately. We were running out of time again.

But there was Wulric, our ugly, mounted Heron, taking Frida from Lise, holding Leo under his other arm. And seeing it, a Norman tried to snatch young Hereward from my arms. I cried out, lashing at him blindly with my fist. It connected, though. I felt a *swish* against my wrist before he fell under another sword, and I whirled to find Hereward's arm – thick, muscled, covered with blood and dirt – reaching down to me; and Hereward's eyes, blacker than the burnt hamlets we had passed, more opaque than the mist itself, fixed unwaveringly on mine.

My hand reached up of its own accord, clutching those large fingers, and then, gasping, I was hoisted, child and all, up behind him in the saddle, and Swallow was moving, galloping under us. And my eyes were closed, my arm fast around the warm, unyielding waist of the man for whom I had done this, the man whose torment, surely, was greater than that of all the men, dead and dying, we left behind.

"How did you get in? Who is with you?"

These were only two of the questions rattling inside my foolishly contented head – in this carnage I was unbelievably, if very temporarily, contented, just because he was here. But I think I must have spoken aloud into his damp, hard back, for he answered me, the words vibrating against my cheek and, from Swallow, up through my body.

"By wading and swimming. We met Tostig to the east."

"Thank God. Where is he?"

"In the battle before the abbey."

Like everything he had said so far, it was quiet, expressionless, brief. But at this, I lifted my head from his warmth, trying to see round to his face.

"The battle is still going on? You were in time to help Thorkell?"

"Can't you hear it? We must have passed you in the fog. It was Thorkell who told us where you were."

I felt his arms pulling Swallow back to a canter. He called some command, softly, and then Swallow was still. There was water in front of us – thick, stagnant, marshy. I could smell it.

Hereward said, "Morcar." And for the first time, there was expression in his voice – pleasure in the survival of another. I peered past Hereward's shoulder.

The young Earl stood there with a handful of his own followers, his hand reaching out almost involuntarily, as mine had, for Hereward's. His eyes were more tragic than ever.

"You," he said, speaking swift and low as Hereward had. "Thank God. And the lady is safe, with your children. I was so afraid . . . But go quickly now. We'll guard your back."

Briefly, Hereward clasped the other's hand, as if giving strength. Then his head turned.

"Siward. Duti. Take your men, and of your love, get my wife to Crowland."

That paralysed me. I could not even speak. But Morcar did, saying the words for me. "And you? Where are you going?"

"To the monastery, of course."

"The battle is lost, Hereward! Our men are nearly all dead or taken! I came only to see you safe! There is no more to be done."

256

"There is," said Hereward with sudden, shocking savagery, twisting in the saddle and all but pushing me, gasping, to the ground. "I'll send that whole nest of clerical vipers to hell."

"You can't!" said Morcar, misunderstanding.

"Watch me."

I said quickly, "No." And handed the child to Lise. Hereward rounded on his kinsmen. "Siward . . .!"

"Hereward, they're monks!" Siward exclaimed. "And we locked them in!"

"Then pray for their souls. Let go, Torfrida." The last because my hands clung to Swallow's bridle.

"Not for this," I said shakily. "Not for this, Hereward. You might burn the abbey, but what in God's name would that achieve? Even as revenge, it is scarcely fitting."

I did not get near him. He barely looked at me. "I shall be the judge of that."

"You would kill yourself – for mere spite – rather than fight another day in the cause they all died for?"

I don't know where I found the words, but they brought his eyes quickly back to mine. Suddenly they were naked, desperate. And I had dropped the bridle, moving swiftly to stand beside him, reaching up blindly for his hands. Releasing the reins, they twisted, catching mine.

"Forgive me," I whispered. "I tried. I tried, but I could not hold it for you . . ."

He swallowed, convulsively. "Torfrida, don't. Just take the children. Please. Forbid me to burn the abbey, and I'll obey. But don't, don't forbid me to lead the men who still fight in my name . . ."

Gasping, I pressed my forehead, my lips, to our joined hands. Never, never, had I needed strength like this before.

"Come back," I found myself saying over and over again. "Come back; come back . . ."

And his hand pulled free to catch in my hair. He bent right down from the saddle, to kiss my mouth, once, and then, released, I was pushed into Siward's arms.

I heard him say, "Morcar? You had best follow them at once. Don't wait for us, but go on to the Bruneswald. I'll find you there."

Morcar's smile was slightly odd. I noticed that, even through my own anguish. He said, "I won't do either of those things. The cause is lost, Hereward. I shall make my peace."

This was unfair. To do this to him now . . . Yet poor Morcar was only trying to be honest. Perhaps he did not even know the bitterness of Hereward's memory of that earlier betrayal, when Morcar's grandfather had sent him into exile. Try as he would, Hereward's old loyalties would not leave him, nor the old expectations that went with them. His lord had betrayed him again.

He said in a strange voice, "Even if I survive, you will not come with me?"

And Morcar's throat jerked. "I have a life I cannot waste. I will not come with you."

And Hereward gave a brief contemptuous laugh. I thought it would stay with Morcar till the end of his days. "Then you waste it all the same."

And he rode off in the midst of his small group of followers. I saw Leofric the Deacon, Martin Lightfoot, Wynter, the inseparable companions, each with a life to waste for him. If not for his cause.

"Lady. Torfrida." It was Siward the Red, holding me by the arm, urgently tugging. Turning, I followed as best I could. It was difficult when I could not see.

CHAPTER 38

The journey was unspeakable. I do not think I could have borne its physical hardships had the spiritual pain been any less. What harm was the icy, cloying water lapping around my thighs after all the death and suffering I had just witnessed on Ely? My freezing, soaking discomfort was of no significance whatsoever when compared with the cause of a people broken forever. I had no right even to notice the painful abrasions on my feet, let alone my sliced-open wrist where the Norman's sword had caught it, when Hereward could already be taken, lying bloody and unattended in some bare dungeon. What did mere exhaustion matter, when he might be dead?

So, we walked on through the night. Twice, I stepped into sinking swamp and had to be pulled out, covered in mud and filth, shivering to the bone. Once, Frida did the same, which was when I realized my soul was not yet dead.

On and on, one foot before the other. I had no idea of the time. I did not even see the turver's hut until I heard Siward saying, "Can you give shelter to the women and the children?"

And then, stumbling down the step, I was inside, out of the wind. There was even a smoky turf-fire in the middle of the room, which some silent, stocky man built up while his wife and another woman spread rough blankets and skins for the children and for me. They asked no questions, even when they quietly and efficiently bound the wound on my wrist, even when Duti and Wulric the Heron sat guard by the door. But by then I was asleep, with the baby cuddled in to me and Frida's hand thrown out over my face.

"Lady. Torfrida. It's time to go."

My eyes opened quickly into Siward's. I sat abruptly. I was not only dry, but warm. The pale, red light at the window told me it was dawn. One of the women of the house silently gave me bread. Frida and young Hereward, wide-eyed and smiling, were already devouring theirs. On a stool under the window, Sigrid was feeding Leo.

Siward said grimly, "Get your things together quickly. There are soldiers coming this way."

That roused me. "How close?" I demanded, rising to my feet while swiftly coiling my hair and stuffing it under the veil Lise had given me for decency.

"Close enough to be tracking us. On the other . . ." He broke off as the door of the hut swung open and a man came in – the man who had built up the fire last night – with Wulric the Heron hard on his heels.

Wulric said, "*He* claims to have seen the soldiers close-to. He says they carry a standard – a black dragon's head on red."

For the space of two loud heartbeats I tried not to let myself hope. I found I was gazing at the turver, a typical product of the fens – taciturn, poor, unafraid and unimpressed.

I said to him, "Do you know whose standard that is?"

He nodded once, impassively. Would he have told us at all if he had not known, if he had not been sympathetic? Unless it was a trap. There was only one way to find out. But we could wait for the soldiers anywhere on the road – whether or not the turver knew my identity, he had already risked himself and his family.

I said, "You have been most kind to us. We thank you, and shall trespass no longer . . ."

"Wait for him here," the man advised. It was the first words I could recall hearing him speak, and they seemed to refer directly to the man at the forefront of all my thoughts.

I said doubtfully, "Do you know who I am?"

And he actually smiled.

Leaning against the open door of the listing hut, I gazed into the rising morning. The mist of yesterday had vanished, and the pale gold sun shimmered in state at the centre of a spectacular array of reds and pinks and bright, hard blues. While Frida galloped around the muddy ground in front of us, and young Hereward trotted after her, I raised my face to the cool sun, taking heart and courage from it.

Today we began again, he and I. Soon. Just as soon as he came.

To make sure we were not waiting merely in a sprung trap – after all, had we not just learned that it was unsafe to trust anybody? – Wulric had slipped off through the reeds to either spy on or join the coming soldiers. He had not come back. So, unless he was dead, the approaching soldiers were led by Hereward. They had to be.

As the sun climbed, releasing its early colours, which gradually faded and merged into the paler, softer blueness of a pleasant autumn morning, my eyes became fixed on the distant trees. They alone cut off the vastness of the fen, prevented me from seeing miles into the horizon. Through these trees, at any moment, he would come, with his men, wounded probably, and exhausted, but alive and needing me, perhaps, as never before. Please, God. Please.

When they came, it seemed almost casual. A man simply stepped out of the trees, then two more on horseback, then a whole stream of them, some mounted, others walking or limping at their side. And somewhere in the middle I saw the standard that identified them. It was black on red. My eyes focused on that as I said, "Siward."

Siward the Red came out of the hut, stepping past me to gaze at the approaching column.

"Not many," he said, and his voice suddenly cracked. "Dear God, not many . . ."

He was right. If that pitifully small group of men was all that was left of Ely's defenders, then how many of our followers, our comrades, our friends, had died in this?

Was it worth this? A small but insistent voice was whispering demandingly in my head. Was anything worth the tragedy – all the tiny, individual tragedies that swelled to cover so many lives, so much grief, so many deaths?

But not his, not his. The black dragon proclaimed that, and even without it now, I could make out the soldier on the leading horse. Though his posture was odd enough to convince me of grievous hurt as well as exhaustion, and some trick of the low sun had bleached the golden lights from his hair, I knew he could only be Hereward. Who else would ride at such a time without his helmet on?

I wanted to rush forward, to throw myself at him in comfort and compassion and mutual grief, but some leaden weight seemed to keep me pinned where I was. If it had not been for the door frame, I would have fallen over.

Lise came out with the baby in her arms. Frida and young Hereward stopped playing, sitting back on their heels like urchin children to watch the soldiers.

I don't remember precisely when I knew, or what told me. Perhaps I had always known. Perhaps the very paralysis which kept me rooted to the spot was the result of knowing. I only remember when I couldn't pretend any more, when my aching eyes had scoured the approaching company, picking out, with a relief that would come later, the strained, wasted features of Outi and Wulric the Black, and Wynter, and then looked back to their leader. He rode just then through the blinding glint of the sun, and revealed himself not Hereward, but Siward the White.

The paralysis broke. I was already across the muddy ground as Siward the Red reached his cousin and friend, their hands gripping in silent, intense welcome.

I heard Duti cry out, his voice harsh with relief, "Couldn't the bastards kill you even without me there to protect you?" And Outi's equally unflattering response.

But by then the Siwards had seen me. The Red stepped back quickly, allowing me access to his cousin, who met my eyes with direct, difficult pain.

I said warningly, "Where is he, Siward?"

"He is not with us, lady," Siward said quickly. "He went a different route, to Crowland, with Martin and Leofric. We are the decoys, if you like, to lead any pursuit in the wrong direction."

No. No, that was wrong. I felt myself frowning with the effort of reasoning.

I said, "Hereward would not have ordered that."

"He didn't. Leofric and I did." Siward swallowed, and the great fear I had been so desperately squashing, broke loose in a rush. Seeing it, Siward said swiftly, "No. He is alive, lady; he is! But – wounded."

Kicking his heels free, he slid out of the saddle and down beside me. His hands held my shoulders, as if giving me courage. Me. When I should have been supporting theirs, as *he* would. My drawn breath shuddered in my body, but at least it pulled me together.

I said, "How wounded?"

Siward hesitated till I said sharply, "The truth in God's name. Nothing can be worse than what I first imagined."

"Badly," Siward admitted. "A sword opened his head. I left him unconscious. There are other hurts, but that is the most serious."

Briefly, I searched his eyes, looking for his own opinion as to Hereward's chances. But I saw only his own pain and fear, and beyond that, total exhaustion.

I said, "Forgive me, Siward. It gives me joy to see you, and the others. You will never know how much. I have been an unnatural friend not to say so at once."

Siward smiled, with difficulty. "But a natural wife."

Ignoring that, I said, "Come, let me see to your own hurts before we start."

Crowland, where Hereward's mother and sister had been since Bourne was taken, unfortunately can only be reached by boat. There are no secret, treacherous paths as there are on to Ely. This was bound to bring us out into the open, advertise our presence to any watchers. But then, as Siward said, any Norman pursuit was likely to be several hours behind us.

Likely to be.

"Norman soldiers," said Wulric the Black laconically as he slunk back through the reeds to join us.

"Many?" Outi demanded.

"Too many for us. Like this."

"Very well. We'll sit tight till they go away."

"It looks to me as if they are the ones – er – sitting tight."

Siward frowned. "Waiting for us?"

"Or him," I said.

Siward's gaze lifted from mine to his cousin's, then took in the twins and the rest of our pitifully small and injured band. He sighed.

"Let's pick them off then. Till they're down to the sort of numbers a few girls could manage. It seems that's all we're fit for right now."

We moved cautiously through the reeds after Wulric, keeping close to the water's edge, though not often in sight of it, until, abruptly, we halted in the shadow of a tall willow. Over Duti's ducked head, I saw two conical helmets.

Now the killing would begin again.

I moved to the children, my finger to my lips. Sigrid turned the baby into her breast, and we all prayed.

I saw the Siwards standing straight, stretching their bows, taking careful aim. Still the Normans watching the water had their backs to us. Then I heard the whine of the arrow in flight. I saw the Normans half-spin, alert and alarmed; and then they fell, one after the other, with only a tiny, choked cry between them.

And the Siwards, their arrows still threaded and un-shot, lowered their bows in confusion.

"What the . . .?"

The willow branches beside us shook, depositing Leofric the Deacon and Martin Lightfoot among us.

Leofric grinned. "You're too slow," he complained to the Siwards. "And unobservant enough to be horsewhipped by Hereward."

And abruptly, at the sound of that name, the relieved grins of welcome froze on the men's faces.

Siward said, "How is he?"

Leofric's eyes flickered till they found me. At once, in pity and comfort, his arm stretched out. "Come," he said.

I went forward blindly, stumbling over rough ground, splashing wet mud up over my grimy skirts like streaks of black dye. I concentrated on those little things because just at that moment I could not cope with the larger.

They had left him in a boat, a small, insignificant fishing boat, hidden in the reeds. Halting at sight of it, I glanced interrogatively up at Leofric. I could see my own reflection in his light, veiled eyes.

"We need it," he said apologetically. "And it's been useful for dragging him around. Torfrida . . ."

But I could not wait for more. I heard their voices, but not their words as I ran the short distance left to the boat – and saw that he was indeed inside it, lying stretched out along the bottom. My hands gripped the boat's side. His golden hair spread out like an angel's, bound only around the head with a dirty bandage; his body, clothed in stained, bloody remnants, did not move; his face, still achingly beautiful to me, looked curiously peaceful, without frown or pain.

They had even closed his eyes.

I remember falling to my knees at his side, although I don't recall climbing in to the boat. I didn't mean to. There was just nothing else I could do. Gazing at his face, so pale and still and far beyond now the great, tumultuous life he had led, I felt it almost like an echo, the desolation of my life after this moment.

I had his children. But I didn't have him. How did women live with that?

I remember my eyes moving over the streaked bandage at his head, then down over the wounds in his body, and wished as I had never wished for anything that I had been there. I thought I might have made it easier for him to die thus in defeat. But I had been wrong: I had placed too much credence in the stars. It seemed he had been right about that too.

Slowly, my sore eyes moved back to his face.

And were held by his, open and staring, not with the blank coldness of death, but the anguish and misery of life.

I don't think the new shock had even hit me before he tried to smile.

He said, "Vain fool that I am, I always thought you would weep for me."

He knew, he always knew what I was thinking. Soon, the relief would flood me, like joy. I could feel it coming. I swallowed.

I said, "Some things are beyond tears. And you are not dead."

And then they came, like a river, spilling over my lashes and cheeks, and over his as, hiding them, I bowed my head to him, and kissed him, as if breathing my own life into his mouth.

"How many times," asked Hereward, as I smeared the healing ointment over his gaping, sluggishly bleeding head-wound, "have you done this for me?"

"Too many," I said tartly. I had recovered, mostly, and he, after his sleep, had found the strength to sit, with Martin's help, his back propped against the side of the boat while I tended his wounds. The dead peace of his sleeping face had vanished into a massive frown that consumed his whole face as he coped with a headache of horrendous proportions. Yet below that he was smiling at me, faintly, lazily, and I was still too shaky to bear that without steadying dryness, without humour.

Calmly, I took the proffered bandage from Lise, and began to wind it around his head. I was aware of his smile slowly dying, while his eyes still watched me, as they always did when I performed this service for him.

He said casually, "Will I live?"

I nodded once, because I could not trust it to speech, but still confidently enough for him to return provokingly, "How do you know? Did the stars tell you?"

"Yes."

He blinked. I felt that, though my attention was all on the bandage. And when my fingers fell away at last, he said curiously, "You really think you know when I shall die."

"I am a skilled astrologer."

"You are a terrifying wife. Do you know how? Or where?"

"In your own home. Be still."

"You're right. I don't want to know. I don't even believe."

And then some urgent voice was speaking outside the haven of our boat: "They've found the bodies, Leofric. They're looking for us."

My hand stilled, dripping water on his arm. My eyes met his.

"No," I said. "No."

And his smile was just a little twisted. "Have faith. I am not in my own home." And then he rose up, unaided, and climbed out of the boat.

Without Hereward, I don't believe they could have done it. It was not just his ingenious deployment of our few men, but his spirit, indomitable although he could not stand unaided for more than a few minutes, let alone charge and fight hand to hand. Instead, he stood still and shot arrows with devastating effect, and shouted instructions, encouraging, bullying, forcing, until Martin, unable to hold him any longer, fell; and Hereward slid to his knees by his side. Still stretching and shooting, his arms steady, his strength apparently eternal, his sight, despite the awful wound and pain, as clear as ever.

And though the men fell around him like rain, he would not surrender, would not stop until the last enemy lay dead.

Then he put down his bow, carefully at his side on the ground, and waited, patiently, to be carried back to the boat.

CHAPTER 39

Storming furiously into Hereward's cell, I found him with his head-bandage rakishly askew, pacing again, round and round the tiny chamber. It now looked barer than ever, for his few belongings – clothes and weapons – had gone.

In the two weeks we had been at Crowland, learning to mourn the dead of Ely and to hope for those who were alive, at least when last seen, Hereward had hardly noticed me. The children and I shared the guest quarters with Aediva and Lucy, but Hereward had chosen a cell rather than the infirmary, and I knew why: he could grieve and endure and recover away from eyes that might see too much, before which he might otherwise have lost face and, therefore, power over his remaining men.

For what? I wondered bleakly. The old life was dead, as dead as Tostig and Thorkell and a hundred others. Everything, it seemed, that had made him what he was over the last three years, had been taken from him. Even Swallow, his swift, ugly, mare had gone lame in the battle. In his flight afterwards, Hereward had had to cut her throat.

Now, as he glanced over his shoulder at me, I saw that he was still terrifyingly white and weakened. His men, and his mother, had grown so used to seeing him bruised and cut that they had come to assume he could not be killed, nor even seriously damaged. But he could; he could.

Worse, he actually looked surprised to see me.

"Torfrida."

"Your wife," I reminded him sarcastically.

"Mother of my children," he agreed with flippancy. "In time to bid me farewell."

"To bid you stop behaving like an imbecile!" I said furiously. "Even if you are stupid enough to go to the Bruneswald now, do you really imagine you can do so without *me?*"

Abruptly, he stopped his pacing in front of me, frowning. If he could physically do this, I was so afraid, for him and for me, that we would find nobody else there . . .

He said carefully, "You want to come with me? To live in forest camps with my 'gang'?"

I said, "No. But if it's all you will provide me with, I suppose I'll have to."

What I remember most about that journey is the storm, so fierce that the trees afforded us no protection whatsoever, forcing us to march on and on through the night in search of some shelter. I remember losing our way in the darkness, searching and failing to find any form of habitation. The wounded men – all but Hereward – took it in turns to sleep for an hour in the cart with the children.

And the dog, of course, the white dog that appeared out of nowhere, right beside me, its eyes glowing, its fur gleaming palely.

I never told anyone, because I thought no one would believe me. But I knew that 'dog' at once for a wolf, a white wolf, fully grown and sleek. Involuntarily, because I was tired enough to be insane, I held my hand down to her, and as though she knew me already, she deigned to sniff at my fingers, her nose wet and icy cold.

And it was that act, I think, which made the others say, "Look, it's a dog!"

"Aye, and a friendly one."

"It loves the lady, at least . . .!"

"Follow it – it's tame. It's bound to lead us somewhere!"

They assumed it would take us to its owner. It couldn't, of course, and it didn't. But: "She knows the woods better than we do in the dark," I said to Hereward who, meeting my gaze briefly over the heads of his men, shrugged and nodded.

The clouds had seemed opaque until then, but suddenly, as we began to follow the wolf, the moon rolled out, like a sun in that blackness, glinting on the men's helmets and spears. And at the same time the trees seemed to thin, and through their bare branches, the weird, glimmering lights of the marsh winked like fairy lights.

Superstitiously convinced now of the 'dog's' benevolence, the men were happy enough to follow it off the paths altogether. Once or twice the wood was so thick that it had to be broken with swords, and even so, briars and thorns scratched at my face and hands.

And then Hereward said, "Listen."

We halted. But all I could hear was the wolf's panting breath as she turned her head and looked at us.

"Men," Hereward said impatiently. "I can hear men's voices. I believe I shall keep that dog! Follow on!"

We began to move again. Briefly, I felt the wolf's silken head under my hand, but when I glanced down, surprised by the affection of so wild a beast, she had gone. I think I would have been sorry, except that by then I too could hear men's voices.

Until, as if suddenly they had heard *us*, they stopped.

Beside me now, Hereward lifted his hands to his lips and made a call like an owl, three times. There was a pause; then it came back like an echo. I heard the faintest hint of gasp from Hereward, or perhaps he was just collecting his breath for the next two hoots. But before they too could be returned, the undergrowth seemed to snap and crackle with life as men erupted out of the trees, some carrying torches which flared and lit up the desperately hoping faces on both sides.

266

"Wynter," said Hereward. Wildly, I wondered how he could tell, for the flames lent a curiously inhuman sameness to all the faces. "Thank God."

Both his arms had gone out, unbearable relief forcing uncharacteristically physical expression to his affection. But Wynter fell to his knees, as if he couldn't help it, great tears rolling down his craggy face as he seized Hereward's hand and pressed it to his lips.

The forest rang with it, the joy of the men at their captain's return – his survival, even, for they had not known if he lived or died on Ely. One by one they came up and were embraced, for after the shock of Wynter, Hereward would allow no one else to kneel to him.

With new joy of my own, which was surely only an easing of grief, I recognized Gaenoch, and Leofwin the Crafty, and Hurchill, and Hogar the cook, and many others of greater and lesser degree.

And after Hereward, of course, they greeted me with shyer if still flatteringly genuine pleasure before they fell into their old comrades' arms. Because of what had gone before, the joy of their reunion was out of all proportion. I felt the intensity of it myself, and I knew Hereward did too. It was in the odd stillness of his posture as he watched and spoke, and in the peculiar pain of his smile as the jollity raged around us. And yet, because of the way he had been with me at Crowland, I was afraid to touch him, to give him my understanding. It was he who moved, who found my hand with his fingers and squeezed so hard it hurt. Only then did he turn his head and look at me.

"It could have been worse," he whispered. "It could have been worse."

And I realized, through the rain, that he was weeping.

And so began probably the oddest phase of our life together. Certainly it was the most difficult, for never in my life had I known such physical hardship, such deprivation of the luxuries I had taken for the necessities of life. And inevitably it was made worse by guilt, for I was forcing this life on my children as well.

Not that they found it hard. They loved it, tumbling and running with a freedom they had never previously been allowed. They never seemed to feel the cold or mind the mists and rains.

And it must be said we rarely went hungry or even without shelter, for everywhere we went – and we had to move far and wide about this and neighbouring counties – the local people pressed food and drink upon us, gave us places, often in their own homes, particularly the children and me. At first I was embarrassed, thinking they did it for fear of Hereward. But they didn't. They did it for love of him, or pride in him. Or both. And once their awe of me was overcome, I even became friends with many of the women, a few of whom I had known before, helping their sick children and repairing their husbands' injured limbs, or just gossiping as women of all ranks do all over the world about the things that truly matter, that are not great or glorious but just part of all our lives.

But I am running ahead a little. Before I got to know the women, before we even left that first camp, the others came, the other survivors of Ely who knew to find us here. These were the ones William had captured, in battle or surrender; the ones who, in his mercy, he had allowed to live in freedom; the ones who lost their hands or their eyes.

I had thought I was accustomed, if not hardened, to war by then. But it seemed I wasn't. Some of them died of their injuries, of course, but I believe we saved the lives of most. Some, Hereward sent with guides to Crowland. Others he helped get home to wives or mothers. Those who wanted to stayed with us, despite the half-pitying, half-resentful objections of some who feared they would slow us up and endanger themselves and everyone else. But Hereward was adamant. With humble or angry difficulty, according to their natures, they learned new skills to aid him in the cause he would not leave.

It was from the maimed ones that we learned what happened to our treacherous monks. When the King had arrived, they were still locked in their refectory. The lord Gilbert de Clare had interrupted them, unlocking their door and strolling in to enquire sardonically whether, since the King himself was actually gracing their church at this moment, they might not choose to dine at some other time.

The poor, hungry monks had fallen over themselves to get to the church, but the King had already gone, leaving only one mark of gold on the alter of St. Aethelthryth – and instructions for the building of a castle within the abbey's precincts. The monks had, apparently, gone chasing after him to Witchford, though rumour said they had not been treated kindly. To me, the King's behaviour to them spoke of sheer distaste, of contempt for the men who may have delivered Ely to him but who, in the end, had betrayed a better man to do it.

Hereward himself, smiled sourly. He did not react at all when they told us that Morcar and the other great nobles had been taken away in chains.

In less than a week, Hereward – suffering frequent, blinding headaches and chronic exhaustion which he could hide from everyone except me – was training his men again, keeping them active. And before two had passed, he had led them in their first successful raid on a Norman-owned estate. Gone were the days when he supplanted such a lord with the rightful holder. Now, it seemed, there *was* no one else, so he just took the Norman's gold and as much treasure and supplies as his men could carry, freed the slaves, some of whom joined us, and the men came back jubilant.

The next day we broke camp and moved north.

* * * *

268

The damp, choking mists of autumn gave way to the icy winds and frosts of winter. I was convinced that I would die, that we all would. In fact no one did, although we all coughed and wheezed and sneezed our way through the short, shivering days and desperately cold, long nights.

With the spring, I could begin to replenish my sadly depleted stock of herbs, and although our numbers were tragically less than before, my life was no less busy. In fact, I had begun to think of myself as really quite a great lady, with so many souls in my care. It was just that I had no hall. And a great lady, I suppose, would have had no need of the little dagger I had hidden in a specially made pouch at my ankle. That had been Hereward's idea.

"For your own protection," he had said, just a little abruptly. "When I cannot be there."

I think it was before Easter that we returned to the Bruneswald, setting up camp near enough to Bourne to remind me of the way my life could have been. Walking back one afternoon – with my cold and my basketful of plants, and accompanied only by Edwin, one of the very young blinded men from Ely whom I was teaching to recognize herbs by smell and feel – I was intrigued to find a very stately carriage, and a good deal of excitement in the camp.

I stopped to examine the former, which seemed to be abandoned at the edge of the camp, and amused Edwin by describing it in awed detail.

Then: "What is this?" I asked flippantly, as Leofric ran down to meet me. "Does Hereward imagine we will make use of it? Travelling to the King's court, perhaps?"

Leofric was grinning. "It hasn't come from Hereward. We found it – together with its owner – in the woods, looking for us, so we brought the whole equipage here. Blindfolding the lady, of course. You'll never guess who she is."

"The Queen?"

"Better than that. The lady Aelfryth."

"Of Worcester?" I demanded, entertained. "Has she actually come here in pursuit of him?"

"Apparently."

Edwin was grinning too. "What is she like?"

"Breathtaking," said Leofric promptly.

"Take me to her," I commanded. "The anticipation is unbearable! You're not so unkind as to laugh in front of her?" I added with a trace of contrition, as we walked into the camp.

"She wouldn't notice if we did," said Leofric. "Behold!"

I beheld.

She was standing aloofly under a large lime tree, her frightened women clinging and trembling at her back, although the lady herself looked as if

269

she had never been afraid in her life, and saw no reason to start now. And why should she indeed? Her obvious wealth, if not her beauty, would have protected her from just about everything since the cradle.

And she *was* beautiful, probably the most beautiful woman I have ever seen. Although elegantly, modestly veiled, I could tell from her colouring that she had bright, flaxen or golden-yellow hair. Indeed, I could just discern a tiny curl peeping out at her cheek. Her face was heart-stopping, delicate boned, even-featured; her perfect skin was white and rosy in all the right places, her eyes large and limpid cornflower blue between long, curling dark lashes; her lips, even when drooping with discontent as they were now, sculpted full and shapely, the prettiest, most kissable lips a man might wish to encounter.

And as if this wasn't enough, the loveliness of her person was draped in a gorgeous pink silk travelling cloak, lined with ermine. Jewels glittered at her throat and breast, fingers and wrists.

Her beauty alone was enough to stop anyone in their tracks, but our men, and the scattering of women who had joined us, had more reason than that to stare. Clearly they were vastly entertained by our splendid visitor, and were giggling and chuckling to each other. Those nearest fell back for Leofric and me, grinning and winking at me. In spite of myself, I felt my lips twitch.

I said pleasantly, "My lady Aelfryth?"

And the disdainful blue eyes turned on me. "Who else would I be?" she snapped.

"Who indeed?" I murmured, and sneezed through Wynter's snigger. "Hurchill, don't stand there gawping. Bring the lady a stool. Hogar, a cup of wine for our guest – the good stuff from the Abbot of Peterborough."

They scuttled off to obey me, imperfectly hiding their grins. I can't say I minded, since their rudeness appeared to be easily out-matched by hers, but I felt compelled to frown at them severely before turning back to the imperious lady.

Her gaze was still upon me, though now with marginally more interest.

"You have some authority over these men?" she demanded. I inclined my head, but before I could speak she went on petulantly, "They are infuriating! I have come to see Hereward of Bourne, and they deny he is here! Yet *they* brought me here, and I am well aware that this *must* be his camp! *You* bring him to me."

I blinked.

"I cannot," I said mildly. "He is not here. Sit, my lady," I added as Hurchill placed a stool for her, exaggeratedly wiping it with his sleeve. If anything, that made it dirtier, but the lady never even looked before she sat, still talking to me.

"Then where is he, pray?"

"I could not say, precisely. But if you tell me where *you* may be found, I shall pass the information on to him."

"You'll get it wrong. I'll wait."

Unused to being assumed quite so dull witted, I felt my lips twitch again. I said patiently, "You will be uncomfortable here. Especially after dark. I doubt, you see, that he will be back before morning."

She stared at me, as if it were my fault she had been offered such an affront in return for her graciousness and trouble. Then, unexpectedly, her eyes glazed over, imagining, I am convinced, what romantic or daring exploits Hereward was engaged upon all night. Suddenly afraid she might ask me, I said hastily, "Or you could leave another letter for him."

That got her attention. Her eyes widened, while the men fell into another communal paroxysm of laughter.

She almost blurted, "You know about the letters?" And I believe I was relieved that she *could* be put out.

I said calmly, "Oh yes," and hoped she did not hear Gaenoch's "*Everyone* knows about the letters!" She did not appear to. Her tongue, little and pink, darted out, wet her pretty lips and withdrew from view.

"Very well," she said with decision. "I need material to . . ."

But just then a shout went up at the other end of the camp. My eyes flickered, meeting Leofric's. He nodded. And just for a moment, my emotions were too confused to sort out. I was glad, as I was always glad when he came back. But I realized that I did not want him to find her here, and not just because she would inevitably claim some of his attention. There was something about her, now I had met her, that niggled uneasily through my head: a feeling that reminded me of another, that made me want to shoo her away like an importunate dog.

She said excitedly, "Is he coming back? Is that Hereward?"

"I believe so," I said calmly, and she jumped to her feet with the biggest show of animation I had yet seen in her. She was so clearly intending to trot off after Leofric that I stepped instinctively in front of her.

"Please wait here," I said as pleasantly as I could.

She looked surprised. Then: "You forget yourself, woman. Stand aside!"

It could not even be called contempt. I was not worthy of that; I was merely some irritating dirt in her path. I found it a trifle disconcerting, but I had not been an outlaw's wife for so long without learning anything.

I said steadily, "Lady, if ever I am misguided enough to visit you, I will submissively go where I am put. Here, that is your prerogative. Your only prerogative."

That won a spark of surprised anger. Clearly she was unused to being addressed in that tone, whether or not she understood the words. One of her women began to twitter with outrage; another gave a very strange noise, a cross between a hicough and a laugh, swiftly smothered. Our own women were grinning openly.

"How dare you speak like that to me?" she demanded, shocked. "Have you any idea who I am?"

"Every idea. On both issues. Now, sit down, if you please. Even you must see that I have the means to compel you."

Her lips fell open. Her wide, entrancing eyes flew up to and around the looming soldiers watching us with such interest. Her women clung tighter.

"They would not dare!" she gasped.

"They are Hereward's men," I mocked. "They would dare anything. But never think I would subject you to the handling of rough soldiers. Lise, see to the lady's needs. If she's troublesome, sit on her head."

And I strolled away, leaving her spluttering, but seated, and her women twittering, as Lise and Gaenoch's wife stood before them, arms akimbo.

I had wasted too much time pinning her down. He was already riding in to the camp on his ordinary, handsome white mare. Behind him, the men were full of excited glee – clearly a successful expedition.

Leofric was beside him, regaling him with the entertaining news of his fair visitor. For a second, astonishment blanked his face. Then he threw back his head and laughed. These days, it was a rare sound.

He dismounted and came to meet me, smiling still. As was his habit now, in this time of so little privacy, he simply took me in his arms without formality and kissed me, before moving on with understandable curiosity to meet his guest. He kept his arm about me as he walked and, childishly, I found I was glad of that. Now that I disliked her I had fewer objections to her feelings being hurt.

His awed whistle of appreciation told me he had seen her. Then his laughter bubbled up again. "The Devil! What a reputation I must have in Worcester!"

It was the old, wild, reckless humour, so unusual now; yet it could still catch me up as it had when we were children. And Aelfryth's voice, almost childish with amazed curiosity, piped up: "Is she – that woman – is she his mistress?"

The men doubled up. Lise and Gaenoch's wife smiled sourly. We came to her, his arm still loosely about my waist. Her eyes were devouring him.

He said gravely, "No. She is my wife."

"Mother of his children," Leofric added helpfully. There was a cruel streak in him sometimes.

"The lady Torfrida," Hereward said. "And lady Aelfryth, how charming, how – astounding – to meet you in person."

The lady rose slowly, as if in a dream, her entranced eyes locked in his mocking gaze as she curtsied low, offering her hand at the same time. Hereward took it gravely. She swallowed, and rose, still in his gaze.

"You must forgive me; I am speechless," she said without any noticeable truth. "It is not every day I meet a hero."

"You must introduce us, too."

"I mean you," she explained patiently, and Hereward's lips twitched.

"Don't imagine I am not flattered," he said.

"He is," I confirmed drily, and the men sniggered. Hereward looked at me quellingly, and they sniggered again.

He said, "I am, naturally, overwhelmed by your kindness, your beauty, your – er – presence. Only – er – what do you want?"

"To be by your side," said Aelfryth, as though stating the obvious. "To help you and comfort you and inspire you."

I could not quite believe I had heard that at first. I think neither could Hereward, for he took a moment to reply. The men's mouths had fallen open. No longer sniggering, they were looking at each other uneasily.

Hereward said flatly, "You can have your *dinner* at my side, and leave your jewels and your gold on the table when you go. Where are the children, Torfrida?"

He didn't even trouble to nod as he turned away from her. Walking by his side towards the tent that was ours, I was aware of the men drifting away too. She was no longer an amusing, decorative curiosity, nor even a beautiful woman with the good sense to be pursuing their captain; but one who had been blatantly insulting to their captain's lady. And for that, they were more than happy to follow his lead.

A wave of something – exaltation, relief, gratitude? – washed over me. It was months later before I realized why.

"You are very jolly," the lady Aelfryth observed without enthusiasm. Like everything else she had uttered since his arrival, it was addressed to Hereward who sat beside her.

As we sometimes did for feasts and celebrations, we had spread out big, makeshift tables around the camp; the food and ale and, when we had it, wine, were set out upon them, and everyone sat down and served themselves. Hereward, hovering between the gracious, the mocking and the downright rude, occasionally remembered to serve the lady Aelfryth. The rest of the time, Leofric, on her other side, performed the service, since she either could not or would not do it herself.

Her women, giggling a little lower down the table, appeared to be succumbing to the wine and blandishments of the men, particularly Outi and Duti who were growing more outrageously bold by the cup.

"Of course we are jolly," Hereward responded, tearing venison off a large bone with his strong white teeth while she watched avidly. "We have just stolen a large quantity of excellent wine and killed three Frenchmen, after which we caught some gold tribute destined for Peterborough. We have had an excellent day."

If he had hoped to shock her by such revelations, he was disappointed. Clearly, she revelled in them. An admiring smile lit up her face, lending her already startling beauty the spark of animation that made all the difference.

"You are very brave," she breathed. "I have heard often what a fierce, and fearless, fighter you are . . ."

"For a worthy prize," said Hereward, bored, breaking off to shout something encouragingly rude to the twins. An apple was flung back at him, and deftly caught in his right hand. He offered it to me with exaggerated courtesy.

Aelfryth said archly, "And do you ever encounter beautiful ladies on your adventures?"

"On my *raids*," Hereward corrected. "Oh, frequently."

"What do you do? Do you treat them with chivalry?"

"No. I bring them back to camp and ravish them under my wife's nose."

Aelfryth's eyes widened. I wondered cynically if it was shock or opportunity. "Doesn't she mind?"

A breath of laughter caught in my throat. Hereward smiled directly, devastatingly, into her eyes. "Would you like to find out?"

"Hereward!" said Leofric sharply. And in truth there was a new flush to the lady's cheeks. She was not, it seemed, quite so hard, or so sophisticated, or so stupid, as I had imagined.

She said bravely, "It is your humour; I know."

Hereward laughed unkindly, and turned away from her again. I leaned forward, looking past him to her. I felt just a little sorry for her now. I suspected that she was only just realizing how far out of her depth she was.

I said, "What of your husband, lady? Does he not object to your somewhat – *unconventional* – expedition?"

"Oh, I have left him at home. I am visiting with the Bishop of Worcester. We are staying at Folkingham. Do you know it?" she asked Hereward.

Abruptly, the very name of the place seemed to sober him. As if suddenly tired of his rather cruel game, he took a last draught of wine from the purloined gold cup, and rose to his feet.

"Time to go," he said to her briefly, and walked away from the table with only a nod to me. Aelfryth, like a lamb to the slaughter, trotted obediently after him.

It was dark by the time he came back, and I was already undressed, lying wakefully on the bedding roll I shared with him.

"Did you get a kiss?" I enquired as he sat down beside me. By the light of the lamp, his eyes gleamed with curious darkness. His fingers held a little leather pouch which he emptied on to the blankets.

"Better than that," he said blandly, and I gazed at the tumbled rings and jewels and gold coins.

"It should buy us some more dinners," I observed, closing my eyes again.

"And William some more troubles. Torfrida?"

I felt his finger, unusually soft on my hair, smoothing it off my cheek. I opened my eyes. "Yes?"

"Are you tired of living like this?"

"Yes," I said again.

His lips were smiling, but it was an odd, sad little smile, with no mirth in his eyes.

He said, "We are all that is left. William has gone to sort out Malcolm and Edgar in Scotland; and Edric the Wild, of all people, has gone with him. I wonder, sometimes, what I am doing. To all of us."

I said low, "I know." There was nothing else I could say.

"It is a habit," he said. "And pride. Because I will not bow to a man I once greatly respected, as a soldier and a ruler. I wonder, Torfrida, who is the bigger fool? That silly girl, or me."

I knelt, wrapping my arms around him, pressing his beloved head to my breast. I could tell by the tight lines above his eyes that his head was aching again. When he let me, I laid him back on the pillow and rubbed gently with my fingers, rhythmically, over and over, almost willing the pain away, until, at last, he slept.

Slowly, my stilled hands dropped. His sleeping face was peaceful, yet it brought an ache to my throat. I lay down at his shoulder, touching my cheek to his bare flesh, and closed my eyes.

He was lost, as he had been lost since Ely had betrayed him. The only new part was his admission. But while I wept for that, and the struggle that had brought it about, I thought too that it might be the beginning of something greater.

CHAPTER 40

The boy was unconscious. He had lost so much blood from a body already undersized and malnourished that he looked to be made only of white dust which would blow away if I breathed on him too hard. On top of that the wound was infected.

Slowly, I took my hand from his forehead and lifted my gaze to his mother, gaunt, haggard, old before she had reached her prime. I swallowed.

I said, "Forgive me. There's nothing I can do for him."

"I know," she whispered. "I knew he was dead as soon as they brought him home . . . It's his father can't give up hoping – he's our only son, you see, and I doubt there'll be more now. Who would bring a child into this anyhow? Only it's hard to lose one already here . . ."

In Flanders, as well as here at Bourne, I had seen many mothers lose their sons. One never became inured to it, but over the years, I had learned the right way to cope, the right things to say and do. But for some reason they all deserted me now. It might have been the emotion of coming back here which had knocked me off balance. Certainly it had been hard to watch the people weep with joy just to see Hereward. And I could not brush off the ache of feeling him beside me, unnaturally stiff, his face set, his eyes black as he took in the new poverty, the sheer misery of the people who had been his and his family's for generations.

I didn't know why we were here. We had both known it would be painful, and I had doubted Hereward was strong enough to bear it right now. But he had come, and seen, because he had to. Even after the debacle of yesterday's storming of a Norman carriage, which had turned out to contain none other than the lady Matilda of Ghent, palely staring at Hereward through the wrenched open door. He had ordered his men off, of course, and ridden away. Siward the White, however, had carried to me her messages of love and desire for reconciliation, if only Hereward could be persuaded to it. I had sent back my best advice: that she should make use of Aelfryth.

As for Hereward, although he never spoke of it, I knew the experience had shaken him, and coming to Bourne on top of that was probably more than most could have endured.

While the people of the village clustered about him, throwing themselves at his feet, kissing his hands, he had stared white-faced around them and said only, "Forgive me," his voice little more than a broken whisper which few can have heard.

It had got better after that. He was used to hiding his emotion, used to leading, and he had forced himself to smile, to greet them, to ask after them all and their families, to listen to their troubles which were legion. That was when the story of Aelfric had come out. A pig had wandered off into the forest, which had been common land before the Normans came. Aelfric had been sent in pursuit, and since he was an enterprising lad, and since his family were all but starving, he had taken the opportunity to kill a bird at the same time. That was when the servants of the new lord, Oger, had chosen to reveal themselves. They had amused themselves for some time, chasing him through the forest before eventually they caught him in a hail of arrows, one of which had pierced his heart through the back.

The boy's father had told me this, stutteringly, determinedly, before it came out in a rush, his plea that I look at the child. And Aelfric was a child, not eleven years old, and already, to all intents and purposes, dead.

"Murder," said his father, low-voiced, from the door of the hut, where he stood with Hereward. "Is it not murder, my lord? In any law but this one . . ."

There was a pause. I looked at Hereward, his head bowed to stand inside the low, bare hut. His eyes were fixed on Aelfric's white, senseless face.

He said, "If I made the law, it would be murder."

Aelfric's father said, "And you would hang the bastards who did this, from those who shot the arrows up to Oger himself . . ."

Hereward's eyes moved to the face of the tortured man. For a second, even in the dark of that vile, smoky hut, I saw the veil over his eyes lift, saw the storm clearly raging. His lips parted to speak, but before the words came, Aelfric's mother was saying tiredly, "Aye, hang some other mother's son . . ." And Hereward's eyes moved quickly to her.

He looked at her a long time, unblinking, saying nothing, till she became aware of it and said in a frightened voice, "Meaning no disrespect, my lord. We always had justice from your father, and from you. And we never forgot that you would stand up for us when no one else would. We always remembered you, all the time you were away . . ."

Hereward's lip curved slightly. It was not quite a smile. He said, "And I am still away, am I not? I have done you no good, in the end; I have done no one any good. But I do feel for your loss."

"We both do," I added, finding my tongue at last. It was easier if I did not look at the boy's face, if I did not think of it, or imagine the features of my own sons imprinted there instead. "I have never felt the uselessness of my skills so much. If he wakes, I can give you this for his pain, but it will not affect the outcome . . ."

"Bless you, lady," she whispered. "And the lord."

Hereward cleared his throat. "As it stands, I can do nothing for you. I could kill you Oger, but God knows who you'd get in his place. All I can offer you now is food, and shelter if things get worse, and those we give gladly. You know where to find us."

"Aye," said the father. "Aye." Dragging his eyes from his dying son to Hereward, who was already reaching up to lift the dirty hanging from the door, he managed a smile. "It does me good to see you though, even with – this. The woman's right. We'll always remember you."

Hereward paused only to glance back over his shoulder. He said, "Before God, I wish I gave you better cause."

"What will you do?" I asked. "Drop from the trees into some secluded spot in the vegetable garden?"

Hereward smiled faintly into the gathering dusk. He had brought me out walking with him that afternoon, before our usual meal. But it was only when I realized we were skirting the road to Folkingham that I began to suspect. I knew there had been a letter from Aelfryth, of course, but this time he had not let me read it; nor had he joked about it with his men. I had had no idea until now, when the hall was almost in view and he told me about the assignation, whether it had been the indirect invitation I had suggested to Matilda, or just one of her lovelorn epistles, further inflamed by having finally encountered his handsome if insolent person. Actually, I still wasn't certain.

He said, "Not at all. I shall knock at the front door like any respectable suitor."

I blinked. "Do respectable suitors bring their wives with them?"

"Well, I thought you might like to chatter with Matilda while I seduce the young lady."

"Hereward, she is already seduced."

"So she is. Perhaps I could talk to Matilda too."

I looked at him quickly. It seemed my stratagem was working and he was indeed using Aelfryth as an excuse to visit his old friends. I wondered why it had to be so complicated. But certainly, beneath the banter, he was seriously preoccupied.

So was I. I had not been here since I was thirteen years old when I had finally left my betrothed's grieving parents. I was glad it was growing dark. The yard where I had first met Robert and first seen Hereward fighting, and rioting, was empty, apart from two men-at-arms who nodded at us without much interest. I suppose we appeared little threat. They had no way of knowing that Hereward the Outlaw had just walked up to their hall.

A servant I recognized opened the door. He seemed to recognize Hereward too, for his mouth fell open before he could speak. Hereward kindly shut it for him with one finger, and enquired for the lady Aelfryth.

"Here I am!" her childish voice sang out, and she appeared in front of the servant who was brushed aside without a word. She wore azure silk and red, and precious gems that winked in the lamp light. The effect was stunning

"Are you coming out?" Hereward asked. "Or am I coming in? I'm sure you know I am not on visiting terms with the lord Gilbert."

"Oh I know all about that. Come inside." She had seized his arm before she noticed me. Her eyes widened. "Oh."

"Don't mind me," I said blandly. "I'm only here to chatter to the lady Matilda."

"Oh," she said again. I thought she sounded relieved. Certainly, she turned from me as soon as the door was shut, and smiled up into Hereward's eyes. Beyond them I could see Matilda and Gilbert himself standing in the middle of the hall. Matilda began to move towards us, nervously. For several seconds, the only sound in the hall was the rustling of her skirts in the rushes.

Then Aelfryth said softly, "Will you not give me the kiss of greeting?"

Her blatancy was breathtaking. If she had not already acknowledged me, I could have imagined I was not there.

Hereward lifted one slightly mocking eyebrow. "I doubt we are on such terms of intimacy, lady." Abruptly his eyes lifted, found Matilda's unerringly. "Are we?"

Aelfryth span round, irritated, but neither Hereward nor Matilda paid her any attention. Matilda swallowed. She said, "If we are not, it is not my doing, or of my wish."

And Hereward crossed the distance between them, placing his hands on her shoulders and gazing down at her before he bent and kissed her mouth.

"It has been too long," he said quietly, and she nodded unable to speak. Her eyes looked bright with unshed tears. In fact, she looked fragile enough to break at any moment. Then he smiled. "I brought Torfrida," he said. "As chaperone."

With just a little effort, Matilda smiled back. "Very proper. The lady Aelfryth is in my charge, you know . . ."

Hereward looked surprised. "On your account, not hers," he corrected, standing aside to let Matilda embrace me. It choked the laughter or the tears or whatever caused the noise in her throat. Hereward watched us benevolently. He appeared to have no interest in the bewildered Aelfryth behind; and he would not yet look forward to Gilbert.

It was left to me to walk up the hall to our host, holding out both of my hands. I said softly, "I take it we are here of your invitation?"

Gilbert smiled ruefully and kissed me. "You are a devious child, Torfrida. But no one could accuse you of misunderstanding your men." His eyes lifted over my head, and locked with another's. He did not need to tell me whose. He said, "Would you have come if *I* had asked?"

I glanced round at Hereward, who had raised his eyebrows. "I thought I had."

Gilbert smiled lopsidedly. "You saw through our little subterfuge?"

"My wife is not so subtle as she likes to believe. On the other hand, I have to give her credit: there aren't many women who would arrange assignations for their husbands."

I looked at the ceiling.

Gilbert said, "And yet you came."

"And yet," said Hereward, "I came."

Matilda said nervously, "Then you will sit down and sup with us?"

Hereward glanced at her, then back to Gilbert. He said, "A man in your

279

position must have enemies. You cannot afford to have it said that Hereward supped at your table."

"I believe I can stand that," said Gilbert. "In fact, I believe the King himself would do the same."

"I could wave my sword around a little, if it would help," Hereward offered. A smile was hovering faintly around his lips.

"It wouldn't," said Matilda firmly. "We have all seen quite enough of your sword over the years! Even at the supper table!"

"*Particularly*," I corrected, "at the supper table."

Aelfryth, unused to being ignored, could not understand what was going on, though she took her place beside Hereward with alacrity. He, however, was looking about the hall, empty but for serving men and women, and frowning.

"Where is your household?" he asked eventually. "Where, indeed, is the reverend Bishop?"

"The household ate earlier," Gilbert said calmly across Matilda. "And the Bishop has gone home."

"It will look like conspiracy," Hereward warned. "Eating in private with me."

Gilbert shrugged, drying his hands and sitting back in his chair. "I could not have my men-at-arms here, could I? You might have fought with them."

"It never used to bother you."

"No, but you seem a little more serious about such things these days."

There was bitterness in Hereward's smile, but he said nothing more. The food was being served, a rich array of fish and spiced meats and jellies, pastries and fruits. Clearly, whatever the hour, we were not dining off leftovers.

"What will you do?" Gilbert asked at last, when the meal was over and enough wine had been passed to ease tensions and tongues beyond the slightly brittle banter of our arrival. "Where will you go from here?"

Hereward smiled faintly into his wine. "Who knows? At the moment we are just seeing how many steps we can keep ahead of the King's men – and I have to say the prognosis is good."

"You can't do that for ever," Gilbert said quietly. "You're bound to be caught in the end – the Bruneswald is hardly perpetual cover."

"It's not the woods which cover me," Hereward said frankly. "It's the people."

"People are fickle about heroes," Gilbert warned. "Especially when faced with soldiers trampling all over them in search of you." He hesitated, then: "You know they have called the militia out against you?"

Hereward looked unimpressed. "They're always doing that. It's made up largely of Saxons who have little desire, and no ability, to fight me. We rarely even come to blows. I say 'boo' from a distance, and they run off and tell their masters that Hereward has defeated them again."

"No, this is different. There are seven counties involved, and the commanders will be Normans. Does the name Ivo de Taillebois mean anything to you?"

"Yes. I've still got his blood on my sword."

"Christ, you're an arrogant . . .!"

"I know," said Hereward quickly. "I'm sorry. I talk rubbish from habit, but you needn't fear I'm in danger of believing any of it." He lifted the cup to his lips, swallowed some wine and laid it down again, still held in his fingers. His eyes lifted to Gilbert's. "You are warning me."

It was Gilbert's eyes which fell this time. "I owe you that much," he said, with difficulty.

Hereward shifted in his chair. I didn't know if it was impatience or discomfort. He said, "Whatever, I thank you for it."

"But will do nothing!" Gilbert sounded angry.

"What can I do except face it when the time comes? I will be prepared."

"Will you be prepared for me? Do you imagine I can avoid this?"

Abruptly, Hereward pushed his cup away. "I'm sorry. Your position is intolerable; I know that, and I can blame you for nothing. But what would you have me do?"

Gilbert's eyes came back to him. I heard his breath draw in and knew the most difficult of all was about to come. He said, "Make peace."

Hereward smiled. "How can I do that? Stroll into William's camp and cast myself at his royal feet? I'd never get past the first soldier – to hell with modesty, I'd never get past the first twenty. At any rate, I'd be hacked to pieces before I got near him. And who would look after my gang then? To say nothing of my wife and children."

Aelfryth was gazing at him still, her lovely face curiously blank.

"There are other ways," Gilbert said. "There are – people who would intercede for you. With the King."

It was my breath which caught this time. Gilbert was giving him a way out, a way I had never let myself even contemplate. Wildly now, I wondered if he would take it, if he *could*. I wondered if I wanted him to, what it would mean for him, for us, in the future. I saw the possibility of peace, of a *settled* life, and let myself hope.

Then he smiled, a strange, sad little smile, and said, "No."

CHAPTER 41

"Gilbert was right. They have raised the militia against me already. The forces of seven counties have converged and are marching upon us."

My eyes closed. I could hear the children breathing peacefully in their sleep, the muffled arguments of soldiers outside the tent. When I could speak, I said, "What will you do?"

"Fight," he said inevitably. I felt his weight on the bedroll beside me, his hand on my hair. "One last time. And then I'll find a way to end it."

"Hereward don't!" I whispered, turning suddenly into him. "I would stay with you on a battlefield! Just live . . .!"

But that was the one thing he could not do, the one thing over which he had no control.

With Gilbert's warnings still ringing in my ears, I think I was relieved when the local men rallied to Hereward's standard, so that he now commanded far more than the two hundred or so of his old 'gang'. But it didn't make the following days any easier to bear, and the waiting was made worse by the fact that I had nothing more difficult to deal with than the revival of my cough, and yet another letter from the lady Aelfryth. In a fit of sardonic humour, I placed the latter under his pillow to await his return.

When Martin came running into the camp I had just delivered a fifth baby to Gaenoch's wife. With the baby still in my arms, I walked to the open door of the tent to see what the fuss was about.

He was yelling something as he ran, causing my heart to jump painfully into my throat. I had to catch at the tent pole for support.

"Martin," I said, weakly enough, and seeing me, he switched direction towards me without even interrupting his stride.

"In good order," he said quickly. "Not pursued, though he is in a tearing hurry!"

Pausing only to give back the baby to its anxious mother – together with an apology and Martin's news – I ran off to find my ready-saddled horse, and rode out with Martin to meet the warriors.

Under the great black dragon banner, they were indeed in a tearing hurry. But they were jubilant, singing and chanting at Hereward's back as if they had thrown King William out of England for good. And at their head, Hereward himself, his bare head shining in the late afternoon sun like a beacon of fire. He was not singing, nor even joking with the men, and the storms were still in his eyes when he met and kissed me, as if the great victory his men were so desperate to describe to me was only one stage in a larger plan.

It was.

* * * *

At dawn, he woke and kissed me, and said he was leaving again to get Bourne back for us. I blinked sleepily. I think I even smiled, because after the euphoria of victory and the joy of last night's love, anything was possible.

I said, "How will you do that?"

"I shall go to the King," he replied.

When I could speak, I was sitting bolt upright in bed staring at him. "You have finally run mad."

"I had a message from him. He is offering to discuss terms if I go to him."

"It is a trap! You cannot even trust that such a message is truly from the King!"

"Oh it is. Our friend Deda brought it. After the battle, naturally – no point in offering me terms before, in case they won . . ."

I was speechless again. Hereward watched me sardonically, though he didn't stop dressing. I didn't want to be watched. I had bad feelings about this sudden offer of peace; it was too exactly what I wanted.

Eventually, I said suspiciously, "Why should the King offer you terms remotely acceptable to you? Why should he even believe you *want* peace?"

"I suspect someone told him so. Someone who has his ear and his trust."

My eyes widened. "Gilbert?"

"Off-hand," said Hereward, "I can't really think of anyone else." He finished fastening on his belt, and sat down on the bedding-roll beside me. "Don't you want this, Torfrida?"

I swallowed. "Of course I want it. But my instinct is to mistrust it."

"There is nothing else to do. Malcolm of Scotland surrendered without a fight and threw out the Aethling his brother-in-law. No one in England has the stomach for rebellion any more, and to be frank, Torfrida, I'm not sure I have it myself. Not without a point, a realistic goal. I cannot even live as a carefree forest outlaw while my own people starve and die under another's ill treatment. For the truth is, I am not carefree. I have the same ties and responsibilities I always had, and it is time I took up their burden."

He smiled a little sadly into my helpless eyes. "You see, I have set my sights rather lower: to look after my own."

I whispered, "It is not an unworthy goal, Hereward—"

"So I must go to York, to the King," he interrupted, as if he could not bear to hear that. The storms were still raging inside him, rigidly under control. I thought if he let go for an instant, their power would annihilate me.

"Let me come with you—"

283

"No," he said at once, standing up with finality. "I won't have my wife holding my hand while I submit to the Bastard. I won't have you any where *near* till I know it is safe."

"Then you *do* suspect a trap?" I pounced.

"No," he said patiently.

And it was the patience that warned me to leave it alone. This was not easy for him. In many ways it was the hardest thing he had ever done, and I had to let him choose his own way to do it.

I summoned a smile – after all, it was just another battle he left me for – and reached up to kiss him. "Kiss the children before you go."

"Of course."

He touched my cheek once, and released me. At the doorway, I stayed him. "Hereward?"

He glanced back over his shoulder, his eyes already somewhere far away.

I said, "Don't take *any* terms. We are not so desperate."

His eyes smiled, briefly returning. "I love you, you know," he observed, and left me.

Another parting. Another waiting. I lay back down on the pillow and coughed– a permanent reminder, like my sadly roughened and browned skin, of my recent life – and wondered what I would do. Then I remembered Aelfryth's letter, nestling cosily under his pillow. I wasn't going to chase after him with it: it would have to wait for another time. Reaching out with my hand, I felt under his pillow for it. There was nothing there.

He had taken it with him.

Some three weeks after his departure, while I stood by the fire tasting soup, Hurchill, not Martin, rode into camp, whooping like a boy with his first sword.

"We've done it!" he yelled, loud enough to inform all and sundry, although it was to me he addressed himself, spilling off his horse and landing at my feet with a crash. "We've done it! We've got Bourne back! Bourne, and all the other lands! Lady, we can go home!"

I could not quite believe it, but apparently it was the case. William had returned Hereward all his old lands, including Bourne. The only condition was that Hereward come into the King's peace and remain there. He and his men were free. In fact, said Hurchill, Hereward had even negotiated that he need never serve William in arms in England, although he was prepared to do so anywhere else.

I felt numb. While Leofric and the others shouted and laughed and feasted, clowning about like children, I sat smiling, wondering when the joy would come. Was I afraid of this peace? Was I afraid that after so long we could not be happy in a settled life?

It came later, in the night's solitude: a slow, creeping pleasure. *"We can go home,"* Hurchill had said. And we could. In peace, and honour, to look after our own and find the dream we had been searching for since Flanders.

The night was clear, and the sky so massive that I could imagine myself sucked up into it. I liked doing that. Normally, I could spend hours in this mixture of knowledge and imagination and pure light-headedness. But tonight, in the garden at Folkingham, Gilbert stood only feet away and I had things to say.

Hearing me, he turned quickly and smiled. The faint torchlight from the hall was kind to him, making him younger, smoother, darker. And less forbidding.

I said, "Stargazing, my lord? You told me once it was nonsense."

"I said it was nonsense for a child to be studying such things," he corrected. "We all look at the sky sometimes. Besides, I was expecting you."

I walked forward to stand beside him. "You knew I would come to thank you."

"You have nothing to thank me for. I wish you had."

I smiled into the night. I thought there was a light there I had never seen before, behind Orien's belt: small and so faint that I could easily have been mistaken.

I said, "You call helping Hereward nothing? After all he has done?"

Gilbert said, "I would gladly do all in my power to help him – and not just through guilt. But I very much doubt he would accept anything that came from me, however indirectly. He has not softened that much."

"He is a wiser man, Gilbert, than he was. Time heals most wounds, takes the edge off most guilts. Alfred was always his more than yours, and in his heart he knew it. And now he has a whole new set which he can blame on nobody else."

"Ely."

"Ely."

From the corner of my eye, I thought the strange light flickered in the sky once more, but when I looked properly I could see nothing. I transferred my gaze to Gilbert instead and found him watching me, a faint, enigmatic crease between his brows. He had looked at me so quite often since I had arrived, but I was at a loss to understand it.

With difficulty, I said, "It is hard for a man who has lived all his life in such violence. I believe it is all the more to his credit that he has come to see the advantages – the necessity – of peace."

Gilbert smiled faintly; yet I thought I saw a loss in his eyes that amounted to pain, as though grieving, finally, for the boy Hereward had once been.

He said, "Yes. In his own way, he was always a realist."

"Is that why you did it?"

The frown deepened. "Did what?"

"Interceded for him with the King! Don't be modest, Gilbert, we know it was you! He knew when he left for York! Who else would be brave and good enough to do this for *us?*"

His eyes did not blink. They were gazing straight into mine, and with surprise I finally recognized the expression which had been there all evening. It was pity.

He said, "*Who else?* Torfrida, do you really not know?"

At last, belatedly, unease began to seep through. "Know what? Are you telling me it was really *not* you who spoke for Hereward? Nor Matilda?"

"Not I," he said quietly. "Nor Matilda. Torfrida, it was Aelfryth of Worcester."

We arrived in York, Leofric and I, a little after mid-day. Leofric had tried to talk me out of it; so hard, in fact, that I eventually worked out for myself what Hurchill had told him – that Hereward was behaving badly. Only when I pointed out that I had seen Hereward in varying degrees of drunkenness since I was twelve years old, did he give in with one of his engagingly rueful grins.

Now, added to the rest of my impatience, was the desire to wash, to rid myself of the dirt I had collected, mainly, at the dreadful alehouse in which we had passed the previous night.

But York almost made me forget that. Somehow it was a surprise to me. It had been so long since I had lived in a city that the sheer noise and intensity of human smells bewildered me. Crowded horses and carts rumbled through the muddy streets – for though the rain had gone off, the whole city was still damp; hammers thudded and banged intermittently, with what purpose was open to the imagination, for I could see nothing of them through the throngs. Raucous laughter, a thousand talking and shouting voices assailed my ears with the immovable force of a stone wall. Somewhere, cattle lowed, and chickens ran clucking in front of our horses as we picked our way through the effluence.

Further in, there were traders yelling their wares, undernourished women fighting over what looked like a scrap of elderly meat but which one of them definitely called a duckling. Here and there I caught a flash of colour, like a glimpse of sunshine in a storm, clouded and muddied by what had gone before. All around, it seemed, children cried, scavenging dogs snarled and barked over trifles. For though it was summer, this was a city ravaged by war, surrounded by a countryside laid pitilessly bare as we had already seen, deliberately ruined to starve rebellious subjects into submission. It had worked too.

Forcing his way through the crowds and the rancid, evil-smelling rubbish till we reached a more respectable neighbourhood, Leofric stopped a stranger, a jaunty, slightly raffish young man, and asked him civilly if he knew where one Hereward of Bourne was lodged.

Somewhat to the surprise of both of us, the stranger was not only familiar with the name, but supplied us with detailed directions. Leofric and I exchanged glances.

I said wryly, "Is he known for his past deeds, or his present ones?"

"Both, I expect . . ."

The directions were faultless. Hereward appeared to be residing in quite a large hall, inconspicuous among the others in its street except for the fact that Wulric the Black lounged outside its door, picking his dirty teeth while his eyes looked all the way along to one end of the street, then turned and checked the other. Eternally looking to his captain's safety.

Then he saw us, and the effect was startling. His mouth fell open like an enormous fish's, and I have never seen eyes dilate quite so obviously over such a distance.

He uttered, "Jesus Christ and Woden!"

"Neither," I said tartly, reining in before him. "But I, at least, shall take it as a compliment. Am I to dismount completely unaided?"

Wulric started forward with alacrity, then fell back and banged on the hall door with the side of his fist before coming once more to hand me down from the saddle.

"Forgive me, lady," he said quickly. "It is just that you are so – unexpected." His eyes went over my head to Leofric, glaring accusingly.

Leofric sighed. "As bad as that, is it?"

"Worse," said Wulric succinctly.

At which point, the hall door opened to reveal his friend the Heron, who stared at me as if I were some shade worthy of a quite uncommon level of terror, and promptly shut the door again.

"Oh for the love of God!" I exclaimed, torn between irritation and amusement.

"He's ashamed of the mess," Wulric said hastily, excusingly. "We have been lax with no lady to order such things . . ."

"Blame it on Hereward," I advised. "He is big enough to stand it."

"Can't, lady," said Wulric apologetically. "The thing is – he – he isn't here. Stepped out." Cunning intelligence dawned. "So why doesn't Leofric take you to – to – look at the churches! – while we clear up? And when you come back, he will be home."

Clearly he thought this a very clever plan. He was counting, however, without a long and arduous journey, and a constitution no longer quite so hearty.

I said firmly, "I do not want to see churches. I want wine, a change of clothes, food and my husband. Probably in that order. So why don't you just open the door and let me in?"

As I spoke, I walked smartly up to the hall, turning back in time to catch Wulric's expression as he gazed at Leofric. Panicked. And pleading.

My lip twitched.

Leofric said, "Oh God."

I knocked at the door myself, and when it opened a cautious crack, I thrust it open forcefully and stalked inside.

They were right.

It was a horrible mess. Several tables stood in the middle of the grubby, cluttered hall still with the remains of last night's repast. One had fallen over. Others had been pushed haphazardly aside, to allow sleeping space, I could only assume. In fact, under a dubious heap of faintly heaving cloaks and weapons, I thought a body still lay snoring. Certainly something was.

Tumbled cups, bits of food, pools of spilled wine, all too numerous to count, were scattered liberally across the floor. I could smell stale meat and staler wine. A girl, scantily clad, bolted out of the shadows, and fled past me to the door, clutching some ragged garment to her bosom.

"Sorry, lady," said Martin Lightfoot, appearing behind Wulric. For once, I thought, he looked it too, which softened me slightly.

I said, "So you should be. Is there any chance of food and wine before we swoon from lack of both?"

"Of course," said Martin at once. "The girl is seeing to it."

I didn't even blink at that. I had assumed she was sent off to drag Hereward out of whatever low alehouse he was carousing in. I said amiably, "Well, while she does, I shall wait in there. I take it that is Hereward's chamber?" I waved vaguely at the door at the far-end of the hall.

"No!" said Wulric and Martin at once. Then, as my eyebrows lifted enquiringly, Martin smiled slightly. "That is, yes. But it's in a terrible state. Worse than here. Let me take you to the guest-house instead . . ."

"Don't be ridiculous," I said, with only half-amused frustration as I brushed past him. "I am well acquainted with Hereward's mess."

Martin said harshly, "Lady, spare his blushes for once! The guest-house is really much more suitable . . ."

I laid my hand on the door. "Martin," I said, polite but firm, "he never blushes." And pushing open the door, I ended my life.

CHAPTER 42

Fate was unkind to me. It did not allow me even to absorb the situation little by little, by degrees that might have provided warning enough to ease the whole just a little. Instead, the picture was complete in the first glance.

The gloriously rumpled bed, with sheets and furs and odd pieces of bright clothing scattered higgledy-piggledy; the two people upon it, naked, kneeling, their profiles quite clear and recognizable.

Hereward, betraying sweat still glistening on his broad, rippling back, a silver cup in one teasing hand, was drizzling blood-red wine on to her nipples, sipping from there with smiling lips because he had thus two pleasures at once.

And Aelfryth, head thrown back, eyes closed in languorous, sensual ecstasy, was holding his golden head in her hands, running his hair through her elegant, ringed fingers.

The whole scene, gathered in that first instant, seemed to freeze and stretch into hours.

Behind me, Leofric said savagely, "Oh Jesus Christ, you stupid *bastard.*"

And the two heads jerked round. Aelfryth fell over with a clumsiness that would have been funny in any other circumstances, her tiny cry degenerating into hysterical giggles.

Hereward did not stir. His eyes stared at me. I realized with a strange, unworldly sort of detachment, that his face was very white. After a while – I don't know how long – his lips moved, but no sound came out.

I had no thought, none that was bearable, so my mind went blessedly blank. I only had instinct, and that spun me on my heels and swept me out of the room.

"You see?" I even said vaguely to Martin. "Not a blush in sight."

"Torfrida."

That came from the bedchamber, low, almost unrecognizable as his voice. But then, my ears were singing. I walked past the silent, pitying faces, Leofric, Martin, Wulric the Heron, Wynter, who had obviously been called in to deal with the emergency, the girl, with all her clothes on now, desperately clearing off a table.

I said, "I believe I have changed my mind, Wulric. I'm going home." And though I sounded odd, my voice did not tremble. I wondered vaguely if I might be glad of that one day, if I ever felt anything again.

Leofric said urgently, "Wait, Torfrida. Wait in the guest-house till I come . . ."

"Why, where are you going?" The words came of their own accord, without meaning or interest to me.

"To punch his damned head in!" said gentle Leofric savagely.

289

"Don't be silly, Leofric. He won't let you."

"Oh yes," said Leofric, "he will."

I walked out of the hall. And stopped. My horse was not there, or I would simply have hauled myself into the saddle and ridden away. But then Wynter was before me, muttering for me to follow him. I obeyed, because there seemed nothing else to do.

By the time I walked past him into the guest-house, I was shaking all over. I didn't hear what he said to me. Without speaking, I watched him pour wine for me, watched him leave. After a bit, because my legs seemed reluctant to hold me up, I sat down and waited for Leofric.

Somewhere, I think I knew already that this was beyond me. The very fabric on which I had drawn my life had split and torn into rags. He had torn it. But it seemed it had always been rotten, corrupt, and only I, lost in a foolish, childish love, had refused to see it. I supposed I would be angry with him later, when I could put off thinking no longer. The anger might help. It would be something to hold onto in a life that no longer had an anchor, a life I no longer knew how to live.

The door opened quickly. A shaft of light flashed across the floor towards my chair, and was gone with the decided click of the closing door.

I said, "Where are the horses, Leofric? I'll take the men back with me, but you can stay here if you . . ."

"Torfrida."

Not Leofric.

My eyes closed involuntarily, because I could not bear the sight of him; but then I remembered he could see my reactions, and slowly forced them open again. Raising my head, I looked at him.

His breath caught.

He was dressed now, though hastily enough, still bare legged, a crumpled white shirt showing beneath a belted blue tunic which had, I noticed, a large wine-stain on the sleeve. I suppose his long, bright hair was no more tangled than normal, but his face still had that unhealthy pallor. He had, clearly, been indulging in some serious debauchery. Dark bruises shadowed the puffy skin under his turbulent eyes, speaking of many sleepless nights – but at that realization a pain twisted through me so sharply that my fingers gripped convulsively on the chair-arm.

I could have borne it, just, except that I knew it was only the beginning, a taste of what was to come. So hastily I tried to thrust it back, ignore it, while searching desperately for some distraction.

I found it, in the end, in the red swelling above his left eye.

I said, "Leofric did hit you, then." And my voice sounded cool, sardonic, lending me courage. For a second he looked confused; then, as if recalling something distant, his hand reached up, touching the spot. I noticed it was shaking. I wished there was solace in that.

He said distractedly, "Leofric? Yes. I let him."

"He said you would. What's the matter, Hereward? Can you not fight with your trousers off either?"

He said, "I don't want to fight Leofric." And the words sounded difficult. I was glad, suddenly. I didn't want any of this to be easy for him. But he was moving now, crossing the floor towards me. I forced my eyes to watch him, to keep my face still, so still that I felt like the woodcarving above the door.

He said softly, "Forgive me, Torfrida."

"Forgive you?"

Abruptly, the words spat out of my mouth as the anger rose up, galloping, from my toes. Relief at finding it made me laugh, a frightening, insane sound that sobered me almost instantly.

"Oh I forgive you, Hereward. I forgive you the disgusting mess you have made of your house and your person. I forgive you the embarrassment you have caused your men and servants. I even forgive you your adultery, for I am a broad-minded woman. What I cannot understand, let alone forgive, is your appalling, lamentable lapse of taste. *Aelfryth*, Hereward!"

"Stop it, Torfrida," he said quickly.

"Stop what?" I asked innocently, my eyes deliberately wide. I think I was actually enjoying acting. It kept at bay the only too real things churning just beneath the surface.

"Stop twisting the knife. I have hurt you. We both know it, and I am sorry."

"Sorry?"

One hand waved helplessly. "I know. Inadequate words, but the truth is I don't know yet what else to say."

Neither did I, so I said nothing. With an effort, I relaxed my fingers on the chair arm, but when they started to shake again I had to tighten my grip once more. He moved closer, crouching down by my side. I looked away.

"Torfrida, I have no excuse. I have been behaving badly, as Leofric says, throwing off for a month the responsibilities that are my real life. I have not been sober for two weeks. Till now. I lost all my money – twice – playing dice. I have brawled in the streets and fought in the halls of my hosts. I have been rude and charming and outrageously amusing – at least to myself – whenever the notion took me; and no one very much has opposed me. I am lionized by fools and mountebanks of all races, and the women throw themselves into my arms. I throw most of them back."

"How noble," I said politely.

"Torfrida, she is just part of this whole – mess!"

"You mean she is not the only one?"

"Of course she is."

Involuntarily, my eyes closed again. I wished that there were twenty others, so that she didn't matter, so that she was reduced to the status of passing whore, or camp follower. The pain was gnawing again, waiting to engulf me.

His finger touched my cheek, shocking me, jerking me back from him, not just with revulsion but with the suddenly flooding memory of his naked back in that bedchamber, and a desperate, shaming spurt of desire. Was there no end to this?

I drew in one shuddering breath.

"Go away, Hereward," I said with loathing. "Just get out."

He said quietly, "I'll take you home. To Bourne."

"You'll take me nowhere!" I cried out. "Nowhere! Ever again. You will never come *near* me ever again!"

The force of that surprised him. It surprised me, and not just because I meant it. I was staring at him, panting, God knows what madness glaring out of my eyes. For a second I thought I saw my own torment reflected in his, but which of us the emotion belonged to, I hardly cared.

Abruptly, he stood, dragging his fingers through his hair. "I have behaved appallingly; I know that. But, Torfrida, don't make it worse than it is – how many men do you know who sleep only in their wife's bed?"

Stricken, my breath caught. I fell back into my chair, dragging my eyes away from his.

"I thought I knew one."

"Torfrida," he whispered into the silence, and there *was* pain there now. "In my heart, there is only you. But I have never been a saint."

Once, in Flanders, when we had lived so much apart, perhaps I would have forgiven him. But we had grown since then. I had grown. Yes, it had a name after all, the snarling pain fighting its way out from all the others: one he knew too well to have inflicted such cruelty on me. It slid in gently, twisting and curling, squeezing about my heart until I thought I would not be able to speak. But I could.

I said, "You have betrayed me, Hereward. Beyond any betrayal you have ever suffered, you have betrayed me."

It was the door crashing open which jerked my head round. Leofric stood there.

Hereward said again, "Torfrida."

"Go back to her," I said contemptuously. "Go for good. Because I cannot live with you now. Not in a battlefield or a prince's palace." And I stood up, on legs that trembled so much my skirts shook, and walked with some dignity, I hoped, out of the house.

It was raining.

My horse was there. Wordlessly, Leofric put me in the saddle and mounted his own mare. My eyes inevitably strayed back to the guest-house door, but he was not there. The man who hated any scene not of his making.

I was glad.

We rode away, the men-at-arms following. I did not look to right nor left as we passed along the street, through the noisy, struggling city and at last back to the open road.

The rain was heavier.

I pushed my horse to a gallop into the springing wind, uncaring whether or not Leofric kept up. My mouth began to open of its own will, silently gasping in the torrents of rain in huge, shaking sobs that seemed to tear my body apart.

Present: March 1076

CHAPTER 43

It was difficult to concentrate when my memory was again flooded with the past, particularly *that* past, that betrayal; so, forcefully, I shovelled my mind clear, and bent it instead to the problem of the bear brooch, and how it had found its way into Martin's burned hand.

If Hereward himself had placed it there, how and when had he managed to do so in the midst of such a fight? Had he suspected the man who now lay asleep in the men's guest-house, guarded in turns by the twins and the Siwards? Would Asselin's story, when at last he told it, confirm whatever this brooch was meant to tell? Gilbert had ordered the questioning to wait for the morning, and weakly I had given in. So, after visiting Aediva, still isolated in the depths of her grief, I had come back to my own guest-house, restless and consumed with unwanted memories, to wrestle in the lamplight with thoughts of bears.

And I was getting nowhere. I began to think I was wrong. I had found a gold brooch clutched in the hand of a dead man. The fact that it was not burned into his hand may have been a freak but it hardly proved that Hereward was speaking to me from beyond the grave.

Besides, Martin had been in the store-house. Hereward had been found in the guest-house, close to where he had jumped from the roof in among his enemies. Was it likely he had darted around so much in the ensuing chaos that he could have run into the still smouldering store-house, left his brooch with Martin, and run back to the guest-house to die?

I began to feel a little silly. The last two days had surely turned to jelly what was left of my brains.

So had it been left by an enemy? Someone who regretted their actions and wished to give a secret clue to – somebody? Ivo? Asselin? But what did they know of Harold the bear? What did bears mean to them? What in God's name did bears mean to me, apart from Harold and Hereward's courage and fury, and Robert, and all that went on over that Northumbrian winter . . . Northumbria.

There came a time when I realized that I was holding my breath, that my heart was beating as it had not since I had walked into the hall at Bourne and seen the yellow ribbon. A suspicion more terrible, more unbelievable than all the others put together, had begun to form in my head, twisting everything else I had learned about his death into confusion.

Eventually, from sheer dizziness, I was forced to breathe out, but it did not help.

I needed, I realized, to speak to Asselin. Now. I could not wait for morning, not with *this* churning in my head . . .

Abruptly, I stood up, and seizing my cloak I threw it round my shoulders before crossing quickly to the door and going quietly outside into the yard.

There was very little light from the sky. A fine drizzle of icy rain trickled down my face as I walked quickly towards the men's guest-house. Two figures sat on either side of the door. I knew it was the twins. I knew too that Gilbert's sentries, regularly patrolling the stockade, were keeping their eyes on Asselin's self-appointed guards to prevent any premature acts of revenge. Or any premature visitors, for all I knew. Until I had spoken to Asselin I did not know what secrets Gilbert had to keep. If any.

The twins rose quickly as I approached, but I hushed them before they could speak.

"Let me in," I said, low. "I have to talk to him."

"Now?" demanded Duti, staring. "It was you who . . ."

"Now," I interrupted. "And quietly. You had better both wait outside."

"You can't go in to him alone," Outi objected.

"Asselin will not hurt me," I said. He couldn't, not now . . .

He was asleep, I think, when I entered. I could see the black mound of his body on the bed as I quietly crossed the floor towards him. At least I thought I was quiet, but before I had reached him, he suddenly said, "Which of you Saxon dogs has come to murder me now?"

"You are too valuable to murder," I said calmly, and he sat bolt upright with far more alarm that either the Siwards or the twins would have inspired in him. "Is there a lamp?"

Wordlessly, he leaned out of the bed and lit it. The pale light illuminated his bruised, dirty face, displaying a vast array of recent cuts and wounds. His eyes were wide as saucers, around a huge frown, his lips slack. His legs swung over the side of the bed so that he sat facing me.

"I never thought you would come to visit me in the night," he observed. "Not recently, any how."

Ignoring that, I looked him straight in the eye. "Did you kill Hereward?"

His eyes fell, then slowly lifted once more to mine. He shook his head. "No."

My heart was still beating and beating. I said, "Who did?"

Asselin's teeth took hold of his lower lip, and bit, though not hard enough to draw blood. There was a pause, a long one, before he said ruefully, "I don't think I can tell you that. I can only tell you what I did."

"And what you saw?"

Without hesitation, Asselin nodded. "And what I saw."

"Will you tell me now? Before Gilbert comes? Without your men or mine?"

His eyes were steady on me now. After a moment he said conversationally, "I have no weapon, you know."

I blinked. "I should think not. What is that to me?"

"Only that being unarmed it would be unfair of you to stick a knife between my ribs once I have told you what you came to hear."

"If you did not kill him, why should I kill you?"

Asselin's lips twisted. "I did not behave well, Torfrida."

This time it was I who paused. Then: "You never do," I said steadily. "What did you do this time?"

"I let him rile me. I let ambition drive me to kill him before lesser men beat me to it."

"Lesser men?"

He sighed. "Ralf of Dol. Hugh of Evermouth. It was Hugh's fault, I suppose. The night before it happened we were all drinking together. At Bourne. Hugh got garrulous and waxed lyrical about your beauty, and your daughter's, and then let slip that he had already asked you for your daughter in marriage."

I said, "I know this part. Hereward told him to wait until at least one of them was grown up."

Asselin grinned. "He said a bit more too in the same vein. It was very funny, actually, but Hugh didn't think so." The smile died. "Pity really. I rather think he misjudged his man there. He didn't need to put it like that.

295

He could have made Hugh wait without humiliating him. Hereward could always keep anyone on his side, if he chose to."

That was true, but I doubted it was his judgement which had lapsed; I rather thought it was his temper. Perhaps because I had allowed Hugh to hope, without consulting him. Perhaps just because it was Frida's life . . .

Asselin was saying, "But Hugh was furious. When we left, he was still going on about it, about Hereward's airs and vanities, and how he could nip them in the bud – by killing him, he meant, and when I laughed at him for that, he challenged me directly. Not to fight each other, but to see which of us could defeat Hereward. Ralf joined in then, boasting that he could do it without either of us, and we went on telling lies to each other all the way back to Folkingham.

"I thought no more about it, to be honest. It was the wine talking, and I'm used to that. However, next day, they both came at me again, deadly serious, as if we had made some pact. Perhaps we had. I was too drunk to remember. I could only take their word. They had a plan. We were invited back the next day, you see, to the lady Aediva's birthday feast, and they thought to use the servants to take Hereward's by surprise, then burst into the hall as if it was under attack. After which, the first of us to best Hereward would be the winner."

"Of what?"

My voice was cold and hard, because men could play such games with people's lives, could waste – *everything*.

Asselin did not reply for a moment. Then he said only, "I don't know. It was pointless, really. Stupid. I liked Hereward. Always did. Only – only I had always wondered too, if I could beat him . . ."

His eyes fell before the contempt in mine. He even wriggled slightly, but he was beyond any deeper embarrassment.

"And if the truth be told," he added, "we are all – *were* all – a little afraid of him. Because he had the King's favour, because it seemed he could do whatever he wanted, even though he had been our worst enemy until only a couple of years ago. A double fear really: afraid for our own positions, and afraid that one day he would turn back on us . . ."

Angrily, almost, Asselin shrugged that off. "Before you, lady, I can make no excuses. You always saw straight through me. Mostly, I went along with it because I didn't want Ralf or Hugh to do it."

"It never entered your head to *tell* him? Or even to tell Gilbert and stop it?" But of course it hadn't, and I was wasting precious time asking him stupid questions. I said quickly, "Go on," before he could answer, and knelt down on the floor at his feet to listen.

It was the story Wulric and Deda and Ivo had already told, of the vicious fight in the hall that had turned into something of a farce as Hereward and Martin and Wynter had taken to the rooftops.

"That was when I realized the bastard was enjoying it," Asselin said, in a tone that held both marvel and bitterness. I think he had forgotten I was there. "He was actually singing – it was a French song and very rude! The others – his two henchmen – were singing it too, roaring it out with gusto."

"What did he say to them?" I had asked Wynter. *"I don't know,"* he had answered. *"He spoke in French, very quickly."* Wynter had been to France, and he certainly understood enough of the language to enjoy – and join in – Hereward's obscene ditties.

Asselin said, "When I heard one of our own men singing it too under his breath, I began to realize what Hereward was doing. I stopped throwing things at him, more stupefied than anything else, but the others kept on going." Asselin frowned. "He was alone on the roof by then – I suppose we had knocked the other two off, though I don't remember it. Ralf and Hugh kept trying to climb up to get at him, and he kept knocking them back down with some insolent joke.

"Once, I remember, Hereward threw his shield at Ralf, who fell yet again, cursing with frustration; yet immediately he was back on his feet, starting all over again." He paused, sparing me a glance from his mind-picture. "Hereward *let* him. He was being merciful; deliberately so. But when Ralf's head cleared the wall this time, he found Hereward crouching above him, sword in hand, ready to strike.

"'They're all coming now,' Ralf snarled. 'You might kill me. But *they*'ll get you.'

"And Hereward just looked at him tolerantly. 'And who will then – er – *get* them?' he asked. '*My* men, of course. Only then Gilbert's will come and arrest – or kill – mine. I may be getting old, but isn't that rather a dull end to a feast?'

"I was angry with him now for spoiling the fun, so I said tauntingly, 'You never used to find it dull.'

"'What do you mean?' says Hereward. 'I have never before *been* in this position, facing quite so much treachery in one place.' There was a faint, aggressive ripple among our men at that, a movement to advance. Then, quite casually, Hereward pushed Ralf's head backwards and he dropped on to the ground.

"Ralf said furiously, 'There is no treachery here!'

"Hereward just stared at him. And for some reason we all let him. Then he said quite deliberately, 'No treachery? You ate at my table, you bastard. What would you call it?'

"I felt that one like a blow on the face. We all did, for we knew he was right, whatever feeble justification we'd been giving ourselves. Even the men began to look . . . uncomfortable. And seeing it, Hereward waved his sword, almost apologetically. 'Forgive me,' he said, amazingly enough. 'I refer to the men who thought to assassinate me in my own hall. Not to the rest of you who are just joining in to support unworthy comrades.'

"'Who is unworthy?' Hugh demanded angrily.

"'You are.' And he turned to all of us with really quite a comical air of confidentiality, explaining about Hugh: 'He thinks to marry my daughter by killing me. So whatever one's opinion of his morals, I'm afraid his intelligence is certainly suspect.'

"*You* know the way he talks, clowning, manipulating. Certainly, he won a few sniggers; even a sardonic smile from none other than Ivo de Taillebois who had come along to watch and stood now a little apart from the rest of us, sword sheathed. But none of them seemed to realize what he was doing, so: 'Don't let him talk!' I raged. 'He talks and talks until you believe anything he says!'

"Hereward only laughed. And God help us, it was infectious. It infuriated the three of us. I said, 'I can still kill you.'

"'Or I can,' said Hugh grimly. And Ralf opened his mouth, no doubt to claim his own boast, but quite suddenly Hereward had stopped playing.

"'*Enough!*' he roared, so loudly that it soared over all the sniggers and laughs and vain, stupid boasts. There he stood on that ridiculous roof, stretched to his full height, his sword raised aloft commandingly while he glared down at all of us. He had never looked so impressive, or so superior, and I hated him for it, even as I fell silent like the rest of them. He had everyone's attention – there was no doubt about that.

"Then, slowly, Hereward's sword came down to his side. 'Enough,' he repeated. 'It is over. It is finished.'

"We were all staring at him, baffled, frustrated, unsure any more how we had got here, and yet I knew, we all knew, that it *was* over. It was Ivo de Taillebois who said it though.

"'He is right,' Ivo drawls, just as damned superior as Hereward. 'It is bad form, after all, to attack a man after eating from his table.'

"And Ralf says, just like a sulky child, 'It isn't his table. The lady Aediva told me. Bourne is his wife's until the marriage of their daughter.'

"'His wife,' Ivo said acidly, 'does not wish him dead either.'

"'That's not what I hear,' Ralf said insolently, and Ivo, oddly enough, cuffed him on the back of the head with enough force to make him stagger."

And Ivo, I remembered quite clearly, had denied hearing any of this.

Asselin was still talking, fluently, as though reliving every detail, every word, telling me how Ivo had called Ralf an oaf before strolling away again towards the hall with an airy wave, even calling over his shoulder to the other Normans, 'You're on your own, lads.'

Asselin said, "Then Hereward spoke again, seriously, making Ivo stop, though he did not turn to look. Hereward said, 'You *could* join us. You and anyone else who has found the night's proceedings . . . somewhat contrary to honour.'

298

"Everyone turned and stared up at Hereward till his lip twitched – genuinely, I'd swear. Join *us*, he said, quite deliberately.

"'What's the matter?' he asked innocently. 'I have seen English and French fight on the same side before. So have most of you. Asselin and I, ironically enough, have even saved each other's lives. Do we really have to decide rights and wrongs now according to our *race?*'"

Asselin's eyes came back into focus on mine, and I realized I was staring at him. A faint, half-excited glimmering of the truth was with me. I thought I knew what he had been about . . .

Asselin said, "Clever devil, wasn't he?"

I only nodded. My voice was hoarse. "Go on."

Asselin said, "I knew. I knew what he was about. I could feel myself being manipulated, yet I couldn't stop it happening, not to myself or to them. It infuriated me all over again, so I only shouted angrily at him, 'You have an alternative?'

"'Well, yes,' says Hereward, quick as you please. 'We could go back inside and get roaring drunk and laugh at Hugh.'

"Hugh flushed bright red, not least because one or two of his own men joined in the sniggers again. And it was funny, you know, the way he said it, but still I wouldn't give in to him. With as much contempt as I could muster, I said, 'What an old woman you've become.'

"'Or we can laugh at him from here,' Hereward said, as though granting me a favour. 'At you too, come to that.'

"I scowled at him. 'I? For what? Being a man?'

"'Being a child. Isn't it time we all grew up? Can't you just step back and look at us? Trying to hack each other to death without anyone – even Hugh – knowing why! *My* head – little enough trophy at the best of times, I modestly concede – is worth nothing won in such a way. If you want to preserve the hatred that will keep us all in poverty – material and spiritual – for generations, then by all means, let us fight some more. But Jesus Christ, the governance of countries, of *peoples,* rests with us and men like us. If we truly cannot think beyond slaughtering each other, we might as well lie down with the pigs.'"

In spite of myself, my breath caught. Seeing it, Asselin smiled, an odd, rueful little smile. "Yes, I know," he agreed. "You can hear him say it, can't you? Can you imagine the spell he had over us? I knew he had won, by then, but I was determined to go down fighting.

"'Very well,' I said, as mockingly as I knew how. 'I never thought I'd live to see it, but here you are making overtures of peace – if I do not mistake?'

"'You do not,' said Hereward quite evenly, 'mistake.' And he glanced down at his own henchmen, I think, and shrugged. 'Somebody has to start it.'

"'Then *you* start it,' I said triumphantly.

"'I thought I had,' Hereward said, pained.

"'Aye, with that great, wicked sword clutched in both hands! Have the courage of your bold words, Hereward! Get rid of the sword and come down here. *Then* we might listen.'"

"So that was it," I said involuntarily. I stared up at Asselin, almost blindly. "You knew he would do it . . ."

"No I didn't," Asselin said quickly, leaning forward in his urgency. "I swear to God, Torfrida, I never thought he would do it. I just wanted him to exert himself to get out of it. It was a challenge I knew he would win – I just didn't know how! And Hereward, God damn him, just looked amused.

"'I suppose,' he said, 'we have nothing to lose.'"

I closed my eyes. *Just you, just you.*

Asselin said, "I didn't know what he was up to now. He always could surprise me. Always. I stared at him till his eyes came back to me. Then I said, 'So do it.'

"And Hereward actually smiled. He lifted his sword, turning it so that the hilt pointed towards me. I just glared into his weird, unmatched eyes, and I swear to God, Torfrida, it was I, not he, who was afraid. Then, still smiling, he raised the sword high. It flew spinning into the air, catching the light of the torches so that it winked like that bright, alien star we saw years ago. Then he lifted his feet, and jumped."

"It was his gift," I whispered, uncaring now of the wetness on my face. "His greatest gift, and I was not there to see it given . . ."

The gift of his life.

"I have never seen it before," Asselin said, later, glancing at the brooch I held in my hand. "Was it his?"

"I don't know . . . Did you see, Asselin? Which of the others killed him? Did you see him die?"

In the end, Duti took me away from Asselin. Entering quickly and peering across the chamber into the pale lamp-light, he looked not unnaturally astonished to find me kneeling at the prisoner's feet, while Asselin held on to my fingers and stared down into my face, totally ignoring the intruder.

However, recovering swiftly, Duti said, "Torfrida – Gilbert is coming. Have done."

"I am done," I said, after only the faintest pause, and began to rise. Yet for a second Asselin held me back, long enough to press my hand briefly to his lips. If he saw Duti's start of revulsion, he ignored that too, as I did.

Outside, although I saw Gilbert coming towards me across the yard, I hurried back towards my own guest-house, Duti trotting at my heels.

"Well?" he said urgently. "Was it Asselin? Did Asselin kill him?"

I shook my head impatiently. "No, no he did not . . . Duti, I am sorry, I think – I'm beginning to think I know what happened, and who did what, but I have to think. I will talk to you tomorrow, I promise – or at least, very soon . . ."

And quietly, resolutely, I shut the guest-house door on his half-intrigued, half-impatient face.

Lise stirred in the outer chamber, but did not wake. In my own bed-chamber I did not undress, but lay down on the bed, still in my cloak, my head buzzing and leaping with Asselin's story. A great wave of desolation, of sadness and shame, was rolling over me, and yet my heart still beat and beat. I thought I knew. I thought I did; but before I decided what to do, I had to go over all I knew of him, all I had heard of him in the past four years, to make sure I was not being unforgivably foolish. If I was wrong, I would hurt an awful lot of people, not least myself all over again. I had to know if what I believed was impossible, or just ridiculously unlikely.

Why had Hereward thrown away his sword and jumped? Because, I was almost sure, it was the natural progression of everything else he had done since retrieving Bourne.

Past: New Roads: 1075

CHAPTER 44

"Ivo de Taillebois."

I looked up into the eyes of the tall man Lucy wanted to marry, and saw something almost like recognition there. It crinkled the corners of his eyes in a manner far from unattractive. He wore a short black beard and short, curly black hair.

"So you are Hereward's elusive lady."

"Oh no," I said sweetly. "I am not elusive at all."

The black eyebrows rose. "No? Yet I have heard you even slipped through your husband's careless fingers."

No one had ever dared to speak of Hereward to me in these terms before and the direct attack was shocking. Somehow I managed to answer evenly, "Is that what you hear?" And even lifted one coolly amused eyebrow.

But Lucy chose, irritatingly, to rescue me.

"We will not speak of my brother, if you please," she said severely. "He has already ruined more evenings in this hall than you can imagine! Has he not, my lady?"

"Infinitely more," Matilda agreed. "And in an infinite number of ways! Torfrida, I'm so glad to see you here! I have grown weary of sending home my guests disappointed because they have not after all met the learned lady of Bourne. I believe they were imagining you a bald old hag who hides herself in the dark, emerging only to berate and cheat over-greedy wool merchants."

"I am not bald," I said judiciously. "But please, bring out the wool merchants."

Ivo de Taillebois laughed. Behind him, someone said, "Might I be presented to the lady?"

He was a little older than Ivo, but sleek, round; the sort of Norman Hereward would once have longed to roll off the roof – though I believed on second glance that he might have had difficulty, for there was toughness behind the plumpness.

His name, as Ivo told me, watching me with some pleasure, was Oger.

Oger smiled at me. It was not a pleasant smile. But then, neither was mine. He said, "I have long wished to meet this lady of Bourne."

"Being yourself," I said clearly, "the one-time usurper of Bourne."

Oger's face flushed, making it mottled in unpleasant shades of purple. He said carefully, "The King gave Bourne to me."

"The King giveth; the King taketh away," I said largely. "There is an excuse for that. There is even an excuse for crass mismanagement. It's the senseless cruelty that sticks in my stomach."

"Oops," said Ivo de Taillebois, twitching his henchman backwards as if out of my reach. My own arm I found in Gilbert's hold as I was urged politely away from the shocked sniggers and haughty glares of outrage from the Norman ladies in the vicinity.

"Are you trying to ruin our feast?" Gilbert asked sardonically. "Or have you just relapsed back to childhood?"

"Sorry," I said ruefully. "I have grown too used to voicing my opinions as they occur. The man is a brutal imbecile, but I apologise for telling him so in your hall. I shall be good now."

"Why does that make me even more nervous? I have placed you, by the way, beside Ivo. He, at least, can take care of himself."

The hall of Folkingham was already full of guests, richly colourful, and too many to all belong to this district. The tables were set out with lace cloths and silver plate, and before them the same carved benches I remembered from childhood. Threading through the guests with nothing more than an impression that they were all French, or at least 'Normanized', I realized Gilbert was taking me somewhere in particular.

"Here," he said, "are two famous knights who claim to know you. I shall not tell you their names – just to test them, you understand."

The man who turned quickly from his companions to face me was immediately familiar. Tall, short brown hair, harsh featured, weathered face and incongruously soft brown eyes. Dressed in elegant, dark green velvet, handsomely groomed, there was little enough to draw my recognition in the right direction. His dark eyes were serious, although they looked somehow as if they wanted to smile. And then, under my frank scrutiny, he blushed.

"Deda!" I said in amazement. And the face broke into smiles of relief when I held out both hands to him in involuntary pleasure.

"Are you surprised to find me in such august company? Or is it my bad manners in claiming acquaintance?"

"Bad sense," I said wryly. "But I am so glad to see you again – we did not even know if you had survived the second assault on Ely . . ."

"I did, because I was not there. They picked my brains after the first then sent me off to Northumbria."

Despite everything, there was pleasure in that. "Then it was not you who . . ." I broke off, shrugging the past away, but he would not let me.

"Who perpetrated the 'witch' charade? I am sorry you could have thought it. Though it was I who told them of your skills, I confess, and the false interpretations that were occasionally made of them. And, I further confess, your husband's – partiality."

I wished I had never mentioned Ely. There were things I could no longer safely recall.

I said brightly, "So have you been in Northumbria all this time?"

"Part of it only. I am just returned from Maine."

Maine. I tried to think how to turn the subject once more, but before I could, Deda said, "I met your husband again on that campaign."

"I expect you did," I said lightly. "Where there is war, there is Hereward."

Laughter, loud and uninhibited, greeted this observation, and following it in some surprise to its source I found another familiar man beside Deda. Still grinning, he bowed to me with exaggerated flourish.

I blinked.

"Good God," I said faintly. "Asselin."

"I told my lord Gilbert! He wouldn't believe I was your suitor before Hereward ever came on the scene."

"Nonsense," said Gilbert. "What I found difficult to swallow was your insistence that you were a *favoured* suitor!"

Asselin shrugged and grinned, unrepentant. "As for Hereward, he may have gained in years, but not in sanity! What he used to get up to over there . . .!"

I didn't want to hear his Hereward stories. I didn't want to hear anything remotely good about him. I was happiest when his name was never mentioned at all, which in fact it very rarely was in my presence. It was only native curiosity that had set me wondering if he was back in England; if he had gone straight home to Aelfryth. I found I wanted to know about the Siwards and Wynter and Gaenoch and the Wulrics, but I could not ask. So I just smiled, recklessly invited both Deda and Asselin to visit my hall at Bourne, and took Gilbert's arm again, steering him, this time, away from yet another source of torment.

"So," said Ivo de Taillebois, sitting back in his chair when he had consumed the last morsel of beef, "have you been poisoning your sister against me?"

I regarded him. "Lucy does not absorb poison," I observed. "She translates it into some other harmless, fluffy substance, quite as mysteriously as the sacred bread becomes the body of Christ."

An involuntary laugh hissed through his teeth. "What an outrageous thing to say!"

"But you do not deny the truth of it."

"She is alluringly sweet. But you have not answered me. *Are* you opposed to our marriage?"

"It is not my place to be. Take it up with her mother. Or her brother. If," I smiled pleasantly, "you can find either of them." Aediva, in fact, was at Crowland, visiting *my* mother for reasons best known to herself.

Ivo was regarding me with smiling, unblinking eyes. He was intrigued. I wondered vaguely if I should wean him off Lucy. Or try to. But then, why should she be denied? Other than the fact that he was Hereward's enemy. On the whole I thought I couldn't be bothered.

"I shall take that as a negative. To opposition."

"Don't let it go to your head."

"If I don't, may I marry her?"

"No, but you may visit her at Bourne until her mother – or her brother – chooses to throw you out with the rest of the rubbish."

"Brutal but honest," he observed, his eyes laughing again. "Though I think her brother is in enough danger without challenging me."

I looked at him carefully. Eventually, deciding to stick to the point, I remarked, "She is not without friends, you know. Nor would it be wise to forget that she is something more than Hereward's sister."

"As you are more than his wife?" The smile began to die. "Or is it less?"

I was ready for him this time. "Surely," I said blandly, "we women can be nothing more than the wives of great warriors?"

"I don't believe I ever doubted it," he said at once. "Before."

I couldn't help it. I laughed. I wished Lucy joy of him.

Her brother is in enough danger without challenging me.

It was late by the time we came to Bourne church, but nevertheless I dismounted and told the men to wait. Pushing open the door, I found a rather touching picture of Leofric bent over the sacred chalice that was the village's pride, lovingly polishing it with a silken rag.

"It is an odd hour," I remarked, "to be polishing."

He jumped up in shock, though a smile quickly replaced his alarm. I pretended not to notice the instinctively half-drawn sword. Despite the peace, he was a martial cleric.

"It's an odd hour to come to church," he returned.

I agreed, cordially, and sat down on the stool opposite him; and Leofric returned to his polishing. Like Hereward, he had large, capable hands, but the Deacon's were thinner, sinewy, more obviously careful.

He observed, "Confession is good for the soul."

"I have nothing to confess. Except the usual stuff with which I shall not bore you."

"Well, tell me something. Silences make me uncomfortable."

"Liar," I said affectionately. Then, abruptly taking my courage in both hands: "Leofric, is he – is Hereward in England?"

"Yes," he answered at once, without looking up. He didn't even seem surprised to be asked, although the name had not passed between us since we had ridden out of York together in the rain more than three years ago.

I looked at the reflection of my folded hands in the silver cup, and said, "Where is he?"

"Warwickshire, last I heard. Though in which of his halls, I do not know . . ."

"Leofric, is he in *danger* there?" I interrupted, because I could wait no longer to ask. And at that, Leofric's fingers did still. In fact his head lifted and stared at me.

"Of course he is!"

Something twisted viciously inside me, and was quieted by force. I said calmly, "What do you mean?"

"I mean, what do you think his life is like, Torfrida? The only English-man undefeated save by betrayal?"

"I don't know," I said deliberately. "But then, I wouldn't."

"Then *imagine*," he said shortly.

Rising with uncharacteristic irritation, he swept one thin, bony hand through his fluffy hair. "There is no man of power in this land who does not hate, or fear, or resent him – men who have the King's ear and few, if any, scruples. God forgive me, I do not even exclude the King himself from such a list! He is the target of every ambitious young buffoon who thinks to make his name by besting the great Hereward! He is the subject of plots and conspiracies of vengeance. Warenne, Taillebois, Oger, Dolfin: they are only a few of those who resent his very existence – never mind his behaviour – as a slight against their own manhood, or against Norman superiority in general. There are those jealous of his prowess, or of the King's indulgence to him, or of his *looks* even! Those who lost lands to him or his. Everywhere he goes, Torfrida, he is taunted and provoked – even by the English, who affect to call him a traitor now for making peace, though precious few of them troubled to fight behind us. He has to look permanently over his shoulder. He cannot even dine in his own halls without posting guards from among the old gang, who are the only men he can trust. He can scarcely go *anywhere* without them now. What do you think such – bonds – do to a man like him . . .?

"What's the matter, Torfrida? Did you think it was you alone who suffered?"

The last was hurled at my back, for unable to bear what he was telling me, I had stumbled to my feet and fled, gasping, to the door. I wanted air. And I wanted my mother.

CHAPTER 45

"This is Hugh de Evermouth," said Deda, presenting the only man among my visitors whom I did not know – a very young, fresh-faced man, with a flashing smile. "He has an ambition," said Deda apologetically, "to have his horoscope cast."

Lucy, kneeling on the floor in the middle of the hall with the children, was smiling up at Ivo de Taillebois. Beside him, Asselin was gazing about him with an unusually thoughtful air.

Hugh de Evermouth said, "In truth, lady, I simply have ambition! I am a younger son – a hapless position which Deda here knows only too well! – and since our families are neighbours in Normandy, I have attached myself to his fortunes until I can better my own. But I cannot help being curious about my prospects – would a horoscope tell me if my ambitions were pointless?"

At this point he was distracted by Frida, who had left her immature brothers to join us. She had grown in to a rather pretty child, quite unlike her mother, so I was not entirely surprised that she caught his eye so easily.

"Hallo," she said, smiling up at him. "I'm eight."

"That's funny," said Hugh gravely. "I am eighteen."

"My mother," said Frida dangerously, "is thirty-one!"

"I'm even older," said Deda, "but I don't suppose you remember me."

Frida looked at him. "Yes, I do. You came to the island. My father's friend."

Deda smiled slightly, half-embarrassed after all to be recognized. But he said easily, "That's right. How are you?"

Civilities over, Frida transferred her attentions back to Hugh, who seemed both amused and bewildered at being entertained by so young a lady.

"She will break hearts," Deda observed.

"Don't be fooled by the angelic smile. It's heads not hearts which she likes to break – ask her brothers!"

Deda was beginning to laugh when, abruptly, the door crashed open without warning and the twins strode in, arguing furiously.

The sudden silence, when it impinged upon their quarrel, brought them up short. Identical ferocious frowns knit their brows as they took in the race and rank of my guests. Duti's hand even itched towards his sword, causing my lips to part in swift warning that was never given – for his brother's eyes had become fixed and wide, and he suddenly yelled aloud and rushed across the hall at Deda.

"*Not* dead, by God!" he shouted, wringing the hand of the half-sheepish, half delighted Norman; and then Duti was there too, grinning and clapping him hugely on the back, and they were falling over each other in boisterous, genuine affection.

The other Normans watched, literally open-mouthed.

"Who are *they*?" Outi asked aggressively, becoming aware of it. "Friends of yours?"

"Certainly," said Deda easily. "But we have trespassed long enough upon the lady's hospitality . . ." His glance brought Hugh and Asselin to their feet. Ivo, tolerantly amused, allowed himself to be pushed by Lucy who no doubt feared the worst of her wild cousins.

"Not you!" Duti hissed in Deda's ear as the others made their civil farewells. "We need you."

I stared at them. Belatedly, I remembered their excited entrance, and as the door closed behind my guests I demanded severely to know what they were up to. They looked at each other, then quickly at me again, and away.

I knew.

"Hereward," I said. There was irritation with them; but mostly, there was dread.

Duti said in a rush, "He is in prison."

The story had come, inevitably, from Martin Lightfoot, who had seen and heard it all. And 'it', also inevitably, had grown out of an alehouse brawl. I would have laughed, except that I couldn't. Not even when Martin himself entered quietly, greeting me as his lady as if he had never been away further than the stables, as if he still lived in my hall. Sitting down with all his old economy of movement and nearly all of his usual lack of expression, he began to relate to me what he had just told the twins.

They had left London together, just Martin and Hereward, intending to return to Warwickshire, and had stopped at a harmless looking country alehouse. I opened my mouth, intending to ask with biting sarcasm what had happened to all the old gang who, Leofric had claimed, went everywhere with him for his protection. But before I could, Martin explained that they had been sent ahead, on the straight road, as decoy. Hereward would not have been sorry. Like me, he needed solitude and space . . .

And at the alehouse, as it grew busier, he had been provoked into a brawl.

"It wasn't his fault," Martin said defensively. "He was goaded to it by some vainglorious swaggart who offered him more insults than a *saint* could have borne in peace – and who was certainly paid by Warenne to do so."

I looked up quickly from my hands. I had been watching them unblinkingly, unseeingly since Martin had opened his mouth.

Martin said, "I saw the Earl come into the house. Hereward still sat over his dinner, ignoring the soldier who was yelling filth at him from behind his back. But I sat opposite Hereward. I saw this soldier exchange looks with the Earl, and I *knew*. The man was a famous brawler, but still I'd swear before the All Mighty that he had been paid."

"To *kill* Hereward?" said Deda, staring, as if he could not believe great men could stoop so low.

Martin said impatiently, "Kill him – or not. Either way, they win. If Hereward dies, they are avenged; he is out of their way. If he kills their man, they haul him off to prison for murder – which is, in fact, better, for then he is in their power and may die more slowly at their hands."

Abruptly, because I could not control it, my fingers showed white on my new, amber gown.

"Sorry," Martin said unconvincingly.

Deda said quickly, "Then he was forced to fight in the end?"

Martin nodded. "He knew from my eyes that someone else had come in. So he turned and looked over his shoulder, beyond the taunting soldier and his jeering friends and the audience who had gathered; and he saw the Earl. I think he knew at once, for he actually smiled. Then he glanced up at the soldier. He even waited politely for the end of the latest stream of abuse before he said, 'Do we have to? They are our necks, not his.' Just for a second the soldier looked taken aback, then ashamed. Because of that, he was furious. Certainly, he was bright red as he dragged out his sword.

"So the fight began – and went on and on till most of us were heartily bored, and Warenne in the corner was definitely restive. They were both bloody from minor wounds. Then suddenly Warenne leapt up furiously, shouting, 'Enough! You are both under arrest for breaking the King's peace!' And the soldier's eyes flew to him as if he had forgotten his very existence. Then he let out this weird cry, and his sword thrust wildly at Hereward's heart. But Hereward was quick. He knocked the soldier's sword up, so that it only grazed his chest, and then finished up the stroke in the soldier's neck. You know the one, boys."

"Yes," said Outi. "We know it . . ."

"So the soldier fell dead. Hereward stood for a moment looking down at the body while they rushed him, all the soldier's so-called friends, disarming him, dragging him away. He let them. But I saw him looking at the Earl over the heads of the others.

"Warenne said, 'Still smiling, Hereward? Still not afraid?' And Hereward said, 'Why should I be? I'm not at home.' "

My eyes closed hard. When I opened them, Deda was frowning. "What did he mean by that?"

"Haven't a clue," said Martin.

Abruptly, I stood up. "Where did they take him?"

Martin looked at me, with just a hint of eagerness. "To Bedford Castle," he said quickly. "The nearest secure place."

"Bedford?" Deda repeated at once. "I know the Keeper. Robert de Horepol."

My lips were dry. I licked them, and wished I could stop the trembling in my body so easily. I would not care about this. I would not. But the effort seemed to be giving me an ague.

I said, "What sort of a man is he?"

"A good man. Brave in battle. Just. Hereward will be as safe as any man confined. Will he bear it?'"

I shrugged, and began to move away. "He has before."

Of course, they would not leave it alone. Leofric, who three years ago had vowed to have nothing more to do with Hereward and kept his word barely six months from what I gathered, was already on his way to Bedford. The twins left me with accusing glares, arguing about the best means of watching the Earl of Warenne for signs of interference in Hereward's custody.

I cast Hugh's horoscope, which revealed him as the ambitious man he claimed to be; also a capable and a successful one. And if I glimpsed a hint of treachery there, well no one was perfect. I presented it to him on his next visit to us. He flashed his smile at me, with thanks, and let Frida sit on his knee.

It left me free to talk to Ivo de Taillebois.

Detaching him determinedly from Lucy, I went straight to the point. "You know, I suppose, of her brother's imprisonment?"

"I believe I heard something. If I hadn't, the agitation of his comic kinsmen might have provided a hint."

"His comic kinsmen," I said, staring at him with an undisguised contempt that wiped the smile off his face, "are also hers. And concerning her brother, your hands had better be clean, or you stand no chance of her."

I turned away at once, having said all – and more – that I intended, but after the tiniest pause, his voice stayed me, lightly mocking as well as curious.

"Where do you fit into this, Torfrida? The estranged wife who still lives with her husband's mother and sister! Are you spurned? Or spurning?"

Just for a second I saw again a naked, perspiring back, muscles rippling as he bent over her breasts. To shatter it, I laughed.

"Like all men, Ivo, you have a small mind. *I* am above all such nonsense."

"One day," he said clearly, so clearly that I thought others might hear. "One *night*, I would like to find out about that. Personally."

Surprise made me glance back at him. The strength of what I saw there caught at my breath. Because I was no longer used to the company of men. Because it had been so long since any one had loved me. Because I had been thinking of *him* and his beautiful, naked, treacherous back . . .

Ivo laughed softly. "Be honest now: wouldn't you?"

With an effort, I forced sanity back. "Frankly," I said, "I would rather read a book."

Aediva came home from Crowland, escorted by Norman soldiers. However, the anxious jolt such news inevitably gave me vanished as soon as I saw her. Not frightened in the least, she looked only embarrassed.

"Oh Torfrida, I have been so *foolish!*" she exclaimed as one of the soldiers lifted her from the saddle and carried her towards me. "I have twisted my ankle and this kind – oh dear, do put me down! I can walk if only you give me your arm . . ."

The soldier obediently did as he was told, while our men stood about the yard and glared suspiciously and jealously. In some amusement now, I stood aside to let my mother-in-law limp into the hall on the blue-cloaked arm of her Norman escort, who glanced up at me in passing in a perfunctory sort of a way. But his eyes came quickly back and he actually stopped in the doorway. He had a small scar just to the left of his mouth that tugged at his upper lip, giving him a not unattractive air of constant if cynical amusement.

"But I know you!" he exclaimed. "You are Hereward's lady!"

"Who else would I be?" I asked, my cool amusement hiding the twist of pain. "Are you not aware that the distressed lady you have just brought home is Hereward's mother?"

As though berating his own foolishness, he laughingly punched his own forehead. Yet it occurred to me that he had known her all along.

Aediva said uneasily, "You know my son?"

"Why yes. I once had the honour to carry letters from the King to Hereward on the Isle of Ely."

"Ralf of Dol," I said promptly, pleased to trace and name the memory, though the scar, I thought, was new. Hereward had liked him. Despite that, I sat down and signalled to the girl to give him wine. He seemed pleased to be remembered.

"I was very impressed by your husband," he assured me, accepting the cup. "I had never come across anything like him before – no great man by the world's standards yet so effortlessly *commanding*, while all his people hung on his words, even earls and bishops . . ." He grinned, the scar shortening and almost disappearing. "And then I met him again in Maine, and he was not like that at all!"

Aediva bridled at such a wanton detraction from her son's glories; and feeling it, Ralf said hastily, "Meaning no disrespect! Only that there is no – *superiority*, no – *distance* about him after all."

I understood perfectly. "You got vilely drunk with him and were induced to participate in some folly he had dreamed up for his own and the world's amusement." Once, I had been part of such follies, even if only to put him to bed when they were done.

Ralf grinned. "That's it," he said sheepishly. "But we never met again, to my sorrow. Is he here now? For I would love to . . ."

"No," said Aediva quickly, with a slightly nervous glance at me. "Not now."

Autumn was falling into a wet winter when Outi and Duti came home again with the breathless news that in Robert de Horepol's absence, the Earl of Warenne had stepped in and was arranging for Hereward's removal to his own custody in Buckingham.

They had sense enough not to say it before Aediva or Lucy, who still appeared blissfully unaware that Hereward was even in prison. I wished they had not spoken before me either. I wished it quite hard, sitting at the hall's high table while the twins, looming, stared down at me, unsure what

311

to do, confident that I would tell them, that I would abandon my prohibition on their interfering in this. And beside me, Leofric looked at his hands so that his eyes did not accuse me. Of what? Of what was I guilty? What in God's name did I owe the man who had betrayed me?

Sightlessly, I gazed at the table, at the clothes I was sorting for charitable distribution among the poor. I repeated the words over and over in my head until I realized my lips were moving silently and had to make them stop.

He was in no danger. The stars said so.

I said, "Where is Robert de Horepol?"

Present: March 1076

CHAPTER 46

Outside in the dark stillness, an owl hooted, bringing me back to my own surroundings. Abruptly, I sat up on the bed, pushing impatiently at the hair in my eyes.

This was achieving nothing, leading me nowhere: my memory was wayward, dragging up all sorts of details and events that were not relevant here. Somehow I had to sift through the flood, extract only what was important to my theory. To prove, or disprove, and quickly . . .

I had found Robert de Horepol, of course, and enlisted his help since I was unwilling to risk the men's recent pardons in the sort of rescue-attempt they were all desperate to perform. A decent man, as Deda had described, he had immediately understood Hereward's danger, and defended him from Warenne in a spirited enough manner to convince me that he and his prisoner had become unlikely friends. Warenne, however, was both powerful and intractable, and in the end the only concession Horepol could obtain was that he and his men accompany Warenne's when they moved the prisoner.

Which I had known was not enough. And so I had been forced to use the old gang anyway, arranging and directing them as once Hereward had done, and yet, although they followed my instructions with blind trust, I was gone, half way back to Bourne, before the prisoner's cavalcade even reached them. This time, I had said coolly to an open-mouthed Siward, Aelfryth could tend any wounds he might have . . .

There it was again: my mind, drifting off on its own when I had never needed it so badly to *think* . . . Restlessly now, I rose to my feet, pacing much as he did. The comparison did not help me.

What *was* important, surely, was that Hereward had tried hard not to kill Warenne's bravo; that he had befriended Robert de Horepol; that during the rescue, according to Leofric, he had demanded that his own men give quarter; and that the result of the whole episode had been a revulsion of feeling among decent Normans against the arrogant, illegal cruelties of men like Warenne.

Another Hereward victory? For was the important discovery of my reunions with Deda and Asselin, of my encounters with Hugh of Evermouth and Ralf of Dol, not this: that these men had also become Hereward's friends? That, I realized clearly now, was what Maine had been all about: building bridges between Norman and Saxon, with the sort of panache of which only he was capable. And when he came home, living on his own estates, looking after his own people while maintaining the friendship he had won with Norman lords, proving that it could be done. Even Ivo, I suspected, had not been immune . . .

Only it had all gone wrong again because of a few careless, tactless words concerning his daughter. He had won these men back, to a degree, during the fight at Bourne, just not enough . . .

Why, though, why would he trouble? For his own amusement, as with Tostig of Rothwell and his other detractors and rivals long ago? Yes, the old Hereward might have done that, but not the man who had commanded the bloodless defence of Ely for so long. For his own safety, then? Oh no, not Hereward, not ever.

A laugh that was part sob rose up in my throat. I could not afford the wave of emotion, the up-rush of pride in the man who had betrayed and left me. Desperately, I pressed my fingers to my temples, forcing my thoughts back to the question in hand.

Why? If not to protect himself, then the children, even me, perhaps? Or Aelfryth? All of us? Grovelling in a noble cause. No; no, even for those he loved, or once loved, I could not imagine that, not unless Aelfryth had changed him beyond recognition, and that was not the message I had received from either his new Norman cronies or his old gang who had welcomed my brief return with such open-hearted joy that the ice of my shields had almost melted.

No, Hereward's motive *must* have been greater: the saving of his own people, the reconciliation of two nations who must now become one. He had been showing the way. Yet he must have discovered, through his imprisonment and a hundred other incidents, that although he had embraced peace, no one would let him have it. For the English and the Normans both, for good or ill, he was the epitome of rebellion.

But I had to give credit to Hereward: he never gave up.

Pausing in my impetuous stride, I turned and went to the plain, oak table and lit the lamp. The light flared and settled back, flickering over my pale, veined hands, and over the bowl of drying ink and the scattering of sharp and blunt pens which lay on the random astrological notes I had made earlier that day. I was guilty, again, of reading in the stars what I wished to see. One interpretation out of many. But Hereward had not come to Bourne for me: he had come, surely, for that greater cause. And yet . . .

Torfrida, did you know there was a bear?

Slowly, I reached out and picked up the golden brooch. It seemed to wink at me as it caught the lamplight. Yes, there was still a bear, and so like the one Hereward had so reluctantly killed in Northumbria. Reluctant killing: there had been so much of that . . .

"Torfrida!"

I should have known better than to expect to creep out without their knowledge: Hereward had taught them too well. Sighing, ignoring Lise's sour, "I told you so", I turned in the first glimmer of the dawn light, and faced Siward the White.

He and his cousin, clearly, had relieved the twins since I had last been outside, but catching sight of Lise and me making furtively for the gate, he had deserted his post to run after us. He stood now towering above me in his billowing cloak, frowning and not best pleased.

"Torfrida? Where are you going?"

"Out for a little," I said vaguely.

"With horses loaded like pack-asses?"

"I have left word for Gilbert explaining . . ."

But Siward interrupted impatiently, his eyes closely searching mine. "You do not – surely you do not intend going after the killers alone?"

"No," I said. "No."

"Then what? What did Asselin tell you? Where in God's name are you going?"

"I will tell you when I come back from Northumbria . . ."

"Northumbria!" He stared at me in disbelief. "Taking no one with you? Even your children?"

"I do not wish a family migration! Siward . . ."

"Oh no, I won't let you go, Torfrida. I mean it."

"And how do you propose to stop me?" I stared him down as intimidatingly as I could, but he was too used to me to be influenced by that.

"By every means at my disposal," he said evenly. "And don't think I won't do it. It is what he would expect."

"In this case," I said carefully, "I believe he would not."

Now it was Siward who was staring. Until this moment I don't think I ever realized just how much of myself I had given to Hereward's men, for it seemed they knew me almost as he did.

Still staring, despair as well as amazement behind the pity in his pale, pale eyes, Siward said, "You think he is alive. You still think Hereward is alive."

Wordlessly, I waved him to silence, at the same time trying to walk past him, but he would not let me even pull my eyes free of him. His were suddenly hollow.

"Torfrida, why will you not let go of this?" he whispered. And now I could pull free, if only to gaze upwards at the slowly lightening sky. I swallowed.

"Because I don't believe men speak from beyond the grave, only from this side of it. Because, in spite of everything, I find I still believe in the prophecies of the stars, and my own skill in reading them."

"He *spoke* to you?" said Siward, his voice resonant with sheer disbelief.

"Siward, I don't have time to explain. I have to go now . . ."

"Wait," he said grimly, already turning his back. "I'm coming with you."

"I thought you wanted to hear what Asselin had to say? He will tell Gilbert everything this morning . . ."

"*You* can tell me as we go," he said over his shoulder.

We did not wait for him, for I did not want to admit that our journey would, in fact, be more comfortable in his presence, but he caught us up before we had even reached the main track.

"If you said a word, even to Siward," I warned, by way of greeting, as he slowed his horse to our pace, "you will have ruined everything."

"I only told him the truth," said Siward with something of his old impudence. "Namely that you had run mad, and I was going to have to go with you to make sure you didn't get into too much trouble. Torfrida, what is this about?"

I said carefully, "The stars predict that he will die at home. Bourne was not his home any more." My eyes flickered to him and away. "I made rather sure of that."

"Do the stars really take account of legalities? In spirit, Bourne was his home. It always was and he had been back some four weeks . . ."

"It doesn't matter," I interrupted. "The time was wrong. It is all to do with Mars, and its angle to the moon . . ."

"I'll take your word for that," he said hastily. "What else?"

My smile was a little twisted. "A faded yellow ribbon."

I felt his eyes on my face, but I kept mine straight ahead. He said, "He always wore it in time of trouble. He thought nobody knew. It was how we recognized the body. It was how you did."

I nodded. "I know. But you did not take it off him, did you?"

"Of course not!"

"Somebody did. Look." Impatiently, I drew the ribbon out from inside my cloak. The twists had straightened now to some degree, but there was still enough to make my point. "This clean bit, this is where he had knotted it round his arm some time before the battle – the rest is dirty with sweat and dried blood." Siward nodded curtly. "But when I untied it, it was not knotted there, but *here,* where the ribbon is dirty all over."

Siward took the ribbon from me and frowned at it a bit before raising his eyes back to mine. His horse jerked its head experimentally, but Siward held it in check without even noticing. "Meaning what precisely?"

"Meaning I don't think that body you found in the guest-house is Hereward at all. I think somebody took the ribbon off Hereward's arm and tied it on another body some time after the fighting had stopped. By which time Hereward was supposed to be dead."

"He could have done it himself, just before he died – taken it off to kiss it . . .?"

"Why? Even if he ever felt so sentimental, he could easily reach it with his mouth without taking it off."

"Someone else could have taken it from him and flaunted it in front of him, knowing it was your token . . ."

"Nobody knew but us." And Asselin? Would Asselin have remembered and recognized it over all these years? Was I right to believe that to be out of character for him?

Siward said discontentedly, "It's still a flimsy reason for your imagining . . ."

"I know. But then I found *this* clutched in the hand of the body from the store-house, the one that we all took to be Martin's." I showed him the gold brooch which I had deliberately used to fasten my cloak. It was one of the few preparations I had made for this journey. "Do you recognize it?"

Siward frowned at it. "No," he said baldly. "Are you imagining it is Hereward's? For I have never seen him wear it."

"I don't expect you did. I don't think he wanted it recognized. But it's a bear, Siward. Think about it. Do you remember when you first knew him at Gilbert's hall in Northumbria? You were a child of nine, and he killed a bear called Harold . . ."

Siward's mouth opened and closed again. He said, "You are clutching at straws."

I said, "Wynter is not dead. He is alive, and Leofric knows it. I think he knew it all along. Now, perhaps I am too trusting, but I cannot believe

316

these two would ever have turned on Hereward. Nor can I believe Leofric would ever have accepted his death so calmly. It is my belief they helped Hereward to fake his death."

I almost felt sorry for Siward trying to take all this in. His mouth opened and closed like a fish's. "Perhaps Wynter ran away during the fight, which was clearly lost, and is now ashamed . . ."

"Wynter would never have left him."

He knew it, of course; everyone knew it. The shame I had sensed so clearly in Wynter during our brief encounter had been at lying to me, not at deserting his lord. With a hint of desperation, Siward said, "But Leofric was knocked unconscious before the fight ever left the hall! He was still under the table when we found him."

"He was *back* under the table when you found him. Asselin told me that Leofric shouted from the gate that the gang were coming. That was when he and the other Normans ran away. *None of them killed Hereward.*" According to Asselin . . . "But the gang was not coming, not yet. They had time to fire the guest-house, dress up a Norman body as Hereward, and place this brooch in Martin's hand, all before the rest of you came."

But Siward had latched on to only one salient point. "*Leofric* was lying to us?"

"Yes. And I only know one man he would do that for. Dead or alive, he was lying because Hereward told him to. Wynter too."

"But why keep it from the rest of us?"

"Because you could not all have acted your parts properly."

"But – but . . ." Floundering, Siward said at last, "I cannot see why he would do anything so cruel and pointless . . .!"

"Cruel," I allowed, "but hardly pointless. His death, real or pretended, was his gift to his people: to make peace as his violent life never could, no matter how hard he tried to change it."

He absorbed that without dispute. Almost as if he understood. I had not expected that. Then: "And the brooch? He just happened to have it with him?"

"No. I think he was expecting some sort of attack. I think he had already planned this."

"But why leave it? Just to tell you the truth, after so elaborately arranging the lie?"

I swallowed. "To tell me where to find him, if I cared to hear it."

Or a trap, laid by a clever and subtle assassin, in order to remove his children and me as well. Which was why my children stayed with the twins and Siward the Red, who would die for them.

Siward poked the dead fire with a stick. "It's recent," he said curtly. "Still warm."

"His?" Lise asked reverently, but Siward did not answer, for his ears, like mine, had picked up the faint cracking sound in the woods beyond this clearing, and he was sprinting swiftly after it. The man he had brought with us from York, Swein – an old servant of his family's, I inferred – stayed quietly beside us, unmoving save for his constantly darting eyes.

Without this Swein as guide we would never have got so far, for the countryside surrounding Gilbert's old residence, always wild and a little bleak, had been laid waste far beyond recognition. Even here, so close to the hall as Swein assured us we were, there seemed to be nothing left of my childhood: I never even *saw* the ravine which Matilda and I had tumbled down so disastrously; the villages were gone, the fields were bare, the population non-existent. Except for whoever had made this fire.

I dismounted unaided and stepped forward slowly to the heap of ashes and charred twigs, kneeling beside it, looking around the ground for clues as to the man – or men – who had been here. There were a few half-scuffed footprints, obviously not Siward's for they were too small.

Hereward had large feet.

In among the ashes were the bones of some small animal; a little distant a couple of fish-heads, still fairly fresh from the smell of them. No other signs of life.

The sharp, spring wind caught at my veil, making me shiver. I could not help wishing that the sky were not quite such an ill-omened grey, but at least the sun could be glimpsed occasionally through the still bare branches when the flying clouds thinned enough . . .

I rose to my feet just as Siward came back through the trees. He had grown taciturn and terse on our journey north, though whether from excessive thought, anxiety or hurt at what Hereward might have done, I did not know. All three probably.

"I could not catch him. Nor even see him. He must know the woods."

"It doesn't matter," I said calmly. "Let's go on to the hall."

We went on, following the track from the clearing through the thicker forest, while memories crowded in on me of the events that had led to Hereward's first true exile.

Sooner or later, fate's urn shakes, casting all its burden over each of us; and saves us a place in Charon's boat on the journey to endless exile . . .

Where had I read that? Or something like that . . . Hereward would have disagreed. He would claim he had made his own fate, his own many exiles, that the final journey, the last, eternal exile from which there could be no return, was his doing too. Or would be, just as this cheat was, if cheat it was . . .

And yet most of our lives seemed to have been exile of one sort or another. Were we really responsible for all of that? Perhaps he was right.

Perhaps true maturity was in recognizing that responsibility. Even the stars, after all, were only guides . . .

"Do you hear something?" Lise whispered loudly, startling me.

"Only you," I said tartly, but she was gazing around her fearfully, into the stark trees on either side, over her shoulder to where we had just been.

"Someone is watching us," she said stubbornly.

"You are fanciful."

"Perhaps," Siward said, twisting around in the saddle. "But we should be on our guard. There is something moving in the woods with us, whether man or animal."

"The man who made the fire?" Or Hereward, eternally watchful, so that fate would not sneak up and spill its urn before he was ready . . .

Siward shrugged impatiently, and increased our pace.

Gradually, the trees thinned out and revealed, almost magically, the old road to Gilbert's hall. In a little, I could even see it, raised high on its mound above the rest of the country.

I doubted that Gilbert owned it any more. Nobody did, I thought as we approached nearer, and nobody cared enough to want to. The once magnificent hall was nothing more than a broken-down, deserted ruin. Our horses picked their own way through the dangling gates which swung vaguely in the light, spring breeze, and I could see that some of the out-houses had been more systematically chopped down, probably for firewood by people who had since fled or died. Weeds and grasses grew abundantly, even between the wall-less boards of what had once been my bedchamber.

Lise said, "Dear God. Who would live here?"

"No one," I said, "of choice."

Unaided, I slid out of the saddle. The poor beast, too tired to go anywhere, just lowered her head to pull half-heartedly at a clump of grass growing out of the mud.

"And how long precisely do you mean us to stay in this – luxurious hall?" Lise enquired with the insolence of long service.

"Sarcasm does not become you, Lise. See if you can find somewhere to stable the horses, and then look around the out-buildings for somewhere habitable for us."

"Why?" she demanded suspiciously. "Where are you going?"

"Into the hall," I said, and without waiting to see if she would obey me, I walked across the yard. For her benefit I tried to look unconcerned, but in truth my eyes were busy, scouring the yard for signs of any living soul, dangerous or otherwise. There is something very eerie about a deserted hall in the hour before dusk.

"Take care," Siward warned, passing me. "I'll look around the back. Swein, stay in the yard and watch."

Unlike the damaged hall at Bourne, the door of Gilbert's old residence was firmly closed. Kicking aside leaves and earth and dead twigs, I pushed it. Nothing happened. Uncared for, the wood had warped. I hoped I would not be obliged to use a window. However, a second, violent effort pushed the door unevenly open, shedding what poor light there was in a pale beam across the empty hall.

For a moment I stood there, my heart beating so loudly that I would not have heard the approach of even the clumsiest attacker. But nothing moved, no one came near me, and slowly, systematically, I forced my eyes to quarter the chamber.

Bare of the hangings and tapestries that had graced it in my youth, it was difficult to recognize. The shields and swords above the fireplace, the silver plate, the trestle tables and benches themselves had all gone, leaving a naked, impersonal hall. A pool of drying water lay in the middle of the floor. Above it, the low loft and the roof itself were open to the grey sky, the only source of light since the windows had all been roughly filled in with nailed wood. Only the high table at the far end had been left. The malevolent carved animal heads glared at me like protective dragons. I could almost imagine I had entered their lair against their wishes.

Taking a deep breath, I began to walk forward, carefully skirting the large puddle on the floor, looking right and left as I went towards the partition, to what had once been Gilbert's own bedchamber. The door opened easily, without any of the creaking protests I expected. I blinked in the shaft of light coming from the window, which was only partially covered, but there was nothing in the chamber to see, save a large, solitary rat which regarded me suspiciously from the middle of the floor. Gasping with distaste, I quickly shut the door again, my eyes darting involuntarily around the hall for any signs of its companions.

Nothing. There was nothing here. I could feel the disappointment growing up from my toes, gathering strength. It seemed I had been wrong. I had come on a wild-goose chase, looking for an impossible answer, deluding myself . . .

Or Lise, or Siward, might be having more luck among the out-buildings . . .

Straightening my shoulders, I began to walk smartly back towards the door. But as I passed the high table, something caught my eye and made me halt once more. It was something behind the table leg, almost invisible from almost every angle but this one. I frowned quickly, in concentration, but nothing moved. Whatever it was, it was not alive. I went towards it, gradually making out a bundle of some sort – wool, or fur.

Crouching down, I reached out and pulled it out. Furs, and woollen blankets. It was a bedding roll, hastily stuffed behind the table to hide it.

My heart felt as if it was beating now inside my throat. I had to swallow, convulsively, to stop my brain running too far ahead of the facts. Yet unbidden, my fingers were drawing the blanket to my cheek, my mouth; I was breathing in the scent of a man.

"Did you weep?"

The voice might have come out of the blanket, unstartling, quiet, interested. My eyes closed, collecting strength, but only for a moment. Then carefully, deliberately, I released the blanket and rose to face the intruder.

Behind him, the door to the bedchamber lay open once more. He had been there all along then, hidden by the door itself from my perfunctory search.

He stood only a few yards from me, in the shadows untouched by light from either door or roof. But I could see that he wore no armour save a stout leather jerkin under a good fur-lined travelling cloak, that beneath those he wore rather torn and stained velvet. I think it was green. I could see the sword and dagger at his belt. Slowly, my eyes lifted to his face.

CHAPTER 47

Ralf of Dol smiled as my heart finally broke and crumbled, because I had been wrong, because I had not wanted to listen to my cerebral, thinking self who had known all along that this would be the outcome of my journey. No loving husband deviously cheating death for noble ends, but this equally devious and terrible young man who had admired him, who had been kind to his mother and whose nobility, if he had any, was strictly for show.

"Well, who cares?" said Ralf when I did not answer him. I could not even remember the question. "Stony-hearted or loving, I am overjoyed to see you. Shall we go and greet your friends?"

Something did stir at that, at least enough to make my lips form the syllable, "No." I knew, somewhere, that I had to begin to think again, to try and save Siward and Lise, and the man Swein who had come so suddenly and faithfully into my world. But I did not know how. At the very least, I thought vaguely, they had to be warned.

Almost mechanically, I opened my mouth. I had no idea what would come out – not words probably, more likely some mindless scream, which was all I was really capable of. And I never found out, for as soon as my lips began to part, Ralf moved, rushing the space between us and seizing me with one violent hand while the other clapped over my mouth.

"Not yet," he said reproachfully. "I am not ready." And his hand in the small of my back pushed.

I think it was the touch of his skin, the smell and taste of his dirty hand – fish, I realized, remembering the fish-heads beside the fire in the woods – which repelled me into something approaching thought. My first instinct was to bite the offending hand, but though my whole body wriggled with the effort, I managed to restrain myself, for it would have brought me little but blows. Instead, while he used his free hand to curtail my wriggling, I used my own to feel for the dagger in his belt.

I had found it too, had even drawn it halfway free before his hand closed over mine.

"Thank you," he said, as though pleased. My fingers were prised effortlessly away, and the dagger was in his own hand, the point at my throat. "I knew," he said, his eyes rich with some mocking amusement, the scar at the corner of his mouth wrinkling up like a caterpillar, "that I had forgotten something."

The fishy hand left my mouth. We had halted behind the hall door, and for a moment his arrogant eyes gazed down into mine. As the amusement died, its place was filled by something like cruelty. The point of the dagger pressed needlessly into my throat, pricking the skin till I felt the tiny trickle of blood.

It was laughable really, in the circumstances. I *would* have laughed, had I been capable just then. Instead, bereft of all humour, I just said curiously, "Do you really think I care?"

"That does not matter, sweet," he said carelessly. He even kissed the top of my head with brash insolence. "They do. *Now* I am ready."

And as he pushed me forward into the doorway and the pale evening sunlight that was suddenly blinding, I realized with panic that I did care, that I would have to, not just for Lise and Siward, but for the children who needed me, who would have to know and understand why their father died. Everyone would have to know, if he was not to have died in vain, and it was my purpose, my duty, to tell them.

My breath caught.

But the yard was empty. No watchful Swein. Even the horses had disappeared. I could hear one whinnying behind, from the place where the stables had once been. Where Hereward had first kissed me, an almost-chaste kiss for an almost-child.

"Call them," Ralf said.

"You call them," I said at once, and again felt the prick of the dagger. This time I did laugh, deliberately. "I told you, I don't care if I live or die."

I *will* live, for you, in endless exile without you . . .

Unexpectedly, I felt him shrug. "No matter," he said, and I felt his lungs inflate. "Hallo there!" he called, almost playfully. "I have your lady here, and I believe she is bleeding! If you want it to stop, I suggest you run to me as fast as you can!"

There was a pause, a silence, and then Siward walked round from the side of the hall. His cloak was slung back over one shoulder; he held his shield in one hand, his sword in the other.

"Very valiant," Ralf approved. "Barbaric but valiant."

Siward came to a halt, saying, "Do Norman knights fight now with children and women? Let her go and do your fighting with me – if you dare."

"But I don't dare. Not with your man skulking around to stab me in the back the moment you have me distracted. Bring him here."

Siward did not say anything. He did not need to. Swein came without instruction, from the opposite side of the hall. After him trailed Lise.

"Excellent," Ralf approved. "The whole set."

Siward said, "So it was your fire in the forest. You who followed us here."

"Actually, you followed me, just at the end. Forgive me, but I have no time to waste in explaining such matters to an English nonentity. Please, step into my hall."

As he spoke, he jerked me backwards, inside once more; and slowly, watchfully, Siward followed, Swein and Lise close on his heels.

"Now," said Ralf, "drop your sword. And your shield. If you want your lady to live."

"Don't, Siward," I said quickly. "What can he do? Is he likely to kill me and risk fighting both of you at once?"

"I don't need to kill you, sweet. But I can make an awful mess of this lovely face of yours."

Siward smiled, suddenly achingly like his uncle. "She is nothing to me. Why should I care for that?"

Ralf did not answer in words. Truthfully, I was so tense I did not even feel the cut, but it sent the breath hissing between Siward's teeth, and made Lise cry out in anguish. My neck felt wet.

Siward snarled, "Leave her alone you . . .!"

The dagger moved again, but before I could speak, Siward swore. I could not hear the words for the clanking of his weapons on the floor – sword, shield and all. I closed my eyes in despair. More slowly, Swein dropped his own belt.

"Good boys," mocked Ralf, and with an unexpected spurt of spirit, I realized his manner was irritating me. When I opened my eyes, Siward's ferocious frown told much the same tale. I wished he had stayed at Folkingham. "Now, walk before me to the table and sit down on the floor, one at each leg. You, Saxon, before you sit, tie your friends."

"With what?" said Swein sullenly – his ancestry was Danish – while Siward and Lise obediently sat.

"There is rope behind the door of the smaller chamber. Bring it."

Swein moved slowly, watching Ralf all the time over his shoulder.

Siward silently moved his legs, positioning himself, I knew, to attack. I tried desperately not to twitch, or even swallow, but the dagger moved anyway, a delicate slice that this time I did feel. The blood trickled down my throat, a twin rivulet to the one already there. They mingled at the neck of my cloak, splashing over the golden bear brooch.

Siward had paused, stock-still.

"Precisely," said Ralf. "And your oaf had better hurry or I'll cut her again." The dagger lovingly caressed my cheek.

"I don't care, Siward," I said desperately. "He cannot hurt me now . . ." But it seemed no one else agreed. While Ralf held me, and supervised, Siward and Lise obediently held their hands behind their backs, and Swein bound them by the wrists to the great table legs. When the knots did not appear tight enough to satisfy him, he nicked my chin, and my cheek. After that, Swein stopped trying, and tied me too, while Ralf smiled and held the dagger casually under my nose.

Ralf tied Swein himself, harshly enough to make the captive wince. I wiped the blood off my face onto my shoulder and kept uncharacteristically quiet. It had struck me, you see, that although we were thus inconvenienced and would have a rather painful time trying to get free, Ralf clearly had no intention of killing us. If he had, he would not have troubled to tie us so carefully. I would have asked him the point, except that I was afraid of annoying him into changing his mind.

"Good," said Ralf, rising to his feet. "It remains just to bid you farewell. Though on the whole, I believe I can't be bothered."

And he laughed, sauntering around the table and stepping off the dais. There, in front of me, he paused. I did not like the glitter in his eyes. There were a thousand questions I would not ask him, because I was so eager for him to go. Yet some pride would not let my eyes fall from his.

"Poor Ivo," he said unexpectedly, and laughed again. In the middle of it, he suddenly swooped to press his mouth roughly on mine. I felt his tongue and his teeth, not just insulting but hurting; and it went on long enough to bruise. Through it, I could hear Siward's furious voice, Lise's squeal. And then the pain stopped and he had straightened, still apparently amused.

"I'd like to stay for more," he said, almost jauntily. "But I have work to do!" And he strode off down the length of the hall to the door, which he closed quite carefully behind him.

Siward exploded, "What the hell is the point of this?"

"Be grateful," I said wryly. "At least from this there is a way out."

"There is?" Lise said shrilly. "Then for God's sake tell us what it is!"

"It's going to be difficult," Swein said mournfully. "I'm sorry, but I dared tie the ropes no looser – I could see what he was doing to her . . ."

"Forget it," I said. Already I was twisting, trying to kneel. Movement had begun to hurt my throat, but I acknowledged it only in a detached sort of a way.

"Wait," said Siward suddenly. "What is that?"

We all paused, listening to a thump on the outer door and then several sharp bangs.

"He's nailing up the door!" Siward yelled. His sudden jerk on the table did not budge it. "Come on! We all have to do this together, pulling the same way . . ."

"Wait," I said. "Wait just a moment . . ." I had my feet out behind me now, my back arched inwards, my fingers scrabbling at my ankles. My cloak had got twisted around them.

"What are you doing?" Siward demanded, but Lise, suddenly, excitedly, was laughing.

"Oh God bless you, lady, you *have!*"

"Hush," I said grimly. "He could still be listening." My fingers finally found the little knife and pulled it free of its pouch above my ankle.

Swein was saying, "He's round the back now. I heard his footsteps . . ."

I said, "The bedchamber window is not quite covered. Perhaps he's nailing that up too."

"Does he mean us to starve to death?" Siward demanded.

"I don't know . . ." I heard something in the bedchamber, too light to be footsteps: a sort of a *swish*, as though something had landed on the floor. For some reason a new, unnamed fear began to rise. But awkwardly, I tried to position the knife at my wrist to enable me to cut the bonds.

"Hurry . . ." said Lise.

There was a pause, then, "I think you have to," Siward said, grimly.

"Well if anyone else had the forethought to conceal one of these about their persons . . ."

"Why should we when you convinced us all we were coming to meet Hereward?"

Hereward is dead. In spite of myself, my eyes closed against the droning words, the pain that would never be any less; and my fingers fumbled on the knife, cutting themselves instead of the rope.

"Torfrida, let's not fight now," Siward said urgently. "I can smell smoke. I think he's thrown a torch into the bed-chamber . . ."

On his last word, Lise screamed, for something else had come dropping through the ceiling, something swift and flaming. It had come through the hole in the roof, a bundle of dry sticks, burning. It sizzled in the puddle on the floor, but did not go out. Another, following swiftly, rolled along the roof-beam and fell into a corner. The flames licked at once around the wall. And in the bedchamber, I was suddenly sure I could hear the fire crackling.

"Dear God, he's burning us alive, just as he did Hereward." Siward sounded savage. His mighty jerk heaved the table half an inch, and made me drop the knife. Wriggling, I managed to seize it, and begin again, determinedly.

"Why?" Lise asked, bewildered. "What is the point? So he killed Hereward. Why kill us? Because we know? We have no proof to satisfy even a biased court of law!"

Almost to myself, I said low, "He must have hated Hereward very much . . . I'm sorry. I risked you in my foolishness . . . ah!" Abruptly, the knife cut through the first rope and I could pull my wrists free. Stumbling in my haste, I hurled myself at Siward's feet.

The hall was filling up with smoke now, billowing in from the bedchamber. The whole building was on fire, the bedchamber, all four walls, the loft and some of the roof-beams above our heads.

"The roof!" Siward panted, as he hacked Swein's bonds. "We have to try and get through the hole in the roof!"

"The roof is burning!" I shouted. "Can't we ram this table through the door? Or a wall?"

They were burning too, but at least if we managed to break free we would be on firm ground and not a crumbling, burning building . . .

By huge efforts, we managed to push the table off the dais, but even if we hadn't been weakened by the smoke, I doubted we would have had the strength to batter our way out with it.

"The roof it is," I whispered, helping to heave the table upright. As soon as we had it, Siward leapt on to it, jumping, reaching for the burning beam above. My mind was appalled at the burns he would receive, and yet there was no other option to survive . . .

And in the end it was no use anyway. The table was not high enough . . .

Unbidden, a memory floated into my tired mind: sitting around a campfire in the forest, while above us three villages burned, and Hereward's 'gang' told me a story of a Viking hero. A serious story we had turned to laughter.

"Thorfinn the Mighty," I said vaguely to the flames, wiping grimy sweat from my brow, throwing aside my torn and pointless veil. Then, suddenly more urgent: "How *did* he get out?" The great Earl of Orkney who had escaped his own burning hall with his wife safe in his arms. "Siward! How did Thorfinn get out?"

But Siward was not listening to me. His head was bent right back, gazing upwards at the gaping, fire-ringed hole. And in the midst of it, I thought I could see a man, a shadow lit against the dark, smoke-filled sky.

I said, "Ralf." Ralf waiting to kill us if we found the only way out. And yet why would he risk that?

"Not Ralf," Siward whispered, so quietly I could barely hear, and then suddenly I saw the rope dropping through the hole, heard Siward's violent sob as he reached down for me.

"You first!" I cried, for the guilt was already too much to bear. But I knew he would not listen, that in disputing I would only waste time that none of us could afford. So I clung to the rope as Siward tied it clumsily around me, dangled as the man above pulled it up as if I were no heavier than a baby. My eyes shut tight, for I was in a burning nightmare of smoke and flame and noise, where I could believe in the reality of nothing. There was heat, crashing, overwhelming, and then blessed cold on my cheek; and my eyes opened on the face of my rescuer.

Strong arms lifting me, releasing the rope, while the tears coursed down my face and I wondered what to do and what to feel.

Hereward is dead.

"Forgive me," I whispered hoarsely, brokenly, the desperate words escaping without permission. "I was not there! I would not come, I did not see . . .!"

"Hush," he said. "Hush . . ."

There was no time, but he moved quickly, bringing his mouth down hard, not gentle on my bruised, pleading lips; yet there was love there, and passion and an instant, surely, among the savagery of the crackling flames, of healing.

"A kiss to die for," he whispered into my mouth. "If I have to."

And then, before the blood could run cold in my veins, his hands were guiding me, lowering me down the slope of the roof. "Jump, sweet heart," he said in my ear. "Jump."

I think he pushed me in the end. I remember lying on the ground, winded and dazed, yet my eyes still riveted on the burning roof, where he stood astride the ridge, stretching down to pull Lise through the hole, while beside him another bit of the burning roof fell inside. Then she jumped down beside me, crying out with the pain, and I could force myself to think again.

Scrambling to my feet, I said to no one in particular. "Ralf. Where is Ralf?"

And Siward, leaping down from the roof, wiping smoky tears from his face, said grimly, "Unblocking the door. He knew there was something going on inside. Wait there . . ."

"We were bait," Lise said, shaking like a leaf beside me while Siward ran around towards the hall door. "We were bait, to bring him . . ."

Only he had come too quickly and too quietly, and Ralf had not seen him.

Swein was down now, turning as soon as he landed to call to Hereward, holding up his hand to help him down. But the fire was cutting him off. Some weird sound came from deep down inside me. Without thought I had propelled myself forward to the burning wall, watching as Hereward, ignoring both of us, peered back into the hole. Behind him, the roof started to break up seriously.

Below, Siward's voice shouted, "Hereward, no!"

Hereward moved one arm in acknowledgement, but he did not turn so much as a hair. Then he tensed his legs and jumped into the inferno.

My mouth was open involuntarily to scream out my rage, but no sound can have come out, for Siward was beside me, talking furiously through it.

"Ralf is in there now – why could he not just leave it? Why not fight out here? Christ, is he still trying to be dead?"

No one ever tried so hard . . .

The salt of my tears was stinging the cuts in my face and neck. I was conscious too of rasping pain in my throat, and yet they were nothing, nothing. With Siward beside me, we were running now to the front of the hall. There was a hole in the door big enough to climb through, but the heat from inside was intense enough to throw Siward back.

"My God," he whispered. And then suddenly he lifted up his face and voice to Heaven and shouted out in pure rage. "Don't do this to us *now!* How many times do you think we can bear it?"

I said, "We can bear anything," and wondered if it was true. I wondered if it would be easier now that I had that kiss, that wordless assurance of his love. When it was over, would that take some of the pain away?

With my hands, I was clawing at the wood nailed across the door, trying to twist myself under it while Siward tried to pull me away. I think we were both sobbing. And then the roof finally collapsed, burying everyone inside. Siward and I were forced back by falling, flaming timber.

And then, when I had begun to realize that I could not bear it after all, another violent crash burst open the burning wall on the right and something catapulted through the air and across the ground, rolling like a ball, then lengthening and straightening, resolving into a man. Two men, one still as death, the other rolling further by his own power with golden streaks showing through the filth of his hair.

And when I hurled myself at his feet, his eyes, looking directly into mine, were wide open. Only his voice was slightly shaky as he said, "Ouch."

But I could play this. I could.

I said, "Is that how Earl Thorfinn did it?"

And Hereward's body began to shake. "Not quite," he said. "Not quite." He moved his smouldering arm, and wordlessly I lay down at his side. I had never known contentment like this.

We were in the most habitable of the out-houses, the old family house, where Robert's little sister had once had hysterics because a bear called Harold had stumbled in upon them, roaring.

The fire was out, leaving the hall merely a pile of ashes and charred timber. Half lying on a bedding roll, I could see Lise and Swein bent over the sorry figure that was Ralf: alive but badly burned and bruised from his encounter with Hereward, he had not yet regained consciousness.

Over his shoulder, Swein said, "Why did you trouble to save him?"

Because it was why he had gone in – not to fight or to kill, but to save. But I didn't say it, and Hereward himself only smiled faintly. I felt rather than saw, because I was still afraid to look. Sitting beside me, he was gently bathing the wounds in my neck. His hands and arms were peppered with burns.

"Why is it," he asked me, "that you never wince?"

And because that was light, bearable, I did move my eyes to his face. Streaked with blood and smoke-dirt, there were new scars, new wounds, new and harsher lines. He was concentrating on his unfamiliar work, work he had forbidden Lise by wordlessly taking the salve box from her hands.

I said, "Because it doesn't hurt."

At that his eyes lifted from my throat. Still disconcertingly different, they met mine. There was a pause, then his lips moved.

In unconscious imitation of Ralf of Dol, he said, "Did you weep?"

And suddenly the tears were there again, trying to choke me. I said, "Not for you. Never for you." And gasped them back. His fingers fell away from my neck, instead touching the brooch which still fastened my cloak. But his lips were smiling slightly. He understood, as he always had.

He said, "I did not know if you would come. I did not know if you would want to. I thought if you did, if you still cared for me, you would look and find the brooch and understand. It was a last service Martin would have been glad to perform."

So Martin Lightfoot really was dead. He must have seen the change in my face, for as if he could not yet bear that wound to be touched he went on a little too quickly. "About Ralf – I am sorry. I never thought he would follow me. I had thought he was long gone with the others, but he seems to have an over-developed sense of vengeance. The weird thing is, it grew out of *honour*. Or his idea of honour . . . I've been playing hide-and-seek with him since yesterday."

I swallowed with difficulty. "Will he live?"

"I don't know," Hereward said candidly. "It's a long time since I have wanted to kill anyone so much. And then I did not know he had abused you first . . ."

His fingers touched the cut on my chin, my bruised lips where they clung. "Torfrida . . ."

"I didn't feel it," I said again. "I don't feel anything . . ."

"Even for me?"

My eyes closed. "Only for you."

And his hand was in my hair. "Then why did you not send for me?"

"Why did you not come?"

"I thought I had killed everything between us." His forehead touched mine. "I didn't want to make it worse . . . And then Robert de Horepol told me what you had done for me with Warenne, and when I got the rest out of Leofric I thought perhaps it might not be over yet . . . Is it over, Torfrida?"

I said, "It is never over – I have learned that. If the past matters – and it does – then it *all* matters . . . Aelfryth . . ."

"Aelfryth!" He was impatient. "I never saw her again. She was just – available! One more lapse in the responsibilities I was not man enough to bear."

"One lapse?" I said, disbelief warring with hope in my voice. It made Hereward smile.

"Three, I think, in the course of that week. I was too damned drunk for more." The smile faded. "Will you come with me again? I have no certainty except that I must stay away for a long time."

"I know." My hand crept into his. "The truth is, there is no exile with you."

Quickly now he bent for my mouth, and my heart leapt again as if I were still a girl awaiting her first kiss. Inevitably, the door swung noisily open and Siward entered with a pile of firewood, carefully not looking at us as he dropped it in the hearth. Hereward drew back, reluctantly, although his hand still held on to mine.

Then, casually jerking his head at his nephew, he said, "Siward can smuggle the children to us . . ."

I sat up straighter. "You will have to tell your mother, and your sisters – it is not fair . . ."

"Whatever you say."

Siward coughed. "The men . . ."

And dropping my hand, Hereward stood up to face him. There was a pause, then: "Siward, the men are part of the problem. I made them so. It is better if they think me dead. It is time to lay down arms and be good, and do a little farming. Disband the old gang, live, and forget what we tried to do. It's the only way we can protect ourselves now."

Siward was staring at him. Angrily, he swiped one hand across his eye. "And you will be content? Just to fade into song, into distant memory?"

Hereward's eyes fell for a moment. It seemed his men knew him as they knew me. My heart welled with pity for him, with irritation at Siward. But Hereward had never lacked courage. His eyes lifted again, directly into Siward's. He even said sardonically, "Well, what is there to sing about me now? History will remember William and the Norman conquerors, not Hereward the Outlaw or his defeated people. It is a new world, even if not precisely the one I would have chosen, and we must all learn to live in it without bitterness."

"*Without bitterness?* Dear God, Hereward, have you any idea how I feel? How any of us feel?"

Hereward's lips parted, but he did not speak. Instead, he swung abruptly away from his nephew – from me too, but I stood up and caught his hand, the blanket falling round our feet. He needed my help, only he had got out of the way of asking. Something inside me ached for that.

With difficulty I said, "He knows, Siward. Of course he knows. Never imagine this is easy for him. I thought you understood; you understood when you thought he was dead."

Tightly, Siward said, "I don't want you to be dead."

And again I answered for him. I had found my way now; I could even smile. "He is not dead. He never will be. The histories may praise William, but it is Hereward who will be in the *people*'s songs, ages after we are all buried. And it is the songs that keep the spirit, Siward, the spirit of what we did, and tried to do."

They were both gazing at me now, Siward with slightly arrested wonder. I would not look at Hereward.

Going forward, I reached up both arms and took Siward by the shoulders. "Accept his gift, Siward. Take it, and pass it on."

Later, much later, as we lay wrapped in blankets with the light from the dying fire flickering feebly against the wall, I listened to his breath and the beat of his heart, and knew that his eyes were wide open. Under my cheek, tied once more around his arm, was a faded and not very clean yellow ribbon.

Into the darkness, Hereward said, "Will the songs really remember me?"

I don't know if he expected me to hear, let alone answer. But I said simply, "Yes; and the stories."

There was the faintest pause, then he turned his battle-scarred head and looked at me with eyes which tried not to care. He had always tried not to care. Yet his smile was gentle, only a little self-mocking.

He said, "Is it in the stars?"

And I smiled back, reaching towards him because I could do nothing else. "Yes. It is in the stars."

About the Author

Mary Lancaster was born in Scotland and graduated with honours from the University of St. Andrews. Her degree is in history, a subject which provides the chief inspiration for her writing. She has worked or studied in Wales, Glasgow, London and Edinburgh, and eventually settled on the Fife coast, where she still lives with her husband and two young sons.

Despite having earned a living over the years as Editorial Assistant, Researcher and Librarian, Mary Lancaster has managed to retain her love of books, particularly old and dusty ones. Her interest has always extended to writing them — although for many years it was only for her own amusement.

**Indianapolis
Marion County
Public Library**

Renew by Phone
269-5222

Renew on the Web
www.imcpl.org

For general Library information
please call 269-1700.

Printed in the United States
44182LVS00003B/169-171

9 781843 192725